THE OTHER CHEEK

THE OTHER CHEEK

Genevieve Lyons

G.K. Hall & Co. • Chivers Press
Thorndike, Maine USA Bath, England

This Large Print edition is published by G.K. Hall & Co., USA and by Chivers Press, England.

Published in 1998 in the U.S. by arrangement with The Sharland Organization.

Published in 1999 in the U.K. by arrangement with Little, Brown (UK) Ltd.

LP
F
Lyo
c.1

U.S. Hardcover   0-7838-0389-3 (Romance Series Edition)
U.K. Hardcover   0-7540-1225-5 (Windsor Large Print)
U.K. Softcover   0-7540-2163-7 (Paragon Large Print)

The text of this Large Print edition is unabridged.
Other aspects of the book may vary from the original edition.

Set in 16 pt. Plantin by Juanita Macdonald.

Printed in the United States on permanent paper.

British Library Cataloguing in Publication Data available

Library of Congress Cataloging in Publication Data

Lyons, Genevieve.
    The other cheek / Genevieve Lyons.
      p.   cm.
    ISBN 0-7838-0389-3 (lg. print : hc : alk. paper)
    1. Large type books.   I. Title.
  [PR6062.Y627O84   1998]
  823'.914—dc21   98-41738

This book is for my dear friend
Marcia Bell, with my love, and Michele

Chapter One

'What do you want, Lydia? What do you really want?'

The girl shrugged her shoulders. She pushed back her hair from her face and turned it to the sun, closing her eyes. The long lashes fanned against the russet tints of her cheek. 'I dunno. I s'pose . . .' She wrinkled her forehead. 'I s'pose I just want life to go on and on like this. Just as it is. On and on and on.' She opened her eyes and smiled at Sean wistfully. 'That's what I want even though I know it's not reasonable.' She sighed. 'Wouldn't it be lovely, though. Sweet summer days like this on and on.'

'No it wouldn't.' Sean Sullivan sounded very sure. 'No it wouldn't at all.' He scowled then said, 'Don't you see, Lydia, everything's unresolved.'

'So isn't it better than Mother finding the right man for me and marrying me off to Mister Perfect?'

Sean's scowl deepened. The idea of Lydia, beautiful Lydia, *his* Lydia marrying another was unbearable. He leaned over and kissed her softly on the lips, treating her as he had always done, with the reverence usually afforded a saint.

At that moment Austin, Lydia's brother, suddenly parted the matted branches of the blackberry bushes. 'Gotcha!' he cried as he peered out of the hedgerow. He looked furious. 'What are ye doin', ye filthy slut?' he hissed. 'Get outta there at once or I'll tell Father Malachy on ye.'

But Austin's triumph at finding them there was short-lived. As he glared down into the blue, defiant gaze of his sister, she looked up at him contemptuously and took Sean's hand, bold as brass, sitting there on the verge of the fallow field. Sean Sullivan had his arm around her and she was obviously enjoying whatever it was he was doing to her. Neither of them seemed in the least disconcerted.

'Get away, Aus.' Lydia sounded amused rather than guilty. 'God, you're a sneaky little gurrier, aren't you?' She looked at him with disdain. 'Creeping around, spying on us. We're not doing anything wrong, so there! It's you who is!'

'Then why are you hiding? Eh? If you're so innocent why are ye behind the bushes?' His face was red and angry.

' 'Cause it's cosy here,' Lydia replied tartly. 'And anyway, it depends on which way you're coming. If it's from your side we're behind the bushes, but from our side it's not, so there!'

Sean Sullivan, sitting beside her, grass in his hair, rose in a leisurely fashion, brushing down his trousers as he did so. 'Don't bother with him, Lydia,' he said dismissively. 'It's none of his business anyhow. Go 'way, Austin,' he growled. 'Leave us alone.'

Austin looked apoplectic. 'None of my business!' he shouted incredulously. 'None of my business! God'n you're a cheeky devil, Sean Sullivan. Isn't that my sister you're messin' with, an' didn't I find you just now in a compromisin' position . . . ?'

Sean burst out laughing. He was a lanky, black-haired youth with merry blue eyes. 'Compromisin' position! Jasus Mary an' Joseph, aren't we the highfalutin' fella now! Me and Liddy were kissin', not carryin' on like Jack Doyle an' Movita!'

Lydia giggled. The great boxer and the lovely film star from *Mutiny on the Bounty*, both married to other people, were living together in a Dublin hotel without the blessing of Mother Church, scandalising the public and infuriating the clergy.

Austin Tracey gave up. These two refused to play his game, refused to read the script his way. Instead of becoming guilty and ashamed they seemed amused and superior. In the meantime they roamed the countryside like gypsies and his mother did not seem to care. Nevertheless he threw a parting shot: 'Yer a disgrace, Lydia, an' I'll tell Mother on ye.'

Lydia tossed her head. Her hair was a glorious cloud of mahogany-coloured waves and curls that caught the sunlight. 'Phooey!' she pouted at him. 'Mother won't say anything an' you know it.'

He did and it was almost too much to bear.

'And who are you, little brother, to *attempt* to

9

tell me off?' She waved her finger in the air and cried, 'Come on, Sean, let's go an' leave this mean-minded half-brother of mine to his prying and poking about. He's got nothing better to do!'

And she took Sean's hand and the pair of them wandered off, smiling at each other and laughing in that united way Austin loathed, as if they could read each others minds! He ground his teeth together, staring after them. Lydia's summer dress was stained with green from the grass and her white ankle-socks were at half-mast. They showed how tanned her legs were. She looked like a labourer's daughter. And Sean! Sean Sullivan was in fact little better than a labourer, a small-holder, an ignorant peasant! Austin shivered.

He hated Sean Sullivan with a passion that frightened him. Sean was everything Austin was not. Tall and rangy to Austin's stocky, raven-haired to Austin's sandy, Sean was a delight to the eye with his handsome face and twinkling eyes, while Austin's appearance gave the impression that *he* was the raw-boned farmer, an uncouth working man. And this was far from the truth and totally unfair, in Austin's opinion.

Austin's father, Martha D'Abru's second husband, had been a respectable solicitor. He, like his father before him, had been an intelligent, ambitious man while the Sullivans were small farmers buffeted by every turn of fate since the tribe began.

They had fought in the Celtic wars, survived Oliver Cromwell, the potato famine, the landlords' drive to rid the land of them and their like. They had fought enthusiastically in every rising, been involved in the illegal activities of the Nationalists before independence, and Austin felt it was grossly unfair that a tribe of gypsies should produce someone so gloriously handsome, while his family, the Traceys, who had always been law-abiding and socially adaptable to every regime that came and went, with the sophistication of the well-educated, should look like thugs. Not bloody fair.

It was a glorious sunny day. The world drowsed under a forget-me-not-blue sky and paused in breathless heat before the harvest. Austin, though, did not notice the beauty around him. He was so full of resentment and hate that he could not see through the lowering cloud of his emotions.

The real trigger to his ill-humour was his sister Lydia. The eldest. Why in God's name the eldest? Born to their mother by her first husband, Bernard D'Abru, she carried the name whence came all their wealth.

Oh, the Tracey solicitors made good money, but they were not in the same league as the *chocolatier* D'Abrus.

Bernard D'Abru, Lydia's father, had fallen head-over-heels in love with and married Martha Daly, one of his best workers. He had seen her first in the small workrooms at the back

11

of the store in Grafton Street, before that part of the business was moved out of town. Her wondrous beauty struck him dumb, and she was the best hand-roller of chocolates he had ever come across. She had given him a beautiful daughter and his cup of joy had run over. But then, out of the blue, Bernard D'Abru had died of a heart attack leaving Martha in sole charge of their highly successful business.

Way back when Bernard's antecedents had been the first *chocolatiers* in Bruges, all the kings and queens of Europe had been customers. Printed beneath the name of D'Abru, *Chocolatiers,* was a list of 'by appointment to' followed by half the crowned heads of the western world. The demand for D'Abru chocolates had grown too big to be met, but the policy of the firm was quality rather than quantity. They had confined their supplies to maintain excellence.

They had moved to Brussels, then to Paris and London. Her Majesty Queen Victoria adored the mouth-watering sweets, and the *chocolatier* found himself pressured into more and more production and at a faster rate than he desired. After the relative quiet of gracious old Bruges, the D'Abru ancestor found the hurly-burly of London, the crowds and the danger, intimidating. The sensitive man hated the prevalence of thieves and pick-pockets, the ever present violence and poverty there, and eventually crossed the Irish Sea to Dublin, where he found to his delight a more peaceful existence, yet he was near enough to supply his royal *clientele* with the chocolates they were addicted to. He bought Mallow Hall and settled to contented prosperity.

The story of how the D'Abru family business became a flourishing enterprise in Dublin's Grafton Street was often related over the dinner table at Mallow Hall and its telling was an unbearable irritant to both Austin and Roland Tracey, Martha's sons by her second marriage. Their family were *solicitors*, God's sakes, creatures of sophistication and intellectual weight, dealing in legal profundities and high-minded subjects, surely above mere sweet-makers!

Then why did they feel inferior, unadventurous and just plain dull when Martha told the story to the family and their guests? Nobody ever asked how the Tracey family started their professional career in Dublin, but everyone seemed interested in how a Belgian family came to Dublin to make chocolates. And the silver dish with its Waterford glass container would be passed around and the chocolates um'd and ah'd over, relished greedily while Austin and Roland seethed.

Austin hated the D'Abrus. He was glad his mother was not of that blood. She had after all only married into the name. 'Bloody foreigners,' he'd mutter, not seeing there was anything odd in lumping the D'Abrus under that heading when they had lived in Ireland now for decades. But there was only one of them now to hate — Lydia, his sister. Half-sister.

After Bernard had died, Martha, to everyone's surprise, remarried within a year. 'Sure I'm used to it now, the married state,' she'd say tranquilly. 'I'd never last on my own.' She married the family solicitor Thomas Tracey, and ran the chocolate business herself, with the help of both Lydia, when she had grown old enough, and Bernard's trusted manager J. G. Moran, called J.G. by everyone.

Martha loved the business. She loved chocolates. She never allowed Roland or Austin to forget where she had begun or that she had been a champion at hand-rolling chocolates — a fact they would much rather have forgotten.

To be precise, Austin and Roland would have liked nothing better than to sell the business and wipe out that memory altogether. They could become the Traceys of Mallow Hall, could forget the D'Abru chocolate business even though it had provided them with this beautiful home, a first-class education, and a lot of luxuries otherwise quite out of reach. So Austin in particular focussed all his resentment on his sister, Lydia D'Abru.

Roland the younger brother, a big stout chap whose name suited him marvellously, was a student at Trinity College, by special dispensation. Catholics could not normally attend this Protestant university but strings had been pulled as Trinity was considered one of the finest colleges in Europe. Roland was a much less intense fellow than his brother but no less averse to the chocolate business and the D'Abru name. He loved his creature comforts, and he loved his food, but although he agreed with his brother wholeheartedly, in reality he adored the exquisite chocolates the D'Abru firm produced. He would, however, have preferred to buy them than be a part of the firm that made them. He, like Austin, hated to be beholden to the D'Abru name for anything at all. But the greed in him was stronger than his dislike of the business and there was nothing he liked better than to demolish a box of D'Abru's best.

He would slide his nail down the cellophane that covered the distinctive brown box with its gold lettering, open it, carefully remove the packaging and the leaves of padded paper with D'ABRU printed in diagonal lines, like ladders, all down them in gold, stare at the rows of chocolates — oblong, square, oval and round — each one in its crisp fluted paper container, each one with a different delicious centre, and choose. The joy of choosing from a full box of D'Abru chocolates was a pleasure that never failed to excite him.

J.G. said only half in jest that the two brothers between them embodied each of the seven deadly sins. He said Austin personified what he called 'dry' sins and Roland the 'juicy' ones. 'Pride, covetousness, envy and anger, that's Austin — dry, hard, tight traits,' he'd say. 'Now Roland, Roland's sins are sloth, lust, gluttony. So self-indulgent. All the girls in D'Abru's avoid his fat fingers like the plague and he demolishes a full one-pound box of chocolates every time he goes into the shop.'

The shop, D'Abru's Fine Chocolates, was halfway up the most fashionable street in Dublin. It had bay windows that displayed the classic brown and gold D'Abru box on a bed of coffee-coloured velvet tastefully draped and scattered with little gold-leaf stars. Gold leaf was used in the box, a tiny clover-leaf shape on the corner of the raspberry truffle.

The chocolates were never put in the window for fear the rays of the sun might damage the quality of the confectionery, but from the street passersby could see the rows of handmade chocolates tempting them in their little sectioned glass containers, enticing and very seductive. Each section had a printed description underneath that in fact was nearly as mouth-watering as the chocolates themselves. Cherry Delight. Caramel Cream with Almond. Milk Chocolate Truffle. Strawberry Fondant. Marzipan Surprise. Praline Dream. All were covered by glass until a customer with a particular preference wanted to choose and then the lid would be lifted and the rich aroma of the chocolate would be released, tempting the buyer still further. The chocolate would then be removed with silver tongs and placed in its special waxed paper in a box, *never* a bag. Each one chocolate purchased would be tucked into tissue in a tiny brown and gold box one inch square made specially for a single D'Abru sweetmeat. Extremely expensive, the chocolates were at all times treated like precious jewels.

The smell of the chocolates as you passed the shop was, next to the aroma of freshly ground coffee from Bewley's down the road, the most tantalising fragrance in Dublin. They met somewhere between the two establishments and mingled, proving an almost irresistible temptation to combine the tastes and bring a D'Abru chocolate into Bewley's to nibble while sipping a cup of the café's finest blend.

The gift of a box of D'Abru's chocolates was considered a supreme luxury and a sure sign of high regard on the part of the giver. The chocolates were expensive, no doubt about that, and the receiver would glance at the brown and gold box with astonished delight.

Austin, dry and intense, hated chocolates. He hated the stylish little shop in Grafton Street. But most of all Austin hated Lydia D'Abru, the sole heiress to the business and Mallow Hall and, to his fury, his *older* sister.

Chapter Two

Martha Tracey sat at her dressing-table in her bedroom at Mallow Hall brushing her long black hair. The action soothed her troubled heart, calmed her somewhat.

Life was not fair! Her mother had often impressed that harsh fact upon her, but enough was enough. Two husbands under the sod and now Dr Fahy that very day had told her the news. She would quite shortly join them, wherever they were. She had cancer. Not long left — a year at most.

Of course she had known. For a long time now her body had sent subconscious messages that all was not well within. There was no cure for cancer, she knew that.

She stared at her face in the mirror. A lovely face. It had been her fortune and, Martha thought happily, Lydia had inherited it. A precious beauty worth more than money or jewels or treasure. A passport to whatever she had wanted. It had drawn men to her like flies to a pot of jam and it would do the same for her daughter. If only Lydia could be persuaded to become seriously interested in love and marriage and stop gallivanting around the countryside with Sean Sullivan. Martha had not worried too much before but time was running out and her daughter's future had to be taken care of. Beauty could bring you your heart's desire but it could also lead you into trouble and shame. Beauty, like money, could attract the wrong kind of men who made promises for the wrong reasons. And Lydia was an heiress. Martha had been very poor and she had always felt that had been to her advantage. She knew what poverty was like and she understood gratitude. Lydia, though Martha had tried her best not to spoil the girl, had a blithe acceptance of the delights of security.

Martha had tried to teach her daughter what to look for in a man. She had impressed upon Lydia the qualities that would guarantee contentment if not wild happiness. Martha did not believe in wild happiness though she herself had had more than her fair share of its milder form. But Martha had been prudent in her choice of men, her poor background making her a vigilant monitor of the men she allowed near. The young locals were discouraged; they had nothing to offer Martha Daly. The teeth-flashing salesmen who wanted a quick fling, ditto. And fortune-hunters were not interested in the poor girl from the cottage in the lane. No, she had been cautious and waited and eventually had the good fortune to have her boss — and not only the boss but the owner of the whole shebang — fall in love with her and marry her. Would Lydia, who was a happy-go-lucky girl, be so cautious when she fell in love? Martha had deep misgivings about such restraint on Lydia's part.

19

She remembered wistfully the tall, black-haired Derry MacCawley from the Liberties — the slums — his swashbuckling bravado, his flirtatious magnetism. She shivered. She had squashed any feelings she had had when he sallied up to her as they came out of the chocolate factory and grinned at her in his saucy way. He had been mad for her, and her struggle with the wild beatings of her heart, the terrible temptation she resisted, had been mercifully successful. It had made her a stronger woman and left her free to marry her boss. She had loved her husbands, both of them, however not with that fierce passion she had felt for Derry. But look at how she'd ended up! Mistress of Mallow Hall, able to afford anything she wanted, cossetted and cared for. It was a very successful result, one had to agree.

Martha smiled at herself. She did not regret for a moment her firm handling of her emotions. She was glad she had not succumbed to Derry's obvious appeal and settled for a hard life of near poverty in the slums. She had adored Bernard. He had been older than she, had taken her from the narrow existence she had led, and guided her into the broader experience of a cultured appreciation of the good things of life. And she had been grateful; her whole world had broadened and she appreciated the beauty and space his money provided. He had worshipped her and that too was wonderful. When to her consternation he had dropped dead from a heart attack she had been devastated. She had been left a widow-woman so soon, too soon.

But Martha was not a woman to dwell in the past. She could not bear to be alone. She loved companionship, the sharing that marriage entailed, and she wore her widow's weeds stylishly. Thomas Tracey had been her husband's solicitor and had always had a *gradh* for the beautiful Mrs D'Abru. Sensing her need, her loneliness, he had made his move, wooed her earnestly and won her. Within six months of Bernard's death she had remarried. The town was shocked, but Martha was content. Let them gossip and rail. She had wanted a companion and she had again chosen wisely. She was very happy with Thomas. Their union produced two sons a year apart and though Thomas was not rich he was comfortably off and their life together was very pleasant.

Martha was not socially ambitious but she appreciated the benefits brought to her by marriage first to a rich manufacturer and second to a respected member of the professional class.

She did not want to leave Mallow Hall and it did not need much persuasion on her part to get Thomas to agree to move into the imposing residence rather than for her to move into his modest home in Ballsbridge. He was easily convinced that it was most sensible and convenient, the obvious thing to do.

Those who were jealous of Martha hinted at all sorts of skulduggery when Thomas followed Bernard to an early grave, but Martha grieved his loss and no one who saw her doubted her genuine sorrow at his passing.

Many a man wooed her after her second husband's death but she said the heart had gone out of her and she cared now only for her children, and indeed devoted all her time to them.

She had been much harder on Lydia, partly because of her beauty and Martha's fear that it might lead her into trouble. Her boys she spoiled dreadfully, fearing the lack of a man about the house. She was aware that there was no love lost between the brothers and their sister but decided that was the way of the male. Men were creatures of violence, of angry feelings at war in their breasts, especially when young. Men went to do battle, got drunk outside pubs on Saturday night and picked fights. That neither of her husbands had been like that did not shake her conviction. It merely confirmed her belief that she had chosen well, that her husbands had been ultra-civilised men.

She would have to find such a husband for Lydia. Martha worried that she had instilled in her daughter too high a standard and expectation and Lydia at twenty-four was still fancy-free. Had she put the girl off? Martha wondered. It was not easy to find young good-looking men who were kind and prudent, men who were well-to-do, so that Lydia's money and inheritance were not the lure rather than Lydia herself. It was difficult to find even one young man with a business or career that was exceptionally successful and who had a sense of humour, an equable disposition and who was intelligent. It was a tall order, and Martha worried that there existed such a paragon. Was there a man in Ireland worthy of her daughter? Martha doubted it.

Martha did not want to die. Not yet. She still had too much to do. Then, as she sat daydreaming about her family, she realised that she did not want to die at all. There was no suitable time. She could not bear to leave this world, for she had loved it so and it had been very good to her. How could she leave it in high summer when the apples were dropping on to the orchard floor and the poppies were nodding in the corn? Not while the blackberries were staining the grass verges purple and the roses were drowning the air with heavenly scent. Not while the sun shone butter-yellow and the waters of the lake danced sparkling-blue under an azure sky. Not now.

But when would it be easy to leave this wonderful world? Not when the autumn leaves fell, amber, bronze, ochre and gold, and the chestnuts hit the grass in the meadow hard and velvet-brown and the first energising frost hit the air.

Nor when the world wore a cloak of white snow and the icicles were gleaming transparent spears dripping slow drops from the eaves and there was skating on the lake.

Or when the first snow-drop bravely pierced the hard earth, holding up its fragile and delicate head, a proof of regeneration and rebirth. Not then. Nor when the bluebells carpeted the wood in a cloudy mauve haze and the first rays of a spring sun fell on her cold cheek. Not then.

Never, she thought, knowing that was impossible, and decided it was better not to know — like Bernard. Like Thomas. Better for death to arrive stealthily, a gaunt black shadow to creep up on her from behind and fell her without warning, that was much, much better. Not like this. Approaching slowly from a distance in front of her, waving at her, in full view. *Here I am, coming to get you.*

She shook her head. She was not going to show her fear. She had always had dignity and she would not allow death to rob her of that. She would do this as she had done everything else in her life, with considered style. 'I will not let you defeat me,' she told her reflection. 'I will not be craven.'

One thing she had to do was make a will. That was essential if the family was to avoid chaos when she went. She had sensed the tinderbox of dissent in her household, dissent generated by the tricky situation of inheritance. Thomas Tracey had died well aware of the violence of the emotion simmering volcano-like just below the surface of their daily lives, but he had avoided the issue, leaving the whole situation in her hands. Well, she had no one to leave decisions to. She had to leave clear and correct instructions, unpopular though that was going to be.

D'Abru's had to go to her daughter. There lay the problem. It was what Bernard D'Abru had wanted and made clear to her. But how would the boys feel about that? Unnecessary to ask. Roland and Austin would not appreciate such a situation. They felt themselves lords of the manor. They were, after all, the male of the species and Lydia a mere girl. A female did not count unless specifically nominated. A wife's property was, in Irish law, her husband's to do with what he liked and let any female try to buck that.

Martha loved her sons but was aware that her daughter held her heart with a special tenderness she could never explain. She tried not to show it, indeed had been harder on Lydia, but she realised that Roland and Austin had always been subconsciously aware of the extra-special feeling she had for her daughter. Women were supposed to favour their sons, she realised that, and had always felt herself odd in how disproportionate her partiality was. She tried to make it up to her boys, to no avail. They *knew*. They took it as a slight upon their father and felt she had somehow betrayed him as well as them. None of this was ever discussed but fermented sourly underneath the daily bustle of their lives. She was well aware of how they felt and was determined to leave her affairs tidy, with no room for speculation after her death. No maybes or perhaps.

On top of that she had always loved the business and was fully aware that if her sons had their way they would sell D'Abru's as fast as they could and she did not want that.

She loved the shop in Grafton Street. She spent time there and had always run the business with delight. Not that she had that much to do — J.G. saw to that. He was the real boss, but she made the decisions and he always deferred to her.

She went in most days, and she knew the workers by name, knew the names of their husbands and wives, their children. Lydia came with her. Lydia enjoyed the shop and the factory, said it made her feel useful. She had a very sound knowledge of the running of the business and the manufacture of the chocolates.

Martha's heart turned when she thought of her daughter. Her daughter was her friend. Lydia would look after D'Abru's for her, after she was gone, she was confident of that.

Where things became ambiguous was in the matter of Mallow Hall. It had been in the D'Abru family for decades, since the first D'Abru had used his profits to purchase the glorious old house in Wicklow. By rights Mallow Hall was Lydia's. She was, after all, the last D'Abru. But the male of the species *expected* to be the heirs. The men in Ireland inherited and her sons were very touchy indeed. Male pride, especially in Austin, was very easily dented.

Lydia had a sweet nature. She would not mind sharing, her mother knew that, and Austin and Roland would never throw their sister out. God forbid! Martha would not even entertain such a thought. Austin and Roland were typically male.

You had to let them think they ran things while in reality you did. No, Martha assured herself, her sons were too kindly and honourable to treat Lydia badly.

However, the problem might not lie within her own family. Her sons would marry, so would Lydia, and everyone knew that in-laws were not to be trusted. They could be greedy and ambitious. Austin and Roland, Martha decided, were utterly trustworthy, but who could predict what their wives would be like? Who could anticipate how they would behave?

So Martha had come to the conclusion that she would have to make a will, write every specific thing down, spell it out in clear English so that there could be no mistake.

She'd go to Pius Brady, her late husband's partner and her sons' godfather, and entrust him with the whole thing. Tracey, Brady and Co was the firm of solicitors who had handled the D'Abru estate and business since the beginning. They were an old firm, a respectable firm with offices in Fitzwilliam Square, and it had been Pius Brady's mother who had invited the widow to the select dinner and sowed the seed in Thomas Tracey's mind that wedding his late partner's wife might be beneficial to them both. The D'Abru account had passed to Pius after Thomas's death and he had taken Austin into the firm as soon as he had qualified.

Martha had deemed this a generous action — Austin was still a fledgling after all but Pius had

had little choice in this matter. Thomas Tracey had left half his business, his half, in trust for his sons with explicit instructions that if either of them followed the family profession he be taken into the partnership. It had been an arrangement that little suited Pius Brady. He had never been that keen on his partner, was in fact jealous of him and his good fortune, but he had no option. He had once hoped to buy out the Tracey share but he could not afford to. The truth of the matter was that Thomas Tracey had been possessed of considerable charm, a quality that Pius sadly lacked, and customers were not that keen to flock to the offices of the edgy solicitor who preferred the races to their problems and whose primary interest seemed to be to get them out of the building as quickly as possible. No, the firm of Tracey, Brady & Co had not prospered since the death of the senior partner.

Pius had hoped that Austin would prove to be a chip off the old block and perhaps take the burden of work off his shoulders, but Austin was a disappointment. He leaned heavily on the fact that until he became articled he could not really do much actual work. He liked the offices in Fitzwilliam Square even less than Pius and dropped in whenever he felt like it, a proper young know-it-all, aware of his power and without any experience at all. The only advantage to Pius in his godson's presence in the office was that he could be relied upon to close his eyes to any irregularities, and that eminently suited Pius.

28

But Martha knew nothing of the ins and outs of the firm of solicitors that handled her affairs, only that her late husband, whom she had trusted and loved, had been a partner there. So she would make an appointment to see Pius, with a view to having him draw up a will clearly stating her wishes, leaving nothing to chance or custom.

As she sat she felt a tide of the terrible pain through her body. She shuddered both from the intensity of it and the knowledge of the decay galloping within her and she decided to make the appointment *at once*. She would insist on seeing Pius Brady tomorrow. Time was running out. Then as she stared at the phone she thought, maybe, maybe I'll recover. Maybe I'll get better. Maybe, just maybe I will be able to live out the rest of my days in this peaceful place I love so much, grow old, enjoy my life. Oh God, she prayed, a miracle. Send me a miracle. Why not? It is within your power. A little miracle wiping out the decay rampaging through my body would be nothing to you. You have all power, so do it.

Nothing happened. Outside a bird sang and she bent her head on her hands and hot tears ran down her cheeks.

Chapter Three

Lydia and Sean walked over the field and into the wood. The trees embraced overhead and the earth smelled pungent and strong, like ripe cheese. The bluebells were gone and the leaves were preparing for their long separation from the trees. Autumn was not far off.

It was late August and harvest time was nigh. Mallow Hall was not a farm but it was set in farming country and all around the stately home there were signs of heightened activity.

'Best be gettin' back,' Sean said, glancing sideways at Lydia.

She was the most beautiful creature he had ever seen but she confused him mightily. Most of the girls hereabouts wanted a tumble with Sean Sullivan more than anyone else, even Tyrone Power. But all he'd ever done was kiss Lydia rather chastely. She did not encourage him or flirt with him as the others did. She treated him like a brother and he could not make her out. Her innate modesty held him back from what he deemed would be taking advantage of her. It was his mother's phrase. 'Ye can do what ye like, Sean boy, an' with half the girls in Ireland after ye I don't reckon ye'll have te stint yerself, but ye must never take advantage of a girl.' She'd warned him over and over, smiling at her gorgeous son, full of pride in his wonderful beauty, his manly body.

When he'd asked her what exactly the phrase meant she'd told him that trying anything the girl was unwilling about was taking advantage and Sean had no problem with that. The girls urged Sean Sullivan on rather than called a halt, but this did not apply to Lydia D'Abru. She was the only one who was not free with him, so she both intimidated him and made him love her all the more.

His mother warned him. 'She's not for you, Sean Sullivan. She's from a different place on the planet.' But it was no use. Love, as Martha Tracey had often said, gave no room to choice. Its barbed arrows hit and willy-nilly there was no decision in it. It was a *fait accompli*.

Sean and Lydia had been friends from childhood. They lived in close harmony with each other and with nature all their born days. Sean had taught Lydia to fish, to identify flowers and herbs, to understand the life of the countryside with all its gentle and cruel ways; the shy things of the woods, the domestic animals, the wild things of the mountains. They'd roamed the countryside together, talked to the travelling men and women, listened to their stories and joined the gypsies singing around the fires in the night. They had climbed trees and played in the rocks on the shore and swum with the seals off the coast in the cold grey sea. They had explored the caves together and Sean knew finally he had fallen in love when they had been trapped in the cave of the Three Old Hags of Burragh and the tide rising. Lydia, blue with cold in her elasticised swimsuit, had turned to him, her eyes huge with fear, and said, 'Save me, Sean, I'm scared.'

He knew then that he would die for her. He had gathered her up in his arms and scrambled sure-footed over the slippery rocks, then, hoisting her high, swum out of the cave into an angry sea. He had borne her aloft with superhuman strength till they reached the shore, and there he'd set her down safely, like a jewel in a box, and she'd turned those huge eyes upon him again and whispered, 'Oh, aren't you the great man!' and he was lost forever. Her slave, her knight.

She had been fourteen then and now she was twenty-four and things had not changed much. There was such innocence about her. She did not seem grown-up to him, did not know how to behave with a fella at all. When she danced on a Saturday night at the local hop she did not flirt or sling her beauty about as the other girls did. She did not use any wiles on the boys, all of whom worshipped at her shrine. In fact she simply seemed full of vibrant life, joyously unselfconscious and totally unaware of the havoc she caused in the hearts of men.

Sean wrestled with the unanswerable dilemma: how to marry her. There was no way he could see that he could ever aspire to being her spouse. Not as things stood. He was a small-time farmer and she was the wealthy and beautiful daughter from the big house, and everyone knew that was not a situation that ever had a happy ending. Yet he wanted her with him for-ever and a day.

In his heart Sean did not believe that there was any hope for him at all. He was too practical and down to earth to believe in easy answers to com-plicated situations.

He could see no way out of his dilemma. He knew Lydia's wish that time would stand still and the summer days never end was a hope that could not, would not be realised. He knew too that he could not marry her and live off the D'Abru fortune in the D'Abru house. He knew too that he could not bring her home to the cot-tage at the crossroads to share a room with him, a curtain dividing them from the living-room, his mother within earshot most of the time. And he could not afford to buy them a place, however humble, of their own. It was a terrible dilemma and however much he pondered the ins and outs of it Sean could see only one answer — for him to leave Wicklow. Leave Ireland. Make some money and return with enough in his purse to ask for Lydia's hand.

'Lydia,' he said, sitting down on a fallen tree-trunk, 'come an' set awhile.'

As usual she obeyed instantly. 'What is it, Sean?' she asked.

'Lydia, I bin thinkin'.' She turned her gaze to-wards him. Her look made his heart beat faster and his throat dry. 'I gotta go away. Leave here.

Make something of myself. Make some money.'

'Money isn't that important,' she said with the assurance of one who always had it. 'When you have it it puts up barriers.'

'Oh, it's all very well, you to talk. You've got it an' plenty.'

'But, Sean, why should things change?' She was staring at him, her cornflower-blue eyes troubled. 'I'm so happy, things as they are. Why should anything have to change?'

Sean looked at her impatiently. 'It's healthy for things to change, Lydia. Look at Dead Man's Pool beyond here. The water's stagnant. Never moves. Nothing blooms there, or lives. Things have to change, Lydia, to live.' She pouted. He continued, 'Honestly, Lydia, you amaze me sometimes. It's like you're asleep. Dreaming. You'll miss out on life, you go on that way.' He shook his head. 'No. I have to make some money so we can be together.'

'We're together now, Sean.'

He sighed. Why was she being so obtuse? 'No, no. I mean forever, all the time. Like married.'

'I don't want to get married, Sean. I'm happy as I am. All that stuff is for later.'

'Lydia, you're twenty-four! Most girls are married by then.'

'Well, *I'm* not!' she jumped up off the mossy tree-trunk, her eyes flashing. 'And I won't be rushed, so there.'

'Sit down, Lydia, and listen. Don't keep interrupting.' She sat down again. 'I'm going to go

34

away. Make some money. Then I'll come back for you.'

'How will you make the money, Sean?' she asked him, sensing his mind was made up and there was no use arguing. Everything was going to change and there was nothing she could do to stop it. She thought idly that one of the reasons she did not want to marry was because she could never really explain to any man exactly how she felt. They never understood, and she always ended up biting her tongue, keeping her thoughts to herself. 'I've heard there's jobs galore in England. Rebuilding the bombed places.'

'That's been done a long time ago, Sean. It's nineteen fifty-five and the war's been over ten years.'

'No. There's still a lot of building to be done. So Paddy Mac says. He's over from London. I saw him in Grady's last evening and him throwing a wad about like he was Rockefeller.'

'Do you have to go, Sean?' her blue eyes pleaded and his heart near stopped with the pain. He put the back of his hand against her cloud of hair. It was soft as silk, a mesh of waves that the sun filtered with light and the breeze through the trees played in. 'You know I do, Lydia darlin'. You know I do.'

She sighed. He was right, she thought reluctantly, everything had to change eventually. Gone forever like dust on the wind. The happy carefree rambles, the unity of their thoughts, the comradeship, walking hand in hand through the woods, swimming in the cove, riding. All of it would slip away no matter how she tried to hold on. These things, these precious moments would become memories, to be rummaged through on dark days. Ah, I was happy then! Would it come to that? She laid her cheek against his shirt-sleeve. 'I want something permanent. Something lasting. Not a seesaw,' she said wistfully.

'Well, Lydia, life *is* a seesaw whether you like it or not, and mebbe it's time you faced that.'

'When will you go?' She stood and so did he. She knew he did not really understand. He would never understand. So she kept her thoughts to herself. She played the scene his way.

The wood was full of the rustlings and flutterings of small creatures.

'I'll go as soon as I can,' he told her.

'Your mam will go bonkers,' she said, smiling. He laughed.

'I'll manage her,' he replied and she lifted an eyebrow.

'Oh yeah?'

'Oh yeah!'

They stared at each other and he moved towards her and put his arms around her. She fitted so neatly into the circle, so snugly against him. 'I'll be back as soon as I can, Lydia,' he said.

'With a wad like Paddy Mac?'

'Yeah!'

'You know I don't care about that, Sean.'

'Oh, I know that. But *I* do,' he said simply.

He stared at the small oval face he loved so well. She was part of him, in his blood, his heart, his very soul. Then he bent and kissed her. It was unlike his usual soft kiss, a mere brushing of lips against lips. It was intense and passionate and her knees turned soft under her, her body dissolved in his arms, and when he let her go she nearly fell.

'Don't you forget that,' he told her.

'As if I could. Where'd you learn that, Sean Sullivan?' she asked breathlessly.

'You jealous?' he laughed. Then, seriously, 'It's so you'll remember.'

Just as seriously she replied, 'I'll remember, Sean.' She looked at him quizzically. 'You really think I'd forget you, do you?'

'No. There's too much between us,' he said. 'I'll talk to Mam tonight. I might be gone in the morning.'

Her heart plummeted. 'So soon?'

'The sooner I'm off the sooner I'll be back,' he told her and, taking her hand in his, he drew her after him out of the woods.

Chapter Four

Mallow Hall was bordered by the wood behind while in front the lawns sloped down to the river. The granite house sat serenely facing the purple mountains, the windows open to the soft cooling breezes.

Martha, sitting near her window in melancholy thought, heard her son clatter up the stairs. The curving staircase was carpeted down the middle but Austin always trod up the side, making a noise and irritating her. He's announcing his presence, she thought, then, he wants me to know he's home and he's angry. But then, she realised suddenly, Austin was *always* angry.

He knocked at her door and she called out, 'Come in.'

'Mother.' He came and kissed her cheek, such a cold, absent-minded kiss, and she could tell he was furious — which meant he'd been bested. She could guess who by. Why her sons did not get along with Lydia she could not fathom. Boys were supposed to adore and spoil their sisters but not Austin or Roland. She knew what was coming and she wished she did not have to listen. She hated to be the repository of Austin's malice.

'Lydia is a disgrace —' he began, Martha held up her hand.

'I don't want to hear any tales, Austin,' she said firmly, but her son was not to be stopped.

'I don't know why you let her run around the countryside with that — that yokel.'

She laughed. 'Oh come along, Austin, Sean Sullivan is not a yokel.'

'He's not a gentleman,' Austin insisted.

'True,' Martha agreed tranquilly. 'He's not had the benefit of a classical education with the Jesuits, but then neither did I have the luxury of the Sacré Coeur like Lydia did. But Sean is far from being —'

'I caught him kissing Lydia in the hedges,' Austin announced, red-faced.

Whatever excuses Martha was about to make on her daughter's behalf died on her lips. That was not good news. Sean was a very handsome lad and Lydia would awaken one day to find she was a woman. It had to happen sooner or later and Martha had hoped to God it would be later.

Martha had allowed Sean Sullivan and her daughter to run about the countryside together because she knew how unawakened Lydia was. Her daughter wore her innocence like a shield, and Martha knew Sean Sullivan was an honourable boy. But the day would come, and she had been on the look-out for it, believing she had all the time in the world to monitor her daughter's development. This was no longer so and steps must now be taken to protect Lydia and secure a satisfactory future for her. And not with Sean Sullivan.

She looked at her son. 'Where were they kissing?' she asked lightly.

'At the edge of the fallow field,' Austin admitted grudgingly. He'd have preferred the barn. It would have made it more secretive, more damning. But he knew his mother would find out if he lied. She had an uncanny ability to sniff out the truth.

'That is rather different matter from "the bushes",' she now said tartly. 'Out in the open? Hardly furtive, Austin, would you say? Anyway, I'll deal with it. Now leave me. I'll see you at dinner.'

'But, Mother . . .'

At that moment Lydia entered her mother's room. She did not knock. Since Thomas Tracey died Martha had given her daughter permission to enter without preamble.

'Oh, *he's* here already!' Lydia cried as soon as she saw Austin. 'Shooting his mouth off. Telling tales. Couldn't wait!'

'Well, Lydia, were you?'

'Was I what?'

'Kissing Sean Sullivan?' Martha asked calmly. Austin could not keep the smirk off his face.

'Yes I was, but —'

'Sean is your friend, Lydia, and he's a very nice boy, but you must not allow him to take liberties.'

'I was kissing him *goodbye!*' Lydia cried triumphantly. It was not strictly true, she knew, but it was worth it to checkmate Austin, see his face.

'What?'

'Sean is going to England,' Lydia informed them. 'He was saying goodbye to me.'

'Good riddance!' Austin muttered. Contrarily he was not at all pleased with the news. Sean Sullivan could have got Little Miss Lydia in trouble, disgraced her and maybe, just maybe, such a situation might have prevented her from inheriting Mallow Hall. A pregnant girl was a disgrace and the neighbourhood would not have tolerated her presence there. Now that tantalising possibility had been removed. Austin was well aware that his wishes were opposite and at times contradictory, but that did not stop him. As Lydia often said, he was forever at war with himself. Nothing pleased him.

'Well then, that's that,' Martha said with finality.

Like Austin, she was both pleased and sorry to hear the news of Sean Sullivan's departure. She was depressed by the fact that so many young men, particularly those from the country, had to leave to make a living for themselves in this new technological age. The old ways were going, the ancient leisurely methods being replaced by machinery and the pace speeded up. Foreign shores beckoned, now not because there was hunger in the land, but because expectations were higher and people were demanding luxuries unheard of ten years ago.

She was glad because it removed the temptation of Sean, the obstacle in Lydia's path. Now other young men, more suitable, could be pressed upon her daughter with a view to matrimony.

It was not that she felt superior to the Sullivans. She herself had come from a similar background and she had never forgotten that fact nor wished to. But, she was convinced, it was different for a man. If Austin or Roland had brought home a girl from a working-class background she would not have given the matter a second thought. She would have helped and encouraged the bride in every way she could. But a man was another matter altogether. A man had pride. And a very dicey thing was pride. It permeated their bones, clouded their every thought.

A man had to be the breadwinner. He had to be head of the household, the boss. Sean Sullivan had not a penny to his name. He could never bow his head to her daughter. A woman's husband had to command respect in the district and Sean Sullivan would be made a mockery of by the populace if he married Lydia. He would never be able to tolerate the ridicule of the country folk and would eventually take it out on Lydia.

And Lydia could not live in the cottage at the crossroads. She was used to the good things in life. It was fine and dandy to roam the countryside adventuring with Sean but Martha knew her daughter needed to come home at the end of the day to a hot bath and a cosy bed and the privacy of her pretty room.

And if Sean were to be somehow prevailed

upon to come to live at Mallow Hall — and her daughter could be very persuasive, Martha was well aware of that — the situation with Austin and Roland would be intolerable. They would kill him. No. Martha had no illusions about that scenario.

Martha now shooed her children away. She had to think, make plans. They left the room reluctantly, softly bickering. They enjoyed being there with her, locked in contest for her approval and her attention, but they left at her request.

She had been writing in a notebook when Austin had disturbed her. Now she turned her attention back to her scribbling.

She had written a list of names there, names of eligible bachelors for Lydia. The problem was Lydia knew them all, had grown up with them, saw them all the time at balls and parties, in the Country Club, at the Horse Show and other functions and she had shown no interest whatsoever in any of them.

Martha sighed. Lydia would have to be prompted. She would have to be pushed, gently of course, but pushed nevertheless. She must make a choice. Twenty-four was an eminently suitable age for a girl to marry — a little old perhaps, but Lydia was beautiful. Now Sean Sullivan was on his way out of her life and the time was ripe. There had been no hurry before but Martha wanted to see Lydia settled before she died.

Oh, that terrible eventuality! It loomed before

her, a spectre influencing everything she did forcing her to hurry, hurry, hurry.

She looked at the names. Michael Donnelan, Cormack McLeigh, Diarmuid McCabe, Orlich Fitzmaurice. They were her favourites, but how did Lydia feel about them? All came from good families, all had been well-educated. All were comfortably off. Of the four Orlich Fitzmaurice was the one she hoped Lydia might pick, the one she was going to try to manoeuvre into marriage with her daughter. Orlich was kind. He was sensible. He had a sense of humour and was good-looking. What more could a girl want?

Love, a little voice screamed within her. Love. But she stifled it, that little voice, stopped it dead.

There was a knock on her door. She smiled. It had to be Roland, her youngest.

'Come in, dear.' Roland squeezed through the door. He was chubby, there was no doubt about that. She wondered briefly why she so preferred this son to the other despite the excesses so clearly revealed on his face. Perhaps it had something to do with his enjoyment of life, an enjoyment Austin seemed incapable of.

Roland was a jolly young man who relished his earthly pleasures and indulged his appetites. When exactly he studied was a mystery. *If* he studied. Sometimes Lydia doubted it. He was a popular, good-natured fellow who gambled rather recklessly and infuriated the frugal Austin by continually begging loans from his complacent mother, loans which he never paid back.

Roland was the perennial student. He saw no reason why he should ever stop being one, grow up to responsible manhood, and he spent most of his time hanging around Trinity with his mates, drinking, chasing skirt and generally leading a slap-happy kind of existence. He spent a great deal of his time at the races, careering from Leopardstown to Dublin, the Curragh and Davy Byrne's, and even across the water to Ascot and Aintree. It was a round of eternal pleasure, paid for, as his brother was fond of pointing out, with the family funds.

Martha refused to worry in spite of Austin's dire predictions. She knew that boys would be boys and was confident that Roland was simply sowing his wild oats and would eventually settle down.

Today as always Roland had his Trinity scarf around his neck, in spite of the heat. It was a status symbol he was never without. He wore a linen blazer and trousers, a pink cotton shirt open at the neck and a carelessly knotted college tie at half-mast on his chest.

Roland's clothes always seemed too small, even when sizing was meticulously accurate. He resembled a bag of laundry and there was nothing even the best tailor could do to rectify that. Roland, however, did not care. He was oblivious to his shortcomings, thought he was stylish, knew he was a member of the 'in' clique, a student at the top college in Dublin. He had enough money to spend so he found it easy to collect about him quite a little *entourage* of fellow-students, hangers-on, and girls. They yo-yo'd between Trinity, the Bailey, Jammet's, the Shelbourne, the Red Bank, Landsdown Road, Mrs Lawlor's of Naas and The Goat. They rollicked from various clubs to dances and parties. They were heedless, irresponsible and felt themselves a cut above the rest, a smart set with little to do but enjoy themselves and get drunk.

'How are you, Mother?' Roland, although normally boisterous, was always gentle around his mother. He adored Martha and to him she was an icon, an angel.

'I'm . . .' She looked into her son's eyes and the glib reply died on her lips. 'I'm a little tired, Roley.'

His look of instant consternation alarmed her. Oh dear God, how was she going to tell her children the terrible truth? She'd have to do so eventually, that much was sure. They'd have to be prepared.

'No, Roley. It's all right. Come, let's sit over here.'

She went to the chaise longue and draped herself upon it, crossing her slim silk-stockinged legs, making room for her son.

'No, Mother, I'll get a chair,' he said, looking dubiously at the small space she seemed to think would be adequate for him. He pulled over one of the Louis Quinze gilt and blue velvet chairs and sat on it facing her.

The room was decorated in light blue and white. Martha loved the cool colours. There were huge arrangements of white flowers in out-size vases everywhere — carnations, roses, lilies and stock — their purity broken only by the soft green of the leaves. The windows were open and the white gauze curtains billowed in the breeze. There were heavy blue velvet draperies fringed with gold looped back from the windows with gold ropes, and pale blue silk carpets, Persian, with a pattern of gold and bronze, on the heavy walnut floor. Two bevelled Venetian mirrors, gilt-framed, graced the walls and a carved walnut bed with a blue and white satin-covered eiderdown stood solidly against one wall.

It was a restful room, a tranquil room, the room, she reflected now, that she would die in.

'Are you sure you're all right, Mother?' Roland asked anxiously. She seemed so far away, so pre-occupied.

She looked at him. She wanted to tell him the dire news, tell *someone*. But she knew pandemonium would break out if she confided in Roland. How she was ever going to be able to do it she did not know and decided this certainly was not the time. She was not at all in command of herself.

'I'm fine, Roley, really,' she said softly, patting the hand he'd given her. 'Don't you worry about me. Now tell me about your studies.'

Roland grimaced. He thought of the mellow buildings in College Green and how he really only used them to boost his social life. He sighed and began to spin her a yarn about the hours he spent poring over dusty books and how dedicated he was to his study even in this hot weather. They both knew he was lying.

When he had left her Martha returned to her thoughts. She was aware of the gun in her back, the urgency her illness imposed upon her to tidy things up before she left this world she loved so well. 'God give me acceptance,' she prayed. 'I don't want to go, oh sweet Jesus I don't want to go.' She wanted to see her grandchildren, spend twilight years in a chair smiling at the rosy up-turned faces of Lydia's and Roland's children. She did not think about Austin's offspring and when she realised this she frowned and wondered why. She hoped there was an afterlife, somewhere her spirit would fly, then debated, who would be there to greet her, Bernard or Thomas? She hoped it would be Bernard, then gave up the debate.

She felt so tired, so very tired. But she had things to do. She picked up the phone and made an appointment to see Pius Brady the next day.

Chapter Five

She had to wait, which irritated her. Of course no one knew how she suffered, how restless pain made her, but nevertheless she had hoped for swifter service, for Pius to be prompt. She wore a flower print voile dress, light and gossamer, full-skirted, silky against her legs. Light though it was, the dress stuck to her back, and her face, pale as milk, was covered in a cold sweat.

No, she did not feel well as she waited in the dark panelled room on a leather chair that she was sticking to, idly turning the pages of *Tatler & Sketch* and *Country Life*. So much of her energy went into holding herself together so that the façade would not crack. She felt tired all the time.

The waiting room was cool and dark. She had often waited here in the old days for Thomas to finish with a client. They would have dinner in town and go to the theatre, then return to Mallow Hall, always the thing that gave her most pleasure. At the end of every day there was always Mallow Hall.

But that was once upon a time and it seemed very long ago now.

Pius Brady came out of the office into the waiting room, hands extended, a huge grin on his face.

'Welcome, welcome, Martha. How good to see you here. Like the old days, eh?'

He had a large round head and his skin was ruddy-brown from playing golf. He was a big bluff hearty bloke, and though his manner was effusive his eyes rarely met those of his clients but danced uneasily about the room, sliding into the corners of the ceiling or fixing on a door-knob, a book or a wastebasket.

He ushered Martha into his office, which was furnished in the same style as the waiting room — wall-to-wall law books, dark panelling, heavy mahogany furniture and padded leather chairs.

Martha sat. He faced her unctuously, rubbing his hands together.

'My dear Martha, what can I do for you? A cup of Earl Grey? Eileen, can get you some tea? Eileen . . . ?' He flicked the intercom as Martha protested.

'No, Pius. No. Please don't bother Eileen . . .' Eileen Skully, his secretary, was a neat little woman of thirty-nine, with a small, pretty face no one noticed. Unmarried, she had been in love with Pius Brady for twenty years, devoted her whole existence to him, but had not been desired by him. Whether he was aware of this passion was debatable and Thomas and Martha had often speculated about it but had never been able to come to a conclusion. Certainly it was a convenient state of affairs for Pius. Eileen was happy to do the work of two, devote all her waking hours to his service, and would if pushed probably have died for him. Her efficiency was breathtaking.

'Eileen, will you bring Mrs Tracey some tea, please.' Pius ignored Martha's protests and settled back in his chair.

'The boys well? I saw Austin this morning of course. Lydia well, I trust?'

The door opened as Martha was reassuring the solicitor that all the family were indeed in good health, and the secretary entered carrying a tray upon which rested a silver teapot, two cups and a plate of oval digestive biscuits. The woman greeted Martha with sweet grace. There was an obvious and pathetic desire to please in her every move and gesture.

'I knew you'd be requiring tea, Mr Brady, with Mrs Tracey coming in, so I had it all ready,' she announced triumphantly.

'Hello, Eileen,' Martha smiled. 'Thoughtful as ever.'

'Oh Mrs Tracey, it is nice to see you here again. Like old times. Will I pour? Or will I leave it to you?'

Martha knew she had not the strength to lift the heavy teapot. 'Please do it for me, Eileen,' she asked as Pius was telling his secretary to leave. Martha smiled at them both so charmingly that they forbore to comment on her departure from the norm. Martha always poured the tea.

'I will leave you alone now, Mr Brady, as soon as I've poured this.' And Eileen filled the delicate little cups, added milk and sugar and brightly handed around the biscuits. Then, smiling at them both as if she was a benevolent aunt, she bowed herself out of the room.

Pius looked at Martha, his smile still in place. Martha sipped her tea. 'She's a treasure,' she remarked.

'Don't I know it,' Pius said fervently, smiling a self-congratulatory smile.

'Sometimes I think you take her for granted.'

'Not really, Martha,' he replied. 'But employees have to be kept in their place,' he shrugged. 'Otherwise . . .'

'Anarchy?' she remarked archly.

'You know what I mean.' He sounded irritated. Martha decided to let it go.

Pius had put aside his smile and his expression switched to serious. 'Well now, Martha, what can I do for you?' he asked earnestly.

'I want to make a will, Pius.' He did not bat an eye, though there was no reason why he should. People required wills drawn up every day.

'Well now, would you like to tell me how you want it and I'll put it into legal jargon and then you can sign it? How about that?'

Why don't I like him? Martha wondered. I never have and I never will. Yet their lives were closely bound together. He had been Thomas's friend and partner. He was the best man at their wedding. He was Austin's godfather. He was always charming to her, looking after her with courtesy and kindness, yet there was something about him that repelled her. A phoniness. A slip-

52

periness. She brushed away her thoughts and told him what she wanted. He made notes, nodding now and then, and when she'd finished all he said was, 'That's simple enough. Clear-cut. I'll have it typed out and ask you to come in again to sign it and check that everything is as you want. Or perhaps I should bring it up to Mallow Hall?'

Mallow Hall, she thought. No, not there. If the boys or Lydia saw Pius Brady they would be curious. No, not Mallow Hall.

Pius was leaning across the desk, speaking to her. 'It's not up to me to comment, Martha, but don't you think your boys come out of this rather badly?' He hesitated. 'After all, Lydia is a girl.' There was no contempt in his voice, he was merely stating a fact.

'I've thought about it, Pius. I've prayed about it. But however I twist and turn it Lydia is the one who *should, must* inherit D'Abru's and Mallow Hall. It is her heritage, not theirs. But I want you to make it clear that the boys have the right to occupy the house until they marry.' She paused and bit her lip, then looked at him earnestly. 'You see, Pius, I feel it is time both of them realised that they should work harder. Make careers for themselves. Really put their backs into it.' She looked at him, sighing. 'You know better than anyone how little they do. Austin should be here this morning.'

'Well, he had to . . .'

'Don't make excuses for him, Pius. I know my

son too well. And Roland, dear boy though he is, is probably as we speak in Davy Byrne's preparatory to going to the races. No. You'll have to encourage them to work, Pius, you really will.'

Not bloody likely; Pius commented to himself, but he kept his bland smile in place as she continued, pulling on her white cotton gloves as she spoke, 'Lydia, as you say, is a girl. She needs security.'

'Surely her husband will provide that.'

'Perhaps. But she needs a dowry.'

'Dowry!' For a moment his laidback façade cracked and he almost shouted, 'Jasus, Martha, D'Abru's and Mallow Hall, some dowry!'

'I would hope the boys would look after her but they don't get along, and whatever I may think, or want, Mallow Hall is hers — and the business. Bernard would have wanted it that way, and after all, Lydia is the only one who has shown any interest in the firm. You know and I know, if we are honest, that Austin and Roland would sell it lock, stock and barrel tomorrow if I left it to them.'

'Well, please God it is all in the future, Martha, and you won't have to face these problems for many years to come.' As he mouthed these platitudes his eye caught hers and he realised in a blinding moment what was coming next. She gave him a level look.

'I'm dying, Pius,' she said simply.

'Aren't we all,' he blustered. 'Aren't we all, Martha.'

She shook her head although she could see that the truth of what she said had sunk in.

She was for the high jump, that was obvious in her eyes, and he gulped back his shock and muttered, 'I'm sorry, Martha. I'm truly sorry.' His professional polish deserted him and he stretched out his hand over the desk and took her gloved one in his.

'I'm afraid being sorry won't help,' she told him.

'What is it?' he asked, horrified at the knowledge that was now his. God, Martha, still young, younger than he. It made him nervous to think about it. He shuddered. If it could happen to her it could happen to any of them.

'It's cancer, Pius.' Then she added, 'But mum's the word. You must give me your solemn promise. The children don't know yet and I have to tell them at the appropriate time. I do not want them finding out from any other source. It will be shocking enough from me. But I needed to get the will organised first. You must promise.'

'Of course, Martha. You have my solemn word. But how awful . . .' He did not know what to say, how to talk to her. He was a glib man but words deserted him now and he stared at her, unable to keep the horror out of his eyes. He hoped fervently that she would leave.

'Now I must go,' she told him to his great relief. 'It's too hot to be in town.'

'Of course, Martha. I'll telephone you.'

He shook her hand, saw her to the door and,

bidding her goodbye, felt overwhelming gratitude that he was well and full of life.

When he returned to his office Eileen was
there gathering up the tea things. 'Shall I type up
these notes, Mr Brady?' she asked, picking up
the paper he had been scribbling on as Martha
spoke.

'No!' his voice rapped out, harsher than he had
meant. More gently he said, 'No, Eileen. Not
those. They're just scribbles. I want to deal with
it myself.'

'But I could —' Eileen was, as always, eager to
help, make things easy for him, but now she was
irritating him.

'No, no leave it,' he ordered.

'Mrs Tracey not on business then?' She spoke
casually and he glanced at her suspiciously.
Then he shook his head. She was involved in all
his business, there had been no secrets between
them — until now. She was utterly trustworthy,
he knew that, but he did not want her to know
about this. This had to be kept private. He was
not thinking about his promise to Martha as he
decided this. He was thinking of something else,
something long buried in his mind.

'No. It was a social visit,' he said firmly. 'And
about Austin. As you know, I'm his godfather.'

Eileen pursed her lips in disapproval. 'Oh Mr
Brady, he's shocking. Why you give him a salary I
don't know. He's useless.' She glanced, suddenly
apprehensive, at her boss, hoping she had not
gone too far, but Pius was smiling.

'Yes, I'm afraid you are right. He's a wash-out as a solicitor, but there's time yet, Eileen, and there's loyalty. Dear old Thomas would have wanted me to look after his son. His sons, Eileen, are fatherless. And young. They'll settle down. Eventually.'

He'd got her going. There was love-light in her eyes and she looked at him with adoration. 'Oh, you are so kind, Mr Brady, such a kind man,' she whispered. 'So loyal. There's not many would have your patience with the likes of the Tracey boys. Don't know when they're lucky.' She shook her head in criticism and, seeing he was not averse to her remarks, continued, 'Many's the young solicitor fresh from college would give his eye-teeth for a position in an office like Tracey, Brady & Co. But is he grateful? No. And I've seen you talk to young Roland and him at the best university in the world, wasting his time, doing nothing.' She glanced at Pius. 'So I've heard. Not grateful for their opportunities, if you ask me.'

He totally agreed with her, but what she did not know was that the boys' behaviour suited him eminently.

'You're a treasure, Eileen,' he told her and saw the pleasure fill her anxious face. It was so easy to please her.

'Is there anything else you want?' she asked.

'No, Eileen. You may go now.'

He waited until she got to the door, then, putting on his most charming smile, he called,

'Eileen?' She turned around, the tray in her hands. 'Thank you,' he said sincerely.

She glowed. 'Oh, it's nothing, Mr Brady. Like you I think loyalty is very important,' she said and left him alone.

She went into her little office annexed to his and put the tray down. The room was small and cramped and lacked comfort, but Eileen felt that that was as it should be. He was the great man deserving of space and mahogany, and she, his servant, naturally lived in cramped discomfort. It was the order of things. There was a square stone basin beside her desk and she turned on the taps and rinsed out the cups. She was thinking.

There was something going on. Of that she was sure. She had not worked for Tracey, Brady & Co for twenty years not to be able to smell out something amiss. She'd come to the firm as a shorthand typist when she was eighteen and by now knew Pius Brady inside out, could tell what he was thinking before he thought it. Today in his office she had sensed concealment, reservation, something he did not want her to know.

She did not mind his reticence. Her boss had to think that there were some things secret from her, but there were none.

Like his gambling, for instance. He did not realise she knew all about that. Oh, Mr Brady loved the horses. He tried to work around the race meetings, fit his schedule to suit Fairyhouse, the Curragh and Leopardstown instead of the other way around, and he often lost heavily. Then he was bad-tempered, irritable. She did not mind. It was to be expected. It was what he had in common with Roland Tracey. The two of them were a right pair. But that was okay. He did not have a wife and family to support, only his old mother in Donnybrook and he looked after her a treat, mind you. She could not cost him very much and the house was hers and paid for. Pius lived there with her, and she hardly ever went out. People always said that Pius was devoted to his mother. They said she was the only woman in his life. Eileen smiled indulgently when she heard this as one would at the antics of a naughty boy. Oh, his mother was the only woman in Pius Brady's life all right, except for the floozie. People did not know about her and Pius did not know that Eileen knew all about Dolly West.

She wrinkled her nose thinking about Dolly West. Hateful, vulgar floozie. Pius had her tucked away in that little huckster house in Drumcondra. Ugh! Eileen shuddered. Yet while her fastidious soul shrank from the idea of the woman she was well aware that men had carnal needs and it suited her much better that Pius had a person of that calibre than that he got himself a respectable girlfriend or, heaven forbid, a wife. A wife would queer Eileen's pitch something shocking. While things remained as they were there was hope. Hope that someday, sometime Pius would look at her, the truth dawning in his eyes as she had seen it in countless movies; Clark

Gable looking at Vivien Leigh in *Gone With The Wind* or Charles Boyer looking at Marlene Dietrich in *The Garden of Allah*. Looks that made her knees go weak. A look that would tell her that Pius at last realised that he loved her, Eileen. Yes, hateful as the thought of Dolly West was, she did not, Eileen felt, interfere with her boss's *mind*. Only she had that power. Only Eileen and his mother, and his mother didn't really count.

She cast her mind back to the interview. Mrs Tracey. Now there was a lovely woman indeed, but a threat. Eileen, who was nothing if not realistic, knew that if Pius Brady could he would marry the widow and Eileen's chances for the 'look' to happen would fly out the window. And it could happen. Mrs Tracey was a widow-woman, a woman who embodied all the attributes most desirable in a wife. Her graciousness, her beauty, her money and her home all made her eminently attractive. No one would blame Mr Brady for aspiring to marry Martha. And Martha liked marriage. She had said so many a time. Eileen bit her lip and retraced her mental steps. Now where had she been?

The notes. Making notes for the stuff he wanted. *Mora ya!* As if! When had he ever done that? There was something fishy there and she did not know what it was but she knew she would not rest until she found out. He'd throw the notes in the wastepaper basket and she'd retrieve them.

60

His voice came through on the intercom. 'Get me the Shelbourne, Eileen, please.' His voice was sharp, his tone urgent. There was something up. Eileen smiled. So he thought he would conceal what he was doing? Some hope. She'd find out, she always did.

Chapter Six

Austin sat on a stool at the Horseshoe Bar in the Shelbourne Hotel. He'd avoided Davy's, fully aware that his brother and his cronies would have dropped in there for a jar on their way to the Curragh. Oh yes, he knew his brother's movements, and he scowled in disapproval as he thought of Roland carousing around Dublin and its environs, the whole of Ireland for God's sakes, merrily ignoring everything except his own pleasure, never even opening a book.

Austin was still fuming that Sean Sullivan was leaving Ireland. In the perfect scenario he had envisaged of the farmer getting his sister pregnant, his mother and the neighbours ostracising Lydia and Lydia *having* to live with Sean and Peggy Sullivan or overseas, his mother would have looked at him, Austin, her huge eyes pleading. 'Help me with Mallow Hall, Austin. I need your help.' And later, 'Do you really advise selling D'Abru's? Well, dear, if you say so, then go ahead and invest the money for me, dear, whatever you think safe. I trust you. I know you'll be prudent . . .' Austin had sometimes been carried away with his fantasy, Martha's pleading and his magnanimity reaching unrealistic proportions. Now he sat at the bar, morosely nursing his drink.

He was shaken from his daydreaming by his name being called. The bell-hop in his wine-coloured uniform with its gold-braided peaked cap was shouting in a piercing nasal voice, 'Mr Tracey, pl-ease. Mr Austin Tracey to the telephone, pl-ease.' Austin tackled him and the fresh-faced youngster told him he could take the call in booth number two.

At first he did not recognise Pius Brady's muffled tones. The man was obviously unwilling to be overheard. Austin immediately clocked that his boss didn't want Eileen to know about the call. He smiled to himself at Pius's caution.

'Hello, that you, Austin?'

'Hello, who's that?'

'It's your boss, it's Pius Brady, you fool.'

'Oh!'

'I knew you'd be there. Whiling away the time, are we?' the tone sarcastic.

Austin suddenly began to sweat. Although he was a partner in Tracey, Brady & Co, Pius was undoubtedly the boss and had power over him. Austin knew he could be pushed quite far, but there was a limit. Pius could stop his salary and that was something Austin could neither endure to think about or afford to tolerate. *Some* work was expected and Austin was uncomfortably aware that he had not pitched up for work at all for the past four days. Jasus, Pius was ferreting him out, here in the Shelbourne, and now, having taken the phone-call, he couldn't deny being here. The staff had probably said he was in the Horseshoe Bar, the way they did, thinking they were being helpful. They may even have told Pius that he had arrived an hour ago. Bloody Irish charm! Always ready to be informative.

'Yes, Pius. I'm meeting with someone. A case. About some land in Limerick. I hope this guy arrives. I've been waiting an hour for him,' he lied. Pius would know he was lying but it saved face.

'Listen, Austin. Something has happened. I have to see you. Hang on there and I'll join you.'

Austin gulped. This was a turnup for the books. 'I don't want another lecture, Pius,' he protested. 'Not another lecture, please.'

'*Listen*, Austin, will you listen! This has nothing to do with your work.'

'Oh come on, Pius . . .'

'Shut up and listen, Austin. Your mother has instructed me to draw up a will.'

'What!' Austin was startled enough to forget his preoccupation with himself for a moment.

'Yes. She wants me to —'

'Is it unfavourable to us?' Austin asked, nervously lighting a cigarette. He knew Pius would know whom he meant by 'us'.

'Yes. Very much so. See, there's nothing extant at the moment. It's not on paper, so it, the estate I mean, would be negotiable. But she wants it all carved in stone. I'll have to do as she says. So. I think we should talk, Austin. Form a plan of campaign.'

'What's your hurry? She may change her mind

again. She's off me just now because I squealed on Lydia. I caught her —'

'I'm not interested, Austin.'

'But she'll get over that and I'll worm myself back into her good books —'

'Austin, there might not be *time*.'

Austin frowned and took a pull on his cigarette. 'What on earth do you mean?'

Pius hesitated. There might be someone on the exchange listening. So far anything said could not be deciphered unless by the knowledgeable. 'I'll explain when I see you,' he said. 'I'll be with you in fifteen minutes.'

The phone clicked and Austin realised Pius had cut the connection. Puzzled, he returned to the dimly lit bar, ordered himself a large one and took it over to a booth at the back. If Pius wanted a confidential chat then the counter was no place to have it.

What the hell was going on? His mother making a will? Why? Austin shook his head and took a belt of the whiskey.

Fifteen minutes later he saw Pius coming towards him. He looked so like a solicitor that Austin nearly laughed. He'd take anyone in in his well-cut three-piece suit, with his well-groomed appearance, his silver hair, his pure cotton shirt and the corner of a paisley hankie peeking from his breast pocket. True, his face was a mottled red, but on this hot day he managed to look cool and in charge of himself. He would inspire confidence in anyone.

Only he did not look directly at Austin when he breezed in, nodding to the bartender, who knew his tipple and smartly mixed a Bloody Mary with an extra dollop of vodka because of the thunderous brow Mr Brady had on him this day. He brought the drink straight to the solicitor, who had seated himself beside Austin Tracey, and scuttled away again pronto as the air in the small booth was palpably thick.

'Now what the hell is this all about?' Austin asked when the bartender was out of earshot. He sounded irritable and Pius glanced at him, the enormity of the news he had to break only now dawning on him.

'Austin, I don't know how to tell you this, but I have to.'

Austin sensed something was very wrong. Pius Brady was as smooth a man as you could meet and he could lie and cheat without turning a hair, but there he sat, lost for words, opening and closing his mouth like a landed salmon. Austin's stomach turned and he stared at Pius apprehensively.

'What the hell you talkin' about?' he asked.

'Look, Austin, if there was any way I'd not tell you this, but, well, I have no choice.'

'Spit it out, for God's sake, will you?' Austin cried impatiently.

'It's your mother, Austin. She's . . .' Pius paused and pursed his lips, then spat it out, 'She's got cancer. She's not got long to live.' He stopped and picked up his glass and gulped down the Bloody Mary, glancing swiftly at Austin out of the corner of his eyes.

Austin paused at his words, the glass halfway to his mouth. He did not speak but remained immobile in that position.

Pius stood up, muttering, 'I'll get another.' He went to the bar and ordered a large one for Austin and surprised the bartender by asking for a double vodka straight for himself.

'Bit early for you, Mr Brady,' the bartender remarked jovially, then, seeing the look on the solicitor's face, he hastily cried, 'Yes, sir. At once, sir. I'll bring it over to you, sir.'

When Pius returned Austin was sitting in exactly the same position though the empty glass was now on the table.

'What did you say?' he asked Pius. He seemed as if he was in a fog, a totally bewildered look on his face. Pius decided on masterful tactics.

'I'm sorry, Austin, to break it to you like this, but your mother has cancer. She's not got long to go.'

Still Austin sat and for the first time Pius forgot the D'Abru business, Mallow Hall and Lydia's fortune and concentrated on the younger man. For one fleeting moment he thought of his own mother and what he'd do if their situations were reversed and Austin was telling *him* that *his* mother had cancer and he squeezed his empty glass so tightly he cracked it.

'It's all right, Mr Brady,' the bartender, who had arrived beside them, said cheerfully. 'It doesn't matter. Sure we've lots of them. Here's the fresh ones an' I'll bring ye some nuts.' He wiped the table efficiently, placed the drinks on the Shelbourne coasters and put a bowl of salted peanuts between them. Then, still conscious of their silence, pregnant with dire emotion, he hurried away muttering, 'Janey Mac, like a bloody wake there,' not realising how accurate he was.

Austin finally looked at Pius, at last catching his eyes for a second before he looked away, surprised to find there an expression of sympathy.

'My mother?'

'Yes, Austin.'

'Jesus, why?'

'Austin, we don't know why.' Pius's voice became avuncular, soothing, oily. 'How can we explain these things?' He spread his hands. 'Only God in His infinite wisdom knows *why*.'

Austin looked at him with distaste. He'd heard that tone so many times. 'Oh cut it out, Pius. Don't give me any of your spiel. You don't mean a word of it.'

'But it means if I make out this will, Austin, that you can't lay your hands on a penny. Not a farthing. Everything will dry up.'

Austin swallowed. 'What can we do?' he asked. He did not doubt that Pius had a plan.

'Nothing! As long as your mother had made no will your claim on the estate and the business could have been manipulated. Lydia is after all the distaff side. But now . . .'

'Isn't there anything you can do? Delay the signing . . . ?'

'Your mother, Austin, is sharp. She's not going to be delayed. No. She'd smell a rat instantly. No. I just thought . . .' He let the little phrase dangle a moment.

'What, Pius?'

It was amazing how Austin's shock was so soon overtaken by his covetousness, how soon his horror at the news was replaced by desire for a plan to satisfy his avarice.

'What I thought . . .' Pius glanced around the room, then leaned forward, 'is that I make *another* will. The one that I will read.'

'But that would mean forgery.'

Pius nodded blandly. 'We need not call it that. Just . . . righting things. Redressing the natural balance. I'll draw up the will Martha wants. It will be witnessed, I expect, by the servants.'

'Noonie and Eilish. Bound to be.'

'It doesn't matter. I'll have the last page with only the codicils and the bequests to the servants. She has a few. She forgets nobody. The signatures will be there. The other pages will be initialed and that can easily be duplicated. I'll replace the first pages with our own creative version.'

'So how will it . . . ?'

'I take the will as she wants it and get her to sign. Then I'll destroy the first pages, keeping the last page with the authentic signatures intact and substitute the other pages, initials traced on to them, and then we'll all benefit.'

'Suppose someone queries it?'

'Like who? Have you ever heard anyone query-
ing initials? And I doubt Lydia will question me.
She trusts me. There's no one else.'

'There's Roland.'

Pius smiled. 'Ah yes, Roland. I don't think
he'll give us any trouble. I'll leave him to you. I
don't think he'll want to have all monies cut off.
He's used to the high life, Austin old fellow —
he's not going to want it suddenly to cease.'

Austin nodded. Roland would pose no threat.

'So as I say, everyone will benefit. Including
me.'

'Surely.' Austin glanced at the florid face, the
eyes now meeting his, gleaming. 'Including you.'
He stared uneasily at the solicitor. 'I expect your
fees will be very high.'

'High? They'll be prohibitive! An even divi-
sion of the money. Sale of D'Abru's, shop and
factory, four ways. You, me, Roland and Lydia.
For we mean to be fair: Lydia will get her whack.
Even. No discussion.'

Austin gulped, utterly winded by this announcement. One fourth to the solicitor. Jesus, it
was monstrous! Utterly out of the question! Ridiculous!

But how could they pull it off without Pius
Brady? That too was impossible. There was no
other way.

Austin clenched his teeth. 'How do you expect
me to explain it to Lydia and Roland?' he asked.

Pius shrugged. 'Don't know. Don't care. Roland, you must know by now, is a self-indulgent idiot, so he shouldn't be too difficult to, er, persuade of what is in his best interests. And Lydia is an innocent. She'll believe what you tell her. I promise she'll not make trouble.'

'I suppose you are right,' Austin said doubtfully.

'Oh, I'm right. Lydia the charmingly trusting and honourable sister and Roland the hedonistic brother will do as you advise, Austin. The will must not be contested. You have to see to that. You have to guarantee those two — our future depends upon it.'

Austin was nodding. 'They'd never contest the will. You're right there.'

'I believe so. But you'll have to guarantee them, Austin. Understand.'

Austin said, 'We must be careful though. Careful you don't set something in motion that might run away with you.'

'Oh, I won't.' Pius was confident.

Pius Brady felt slightly sick. He was not concerned about the forgery. He could do that easily. With tracing paper. And it was only initials, not signatures. And if he knew Lydia and Roland he doubted they even realised it was possible to contest a will. Roland would give them no trouble if the will was in his favour. The only thing Pius worried about was Roland finding out and talking. He was an irresponsible fool who talked in his cups and that would blow them all

71

sky-high. But Pius was confident this would not happen. Austin was *not* a fool and he would see to it that Roland knew as little as possible about the whole thing.

No, what made Pius Brady feel sick was how quickly Austin Tracey had got over the news of his mother's imminent death. The man was a shit, that was for sure. Swindles, deception, embezzlement, sharp-dealing, forgery — even blackmail — were, if the end justified the means, bread and butter to Pius, but mothers were sacred! How Austin could sit there, forgetting his grief in his greed, was beyond the solicitor. Pius had prepared himself for tears and anguish. Indeed, he had believed that he would have to persuade Austin, who would be in a terrible state, to cooperate in the scheme. But no. The man was ahead of him even: after a short, very short moment of shock he'd adapted and was calmly accepting Pius's proposals, discussing percentages. It was sick-making.

It also caused small undercurrents of alarm to course through Pius Brady's nerves. If the man was so cold-blooded about his own mother was there any humanity there at all? And in adversity would Austin Tracey be manageable? The question caused Pius to pause. He might have bitten off more than he could chew. Don't set something going that might run away with you. Oh yes.

But it was too late now. The conspiracy was underway, the ball had been thrown into the field, and who knew what the outcome would be?

Pius Brady shook Austin's hand and, leaving him there in the dim light of the Horseshoe Bar nursing his whiskey, he went out into the sunshine, picked up his Bentley and drove to the Curragh.

It was essential he got the money soon. His overdraft at the Royal Bank of Ireland was daunting and the manager, a good friend of his, had informed him on the golf course at Portmarnock the other day that his limit had been exceeded and the board would not tolerate any more withdrawals. He also owed the bookies large independent sums which he had to cover soon. A man did not Welch on his debts, especially to his bookie. Pius was in a bind and this whole business with Martha's will had come at exactly the right time. If he could pull it off — and he saw no reason why he shouldn't.

His heart rose. He was glad, speeding through Ballsbridge, that Harry O'Malley the bank manager would not spoil his fun at the Curragh that day. Bank officials were not allowed to go to the races. It was in the terms of their agreement, as it was considered inappropriate for them in their positions of trust and involvement with large sums of money. Pius decided to avoid the golf club, where he was sure to meet Harry, until all this was sorted out and he could settle his debts. Lack of money stinted one so, curtailed activities. Still, not for much longer.

Unless . . . the awful thought descended. Suppose Martha Tracey recovered! Jasus H Christ! Suppose she didn't die! Mother of God, that would be a catastrophe.

Then he quelled the nervous spasm within him. Nonsense. Martha was a very competent woman. She'd never make a mistake like that. Not in a million years. No, she was for the high jump, no doubt about it.

So Pius gave himself over to the enjoyment of the glorious day and his anticipation of the races and the vast sums of money he was bound to make if he placed his bets shrewdly. Yes, life was very good. Very good indeed.

Chapter Seven

While Pius and Austin were plotting in the Shelbourne, Martha visited the shop in Grafton Street then the factory outside Bray on her way home. It brought back memories, tender and happy, just being there, hearing the chatter of the workers' voices, smelling the sweet scent of the confectionery. She nodded and smiled at the girls, for it was mostly girls who hand-made the chocolates.

Brosnan Burke ran the shop in Grafton Street. He was a plump, jolly man, self-indulgent but not selfish. He adored the sweetmeats, often popped a chocolate in his mouth — just to check its quality, he said. People liked Brosnan, warmed to him. The smart little shop with its rows of delectable bon-bons was his empire and he was entirely trustworthy. Martha liked him very much indeed.

J. G. Moran was thin as a rail, serious and dedicated, and he ruled the factory with a rod of iron. But he was a fair manager and though the workers did not warm to him, they respected him.

Martha made her usual enquiries and was fully satisfied, but the two visits tired her. It used not to be like that, and not for the first time she deplored her weakening state.

She wanted to get away from people, wanted

to stop driving, to lay down her head on her soft, lavender-scented pillow in her bed in Mallow Hall and sleep, sleep, sleep. However, she had one last call to make.

At the crossroads near the falls and just a mile away from Mallow Hall there was a row of four cottages, each one detached, surrounded by its small plot of land. One of them was inhabited by the Sullivans and one by her mother, Kathleen Daly.

Spray from the falls dappled the car as she drove past. I love the water, she thought, it sings to me.

She parked the car under an oak tree that had been there in the time of Columbkill and St Patrick and walked down the boreen, neatly stepping on the flat stones and avoiding the damp earth and puddles where the stream over-flowed in winter. Not that she cared if she spoiled her dainty shoes in the mud, it was more from force of habit. She could smell the rich moist clay, and a gaggle of geese waddled across her path, honking loudly. The hollyhocks were waist-high because of the hot weather and the hedgerows were starred with daisies and dande-lions and cow-parsley.

'Dias Mhuire gut,' Martha heard as she shooed the geese before her, and there was the beaming face of Sean Sullivan's mother pegging her washing to the line slung from apple tree to apple tree beside her cottage.

'An' how are ye, me dear?' Peggy's periwinkle-blue eyes twinkled and her cheeks dimpled and Martha's eyes filled with tears at the fond expression she saw on Peggy's face.

'I'm . . . well. Thank you, Peggy. And yourself?'

'Couldn't be better. Isn't it grand weather we're havin'?' She laughed. 'Ye could fry an egg on the stone there!'

'Indeed you could.' All my fine ways, so natural up at Mallow Hall, desert me here, where I grew up, Martha reflected, and felt her body relax. 'And how is your Sean?' she asked.

Peggy hung a pair of knickers over the line and turned to Martha. 'Sure an' he's off!' she said, tears suddenly brimming in her eyes. 'To Lunnen. Te make his fortune! Did ye ever? An' isn't he in for the shock of his life. I seen it in fillums, Martha darlin'. Oh, not the American ones. They're all Technicolor, cowboys an' people shootin' each other all over the place. Or else they're in cute little houses with frilly curtains an' swings on the porch. No. English fillums show ye the truth of it, there in Lunnen. Dark foggy streets an' prostitutes gettin' murdered, God help us, an' . . .'

'Peggy, don't upset yourself. Those films you saw, they were probably about Jack the Ripper. Victorian London . . .'

'Did ye ever know any good to come of it? Did ye ever know anyone te come back wi' a fortune in his pocket?'

'I'm sure I could if I put my mind to it, Peggy. Sean is a fine lad and I'm sure he'll make good.'

'He'll get led astray an' him so handsome as to make Valentino turn in his grave. Some floozie'll get her claws inte him an' he'll never come home. He'll get corrupted, so he will. Or he'll be turned to villainy.' Peggy was openly weeping now, wiping her eyes with her apron.

'No, Peggy,' Martha assured her. 'He'll be fine. Everything's not like it is in the pictures.'

'Ah, I know,' Peggy said in a sudden lifting of mood, blowing her nose on her apron and smiling through her tears. 'Sure he's a good boy. He'll be grand.'

'And remember, Peggy, England is not too different from here. The weather, I mean. It's not all foggy, not always winter there.'

A bright grin split Peggy's plump face. 'Sure now I never thought of that. Wasn't I thinkin' 'twas like Siberia or the Black Hole of Calcutta! Thank you, Martha,' she cried. 'Ye were always a lovely person, so ye were. Kindly.'

Martha smiled back at Peggy and patted the work-worn hand. There but for the grace of God and the love of Bernard D'Abru, she thought. If it had not been for him she too would be hanging her washing out on a line beside her small houseen and her hands would be devastated by work like Peggy's. Her own hands were soft and white and slim, the nails pearly, and there were jewelled rings decorating her fingers. Yet, she thought, Peggy's rough hands would be washing and wringing out her clothes and mangling them long after Martha's fair ones had decayed beneath the brown earth and become white bones. She shivered.

'Are ye all right, me darlin'?' Peggy asked.

Martha nodded and dropped the hand she had held.

'Come te see yer mam?'

Martha nodded. 'Yes. Is she there?'

'An' where else would she be?' Peggy retorted and waving her hand went back to her laundry.

Martha followed the wee path to the gate of her mother's house. There were nettles and cow-parsley on either side. She remembered running down here from school and later from the factory. The fruit on the blackberry bushes beside the ditch was not yet fully ripe. She had loved to pick the juicy berries and cram her mouth full on her way home.

The cottage where she had passed her childhood slept in the dappled sunlight, recumbent on the green earth, shielded by the trees. Behind it the cabbage patch was overgrown and Martha knew her mother was being lazy about the vegetables.

'Ah Martha, me darlin'.' Her mother held out her arms to her daughter and held her close in loving embrace, kissing her cheeks and forehead, patting her and cooing over her.

Her mother had refused to leave the small cottage when Bernard took her daughter to live at Mallow Hall. Martha had wanted her mother with her there — the Hall was big enough, but Kathleen refused. No amount of persuasion would tempt her. 'Sure the grandeur'd be the death of me!' she told Bernard and her daughter. 'Yer father brought me here as a bride, Martha, an' I'll leave it feet first, in me coffin. Sure it's me place.'

She now seemed quite content in herself, though she looked older than her sixty-five years. Her skin was walnut-brown and crossed all over with fine lines, and many of her teeth were missing. Yet the old lady had a calm serenity that her daughter envied, her staunch faith seeing her through everything with stoic bravery. She had accepted the death of her husband Liam, and the loss of her two sons — Martha's little brothers Peter and Paul — who got scarlet fever when they were four and seven respectively and whose death near broke her heart. But she knew that for whatever reason the good God had harvested them before their time, it was His will.

She mourned with Martha Bernard's death and accepted too her daughters remarriage, though she and Thomas Tracey never got on. The lack of enthusiasm had been not on Kathleen's part, but rather on the side of the solicitor, who could not but see Kathleen as a liability and found her presence made him uncomfortable. She seemed to be able to read his mind, which for Thomas was not at all acceptable. Kathleen did not trust him, though she never confided her feelings to her daughter.

Kathleen did not like Roland or Austin either, but again kept her own counsel, and Martha knew only that her mother worshipped her granddaughter and that her old age was lit up by the presence of Lydia in her life.

And Lydia spent a great deal of time with her grandmother and her neighbours, the Sullivans. She gravitated there, much to her brothers' disgust.

Today Kathleen had the radio on. It was playing loud modern music with a strong beat. After she'd let her daughter loose from her embrace she twiddled the knob, turning it down. 'Has Lydia taken to rock an' roll yet?' she asked, twinkling at her daughter roguishly. 'Isn't it excitin'?' She pointed to the radio where Elvis Presley could be heard bellowing something about a teddy-bear. 'Makes me want to lep up and cut a caper. Though the Archbishop says it's the sound of the devil!' Her eyes gleamed and she laughed. 'As if he'd know! Sure isn't he the last one to claim that! He refuses to call it music though what makes him an expert I don't know.' She glanced from the radio back to Martha. 'An' yiv got gorgeous legs on ye, Martha child. Every time I see them they gladden my heart an' I remember bein' young meself. They're my legs yiv got an' didn't I say to Lydia the other day, yiv got yer mam's legs, an' mine. An' didn't she look at my old gams' — here Kathleen stuck out her spindly, aged legs and contemplated them with distaste — 'Jasus, will ye look at what time will do.' Then something in her daughter's manner stopped her and she stared at Martha, pulling her near. Suddenly serious and suddenly frightened she pressed her hand over her heart and cried, 'What is it, child? Ah no! What is it?'

'Mam, I've cancer,' Martha told her quietly. 'I've not long to live, maybe a year. At best.'

Kathleen kept her hand pressed against her bosom and bent forward and Martha thought she was going to faint, but she saw it was to touch the crucifix beside the empty fireplace with her lips. The crucifix was worn with Kathleen's touching and now she pressed her face against it and took her rosary from the hook beside it and held it tightly in her crabbed hand.

Martha pulled the fireside stool close to her mother and sat on it and put her arm around Kathleen, leaning her head against her mother's grey hairs. She knew Kathleen's hand on her chest lay on her scapulars. They were on a ribbon around her neck, nestling there in their tiny sachets between her breasts. There was a relic of the True Cross, a relic of St Bernadette's habit, a tiny brown particle curled at the edges in a locket and a relic of the Little Flower, St Theresa, supposedly a sliver of her bone. The relic of the True Cross had been blessed by the Pope. Her mother believed absolutely that these tiny pieces were authentic and Martha had never found it in her heart to disillusion her, for her mother found strength in these things. She was trying now desperately to draw from the inanimate objects the courage and resignation, the acceptance she so badly needed.

'Hail Mary, Mother of God, Hail Holy Queen . . . oh darlin', oh my darlin', my dearest, my sweet, my lamb. Oh Jesus, sweet Jesus, oh help us, dear God help us. Mary, Mother of the Lord, help me this day.' Kathleen cried softly. She left off kissing and touching the crucifix and turned her face into her daughter's breast and sobbed gently against the soft flowered voile and moaned her lament of prayer and supplication and drew her rosary through her fingers and touched her scapulars and prayed fervently and helplessly.

Martha held her mother, stroked her hair and soothed her with the same words Kathleen had used to her when as a child she had been hurt or wounded. 'There, there, darlin', there, there.'

'It can't be true, my darlin', my little one, it can't be true. They've made a mistake.'

Martha shook her head. 'No, Mam. It's true.'

'But it's wrong! It's wrong. It's just not right. I should go first. I should go before ye. It's my turn, not yours.'

In a while, when the first paroxysms of grief had abated, Martha wiped her mother's tears away then said, 'Mother, I need to talk to you. I need your attention.'

The old lady looked sharply at her daughter. 'I'll do anything for ye, ye know that,' she said.

Martha saw that she'd aged. In those few minutes just past Kathleen Daly had put on years. All the buoyancy and joy had vanished and sorrow had laid its heavy hand upon her and she suddenly looked ancient.

'Mam, I've made a will,' she said. 'I don't think anything will go wrong, but . . . well, I want you to look out for Lydia. She loves you and I know you love her. Just keep an eye on her for me. Promise me, will you?'

Kathleen nodded. She felt tired unto death. 'Of course I promise,' she said. 'You don't have to even ask. I'd do it anyway.'

'Thank you, Mam. I feel better knowing that.'

They clung together for a while, holding each other, soothing, murmuring reassurances both knew were quite meaningless. The sun outside faded and the sky over the little cottages darkened and twilight settled, casting its mysterious shadows over field and lane.

Martha at last sighed and rose. 'I must go, Mam. Dinner'll be ready.'

'Sure ye must, *alanna.*'

'Ye'll not worry, Mam.'

Kathleen smiled. 'No, *alanna,* I'll not worry.' They both knew she lied.

At the door Martha turned. 'I'll be back when I can,' she said and left the house.

Kathleen sat for a long time deep in prayer and thought. At last she rose. The arthritis in her hands and legs slowed up her movements something shocking. She went to the door and looked at the sky. It was deep blue and spangled with stars, like a young girl's dress, she thought. The land shimmered in the mauve light and purple mists like ghostly scarves draped the trees. It was the time for banshees and goblins, for wraiths and evil spirits to wander the land. Kathleen thought of the tiny babby she'd held in her arms. Martha. She'd always been so bonny. When Peter and little Paul died Martha was not touched by the contagious fever but thrived and did not succumb. A survivor. She'd survived two husbands. 'Why now?' Kathleen whispered to the twilight emptiness. 'Dear Jesus, why now? Couldn't you leave her to me just a wee few years longer?' Then she amended, 'Ah, I suppose not. We all must go when our time comes. But I'll miss my babby.' Her voice caught in a sob. 'Oh dear Jesus, I'll miss her so.'

She drew a deep breath. She was too tired for tears, too worn out. She had to husband her strength. She'd need it for Lydia. Sweet, sweet Lydia. Then when Lydia was taken care of, when she had found her way on to the right road for her happiness, then and then only would Kathleen let go. Then she could slip off out there where the moon shone and the stars sparkled and losing herself find Liam again, find little Peter and Paul, find Bernard, and with him would be, for sure, her darling daughter.

Chapter Eight

Dinner was a sombre affair that night at Mallow Hall. The dining-room was dark and high-ceilinged and the heavy mahogany table was long and imposed formality. Martha had never liked it.

Lydia, sitting to the right of her mother, was preoccupied with thoughts of Sean Sullivan's departure from Ireland and her life without him, and Austin, at his mother's left, was absorbed with the news he had received that day from Pius Brady and the conspiracy he was now bound up in. He kept glancing sideways at Martha as if he might see her imminent demise heralded on her face or in her movements. But to him she looked the same, though she did appear quieter than usual. Perhaps, he thought, Pius Brady had made a mistake.

Roland did not put in an appearance. Martha always asked him to let them know if he was not going to be there for meals. 'It's not fair on Eilish, dear,' she told him. However, Roland was careless of the servants' feelings, careless indeed of anyone's feelings, so he rarely bothered to phone and the cook had to wing it. Guess and hope and grumble.

Lydia did not notice her mother's quiet. Her mind raced in all directions as she tried to imagine what the world would be like without Sean

Sullivan. His presence had been interwoven in her life as long as she could remember, and an existence without him seemed unimaginable.

Oh, she had always had a life apart from Sean. He did not come up to Mallow Hall, much preferring to catch her at the gates or on the edge of the wood, at the falls, or beside the lake. It was one of those strange things about the pair of them — they rarely had to look for each other. So attuned were they that they divined each other's whereabouts, each other's mood, each other's feelings without speech.

Sean never escorted her to the dress-dances she regularly attended; he did not possess evening clothes. He did not play tennis with the groups that clustered around the courts at Mallow Hall on summer days or join them riding. But he was always there in the background, like an anchor, a harbour, and when she was with him she felt she'd come home. All the rest was marking time.

She supposed now, as she drank her iced watercress soup, that that was true friendship and she sadly admitted to herself that she would miss her friend dreadfully.

Opposite her, Austin's head continued to whirl. It was all right for Pius Brady to sit in the Shelbourne and casually suggest forgery and misappropriation, embezzlement and outright theft as if they were an everyday occurrence, and quite another to sit here in the company of his mother and the sister he intended to defraud.

Quite another! He was in a fever of contradictory feelings. Why did he have to resort to crime to inherit a portion of what was after all his mother's assets and therefore his by rights? Why had his mother made this necessary? Why couldn't she consider her sons, the position she put them in? All she needed to do was write a will splitting the whole caboodle three ways and then this ghastly plot he had become party to would be rendered unnecessary. His mind swerved away from the fact that in order to do this D'Abru's would have to be sold, but in any case it seemed crazy to him to keep the business. Who cared? Chocolates, for God's sake! But his mother had a fixation about it and did not want it sold even after her death! Jasus, how selfish could you get! And now he was being black-mailed by his godfather and his mother was dying. Shit!

He looked at her. On closer inspection she did seem frail and he could see the bones through her almost transparent skin.

'Mamma!' he cried suddenly, overwhelmed by the thought of losing her.

They all looked at him. Lydia was obviously puzzled. 'Aus?' she murmured. Her expression was anxious. She'd forgotten and forgiven their encounter yesterday. Lydia never held grudges. 'Are you okay, Aus?' There was real concern in her voice and he could see sisterly love in her eyes, and it angered him and made him uncom-fortable. It suddenly occurred to him that in all

88

probability even with the will his mother proposed Lydia was sweet enough not to go against
his wishes. But he thrust the thought away. He
could not afford to take that risk.

He became aware that his mother was watching him. She knows that I know he realised, and
winced at his foolishness. Nonie came in with
the lamb. She had been crying, Lydia could see.
Her big plain face was covered in brick-red
blotches and she kept sniffing as she carved.

'For God's sake, Nonie, stop that snivelling,'
Austin growled, then realised that Nonie probably knew too. Mother must have told her. That
would let him off the hook as far as keeping
stumm about Pius having broken a confidence.
He had his answer. Nonie let it slip. His mother
would never check with Nonie.

Lydia rose from the table and went to the dis-
tressed servant at the sideboard. 'There, there,
Nonie,' she said. 'You go downstairs and make
yourself a nice cup of tea. I don't know what's
upset you but we'll sort it all out later.' She
patted the woman's broad shoulders and took
the carving knife and fork from her. 'I'll carve,
Nonie. Eilish can serve pudding.'

Nonie's wail crescendoed and she fled the
room, relinquishing the carving implements to
Lydia, who looked at the meat, then at Austin.
'Maybe you'd be better at this, Austin, than me,'
she said, holding out the carvers to him.

He looked up. 'What?' At first he didn't know
what she was talking about, then he leapt to his

feet and almost snatched the carving knife and fork from her. 'Of course,' he cried, trying to sound jovial. 'Here, let me. It's a man's job, carving.' He glanced at his mother. 'Head of the house. That's me.'

But his remark was lost on Martha, who was deep in thought. Austin carved while Lydia held the plates. When they were served and seated they ate in silence. The ticking of the clock seemed very loud and, though the lamb was excellent, the carrots and celery just tender, the potatoes nicely crisp, none of them finished what was on their plates but instead put knife and fork together in the finished position before they were halfway through.

Lydia rang for Eilish. Her mother seemed lost in a dream. She wished Roland were there to break the concentrated gloom with his ceaseless trivial chatter.

When Eilish answered the call from the dining-room it was obvious that she too had been crying. This was too much for Lydia. 'What on earth's going on, Mamma?' she demanded. 'What's the matter with everyone?'

The cook brought a glorious queen of puddings to the sideboard and Martha said, 'Please, Eilish, leave it there. We'll serve ourselves. You can clear afterwards. Bring a pot of coffee and cups to my room when I ring, will you?'

Eilish dabbed her eyes with her apron. 'Yes, mum.'

Unlike most cooks she was rail-thin and she

quivered now from head to toe, making Martha realise that she could not put off telling the children any longer. She'd told Nonie, who had obviously told the other servants and it had not occurred to Martha that they would be so upset. She should have realised. Nonie had been with her since she married Bernard and Martha had wanted her prepared to cope with the children's shock and grief when she told them the news. Much use she'd be to the boys and Lydia in this condition!

'I want to see you, Lydia, in my room.'

'Now, Mamma?'

'Yes, dear. And Austin, I'll send for you when I've finished with Lydia.'

Austin felt sick. The terrible fact was going to be confirmed and he did not want that. As long as it remained unsaid except by Pius he could fancy it was all part of a bizarre plot as nutty as something Alexandre Dumas might write in a book or a film that Errol Flynn might star in. He watched Lydia leave the room with Martha. Lydia put her arm around her mother's waist and he felt a pang of jealousy at their closeness. She adores them both, he thought, loves them more than me. Her eldest and her youngest. Her daughter and Roland. With me sandwiched between.

He knew she was going to tell Lydia, then him. He'd have to await her pleasure. He looked over at the sideboard and his eye fell on the queen of puddings. The custard was sunshine-yellow under the crested meringue tipped with brown. His tastebuds watered and he got up and helped himself to a large portion, then sat alone at the table eating it.

Chapter Nine

Lydia could not take in what Martha told her. Preoccupied as she had been about Sean Sullivan, her brain rejected the information Martha imparted in a horrified refusal to believe such a thing was possible. If Sean was an overwhelming force in her life, her mother was the heart, soul and mainspring of it. White-faced, shivering in shock, she heard the phrase her mother kept repeating: 'You must be brave, dearest love, you must be brave,' and could make no sense of it at all.

A world without her mother? It was unthinkable. The earth without that warm and loving presence at its centre? A Mallow Hall without Martha would be a bleak and lonely place.

She did not cry, for which Martha was grateful. She was too shocked. She knelt beside the chaise and laid her head in her mother's lap and waited for the horror to pass. It will be all right in a minute, she thought. It will have been a mistake and suddenly Mother will laugh and everything will be back to normal.

But that did not happen, and her mother, stroking her hair, was talking to her about marriage. Marriage! She sat up, staring at Martha, wide-eyed, dry-eyed.

'Marriage, Mamma? I don't *want* to get married!'

'Listen, my darling. I will not be here much longer and I won't be able to go peacefully unless I know you are being looked after properly.'

'If it will stop you . . . going' — Lydia could not say dying — 'then I'll *never* marry.'

'Don't be silly, dearest girl. Now listen to me. I've made a list. They are all nice young men and I'm sure any one of them would treat you well. I thought Diarmuid McCabe . . .'

'Mamma!' Lydia yelled. 'He's a car freak! He's not at all interested in the things I care about. All he wants to do morning noon and night is go to rallies, stock-car races and all that junk. He even forgot to bring me a *corsage* for my dress last autumn when he took me to the hunt ball in Galway.'

'Oh dear, dear, dear, how remiss,' Martha tutted, smiling, and for a moment everything seemed normal to both of them, sitting there in Martha's bedroom chatting about boys and balls. Then the horrible truth hit Lydia anew and she cried, 'Oh Mamma!' Just as Austin had done in the dining-room.

'No, no, Lydia, listen.' Martha tried to divert her daughter, fix her attention on her plan. 'I thought of Michael Donnelan or Cormack McLeigh . . .'

'Mother! Michael can't dance! He can't even manage a foxtrot, which he should have learned to in dance class years ago, never mind rock an' roll and the new ones. They're beyond him.'

'I don't think that being a good dancer is necessarily a recommendation for a good husband,' Martha said quietly, but her daughter was pressing on hectically, eyes dry and hot, face flushed and troubled.

'And Cormack is, well, Cormack is an idiot. An absolute *dope. And* he's always sarky about Mallow Hall. I think he's jealous.'

'Nonsense, Lydia. He's got two delightful homes, one in Blackrock and a summer one in Brittas Bay.'

'But they're *small*. He says he doesn't believe in having big houses that need servants. He says it's oppressing the workers. Exploitation of the masses, he says.'

'What utter rubbish! If I didn't have Nonie and Eilish, and little Tam and Matty to do the garden we'd have to *sell* Mallow Hall.'

'Exactly. Cormack thinks that would be a good thing.'

'Oh dear! And what then do you suppose would happen to Nonie and Eilish and little Tam and Matty? Eh? What would they do? Where would they go? Thrown out into a cruel world!' Martha was indignant.

'I know, Mother. I'm on your side. It's Cormack who says these things and I wouldn't marry him for the world.'

'All right, dear. Then what about Orlick Fitzmaurice?'

There was silence. Lydia could think of nothing bad to say about Orlick Fitzmaurice. As good-looking as Sean in a blond way, as dashing, loving, good-humoured and kind-hearted a boy as you could hope to meet. Lydia, try as she might, could not think of one bad thing to say about Orlick.

'Well then, that's that. We'll encourage Orlick. Not that he'll need any encouragement. You've been the belle of the countryside, Lydia, for long enough. It's time to move on and let some of the younger girls have a chance. That delightful little sister of Cormack's, Millie McLeigh. She's dying to step into your shoes and queen it about the county.'

It was almost as if the terrible news had never been broken, as if everything was as usual and they were just having an after-dinner chat.

An enormous sadness engulfed Lydia, a huge emptiness, as if she were hollow. She felt shrouded in darkness. She shivered, suddenly powerless. She said, 'All right, Mamma. I'll marry Orlick.' Just like that. If it was what made her mother happy then so be it. Then she kissed her mother and fled the room in haste to get to her own before the dam burst. Then like Nonie and Eilish she lay on her bed and endlessly sobbed her heart out. 'Oh Sean,' she cried aloud. 'If only you were here. If only I could talk to you.' It was an idle wish and when at last the storm subsided she raged about her room, alternately shaking her fist at the ceiling and at her little statue of the Virgin Mary, screaming, 'How could you?'

Nonie came in at last with coffee. She had

taken the beverage to Martha, who had sent her to her daughter. She put her arms around the girl without speech and they rocked together and wept in each other's arms.

At last Nonie said, 'Now come on, Miss Lydia. Your mam wouldn't like this at all an' she knows how we're behavin' this minute, miss, believe me she knows. So dry your eyes now an' I'll dry mine an' we'll take a sip of coffee together then you must try an' get some sleep. We must be strong for yer mam.' Lydia was used to doing as Nonie said and she obeyed.

The servant helped the girl to undress. Worn out with weeping, Lydia offered no resistance. Nonie was certain that after all the emotion Lydia would sleep soundly. She kissed the girl and said goodnight, then at the door she turned. 'You go see your Granny Kathleen tomorrow, Miss Lydia. She's gonna need you somethin' dreadful.'

She wanted to leave the girl with an objective and she knew that that was the right thing to say. Clutching the thought of Granny Kathleen to her like a talisman, Lydia fell into the sound sleep of the emotionally exhausted.

It did not prove necessary to tell Austin the news. To Martha's relief he said he'd heard it from Nonie, a piece of information she accepted though she found hard to believe, for Nonie, apart from the fact that she was utterly trustworthy, had been nowhere near Austin since his return to Mallow Hall ten minutes before dinner was served. However, Martha was too tired to care how Austin had found out and when he proved tiresome, quizzing her about what she intended to do with D'Abru's and offering her unsolicited advice on financial matters, she sent him away, saying she needed her rest and wanted to retire to bed. Austin left, bitter that his mother was dismissing him and resentful that she wouldn't listen to him, convinced she would not treat Lydia or Roland so peremptorily.

Martha had had a truly exhausting day and when Nonie came she was almost asleep on her feet.

'I told Miss Lydia to go see her granny tomorrow,' Nonie told her mistress, tenderly helping her to bed.

'How wise of you, Nonie,' Martha whispered.

'Give her a focus,' Nonie added, nodding her head, hoping her mistress would understand her strategy. Martha did.

'You're a great help, Nonie,' she told her, silently acknowledging that Nonie had proved her strength in a crisis, and laid her weak body between the cool sheets. The linen felt clean and crisp against her cheek and she took the medicine Nonie fed her, a strong sleeping draught, and was glad in the knowledge that she would sleep tonight. She was so terribly tired.

Dr Fahy had doubled her usual dose and Martha knew it was because he wanted to make her last days as easy as possible. She was confident too that Gerry Fahy, without being asked, would, when the pain became unbearable, make it possible for her to exit from this life with dignity.

She had done all she could. She had broken the news to her family, all except Roland. But she was too tired to worry about him now. She had seen Pius and set in motion her last will and testament, and Lydia had agreed to marry Orlick. She could think of nothing else that was urgent and she fell asleep at last, setting her problems aside as best she could and allowing her sleeping draught to do its work.

Chapter Ten

Roland did not return to Mallow Hall until the wee small hours. He was not in his usual half-cocked state, and, to boot, his good-humour had been sorely tried this evening. He was angry as hell not only with Varina Gallagher but also with himself for allowing her to get, as he put it, 'the better of him'. He'd taken her completely for granted and it had never crossed his mind that she might have diddled him, trapped him, scuppered him as she appeared to have done.

He'd gone to the races with the fellows, then met the girls in the bar of the Bailey. He'd not noticed anything amiss until Michael Donnelan asked him at the bar what was up with Varina. Roland had shrugged and said he hadn't a clue and they'd taken the jars back to their table.

Roland had looked curiously at Varina and had to admit that although she looked her usual spectacular self she seemed a little nervous. He wasn't concerned, though. Why should he be? Varina was a big girl; she didn't need Daddy's permission.

They'd piled into the cars about eight o'clock that evening and headed for Bective and the hop. They'd be playing rock 'n' roll there and the lads didn't want to miss anything. The girls were all dressed up in their ballerina skirts and their ankle socks, with cardies over their cute little broderie anglaise tops. It promised to be a great night, but Varina went all moody on him, pouting and sulking until, exasperated, he jerked her outside.

The moon lit the playing fields, softening the harsh, functional lines of the clubhouse and turning everything silver. It was hot and Roland was sweating. He mopped his brow with a large handkerchief and asked her point-blank.

'Varina, what the hell's the matter with you?'

'Let go my arm, Roley, you're hurting me.' She sounded petulant. Her face was pale in the moonlight, her breasts rising high in her uplift under the snazzy little top she was wearing. He was mad for her breasts. They drove him wild. He grabbed her there in the moonlight and began massaging the soft round globes. Usually she responded but tonight she pulled away.

'There you are, you see, what you do that for?'

He could hear the band playing 'Blue Suede Shoes' and the screams of excited laughter. One of the boys was throwing up in the bushes and he could hear a girl's voice protesting, 'No, no, Mike, don't *do* that. What would Mam say?'

Varina turned and looked at him. Her blue eyes were dark in the moonlight. 'I'm pregnant,' she told him bluntly. Just like that.

There was a pause while he tried to take it in. 'You sure?' he asked finally.

She tapped her foot impatiently and grimaced, looking upward to heaven as if to plead for support. ' 'Course I am! Think I'd say it otherwise? As sure as I can be, but that's pretty sure. I missed my period now twice.' She shook her head gloomily. 'First time I thought was a mistake.'

Then there's a chance you're not,' he clutched at straws.

'You're not listening to me, Roland Tracey.' She'd put her hands on her hips and was glaring at him, her magnificent breasts heaving. 'I *said* I'm pregnant.' She'd raised her voice and he was terrified someone would hear. He hustled her over to the Morris Minor.

'We can't talk about it out here,' he said. 'Get in the car.'

When they were inside he said the thing he shouldn't have said. He said plainly to her, 'If you think for one moment, Varina, that I'm going to marry you, baby or no baby, then you're making the mistake of your life.' And she'd cried. All over the Morris Minor. Then she'd bunched her fists and begun to hit his chest, screaming. The chap who had been throwing up glanced over. Roland could see him duck his head, trying to see inside the car. Obviously he could hear something, so Roland put his hand over Varina's mouth. 'Come on, you can't blame me. It's not just you, Varina. I don't want to marry *anyone*.'

'Well, you'll have to. You've got no choice. If you didn't want to get married you shouldn't have got me to . . . you know.'

'Oh, so it's "got me to" now. I didn't notice you

being so reluctant.'

'Anyhow, I've got to tell my da,' she cried and jumped out of the car. 'If you think I'm going to slink off to London and risk my life in some back-street abortion place, then you'll have to think again. *And* I'm not going to have an illegitimate little bastard. Be ruined. Oh no, Roland Tracey. You're for the altar even if my father has to drag you up the aisle by the scruff of your neck. So there!' And she'd flounced away.

Roland's blood had run cold. Tom Gallagher was a giant of a man. He was a man to be reckoned with, a man who, they said, could not be bought. Certainly he was a man who when he discovered his darling daughter, his one and only, had been seduced by Roland Tracey would come after him, all barrels blazing, and either make him marry Varina or kill him. It was a toss-up which. Tom Gallagher was the sort of man who'd do that; think nothing of it.

Roland, undressing, sighed. This was the end of what he thought of as his golden days. A wife and a babby! Jasus, Mary and Joseph. Varina Gallagher had truly done for him. No more cruising the countryside without a care in the world, flirting with the lovely girls — the red-heads, the tanned brunettes, the white-cheeked raven-haired girls from Sligo. The smell of them, Chanel No. 5, Je Reviens, Carvan Ma Griffe. *Oh là là*. All over. All finished.

No more Trinity and being a student, boating and dancing, leading the life of Riley. Not with a wife and babby. His mother would insist he graduate, get a job. Jasus, *work!*

Oh God, when his mother found out! Roland did not want to think about that. It gave him goose-pimples. His mother was quite lethal in her contempt of young men who got girls in trouble. Even if Tom Gallagher had not been Varina's father, even if she had had no father to threaten him, his mother would never allow him to wriggle out of his responsibility.

And what was that, exactly? Would he have to marry Varina? Couldn't she be persuaded to go to London and get rid of it? Glamorous girls like Varina didn't want to be saddled with a baby, surely. He shook his head. She had sounded very sure about London. Trouble with Varina was that for all her sexiness, underneath she was a good little Catholic convent-bred girl.

Couldn't he pretend it wasn't his? Deny anything to do with Varina, physically, that was? Tom Gallagher's face came to mind and again Roland discarded the idea. Tom Gallagher would not allow anyone to accuse his daughter of deception. Anyway, why would she choose Roland? If she'd wanted a husband she could do much better for herself. Every boy in Dublin wanted Varina Gallagher. And everyone knew that Roland was hanging out with her and she had favoured him and no one else. It was one of the things that gave him *cachet* with the gang.

He'd lusted after Varina from the first moment she'd strutted into the Rugby Club dance on

Diarmuid McCabe's arm. Wow! The whole room had stopped to stare, every fellow holding his breath. All the girls in their virginal white or sugar-almond pastels gulped, and the boys in their tuxedos gawped at the statuesque blonde with the Marilyn Monroe figure in its scarlet satin sheath. Soft white-blonde hair floated around her head, a shimmering nimbus. Wide china-blue eyes and a pouting mouth challenged every man in the room, and Roland had decided he'd have to have her.

It had not been easy. Every other man in Dublin had come to the same decision. But for all her Jean Harlow come-hither attitude, underneath Varina Gallagher was Daddy's little girl and no easy push-over.

In the end Roland won. He wooed her with flowers and chocolates and he waited. He guessed correctly that the others, driven to distraction by her voluptuous charms, would leap in there too quickly. Girls didn't like that. It made them feel cheap. So Roland, always around, waited until after three months' concentrated effort he finally got to snog heavily with her in the back seat of the Morris Minor, and eventually, by dint of persuasion, he went the whole hog.

He had been careful. He withdrew just as he was about to climax. As they began to do it more often, all the time in fact, not able to stop themselves for she liked it as much as he, she'd tell him when her 'safe' period was. When that time of the month came, when they were sure she wouldn't conceive, they did it non-stop. And everyone knew.

Roland told her he loved her and they'd be married. He'd have promised anything to get turned on like that, get that excruciating pleasure, but secretly he did not respect her. Nice women did not gasp and cry out and seem to climax just like a man. Women having a climax! Whoever heard of such a thing? The very idea amused him. But he didn't like it, either, when she reacted like that. It lessened his pleasure. He wanted his concentration to be entirely between his legs, and her puffing and yelling put him off.

Women were pure, dove-like creatures and men were brutes, and in order for men to have that earth-shattering sensation their women needed to be innocent and acquiescent. Men therefore married them, housed them, clothed them, and it simply would not be fair if these innocents enjoyed sex as well. It would unbalance the bargain.

Roland's head was spinning and the ceiling was whirling around, zooming down on him, receding, whirling around and around like a top, and he collapsed on the bed, his trousers around his ankles, his shirt undone, and passed out cold.

Chapter Eleven

Next morning when he awakened his head throbbed unmercifully and his first thought was for an Alka-Seltzer and a Ferni Branca. He couldn't remember what was wrong, only that something terrible had happened. He lay for some minutes in this state of numbing anxiety, groaning.

When he stood up, which he did with difficulty, he nearly fell over his trousers bunched around his ankles. He sank to his knees and from that position rolled over on to his buttocks and pulled the offending garment off. He removed his shirt and the rest of his clothes, stumbled into the bathroom and vomited just as he reached the lavatory. It was a usual awakening, nothing odd about it — it just had to be endured.

It was not until later, when he had retched for ten minutes, then repaired the night's damage, washed it away, and was dressing slowly that he remembered Varina Gallagher. Varina and the baby. Je-sus!

He'd have to tell his mother as soon as possible, get in first before Tom Gallagher came gunning. When he got wind of his daughter's plight he'd come steaming up to Mallow Hall, creating and threatening. Roland would have to say his say before that happened.

His mother would be cross with him — though

she never stayed cross for long — but he'd slant his version and phrase it so the whole thing came out in his favour. No one looking at Varina would believe she was the shrinking-violet type, the reluctant virgin, yet he knew that that was precisely what she had been before she gave in to him. But no, no one would believe it, her looking like a temptress, a siren. She gave off a flagrant sexuality, the impression that she was longing for it, whereas it had taken him six long months to get his leg over — shit, she had been as tough to break in as Blunder was below in the stables. He paused and pranced and bucked and shied if you as much as laid a finger on him. Sweet Jesus, Varina Gallagher had been a *challenge*. And now it was only his word against hers — and bloody Tom Gallagher's, who sure as hell would not see his daughter like that — to deal with.

He'd taken his Alka-Seltzer but he still felt terrible as he went down to the dining-room for breakfast. Coffee, black, would do the trick. Then he'd tell his mother. He'd be straightforward about it, she'd appreciate that. He'd explain . . . what? That Varina had given him the come-on in a big way and he was a man after all and what did she expect? His mother would no doubt be sympathetic, but there was no way out of it — she'd insist he do the right thing. No matter how biased his mother was she'd expect him to marry the girl and that would tie him up like a trussed turkey ready for the oven. Je-sus!

And he'd have to, there was no doubt about

that. Roggy McIntyre had become engaged to some slag from Crumlin when he was in his cups and when he tried to wriggle out the damn girl took him to court for 'breach of promise' and he'd had to fork out a small fortune. It simply wasn't fair. Bloody women. They should be kept in their place. God created them for man's pleasure and for the procreation of children. In the sanctity of marriage. Not outside it. A girl gets pregnant, shouldn't have anything to do with the bloke. It wasn't rape, after all. Should be *her* responsibility.

He was drinking his coffee, nibbling on some dry toast — all his stomach could stand — ruminating about his sorry position and the mess Varina Gallagher had got him into when Lydia came into the room.

'Jeez! You look awful!' he cried when he saw her. She looked ghastly pale and there were dark circles under her eyes.

She gave him a funny look, then asked, 'Have you seen Mother?'

He shook his head. Not this morning. Or yesterday, come to think of it. She wasn't home when I dropped in to change. I was out late.' He rolled his eyes, then asked, 'Why? You want her?'

He was surprised by the look in her eyes, a look so deeply sorry for him that he was taken aback. 'What's the matter?' he demanded, puzzled.

'Oh poor Roland, you don't know,' she said.

'Jeez, you're scaring me,' he cried, now totally bewildered.

Lydia's hand shook and she put her cup of coffee down on the table with a bang. She stood for moments shaking, trying to speak, then she cried out in an anguished voice, 'Mother's got cancer. She's dying.' And she ran from the room leaving Roland sitting, staring at Lydia's steaming cup of coffee.

He thought at first it must be a joke, but knew the same instant that of course it was not. No one would joke about something like that. He sat helplessly, his coffee cooling in the cup in one hand, his toast between the fingers of the other, dazed and shocked.

Mother gone. It was not possible. Beautiful and feisty, his mother was healthy as a rat and the other fellows envied him her glamour. 'She's gorgeous, your mam. A smasher.' 'Whew, Roley' — Michael clicking his teeth — 'if I was a bit older I'd go for her myself.'

Mam not here. Then she'd not have to know about Varina and the babby. How long had she got? he wondered. He tried to adjust his ideas. What now? The Gallaghers couldn't kick up a stink with a dying woman. Even if they did he could promise the moon and change his mind after . . . after . . . after.

He banged his cup back on the saucer, rose from the table, his face crumbling, and as Nonie came into the dining-room he almost collided with her, then rushed out crying, 'Mammy . . . Mammy . . .'

'Ah God help us, they all know now,' Nonie

sighed, wiping her eyes and clearing up the breakfast things. 'Ah, it's a sorry day, so it is, a sorry day indeed for Mallow Hall.'

Chapter Twelve

Tom Gallagher, as predicted, came roaring up to Mallow Hall in his Rover in a terrible rage. Nonie showed him into the drawing-room.

It was a lighter room than the dining room. Though the mahogany furniture was heavy and the colours dark, the French windows opened on to the lawn which sloped down to the river.

Tom Gallagher waited impatiently, pacing up and down the room, glaring at the portrait of Bernard D'Abru over the mantelpiece, averting his eyes from the gentle and beautiful face of Martha Tracey in evening dress on the other wall. He wanted to keep his anger on the boil. He would not be fobbed off by charm or excuses. Whenever he talked to Martha Tracey he lost the proper use of his tongue. Well, that would not happen today. His little girl, his innocent Varina, the delight of his eye, had been *seduced* by the terrible Roland Tracey, that waster, that young fella-me-lad, and he would have to pay.

Tom Gallagher was a fine figure of a man as he paced the beautiful old Indian carpet. Tall and broad-shouldered, he stood six-foot-three in his stockinged feet and he had the shoulders of an ox. Red-faced and jovial, mustached and beetle-browed, he had abundant brown hair shot with silver and the severity of his countenance was offset by the humour in his light blue eyes.

There was, however, no humour in his eyes today. Tom's wife Mary had been killed in a motor accident six years ago and Varina was all that was left to him. A group of lads — Trinity students like Roland — coming home from a hop absolutely soused having been drinking all night, had crashed into the Ford Mary was driving, carefully and soberly, and she had been killed instantly. The young men had been reprimanded and fined. They had been considered not 'in the full possession of their faculties' by the court and therefore the death could not be considered as premeditated. The judge, who loved a jar himself, added that he hoped they'd learned their lesson and would drive more carefully in future — in a year's time when they were permitted to drive again. Then he banged his gavel and dismissed the court and the boys had filed past Tom Gallagher, eyes downcast but not concealing the relief that radiated from them like triumph.

Since that day Tom Gallagher had been an angry man. People had to tread softly around him. They were careful what they said and used placating tones as if he'd accused them of something. Only Varina acted naturally around Tom Gallagher . . .

'My dear Tom!' Martha completely disarmed him, entering the room in what appeared to him to be a cloud of chiffon and scent. Actually she wore a *robe de chambre*.

'My dear man, sit down please,' she indicated the sofa, then seated herself opposite him in an upright chair. 'To what do I owe this pleasure?'

Then, without waiting for a reply or giving him a chance to explain, she continued, 'We don't see you often enough. Time flies so quickly, doesn't it? I do wish we always acted upon our good intentions, but you know what they say about the road to hell.' She smiled at him, a radiant, intimate smile. He opened his mouth but she went on, 'I cannot tell you how often I've thought I must have you here to dinner, and then' — she shrugged — 'simply didn't. Was too lazy. You must forgive me.' He desperately wanted to keep his anger at the boil and she could sense that. She looked into his eyes, her expression soft and appealing. His were still firing sparks of rage and she wondered how much charming she could do and what on earth he had on his mind. It was something deeply unpleasant, she could tell.

The door opened and a red-eyed Nonie came in with a laden tray while Martha covertly inspected Tom. He would not launch into his grievance while Nonie was in the room, so she had a moment's pause.

Tom Gallagher was the sort of man she fancied. Martha reflected on that with ironic amusement. Why should that dawn on her just now? she wondered. She looked at him, admiring his manly figure, his silver-threaded hair, his clear, tanned skin. It would be soft to the touch, she could tell. There was an exciting vitality

114

about him and she could see how angry he was, the emotion giving him an electricity that permeated the room. She sighed as Nonie poured the tea. Unbidden; there came into her mind a vision of his arms around her, his body next to hers, naked, beautiful, hard. She shivered. Never again would she feel a man's hardness against her, never again make love. She felt a vast emptiness within her.

There was silence in the room, Nonie serving tea, Tom fuming, Martha lost in regretful thought.

When at last Nonie left the room, quietly closing the door behind her, Tom abruptly put down his cup and rose to his feet. Unable to bear it a moment longer he cried, 'Your Roland has got my Varina pregnant!'

Martha burst out laughing. A joyous ripple that filled the room with music. 'How lovely!' she cried.

He had expected denial, anger, excuses, tears even, but not this. Nonplussed, he sat down again with a thump.

'Oh Tom, how wonderful. A new life,' she said and thought: a bonus. I go and a new little part of me is born. How beautiful. Thank you, God.

He had been struck silent. He opened and shut his mouth.

'They must marry at once,' she told him. 'We'll post the banns immediately. Marry in three weeks.' Will I be there? she wondered.

He looked at her, seeing her as if for the first

115

time. She was luminescent. There was a glow upon her, her skin pale and translucent. He stared fascinated at her small even teeth and the blue veins at her temples. Her eyes seemed enlarged, like a drug addict's, and she seemed to him, sitting there in her clouds of chiffon, her halo of hair lit from behind by a shaft of sunlight, infinitely desirable. He felt horror rise within him and shame engulf him as he realised he desperately wanted to go to bed with her.

He cleared his throat. 'Em, yes,' he said.

'You'll want to give Varina a big send-off, Tom,' she was saying.

'Er, yes.' He wondered if his desire was written large across his face. He arranged his features soberly.

'Would you like me to have it here?' she asked, adding to herself, 'if it does not clash with the funeral'.

But Tom was shaking his head. 'No, no. *I'll* do my own daughter's wedding, thank you.'

'I was only suggesting . . .'

'It's very kind of you, Martha, but I am quite capable of organising Varina's nuptials.'

God, she was appealing, so fragile sitting there, yet there was fire in her, steel. You could sense it. She was so feminine, though, he wanted to sweep her up in his arms, carry her to a bedroom and make wild love to her.

He desperately stifled his emotions, fiercely embarrassed at his inappropriate thoughts, and looked out of the window instead of at her.

'I'm so pleased, Tom,' she was saying. 'I've always wanted a grandchild, to be a grand-mother. And Varina is a sweet girl and I'm sure she'll help Roland settle down. The love of a good woman, you know.'

Tom harrumphed and cleared his throat, unable to think of a complaint. He had come for a quarrel and now felt frustrated. The sudden urge to make love to this sophisticated woman had confused him and his intent had been de-flected so subtly that he felt himself floundering, unsure all of a sudden. He had a strong suspicion she knew exactly what she was doing.

'I'll organise the wedding,' he said uncertainly, realising he sounded boorish. 'I'll give her what-ever kind of send-off her heart desires.'

He's a nice man, a good man, Martha thought. His only problem is not being able to accept his wife's death and over-indulging his only child.

'There, drink your tea, Tom, and as we are going to be related, let's talk this thing through.' She stretched out her hand to him and, crossing the room, sat beside him and took his hand in hers. He could smell her perfume, a jasmine scent that seemed to emanate softly from her every pore. Most women's perfume came from behind their ears or their wrists. Martha's wafted like a seductive aura every time she moved, yet it was never too strong.

Her closeness was unbearable. He gently re-moved his hand from hers and folded his in his lap.

She was staring at him with, unless he was very much mistaken, a sudden awareness of his thoughts. He stood, a little unsteadily, and abruptly announced he had to leave.

'Things to do,' he said feebly.

'Oh, do stay, Tom, stay for lunch,' she said, and she seemed amused.

'Can't,' he protested. 'My schedule's chock-a-block, I'm afraid,' He knew this sounded ungracious and added without thinking, 'But we'll get together and discuss things, Martha.'

'When?' She disconcerted him again by her directness. This woman had the ability to throw him completely. She rose and stood beside him, barely reaching his shoulder.

'Well, er, soon. Soon.'

'How about dinner on Thursday?' she asked. Her eyes were twinkling and she seemed to be enjoying herself. He felt at a complete disadvantage and he was blowed if he could think why or what to do about it.

'Sure. Yes, of course,' he agreed.

'Eight o'clock then. At the Shelbourne.' She was not asking, she was announcing.

'Sure,' he agreed. 'Bang-on. Absolutely. Shelbourne, eight.'

'Thursday,' she said, the light in her eyes dancing like the sun on water.

He nodded.

'You know, Tom, I'm glad we are going to get to know each other better,' she told him. 'I've always liked you.'

He thought of Bernard D'Abru and Thomas Tracey and the emotional turmoil inside him churned with conflicting surges of apprehension, excitement, anxiety and exuberance.

Martha pulled the bell-cord beside the fireplace and just as Nonie opened the door she stood on tiptoe and kissed his cheek lightly as a butterfly. 'Goodbye,' she said and Nonie ushered him out of the room and across the hall and he found himself standing bemused by his car in the driveway.

Chapter Thirteen

Roland was given his orders. His mother wasted no time delivering her edict. He was to be married to Varina Gallagher *tout de suite.* In three weeks.

The banns were posted in Varina's local church and announcements were issued, invitations printed, dressmakers consulted, florists and caterers hustled into a sudden flurry of hyperactivity, and no debates were permitted.

Roland's first inclination to deny everything was not tolerated for a second. Martha stamped on that piece of foolishness with the firmness of one who has all authority. 'You'll marry the girl, Roley,' she said with finality, 'and that's that. I am not so foolish as to think you had nothing to do with it. Don't insult my intelligence please.'

Roland was devastated. He had to accept the inevitable and come to terms with the fact that his nightmare had become reality. He had been trapped into the thing he dreaded most, losing his freedom. The good old racketing-about days were coming to an end; responsibility reared its ugly head.

Varina Gallagher was not much more enthusiastic, but she was in the terrifying position of being pregnant. To remain unmarried would be socially suicidal; she would be ostracised. There was nothing she could do except marry Roland Tracey.

She could not understand how she'd ever been so mad about the plump young man she found herself betrothed to. He had pursued her relentlessly, wooed her tirelessly, flattered her shamelessly, and eventually and insiduously introduced her to sex — and that had been exciting. She enjoyed sex and he was a good lover. But that was it. Now, looking at him with disenchanted eyes, she wondered how he'd ever appealed to her.

When she thought about it, she realised she knew very little about her future husband. They had followed the routine of meeting with the crowd in the Bailey or Davy Byrne's, having drinks, piling into cars to go to the races, and she'd hung out with the other girlfriends as the chaps put on bets and studied form, then more pubs or a hop in Bective or a tennis club or a dance in the Gresham or the Country Club, then sex in the back seat of the Morris Minor. Oh, those aching climaxes had been sensational, but worth getting pregnant for? She was not at all sure now.

Varina Gallagher and her father lived in a comfortable, detached house on Ailesbury Road. The house was lonely now without a mistress and Varina, young girl that she was, left without a mother and having no experience, was incapable of exerting her mother's feminising influence. Miss Cobbs, the harsh-faced housekeeper, looked after it, and did a first-class job of running the establishment efficiently, but she lacked taste and understood nothing of the delicate arts of house-decoration and flower-arranging. There was in the house on Ailesbury Road none of the feminine embellishments so obvious at Mallow Hall.

This first hit Tom Gallagher when he returned from the Tracey home to his gloomy study. 'Varina! Varina!' he called from the doorway, looking up the stairs. Miss Cobbs stuck her head out of the door to the kitchens.

'Will I get her for you, Mr Gallagher?' she asked. Tom glared at her with distaste. Her skin was coarse and tough, her chin square and strong, and just now she irritated him, so full was his mind of the delicate beauty he had recently left.

There was, however, no need for him to answer her. Varina appeared on the stairs in her clinging angora sweater, her dirndl skirt, her bobby-socks and ballet slippers. Her hair was a tangled mass of curls and her mouth pouty. She looked sulky and resentful.

'Come in here, Varina, I want to talk to you.'

She followed him into his study, her whole body the picture of reluctance.

'It appears, Varina, that you and Roland will get married in three weeks. September one,' Tom announced without preamble.

'But I don't love him, Da,' she said sweetly, coaxingly.

'Well, you should have thought of that before.' He put up his hand as she opened her mouth to reply. 'And it's no use trying to get round me. It was not an Immaculate Conception, my lady.'

'I wasn't going to say that,' Varina protested.

'Yes. Well. It's married you are going to be, young lady, and that's an end to it.' He relaxed suddenly, looking at her with compassion. 'There are some things, Varina, that cannot be undone. You simply have to accept the consequences.' He sighed and spread his hands. 'I can't think what else we can do,' he said helplessly. 'Can you?'

She stared at him wordlessly for a moment, then, 'No, Da, I can't!' she cried and burst into a flood of tears. She stumbled around his desk as she used to when she was a little girl and, collapsing into his arms, sat on his knee, burying her face in his jacket, and proceeded to drench him with her tears.

Tom soothed the distraught girl and wondered again at the myth he had been brought up with — that money could solve all problems, that if you had enough money you could ward off all evil. It was a terrible lie.

Tom Gallagher owned a string of tobacconist shops across Ireland. Like the Somerset Maugham character, he had been walking down Capel Street one day, dying for a fag, aching for one in fact, and found himself unable to satisfy his craving till a quarter of a mile further on: there was no shop on that street that sold cigarettes.

Seeing a God-sent opportunity, he promptly took all his savings, got a loan from the bank and bought an empty premises on the exact spot where he had felt the overwhelming need, in Capel Street, halfway down.

He never looked back. From then on, wherever he found a gap, a long distance between shops where the weed was sold, he bought a property and converted it, turning it into a little goldmine.

He was a wealthy man when he married his wife, and when she gave him Varina, the light of his life, he had felt grateful, a man insulated against the harshness of life by his bank balance, a man who had everything. And then his beloved Mary was killed. His money could not save her, and from that day forth his world had been incomplete.

He did not like Roland Tracey. The fellow was a wastrel, a playboy, and worst of all, a fool. Tom had encouraged Varina to be friends with Lydia D'Abru, who was in his estimation a delightful young lady, but Varina said she was too old for her and she preferred the rackety lot that hung out with Roley and his bunch of idlers, all into partying and the new music and God knows what.

Varina was a girl with a mind of her own, not one to be pushed. However, Tom knew that in the situation she had found herself there was no need at all to push. Unmarried girls did not produce offspring. If they did, society closed its doors against them. Suddenly they found themselves off guest-lists, not admitted to the houses of their friends. Where once the phone rang, now it would be silent. Where once there were stacks of invitations on the mantelpiece, now there would be none.

The hypocrisy of it was that it happened all the time; the trick was not to brazen it out. Shotgun weddings were very common. Everyone knew why there was a hurry, but faces were saved. The bolder or more desperate or immoral went to London and had an abortion at the risk of hellfire and damnation, but anything was better than public humiliation. Otherwise the girl emigrated and carried her shame with her to England or America, touting some story about a dead husband.

It was always the woman that paid. Tom reflected that rarely was the young buck held responsible. It was the girl who was supposed to guard her virtue, and the fellow washed his hands of responsibility under the banner that she 'let him' and so was 'no better than she should be'.

Tom could not bear Varina to suffer humiliation, so there was no alternative except for her to marry the man responsible. It was a shame that man was Roland Tracey.

Abortion did not even occur to Tom Gallagher. He would never dream of subjecting his daughter to such a thing and in any event it was a terrible sin against the Church. Tom

Gallagher did not believe a lot of the Catholic mumbo-jumbo he had been brought up with, but abortion was another matter entirely. Like divorce, murder and theft, it was against the law of the land as well as canonical precepts, and Tom Gallagher was a firm upholder of the law. Besides, he was quite sure that living with the consequences of abortion would be a terrible burden for Varina. Mary, before she had had their daughter, had had a miscarriage and had suffered deep depression for months afterwards. An abortion, Tom realised, could only be worse.

No, it was marriage to Roland Tracey or exile to a place where no one knew them, both of them starting a new life in a strange land — America probably. Tom did not think he could start again. He was too old. The fire, the hunger in him had been satisfied, appeased by his success, and he could not visualise beginning again with strangers.

Martha met him in the Shelbourne. He felt like a schoolboy on his first date, nervous, apprehensive and very excited all at the same time.

It was silly, he reasoned. Martha Tracey was a mature woman, a sophisticated one. Why on earth then did he feel this gauche?

He was sitting at their table in the Shelbourne when she arrived. He had secured the best table, the one in the window, and he sat facing the entrance, alternately glancing out into the street and towards the archway where she would have to enter. When he saw her his heart seemed to stop and he rose unsteadily to his feet, knocking his glass over in the clumsy motion. She appeared opposite him in a cloud of pale silks and perfume like a divine apparition. She hardly seemed real, so fragile was she.

'My dear Tom.' She extended both hands, holding his above the table, totally ignoring the spilled drink the waiter was trying to mop up. 'My dear man,' she whispered, and he felt alone in the world with her, elevated by this lovely creature to a position of enormous specialness.

She sat down, another waiter holding out the chair for her. She flashed the boy a radiant smile then turned to Tom, who was reseating himself, his waiter having covered the stained damask cloth with a napkin. Tom had muttered, 'Don't fuss! Don't fuss please,' in an aside when the man had been about to replace the cloth. Martha ignored the whole thing.

'Are you getting used to the idea? Of Varina marrying Roland?' she was asking lightly, smoothing the tablecloth with pale, nervous fingers.

'Of course.' Tom pulled himself together. He had to think clearly, sensibly. This was his daughter's life.

'It's a shame they have been so silly,' she said. The word 'they' caused Tom Gallagher to bristle, putting as it did half the blame on Varina's shoulders. Then he reflected that some women would put the blame entirely on the girl's shoulders, excusing their sons with the saying 'boys will be boys'. Tom was a realist and he knew very well that it took two to tango, that Roland was not the type to force Varina to do anything she did not want to do. Persuade, yes. But Roland was too weak to be aggressive. It stuck in Tom's throat to admit it but he realised his daughter was just as guilty as that young whipper-snapper.

However, Martha was continuing, 'Dear Tom, we cannot undo what is done. We cannot waste time in regrets. I'm only sorry for your sake and your daughter's that Roland is not . . .' She lifted her shoulders lightly. 'Not qualified in anything. God knows there is no excuse for him. He should by now have buckled under and . . .' She waved that delicate hand in an infinitely graceful gesture. 'But you know, Tom,' she said with a sad smile, 'it's been hard without a husband. Hard to bring up boys on my own.'

'I know,' he nodded in agreement. 'I know, my dear.'

She sighed. 'Yes. You've been in the same position. Poor Mary. I'm sure like me you sometimes feel quite helpless. Roland thinks, you see, that life is a party and he does not have to do anything at all to deserve an existence of total self-gratification.'

'Don't worry, my dear,' Tom replied swiftly. 'I'll see to all that. Once he marries Varina it's nose-to-the-grindstone time. I'll not tolerate idlers. I'll issue an ultimatum. Either he graduates from that heathen college or he goes into

128

one of my shops. I'd send the pair of them to Tullamore or Castletownbare, only I'd miss Varina so much I couldn't bear it.' He looked at Martha and she could see the love and pain in his eyes. This was a man who felt deeply. Her heart warmed to him and she made a little noise of understanding as he continued, 'They don't either of them realise how lucky they are. They are blessed. Spoiled even. Still, I suppose we cannot blame them. We did it to them. And it wasn't our fault either. We were only trying to make up for the loss of their other parent. Varina did not have the benefit of her mother to guide and support her any more than Roland had a father to be firm with him.'

Martha nodded. 'I know, Tom. Oh, I know.' And they looked at each other in complete understanding.

It had dawned on both of them as they talked how alike their situations were. They had a great deal in common, both of them widowed with children missing the guidance of a parent of the same sex, both with money to cushion the loss. They shared feelings of guilt and failure, Martha over her sons, Tom over Varina. They nibbled their smoked salmon, ate their duck, dunked their strawberries in sugar and cream and sipped Courvoisier with their coffee. There was an atmosphere of warm companionship and understanding between them, a rosy glow of content. And something more. As she had at Mallow Hall, Martha realised that Tom not only admired her, which she took as her due, but he obviously harboured amorous feelings towards her as well, feelings which she knew shocked him and which he did his best to conceal.

And as the evening progressed a little voice within her asked, 'Why not? Why not?' In that romantic room, under the glittering chandelier, in the rosy glow of the candlelight they stared at each other as if seeing the face opposite for the first time.

Although the pain was under control (she had taken a strong dose of the drug before she left home), she could feel the occasional sharp stabs, but to her amazement it was manageable. She felt buoyant, full of life and excitement. She felt much better. And she knew this surge of exhilaration was to be laid at Tom Gallagher's door.

They laughed. It was such a long time since she had laughed that she gasped, surprised at the force of her joy. He lit a cigar and leaned back, waxing eloquent about Irish politics, the government, Sean T. and the latest movies.

'We must do this again,' she told him lightly when at last the lights in the restaurant were dimmed and Tom had paid the bill, all the other customers had gone and the last lone waiter yawned.

Outside, the street-lights glimmered and Stephen's Green looked mysterious across the road. He leaned across the table, looking into her eyes. 'When?' he asked.

'When would you like?' she replied simply. Her

heart beat quicker and she felt suddenly very much alive.

'How about,' he frowned, then smiled at her wickedly, 'how about tomorrow?'

She laughed and shook her head. 'Not possible,' she answered, delighted that he made it as soon as that, but aware she would not be strong enough by then to sparkle so brightly for him. 'Monday,' she said.

'Monday it is.' His gaze was still fixed upon her, and as she stared back he blushed and his thoughts were written on his face. She smiled at him and they left the hotel in silence.

Chapter Fourteen

Martha paid for her outing. She spent the next morning in bed, worn out.

What had she been thinking of? The father of her son's bride-to-be! Red-hot passion for a terminal patient! She was, she decided, insane.

But she did not pick up the phone and cancel the engagement for Monday night. Instead, when Tom Gallagher called, she snuggled down into the pillows and had the kind of conversation she had not had for many years.

'Hello. It's Tom.'

'I know. Hello.'

'Thank you.'

'You're welcome.' Laughing softly.

'It was wonderful.'

'Yes. Great food. Lovely atmosphere.'

'No. You know what I mean.'

'Yes.'

'You. You are wonderful.'

'You too. Oh, Tom.'

'I can't think.'

'Me neither.'

'Listen, Martha . . .'

'Tom, there are a million reasons . . .'

'I know. I know.'

'And we preach sense to our children . . .'

'I know. I know.'

'None of it makes sense.'

'I've never felt this . . .'

'Me neither.'

Nonie came into the room and Martha exclaimed.

'What is it?'

'Look . . . I got to go.'

'Oh! Can't talk. I get it.' Already deception. 'Yes. Goodbye. See you Monday.'

'Monday. I can't wait.'

She replaced the receiver in its cradle.

'Mum, Mr Brady is here. I put him in the music room.'

'Thank you, Nonie. Please help me into a gown.'

'Yes, mum.'

Nonie shivered as she draped her mistress's slim body in a wine silk *robe de chambre*. With infinite tenderness she placed a light cashmere wrap over Martha's shoulders. Unable really to assimilate what was happening, that her beloved mistress was going to die, Nonie savoured every moment with her, relished whatever service she could perform in an effort to show Martha how she loved her.

Pius Brady waited in the music room. He felt awkward there, outsized and uncomfortable. He folded his hands behind his back. He had never thought about his hands but now, suddenly, they appeared to him like great red hams, uncouth and ugly.

The room seemed to him dainty, a fragile, feminine room like fine china. It was as if everything in it were breakable. The carpets were pale yellow and the furniture French. Curved, finger-thin gilded legs supported what seemed to Pius insubstantial chairs that would probably collapse under him. He did not experiment to find out. A rosewood harmonium graced one corner, beside which stood a matching hand-carved music stand. The whole impression was one of luxury, and he knew a moment of acute covetousness. Then he wondered, would he *want* to live like this? With such delicacy? How uncomfortable it would be! The carpets would spoil and stain, they were not hard-wearing as a floor-covering should be. His mother would never have countenanced *yellow* on the floor. She would tut-tut and tell him brown was the colour. Brown was practical thus economical. Well, he sighed, soon — a year, maybe less — he would not have to worry about economical.

The next half an hour was spent in an attitude of assumed patience. He had the will in his brief-case all right, tight and legitimate. He gave it to Martha when she arrived, looking deadly pale but ravishing in her wine silk. She studied the will carefully, checking every dot, comma and sentence. As he anticipated, she sent for Eilish and Nonie when at last she had finished and seemed satisfied, and they carefully signed and initialled the typed pages and signed on the dotted lines at the end. Done. Relieved, he tucked the document back into his briefcase and took his leave, refusing the offer of a drink or a cup of tea.

Martha in her turn was relieved to see him climb into his car and drive off towards Dublin. She sank back on the chaise, exhausted, and Nonie brought her a cup of coffee. 'God between us an' all harm, mum, ye look wore out,' she tutted and when Lydia bounced into the room she cried, 'Will ye keep it down, Miss Lydia, God's sakes, think of yer mam.' Lydia drew to a halt, remembering her mother's condition, and tiptoed towards the chaise.

'Darling, don't,' Martha cried protestingly. 'It's not necessary to pussyfoot around like that. I'm not actually dying yet.'

Nonie let out an involuntary sob and fled the room.

'Oh dear, oh dear, I've upset poor Nonie,' Martha said. She felt, in spite of her exhaustion, full of life at this moment.

Lydia sank to her knees and laid her head on Martha's knee. 'Oh Mamma, don't leave us. I'll not want to live without you.'

'Hush, Liddy pet, hush. Don't say things like that. Now, dear, listen to me. You'll get yourself a husband at last. Orlick will look after you. He'll care for you when I'm gone. That's the way of the world. You'll start a family. You'll have others to love and care for. You'll not have time to grieve for me and I would hate it if you did.' She lifted her daughter's head and, putting her hands

135

on Lydia's cheeks, looked intently into her eyes. 'Listen, my darling, I don't want you to pine for me. I want you to promise. You see, I'll be there, somewhere, keeping an eye on you. I couldn't bear it if you were miserable.' She kissed her daughter's forehead and added, 'Listen, Lydia, life is for living, enjoying. You don't want to be like Austin, poor boy, incapable of being happy or getting joy out of the beauty of this wonderful world.' She smiled sadly at her lovely daughter. 'I've left the house to you. You and Orlick should live here. He can afford the upkeep so that's all right.'

'But Mamma . . . oh Mamma, I don't want . . .'

'Of course you don't, my pet. I know this is the last thing you want to talk about now, but it's necessary. I've just drawn up my will. That's why Pius Brady was here just now.'

'I saw him drive away, but Mamma . . .'

'No, dearest, hush. It had to be done.'

'Well I don't want anything, Mamma. I only want you.' Lydia stuck her chin out stubbornly.

She's so like me, Martha reflected. She's the sweetest girl in the world but underneath all that niceness there's a clear, strong will. She continued, 'I know that, dear, but we've got responsibilities, you must understand that. The staff, the workers, their families. I want it all kept like it is.' She smiled at Lydia. The poor child's eyes were full of fear and filmed by tears. Martha wondered how she would have felt if it were Kathleen who was dying and she shivered.

Lydia bit her lip. Life without her mother would be a dark and lonely place.

Martha, thinking of her mother, said to Lydia, 'Go to Granny Daly if you're troubled, pet, or sad.'

'Does she know, Mamma?'

Martha nodded. 'Yes. And she'll help you, no doubt.' She wanted to lighten her daughter's distress. 'Now cheer up, Lydia. I'm not gone yet. There's lots of time left.' She did not know if this was true or not but just now she did not care. 'Let us enjoy ourselves, savour every moment. Live for the day. Right?' She glanced enquiringly at Lydia, who nodded. They could only be happy a day at a time, and who knew? Maybe her mother would not die. Maybe a miracle would happen and Martha would get better.

Lydia kissed her mother's pale forehead. She loved her so much, so much. She'd say the rosary every night from now on, storm heaven for her mother's recovery. Then everything would be like it was. Everything would be back to normal, like the day she told Sean Sullivan that she wanted the sweet summer days to go on and on and nothing to change, ever.

Chapter Fifteen

That evening groups of girls in pale dresses with long full skirts and elbow-length gloves and boys in evening clothes stood on the verandah that surrounded the Country Club. The moon cast a silver-blue shine over everything and the young people stared at it and whispered romantic things to each other, the boys in the hope of a heavy-petting session, the girls in the hope of proposals of marriage.

A foxtrot had ended and there would be a break before the Ladies' Excuse-me or the Paul Jones, whichever was to follow on from 'You Do Something To Me'.

There had been a meeting of the committee and they had decided to ban the new rock 'n' roll music that threatened to corrupt the young. You could hear that sort of loud and raucous music (if you could call it music!) at the hops in the Rugby Clubs but, the committee decided, not here in the elegant Country Club. Here they would ensure that dignity and style would triumph. Who knew where it would lead otherwise? Jive and jitterbug (such names!) had had their day, come and thankfully gone, and no doubt the same thing would happen to this new stuff. In the meantime the bands they employed would play appropriate *music*. Foxtrots, quick-steps, waltzes, tangoes, even the samba, but not that other stuff, no!

The boys on the verandah gravitated together, away from the girls, smoking cigarettes, sipping their drinks, mopping their brows. They drank mainly whiskey — gin was considered a girl's drink and beer was not allowed in the Country Club on formal occasions. It was an unsophisticated beverage and suitable only for the working classes and the uncouth.

The girls clustered together at the top of the wide steps leading to the driveway, a posy of pale pink and blue and soft yellow and white. Mainly white. They giggled and glanced covertly at the boys, who preened a little, knowing they were observed, indulged in horse-play, laughed louder, swaggered about and generally acted with macho excess. With laughing eager eyes the girls chose the man they'd ask to dance if it was Ladies' Choice. They rapidly worked out the quickest route to the chosen one and how best to cut out any other contenders who might have an eye on him.

A few boys and girls had paired off and Orlick Fitzmaurice and Lydia D'Abru were standing together, leaning on the balustrade. The other girls heaved sighs of relief when they saw that Lydia was firmly attached to Orlick and the boys breathed sighs of disappointment. The girls hoped fervently that Lydia had made her choice at last. She had queened it for too long now over all of them and though some of them cast covet-

ous glances at the tall, fair Orlick they were relieved that now quite a few of the lads would be
available. Diarmuid McCabe for one, and Michael Donnelan, and the delectable Cormack
McLeigh.

Orlick had danced with Lydia, surprised that
she'd agreed to the quickstep *and* the foxtrot,
one after the other. Usually she changed partners after each dance, in order, as her mother
had instructed her, not to favour any one boy
particularly until she had made up her mind
which one she wanted. Orlick took this departure from the norm optimistically and decided
to press the advantage.

'Will you do a line with me, Liddy?' he asked,
crossing his fingers, his heart pounding. 'I mean
go out only with me. With a view to, you
know . . .'

He did not think she'd say yes. He'd asked her
so many times before. All his mates had too, but
she always shook her head, so he thought he'd
imagined it when she whispered softly. 'Yes,
Orlick.'

'What?'

'I said yes.'

'Oh Liddy! Wow! You mean it?'

Elated, he turned to face her and saw her staring up at him, her eyes full of tears, a despairing
expression on her face.

Alarmed, he asked, 'Lydia, what is it?'

'It's Mamma, Orlick. She's dying.'

She leaned forward with a sob and he caught

and held her in his arms. He was overcome by a surge of tenderness, an overwhelming desire to protect her.

'Don't tell anyone, Orlick. She doesn't want anyone to know. But . . .' She leaned back looking at him, the moonlight turning her tears to shimmering spangles, '. . . I know I can trust you.'

'Of course you can,' he said stoutly. He felt very masterful and his heart swelled with sympathy and determination. He would guard her and look after her for the rest of their lives.

Lydia D'Abru, the most beautiful girl in the world, had chosen him from all the rest, from all the boys who'd chased after her since she came out. It had been a long time, a long pursuit, but until now Lydia had not encouraged any one of them and they had faithfully remained her beaux, to the chagrin of the other girls.

Well, she'd chosen at last. Of course, lots of girls did lines with boys they'd no intention of marrying. For some of them it was to fill in time between one love affair — perfectly innocent — and another. The boy, although he didn't know it, poor idiot, was needed as an escort. Others were scalp-hunters — they tried to break as many hearts as they could. But Lydia had always played straight. She'd said, and they all heard her, 'When I do a line with someone it will be because I want to marry him.'

Orlick's heart swelled as he held her slim frame in his arms. He wanted so badly to marry this delightful girl. He came to a snap decision.

'Look, Lydia, let's announce our engagement.' And as she made to protest he put a finger on her lips and led her to a bench against the wall and sat her down. 'No, listen. You've told me about your mother. You're going to need all the support you can get. I can give you that. I'll be there at your side helping you, my darling. And it's not as if we were strangers, or even didn't know each other very well. We've been chums for ever. Our families are friends. So why don't we make it official, and we'll go to Weir's on Monday and get a ring? What do you say?'

It seemed the best thing to do. He was right. She would need his support, his strong arms around her, and Orlick would be very good at that. He was a person who liked helping; an intern in the Mater, he was dedicated to looking after the needy.

Though his family had money Orlick had always wanted to be a doctor. He could, Lydia knew, have led the kind of life Roland found so seductive, but he chose to work, to study hard, to be useful. Lydia looked at him. He was so kind, so good-looking, and her mother was in favour. It was what her dying mother wanted and it seemed to Lydia that the most comforting and reassuring thing she could do was to agree to get engaged to Orlick Fitzmaurice.

'Okay,' she said brightly.

'Oh Lydia.' He kissed the tears trembling on her cheeks, staring at her with passionate honesty. 'I'll never let you down,' he said. 'I'll look after you always.' And she felt a warm flood of relief speed through her as if she'd laid down a burden she'd been carrying. She sighed and leaned against his broad shoulder. She'd made her decision. For years she'd struggled not to but now it had been done, forced on her by her mother's situation. She'd not worry any more. She'd not have to struggle any more. She'd let Orlick do that for her. He kissed her softly on the lips and she could feel herself respond, like a flower opening under the sun, and she knew with certainty that with Orlick at her side she could cope with anything.

Cecie McCabe came swishing up to them where they sat, slightly apart now, a little over-awed by their sudden commitment to each other. She was swinging her voluminous net skirt side-ways to right and left and doing the same with her orange hair. Lydia decided she was trying to look like Rita Hayworth. Unfortunately she looked more like a friendly puppy. 'You dance, Orlick?' she interrupted them. Then, smirking, announced, 'It's a Ladies' Choice.'

'No thank you, Cecie,' Orlick said, taking Lydia's hand.

'But that's not *fair*,' Cecie pouted. 'You're sup-posed to say yes.'

'Lydia and I have just got engaged,' Orlick said. For a second Lydia felt a rush of resent-ment. He was talking for her, telling people with-out her permission, assuming authority. Then she shrugged and accepted it. This was what

143

marriage would be like, not having to make decisions. She smiled at Cecie.

'Oh gosh! Smashing!' Cecie exclaimed unenthusiastically. She had always fancied Orlick Fitzmaurice, and had been sure that he would get tired of waiting for Lydia to make up her mind — then, as she said, she'd be in there quick as a flash.

Lydia could see Cecie couldn't wait to dash back and tell the others. The band was playing a slow foxtrot, 'I'm Getting Sentimental Over You'. Some of the boys looked bored. They'd been snapped up by either girls who were never normally asked to dance, or ones who were not any of their first choices. The Ladies' Choice sort of evened things out for the unpopular ones. Cecie, Lydia could see, wanted to get in there and spread the word. She looked desperately about for someone to ask to dance and her eyes lit on a pimply youth with four large protruding front teeth. None of the girls fancied him, so he'd been left partnerless.

'Jerry!' she cried, rushing over to the startled youth, who was quite used to sitting out the Ladies' Choice. 'Come an' dance wi' me.'

'Wha's the matter, Cecie? You lost your eyesight?' he asked cheerily and hastened to lead her on to the dance floor. Lydia could see her whispering to him.

'It will be all over town by morning,' she said. 'That Cecie!'

'Let's tell our parents then,' Orlick said. 'Let's

144

go now. First to your mother, okay?'

She nodded and took his hand. It was nice being taken charge of. 'Oh Orlick, this is *it*,' she whispered excitedly.

'Yep,' he said. 'Yes, Lydia. This is it. And I'll make you happy. So happy. You'll see.'

Chapter Sixteen

Roland sat with his brother hunched low over his drink in the dark little pub in Booterstown. Austin had chosen it for its privacy. It was unlikely they would meet any of their cronies in the sawdust pub with its low bar and ancient alcoves. The place was mainly haunted by aged locals who eyed the two with idle curiosity as they sipped their Murphy's stout. A sign on the wall advertised Thomond Plug, another Guinness, and yet another some long forgotten game of hurling — Kerry v. Clonmel, an all-Ireland final. That meant excluding the North, the six counties. It went without saying.

The brothers sat, heads low over their whiskey, whispering. Roland had lost a great deal of his buoyancy in the past week and seemed subdued. Austin could barely contain his excitement. Roland listened, at first having difficulty concentrating on what Austin said, even though he knew this was important or Austin would not have chosen such an out-of-the-way spot. Roland had never had the capacity to hold more than one thought in his head at a time and his mind right now was full of the situation he'd found himself in with Varina Gallagher. Notwithstanding the invitations and wedding arrangements, he was vainly trying to escape, and if that was not enough to occupy a man he had received a letter from Tom Gallagher that morning which was, to say the least, alarming.

Roland had not gone to see his prospective father-in-law since the whole business of Varina's pregnancy had come to light. He had not paid the house in Ailesbury Road a visit, despite his mother's strict instructions. Tom had written, 'I have waited patiently for you to have the courtesy to contact me and I have waited in vain. I therefore have to take the initiative and summon you to my house on Tuesday next, otherwise I will be forced to issue a summons and take you to court for a Breach of Promise suit. You leave me no alternative.' And he had signed it simply 'Tom Gallagher'. Not 'sincerely' or 'respectfully yours' or even 'regards'. Just his name.

Obviously, Roland realised, Tom Gallagher was very angry and he was not a man to be trifled with. Roland sighed and sank deeper into the booth as if he would like to disappear. He tried again to concentrate on what Austin was saying.

Then in a moment Austin's words became utterly riveting and Roland forgot Varina and the letter in his fascination with what he heard. At last he said, 'So what you're suggesting, we screw Lydia out of her inheritance, business, house, the lot. Say Mother left it to us. Split four ways. Pius gets a quarter.'

Austin glanced nervously around. 'God, you don't mince words, Roley, do you? Call a spade a spade.'

147

'We're not talking about bloody spades here, Aus, you know. We're talking about fraud. Major fraud. This has got to be mulched over.'

'I don't see what's to mulch over, as you call it. Either we do or we don't. If we do we take certain risks. I have to say that with Pius Brady and the full weight of his legal experience behind us the risk is not too great. Or we don't, and we find ourselves penniless, out in the cold. What's there to mulch over?'

'But we could be caught. I would have thought that was worth a little mulching, eh, Aus?'

'I've said. Pius will deal with the details. Our dear little sister will not contest, of that I'm sure. What else could go wrong? How the hell could we be caught?'

'Suppose Lydia *does* contest the will?'

'Lydia? Are you crazy?' Austin shook his head. 'If she *does, if,* mind, being about as likely as you getting out of marrying that Varina Gallagher babe' — Roland winced — 'if she did, then Pius is sure most judges would smile and rule for us. Judges are, after all, men, and we know women can't run things. It's impossible. She'd make a hash of it. See, women are just not as capable as men and the male of the species has rights over the female every time. Society'd go to pot otherwise. No. There's not a judge in the land who'd rule for Lydia running D'Abru's or Mallow Hall. At worst it would be divided, and that's what we intend to do anyway.'

Roland hunched even lower. He was a coward,

Austin decided, and glared at him contemptuously. 'Oh for God's sake, Roley, what choice do we have? Mother's for the high jump . . .'

Tears filled Roland's eyes and spilled down his cheeks. 'I wish you wouldn't *talk* like that,' he cried in anguished tones. 'You're heartless and cruel, Aus, you always were. A jerk. You're a jerk and I hate you.'

'Oh come off it, Roland. Pull yourself together. Facts are facts.' Austin leaned across the table towards his brother, not a little alarmed by his attitude. Roland was stupid and quite capable of screwing the whole thing up and then where would Austin be? In the poorhouse. Or jail. Jeez! 'If there was anything I could do, anything at all to help Mamma, Roley, don't you think I would?' he said earnestly. 'But there isn't. So either we take it lying down — or we fight. If we don't fight, Roley, you'll have to give up your jaunts to the Curragh and Leopardstown. You'll have to quit those pleasant afternoons in Davy's and the Bailey. You'll have to *work*, Roley, work . . .'

'I'll probably have to do that anyway,' Roland blurted out.

'What do you mean, Roley? Oh, you mean marrying. What makes you think you should have to change? If you have money you'll not need to. Only if you don't. Don't you know that in this country men are still the bosses? We don't live in America, thank God, and once married to Varina you can do as you damn well please. But

149

only if you have money.'

'But Tom Gallagher . . .'

'Don't be such a yellow-belly, Roley. Tom Gallagher can't touch you. What's it say in the Bible? 'And the wife shall leave her father and mother and cleave to her husband.' Something like that. Varina can't stop you going to the races or the Bailey or Davy's. Lack of funds can, though.'

'Mother says I have to work in one of Tom Gallagher's shops. Tom Gallagher is a very determined man, a strong one. Probably a bully. Here, look.' He produced the letter and shoved it across to Austin.

Austin pondered the piece of paper for some time before he replied. 'Yeah. You're in the soup, Roley, no doubt. That is, without money. But don't you see, old chap, if we do this thing, go in with Pius — and if we're caught we can always say he *made* us —' (Roland's eyes brightened. He of all of them could plead innocence to the whole conspiracy. Total ignorance.) 'If we go along with Pius, then in a while you'll be a rich man.'

Austin was waxing enthusiastic. He avoided saying 'When our mother dies we'll be rich men', couldn't bring himself to say that. 'You'll be a property owner. You can call all the shots. Listen, Roley.' (God, why did he have such a milk-and-water brother, a wet, a weasel, an idiot?) 'You marry Varina Gallagher, work in one of her da's little tobacco kiosks and you'll be a football. They'll kick you around. They'll annihilate you.' Roland was wide-eyed watching Austin. He was trembling at the picture his brother painted. 'But if you do as I say you'll be your own master. You'll be able to do as you please and screw Varina and her da. They'll have no power over you. Money, Roley, is power. Without it you are a cripple. Believe me.'

'Oh all right, all right, all right.' Roland gulped down the last of his drink. 'Okay.'

'No going back? You know that?'

Roland nodded and rose to his feet a trifle unsteadily. 'I know that,' he protested. 'Not a complete fool. I *said* all right!'

'Okay.'

'Okay!'

'You all right to drive?'

Roland snorted. ' 'Course I am. I drive *better* when I'm a bit pissed. Sharpens my reactions.'

He left Austin sitting alone in the deep gloom of the snug. A shaft of sunlight played through a crack in the wooden beams. It caught a thousand dancing motes in its beam and spotlit a worn flagstone, beer-stained and strewn with fresh sawdust. The sawdust had turned gold in the light. Austin stared at it and wondered why he could not seem to relax. It was all going to plan, smooth as silk. Pius said the will had been signed, then altered, the initialling copied at the bottom of the new pages and the fake document sealed in his safe. Everything was in perfect order. Nothing could go wrong. It was just a matter of time. Pius said he'd been very careful.

The last page of the will, the one where his mother and Eilish and Nonie had signed with their full signatures, need not be copied. It would be there for examination of signatures by all-comers. Austin wanted assurance from Pius that the original pages were destroyed, but Pius said he could not do that just yet, not until Martha actually died, as at any moment she might demand to see it.

'You needn't worry so, Austin,' Pius had said. 'She may yet do the right thing and divide the business and the estate between you boys and Lydia. I need to be able to produce the original will at a moment's notice. It often happens that people change their minds about their wills. I'll destroy it instantly she passes on.' Austin gulped, uncomfortably. 'Rest assured, Austin, I don't want anything to go amiss any more than you do.' And Austin had to be content with that.

There was nothing to worry about, but Austin could not relax. He did not feel easy in himself and the unease made him irritable. He shifted in his seat and held his hand up for a refill. Then he grinned, thinking of Roland. Poor old Roley, having Tom Gallagher breathing down his neck, having to marry his daughter. Still, Varina was a goer. Those boobs. That pouty mouth. Those sulky eyes promising hell. He hummed:
'If ever the devil was born,
Without a pair of horns
It was you, Jezebel, it was you.
If ever a pair of eyes,

Promised paradise,

Deceiving me, grieving me, lea-e-e-ving me blue,

It was you, Jezebel, it was you . . .'

Oh, Roley had let himself in for one hell of a time, that was for sure. Austin began to laugh. The bartender didn't even raise his head from the racing page. He'd seen all sorts in here, heard everything, managed a hundred scenarios and not turned a hair.

Austin felt better after another jar. Things began to smooth out, seem less traumatic. The trick was, he decided, to shrink the whole plan down to a manageable size — not dramatise it or build it up.

They were simply sorting things, that was what they were doing. Things were being *righted* to what in law they should be. The male inherited, the female's husband provided, that was Nature's and Society's rule and they, Pius and Roley and he, were simply making sure the natural and social law prevailed. Reassured, he paid for their drinks and left. The barman scarcely looked at him. Austin smiled to himself. Roley was a fool, but he was manageable too. Varina Gallagher would give him hell. And it would be all the same in a hundred years.

Chapter Seventeen

Roland stood in front of Tom Gallagher's desk. There was no chair to sit on except the one Tom Gallagher lounged on and two little antique ones standing daintily against the walls, but they looked ornamental rather than useful, and as Roland did not like to carry one of them to the desk he stood.

The room was full of manly things: a cuspidor, a boar's head on the wall, a huge fish in a glass case with the date 1934 underneath and something else in an elaborate scroll Roland could not decipher. There were golf clubs in a holder against the desk and a huge map over Tom Gallagher's head. On the desk was a box of Havana cigars.

Tom Gallagher's piercing blue eyes bored into Roland, making him uncomfortable. 'Well, young fella-me-lad, what have you got to say for yourself?' Tom broke the silence at last. 'You've not behaved very well now, have you? Not in a gentlemanly way at all, at all,' he added.

'Well, sir, I'd, er, like to marry your daughter Varina, er, if I may,' Roland asked rather unnecessarily.

Tom hooted. 'I'd say that takes the biscuit! The invitations are out, boy. There is no chance you'll get out of marrying Varina.'

'Well, it's just that I thought . . . I thought . . .'

'What did you think? Always supposing you are capable of thinking?'

'I thought that's what you wanted me to say.'

'Jesus!' Tom exclaimed incredulously. 'Mother of God!'

'Well she's your daughter, sir.'

' 'Course she's my daughter. You wouldn't be here otherwise.'

'I thought you wanted me to ask your permission, sir.'

'Bit late for that! You've done the deed, haven't you? So what else can you do but marry her? We've sent out the invitations, the dates are fixed and you've not had the courtesy to ask my permission . . .'

'That's what I'm doing now.' Roland protested.

Tom glared at Roland. How could anyone be so stupid? He was acutely aware that this was *her* son, Martha's son. The thought of her tightened his chest and made breathing difficult. It also made it difficult for him to be mad at Roland. 'You better go,' he snapped.

'I'll be good to her, sir,' Roland assured him.

'You better be!' Tom said shortly.

Roland did not know why he was talking like this, all placatory and subservient. He did not want to marry Varina Gallagher, but here he was reassuring the father he was going to be good to her! Truth was, he was afraid of Tom Gallagher. Deep down in Roland Tracey there coiled a

155

snake of fear that he drowned with alcohol and good times.

Then he thought of the hoax, as he had decided to call it. The money he would come into consoled him, was a balm to his predicament as he stood before this stern father who was reducing him to schoolboy status in his study. As if he was a feeble fellow found with his hand in the cookie jar. It was humiliating. Well, with the money that the sale of D'Abru's would bring, this man would have no power over him. Roland could lead his own life, independently, give Varina enough to live in comfort and do as he pleased. She could stay at home and look after the kid and he could go on as he always had, no problem. It was just as Austin said. It would be perfect.

'Look here, Roland, we are going to be, em,' Tom began hesitantly, interrupting Roland's reverie, 'em, linked by marriage, so we'd better try to get on.' He cleared his throat. 'Now, as I understand it you have no job, no qualifications, no profession?'

Roland shifted uneasily. 'Well, sir, I'm studying. I'm at Trinity . . .'

Tom guffawed. It was a loud, infectious laugh that startled Roland and made him jump. 'Don't give me that balderdash! Study! You don't know the meaning of the word! Why, I'll bet you haven't opened a book in years!'

This was true but Roland shook his head vehemently. 'I work hard. Very hard, sir. I should have

156

qualified before but . . .'

'Don't give me that guff,' Tom Gallagher stopped him, raising his hand. 'It's no use trying to impress me.' He leaned across the desk and said confidentially, 'I've had a chat with your mother and we've decided that the best thing would be for you to come and work for me. That way I can keep an eye on you, see you use your, er, full potential.' He watched Roland's horror-struck face as the whole impact of that news sank in. He felt a sudden sympathy for the boy. To be cut off from all he thought of as worthwhile must come as a severe blow. Curtailed so early in life.

'It will do you no end of good,' he told Roland firmly. 'Show you how the grown-ups behave. I'll start you in the kiosk in Drimnagh.'

Tom Gallagher said it like it was nothing at all and Roland clenched his teeth. This was totally horrendous. A foul little kiosk in a horrid place; he would be trapped there all day, this monster checking up on him. Whatever reservations he had had about Austin's plan now simply evaporated.

Oh, he'd been warned about it, that that was what Tom Gallagher would propose, but hearing it now in the cold light of day, hearing it stated, unnerved him. What did the old geezer want? His life? Did he expect him to stand in that two-by-four booth selling fags to exhausted workmen and their worn-out wives? Roland shuddered. Nothing could be worse than standing in a Gallagher tobacco outlet serving cigarettes to the riffraff of Dublin. Not even prison. He would be reduced to a gibbering idiot within a year — no, a month.

So what was he to do? He'd marry Varina, he had no choice. Then he'd have to go along with Tom Gallagher's plan, at least verbally if not in actuality. He could plead flu, a toothache whatever, until . . . until . . . well, until the plan came to fruition. Then take off. But *pianissimo*. Simply go his own way, but see Varina had plenty. That's what he would do. Austin was right. Money was power. He would be lost without it. Utterly at the mercy of this blue-eyed tyrant. Roland thought Tom Gallagher's eyes reminded him of someone else's, someone threatening. Who? They were cold and blue and merciless. Then he remembered. Varina. Of course. Varina Gallagher had her father's eyes.

'You'll be married in three weeks,' Tom said coldly. 'Have you by the way *seen* the invitations? Do you know *anything* about your own wedding?' His voice was heavily sarcastic.

Roland shook his head. 'I thought that was your bag, sir. Father of the bride . . .'

Tom threw him a withering glance. 'As I've said. I've spoken to your mother,' he began, then hesitated, seeing her floating towards him swathed in chiffon, feeling his body grow weak at the thought of her. 'The ceremony will be held in the Holy Child down the road and I plan to have the reception at the Royal in Bray.'

Roland said nothing. He simply nodded,

something he intended to do a lot of in the future. He'd agree to whatever Tom Gallagher demanded then do precisely what he wanted. Before Tom Gallagher had sussed this ploy the whole matter of the money would have been resolved and Roland would be free to carry on the old and much loved regime. Those marvellous mornings in the pub when daylight streaked through the doorway as the first customers crept in. The first sharp taste of his beer. The ritual of selecting the runners for the day. The wonderful, comfortable feeling he always had, his bunch of friends around him, piling into their cars, laughing, warm and mellow inside, full of goodwill and the prospect of the day before them. Oh, it was a grand life, a life he had no intention of allowing Varina Gallagher or her father to seriously disrupt.

He nodded again and when he finally left the room Tom Gallagher sighed. No fool he, he knew what little effect he'd had on Roland Tracey. 'Well, well, well my boy, just you wait and see,' he muttered to himself, then gave himself over to a reverie about Martha.

Lovely, fair, adorable woman. She enchanted him. She dazzled him. He knew it was an untenable situation, impossible and outrageous, yet he had no control over himself. For the first time in his life he felt irresponsible and capable of giving in to his wildest whims. He was like a teenager, intoxicated and unable to think clearly. And he loved the feeling.

He grinned to himself. He was seeing her for dinner tonight. He felt young and virile and excited. He dismissed all thoughts of Roland and began to plan his evening with care.

Chapter Eighteen

Eileen Skully riffled through the file connected with the D'Abru will. *Her* file, not Pius Brady's. She had tucked away some crumpled pieces of paper found in her boss's wastepaper basket along with copies of documents hastily jettisoned by Pius. It had taken some time to put it all together.

First, the notes. Those screwed up pieces of paper discarded by Pius after Martha Tracey had left the office, the notes he had made at the time. Then, more tellingly, the practiced initials. She had saved everything, nothing was thrown away.

In her jealous hoarding and by diligent listen-in to her boss's phone calls she had put together some, if not all, of the plan. Sitting in her tiny office she had oo-ed and ah-ed aloud at the audacity of it. They planned, Pius and the sons, to cheat Lydia D'Abru of her inheritance.

Pius had asked her to type up the original will. He seemed to think she was a robot and had no thinking powers at all. Then she had found discarded carbon copies of changes he had made to the contents, with the initials forged at the top. She knew he had unpinned the last page and added it on to the counterfeit will and tucked the document safely into his safe. She knew the combination and had access whenever she wished. But Pius did not know that. She would not meddle with it yet though; she would bide her time.

Hugging her narrow chest, she allowed herself to realise that for the first time Pius Brady was within her grasp. It was a determined and greedy grasp. Eileen Skully had not loved her boss so passionately for so long without indulging in the fantasy of one day marrying him. And fantasies, if indulged in often enough, can come to seem more realistic than real life. Eileen Skully saw nothing outrageous in her desire to settle down with her boss — after all, it happened in the movies all the time. No, what she felt was unfair was the fact that Pius did not credit her with more intelligence. Did he really think her so dumb? Or was she in fact brighter than most secretaries? On reflection, she plumped for the latter. She was, she knew deep inside, a very clever woman, brighter than anyone gave her credit for. If only they knew!

And she was patient. She had waited so long, another few months, years even, would not matter to her.

She tidied the desk in her small, airless office. The roses she had put in a vase beside her type-writer that morning had withered from lack of oxygen. Their heads flopped over and their pink petals fell slowly, one by one, on to her desk.

She sighed. She had not seen Pius that day. Away with the horses, no doubt, or away with the conspirators. Ah yes. That little group, up to no good. She smiled to herself.

162

In her heart she condemned what they were about to do. Everything in her shrank from such perversity, such evil. It was appalling. Yet she could not help but rejoice. It never even occurred to her to try to reverse the process, to prevent it. That might mean the loss of her job, which she could not countenance, and what they were doing, were about to do, was her passport to happiness.

Long days and nights of unrequited love, of plans to entrap Pius, plans that she never had the courage to put into practice, of delirious dreams about him, had honed her spirit to a sharp and steely determination. Had blinded her to all else. And she had the answer now, her master plan, her script.

She looked at herself in the small cracked mirror over the basin. The pale face stared back at her, eyes wide and feverish. She did not see that lean, voracious face. Linda Darnell looked back at her, Dorothy Lamour or Hedy Lamarr. Yes, a film-star face smiled back, a face Pius Brady would desire, luscious lips he'd ache to kiss.

With a grin she put on her hat, stuck a pin through it and, turning the light off, locking the doors, she sauntered out into the street with a spring in her step and a bright light in her eyes.

Chapter Nineteen

It was raining when Martha arrived at the Shelbourne. The doorman took her umbrella, shook it out and helped her off with the light mac she was wearing.

She patted her hair in the mirror outside the restaurant and, reassured, entered. Her breath quickened when she saw him. He rose and stood awkwardly, his smile of welcome trembling on nervous lips. She hurried over and their hands touched then jerked away, as if an electric current had shocked them both.

They sat. He feasted his eyes on her, on the small bones of her face almost visible under her fine skin, on the pearly teeth and the dark lashes curtaining her eyes. She wore a black suit in silk grosgrain and a string of pearls lay warmly around her neck.

'You look very well,' he said, and a brick-red stain swept over his face as he realised how daft he sounded, how gauche.

'Thank you,' she said without humour, glancing up at him under her lashes.

The waiter brought the two-foot-long menus which separated them by their sheer size and for a moment they both disappeared behind them.

'What will you eat?' she asked, then she too

blinked at the stupidity of her question. 'Oh, I didn't mean . . .'

He stared over the top of the menu at her. 'I'm not as hungry tonight as I was the last time I met you,' he said.

She nodded in agreement, fingering the pearls at her throat. 'A little salad maybe.'

They ordered salmon mayonnaise. They were awkward with each other and lapsed every so often into silence. They tried to talk about the wedding but neither of them was that interested in it. Except that Tom was anxious about Varina. 'I don't think she's in love with your son,' he told her. 'Not what I'd call love.' Looking at her, then glancing away, embarrassed.

'You are most probably right, Tom, but what are we to do? There is no other course that we can take.'

He nodded in agreement and once more the conversation petered out. They skipped dessert, drank coffee and brandy, then left.

By now the silence between them was absolute. He took her arm and they walked down the Green. At first Martha did not notice how far they went, she was too content, her arm in his, the close contact. She felt part of him, strolling along beside him, attached to him, serene because he guided her along, taking charge. Then the pace began to tire her but she did not want to stop, to tell him she was tired, break the spell.

The streets were dark and the light from the street-lamps made the puddles left by the rain shimmer in the dark. A full moon hung in a velvet sky and the only people about were courting couples unable to bear parting for the night. They strolled into Grafton Street, down D'Olier Street.

At last they reached O'Connell Street and Martha was out of breath. She leaned against the parapet of the bridge, gasping.

'Oh my dear, I'm sorry. I wore you out.' Tom looked at her aghast, seeing her exhaustion. Her face was pale as death, her eyes feverish. 'What is the matter?' he cried. 'Oh my dear, are you all right?'

'I'm fine,' she whispered. She turned, sucking in air, staring at the river's murky depths, the Halfpenny Bridge beyond, trying to get oxygen, feeling the world spin slowly around her.

'What is it, Martha? What is wrong?' he asked again.

She smiled at him soothingly. 'I'm all right really,' she told him reassuringly, her voice normal.

He put his arms around her and held her close against him. He had never felt so protective before. He touched her hair, kissed her cheeks, not passionately but tenderly, aching to care for her, make her feel better.

'I'll get a taxi,' he said when her breathing was normal. She did not protest. She was too exhausted.

The taxi smelled of stale smoke and the doorhandle did not work. They smiled at each other, sharing their feelings, shaking their heads over the state of taxis these days.

Tom paid the taxi off at Ballsbridge and carried her to his car. He had never seen anyone so frail. She seemed like a doll to him; a piece of Dresden china. He settled her tenderly into the front seat, tucking a rug around her knees. She smiled feebly at him. 'I'm sorry,' she whispered, and he bit his lip to stop himself from hurting.

'Oh my dearest one, never apologise.'

He drove her home in silence. She half dozed in her seat beside him, her head against his upper arm. His hands clenched the wheel, white-knuckled.

When they reached the Hall he cut the engine and looked at her. She lay back in the seat, pale and fragile, staring at him, her eyes huge in her small face. He caught his breath.

'Are you all right?' he asked.

She nodded, her eyes full of tenderness. 'I've been under a strain recently. It's not easy, a woman alone. The boys. This estate.' He nodded. She was a little woman battling the big world alone. They looked intently at each other for a long moment.

'What's happening?' he asked huskily, like a child.

'I don't know,' she whispered back.

Things, she realised, had gone much further than she dreamed possible in so short a space of time. How had they reached this point so quickly? It was no longer a game, a delicious flirtation, a passing brush with a passion that had been lost somewhere in the mists of time. Both knew they were utterly vulnerable, at each other's mercy, without guile or defences.

He took her face carefully between his hands and they inspected each other slowly, intently, examining bone and hair and eyes, their portraits seen in minute detail as by a painter seriously and gravely. Then he kissed her on her lips, so softly, so gently, so reverently that it felt like the most tender gift of love she had ever received.

They did not speak, did not utter a word, and he helped her out of the car and up the steps. He took her key from her and opened the door.

'Will you come in?' she asked. He shook his head and put his finger on her lips as Nonie came into the hall.

'I'll call you tomorrow,' he said and went back to his car. He drove off into the night, leaving her bemused, touching her lips with her fingers.

Chapter Twenty

'I've got to see you!'

It was hardly nine o'clock and Martha had drowsily picked up the phone to stop it ringing. She cradled it at her ear. His voice, which had never left her all through the night, filtered into her consciousness. His tone was urgent.

'Oh darling,' she replied, because she was so happy to hear him. Because it didn't matter what he talked about, the sound of his voice thrilled her. She could feel it in the marrow of her bones.

She felt fine. She should be overtired, in pain, sick, but she felt, if not exactly energetic, at least ready to get up, get dressed, live life. She smiled at the phone, stretched a little, and said, 'Why don't you come here for lunch?' She giggled. 'Discuss wedding plans?'

'What time?' he asked, serious.

'Twelve. Twelve-thirty.'

'See you then.'

Lydia came into her bedroom, face aglow, to show her the ring Orlick had bought. It glittered on her finger as she waved her hand right and left, showing off the sparkling solitaire.

'It's lovely, darling. Just lovely.'

Lydia sat on the edge of her mother's bed, leaned over and kissed her.

'It's wrong, Mamma, for me to be happy when you're sick.'

'I'm not, darling. Not today. Today I feel fine.'

Lydia felt her heart rise joyously. Her prayers were working. Her mamma was getting better. Why, she looked young and happy and healthy this morning. What could there be wrong with her?

'What are you doing today, pet?' Martha asked, and realised she was plotting, planning.

'I'm having lunch with the Fitzmaurices. They asked you too, Mamma — can you come? We're meeting in the Gresham at one o'clock.'

'No, sweetheart, I'm afraid I can't. I've got a meeting with Tom Gallagher' — be still my heart — 'about Varina's and Roland's wedding.' She laughed. 'It seems like the whole family are getting married. Well, that's a good thing.'

'Can't you and Mr Gallagher come along to the Gresham? After all, he's going to be family too.'

Martha's heart skipped a beat, but she shook her head. 'No. It might be an imposition on the Fitzmaurices. They might not be ready yet to take on the whole tribe!'

'I expect you're right,' Lydia agreed.

'We'll meet up very soon, dear. Make a date for any day next week.'

'Okay, Mamma.' Lydia frowned and said, 'But do I have to be bridesmaid at Varina's wedding? Do I *have* to?'

'Yes, dear. And she'll be bridesmaid at yours.'

Lydia groaned.

'I'm sorry you don't like her, but she's really a very sweet girl.' No, she thought, her father is sweet, and wonderful, not Varina. I don't know Varina at all.

'*Mother!* The last thing I'd call Varina Gallagher is *sweet.*'

'Well, you'll have to grin and bear it. Your brother is marrying her and that will make her your sister-in-law, so you'll be related. I'm sorry, Lydia. We choose our friends, not our family. You'll just have to learn tolerance.'

And will you tolerate me if you find out . . . what? There was nothing yet to find out. The thought that there might be, *would* be something for her daughter to discover made her shiver with a sick excitement.

'Do you know where your brothers are going today? What their plans are?'

'If you mean will Roland be here to discuss wedding plans with Mr Gallagher, then you're out of luck. He went off after breakfast this morning with Austin. They rushed down the drive in the Morris Minor. They said they'd something to talk over together but I don't think so. I think Austin is trying to avoid Mr Brady and I think Roland probably doesn't want to see Mr Gallagher.'

Martha smiled fondly at her daughter. She was glad about Orlick. She was glad the house would be empty when Tom came.

'What are you going to wear?' she asked.

'My silk shantung,' Lydia replied promptly.

'Very appropriate, darling. Tell the Fitz-maurices for me that I'm truly sorry about luncheon. Why don't we ask them here for,' she frowned, 'let's see, how about Saturday? For lunch? How would that suit?'

'Perfectly, Mamma.' Lydia went to the door.' I think you're getting better,' she said. 'I'm praying for you, Mamma, every morning and night.'

'Thank you, pet.'

When she'd gone Martha rose and realised that her daughter might be right. She felt wonderful. She bathed and dressed, putting on a simple cream silk dress with a tan belt and shoes. She wore little make-up.

Later, waiting for Tom in the drawing-room she realised she felt like a young girl again, full of excitement, apprehension and hope. But there was something else too, a kind of certainty, a positive feeling deep down that told her all would be well, that this situation, which seemed on the face of it so wrong, was undoubtedly right.

She had told Nonie to leave a cold lunch and take the afternoon off. 'I'll not need you, Nonie,' she said brightly. 'Or Eilish. I'll rest this afternoon. As long as you're both back for dinner I'll be happy.'

'You sure, mum?' Nonie sounded doubtful.

'Look at me, Nonie. Don't you think I look well?'

The old servant, who had the same hopes as Lydia and was praying as hard if not harder, looked at her mistress and had to agree.

'Ye look like an angel. Sure mebbe the doctor was wrong.' Then she said the same thing Lydia had said. 'I'm praying for ye, missus. Doin' a novena to the Blessed Virgin, so I am. Stormin' heaven!'

'Well, that's very kind of you, Nonie. Lay out lunch then off you go. But don't wear yourself out, will you?'

'No, mum, 'deeding I won't.'

I'm emptying the house, Martha thought. What on earth am I up to? Then she put the thought aside and waited, sitting in her window admiring her roses, her hands folded lightly in her lap.

When Tom arrived carrying a huge bunch of roses not half as pretty as the ones in her garden but infinitely more precious to her, Martha ran to the window and watched for Nonie to leave. Tom asked her what she was doing and she put her fingers to her lips. 'Hush!' she admonished and saw the pair of servants, hats and coats on despite the warm day, trundle off towards the bus stop at the end of the driveway.

'You're like a child,' Tom said, coming up close behind her. 'An enchanting child.'

She turned and was in his arms. Their embrace was fierce, all reticence gone. His lips met hers avidly, tasting her, seeking her, kissing her now gently, now hard and greedily.

When they drew apart he looked at her breathlessly. 'I'm a bit rusty at this,' he said. She said,

'So am I.' But there was no hesitation on either part. He wanted her with every beat of his heart. She wanted him as she'd never wanted a man before. Bernard had been a passionate lover and she had enjoyed their love-making, but she had been a girl then, untutored. Thomas Tracey had liked to be the dominant male and though he satisfied her, neither man had made her feel as she felt now — greedily intense, an unbearable excitement within her rising and overwhelming her. She felt love flowing from her like a torrent of lava. Life flowed in her again. She wanted it all. She wanted to caress Tom, taste him, embrace him and love him with abandonment. She adored him with all the breath in her body, with the essence of her being.

His body to her was beautiful, big, strong, male — fiercely alive. The feel of his muscles, the smoothness of his skin under her hands excited her, aroused her until her intensity turned into an excruciatingly tender and voluptuous sensitivity. Drowsy with passion, with kisses and caresses, with ardent embraces, they at last came into each other, fusing together with cries of ecstasy as at last they were one.

It seemed to them both as if their pleasure in each other could not climax further, yet as they moved together in the ballet of sex the unbearable sweetness rose and rose until at last they came again, a long shuddering orgasm that left them both almost fainting from the sensation.

Later, much later, she turned to his shoulder

and kissed it and whispered, 'Oh Tom. Oh Tom!'

'I love you,' he said.

'I love you too.'

'So much. So much,' he told her.

'Mmm.'

'Oh my beloved, I love you so.'

'I know, I know.'

He was the first to start thinking of the future. Mind racing, he asked, 'What are we going to do?'

'I don't know.' She sounded unconcerned. 'I only know we can't go back.'

'It's too late for that,' he agreed.

'Tom, I don't want to think about it just now. I'm too content.'

'But we must.' He raised himself on his elbow and looked down at her face on the pillow. 'I want you to spend the rest of your life with me.'

'I will, beloved. I promise you I will. Now hush and let me kiss you once again.'

Chapter Twenty-One

The next morning Lydia went to see her grand-mother. She strolled down the lane, taking her time. No one hurried down the lanes. They were magic places to wander in. The ferns on both sides were waist-high, dotted with cow-parsley and tall yellow wild iris. The stream gurgled past somewhere in the undergrowth and the geese, waddling from side to side, honked loudly as they ducked their heads and stared beadily at her, side-ways. Their gaze made her laugh — evil and hu-morous at the same time.

Lydia loved it here. She loved the smallness of it, the neatness, the sheer prettiness. She had always hated grandeur. The cottages, thatched and dreaming, snuggled into the green mounded land. A cat slept on a doorstep, and except for the geese all was still.

She wished time would stop. It was a constant ache. Oh God, let time stay at this moment now and forever. It was of course a vain wish and, as Sean Sullivan had often told her, a silly one. 'If you always want it to be *now*, then what are you worried about? It *is* always now,' he had told her.

How could she explain to him that if time stood still her mother would never have to die? Roland and Varina would not marry. She could stay engaged to Orlick forever and nobody, not even Granny Kathleen, would get any older.

Lydia adored Granny Kathleen, but she was aware that every visit revealed yet more deterioration in the old lady. She'd seen her grandmother slow down, her hands become increasingly gnarled and clumsy, her sight shorten until she peered all the time, and lately she'd taken to cupping her ear with her hand and murmuring 'Eh? Eh?', so that Lydia had to repeat whatever it was she had just said.

But this morning she was shocked. Granny Kathleen seemed suddenly ancient. Her mouth, usually relaxed and kindly, had tightened sorrowfully and her lips vanished in a thin, tense line, comb-teeth lines above and below. Her cheeks seemed sunken, but most of all her eyes were hollows of anguish, staring out of their sockets in mute appeal.

Lydia ran to her and enfolded the skinny frame in her arms. 'Oh Granny, Granny, what are we to do?' she sobbed, and for a while, a long while, they remained like that, clinging close, keening softly, murmuring to each other.

At last, as if by some secret signal, they separated simultaneously, wiping their eyes — Lydia with her fine linen handkerchief, Granny Kathleen with the sleeve of her jersey.

'I came to tell you, Granny, I'm going to marry Orlick Fitzmaurice,' Lydia said after a slight pause.

The old lady bustled herself together. 'Don't

do it, me darlin'.' She turned to her grand-daughter and took her hands in a fierce grasp. 'Look, yer an innocent. Ye run from life. I know yer mam wants ye to, but yer only doin' it to please her. Tell her ye will. Keep her happy. Then don't!'

'But I *want* to, Granny. I mean to.'

'Ye don't love him, pet.'

'I do. I do.'

'Well, I don't think so. Not real love. Not passion. Not head over heels like it should be.'

'Yes I love him, and I don't want head over heels. Sounds very uncomfortable to me. I'm twenty-five, Granny. All my friends are married. Or have careers.'

'You have D'Abru's. You go there often enough. Practically run it, yer mam says.'

'Not like that! That's a sweet factory and shop. No. Jamie McDonald is a doctor in the Mater with Orlick, interning with him. Annie McCawley is a journalist in London. Jessie Houlihan has three children. It's about time, Granny.'

'Is that a reason then?' Kathleen Daly asked and thought of her dead Liam and the fierce love they had had for each other, and for a moment Lydia saw in her the young pretty girl she had once been, firm-cheeked, firm-bodied, eyes full of hope. Then she said to her granddaughter, 'What about bein' in love? Eh?'

'I do love him, Granny. He's the sort of boy I want to be with. He understands me. I'm so happy with him. Quietly happy.'

'But not excited. Not the least bit frightened? You should be.'

'I don't *want* to be frightened. It's the last thing I want.'

The old lady shook her head. 'What about Sean?' she asked.

'What about him?' Lydia snapped back.

'Don't take that tone with me, sassy wench,' Granny Kathleen admonished. 'You know very well what about Sean!'

Lydia's face softened. She had not allowed herself to think about Sean Sullivan since his precipitate departure. 'I don't know, Granny. He frightened me sometimes. He's so . . .' She paused, thinking, 'strong. So dynamic. I'm out of my depth with him. Oh, I love him as a friend. He is very close to my heart. But as a husband, it's not on, Granny, how could it be? It would be impossible.'

'I don't see why,' the old lady insisted stubbornly. 'Your mam married Bernard D'Abru an' she hailed from this wee place —' She indicated the cottage. 'She married above her station.'

'It's not the same thing and you know it. Sean has his pride. He's a fiercely proud man, is Sean.'

'Then more fool he! Isn't he the very one who'll look after your interests, no mistake. An' if I'm not mistaken your interests'll need lookin' after when . . . when . . .'

'Oh Granny, don't upset yourself! Don't upset me. You must see I don't want to marry Sean. I find him disturbing and I like him as my friend. I don't have to *deal* with him. I don't want to live with that.'

'Then more fool you!'

'I want to marry someone who'll keep things as they are,' Lydia told her, trying to explain her feelings and not really succeeding. 'Nice and calm. I don't want conflict, Granny.'

'Life is conflict, child,' Granny Kathleen informed her.

'Well, I don't want it.' Lydia's chin stuck out stubbornly and Granny Kathleen was reminded of her daughter. She sighed. She felt too old and disenchanted to try to make her granddaughter change her mind.

'Well, whatever you think best for yourself, Lydia, I'll not argue with you. Remember what I said. Think it over carefully. Life is not meant to be slept through.'

Lydia tossed her head. 'Oh, I know that, and I don't want to sleep through my life. What I do want is a nice, uneventful time.' She stood up sharply. 'Can I get you a cup of tea, Granny?' she asked and Kathleen Daly knew the subject was closed.

She had done her best. She had tried to help her granddaughter a little way towards facing up to life. Squaring up to the harshness of it. And she had failed. She shook her head and a tear slid down her cheek.

Who would listen? The old knew so much. They could see the inevitable consequences of certain acts, but no one paid them any attention.

But then, she thought, that's what youth and growing up is all about; making mistakes, learning from them. Only Lydia had avoided it for such a long time. She had dreamed her way through childhood and into her teens and twenties, shrinking self-protectively from passion and pain alike, cloaking herself in the serenity of innocence for far too long, in her grandmother's opinion. Granny Kathleen wondered if perhaps Lydia knew something about herself that she wasn't privy to. Could it possibly be that Lydia knew what she wanted and was, with that ruthless determination, going after exactly what would make her happy? Granny Kathleen shook her head, glancing covertly at her granddaughter standing with her hand on the handle of the kettle on the hob, and she hoped fervently that Lydia's awakening would not be too painful.

Chapter Twenty-Two

The wedding took place with undue speed. All Dublin guessed the reason for the rush. 'Bet Varina's got a bun in the oven.' 'I hear Roland Tracey put her up the spout.' 'Varina Gallagher's banged up. Roland Tracey's the one who did it.' Evil smiles on their faces, malicious smirks accompanying their words.

Lydia D'Abru shrank from the gossip. Martha and Tom ignored it. There was no one more judgemental, in Martha's opinion, than the righteous; the ones who led repressed lives hated the ones who broke the rules.

Varina Gallagher hid until her wedding day and refused to face the world. She would square up to it when she was Mrs Tracey and not before. Dressmakers were sent for. A selection of shoes was dispatched from Dolcis. Richard Allen did the bridesmaids' dresses and Lydia squirmed at fittings and said she *hated* green and anyway it was unlucky and did she *have* to have a green dress? Varina insisted. Lettuce green and white. She, the bride, would be all in white except for the green stems and leaves of her bouquet and head-dress and the bridesmaids would wear green dresses trimmed with white. She'd always wanted that, she said.

Roland escaped. He did his minimum duty,

checking in each day to have morning coffee with his bride-to-be in the house on Ailesbury Road because Tom Gallagher said he'd personally kill him if he did not. Then, 'leaving her to it' as he phrased it, he scarpered off to the races and the pubs with his cronies.

Varina was too busy with preparations to care or see in Roland's behaviour a pattern for the future. All she knew was that she was pregnant and she had to get married and the less she saw of Roland until that inevitability the better.

And Tom and Martha, parents of the happy couple, spent all their time making love, wondering at the miracle of their romance, starry-eyed as teenagers and utterly absorbed in the discovery of each other. And no one noticed. No one at all. There was too much else going on.

They went on the top of the tram to Howth, roamed the purple hills, picked heather, had tea in a snug little tea-room, scoffing homemade bread and scones with hearty appetite. They giggled like schoolchildren, admitting they were too old and cautious to make love in the heather, acknowledging that they would have done so twenty years ago.

He was utterly enchanted by her. There was a mystery and passion in Martha Tracey that reached his soul and slid in there, into the essence of him, twining with his every thought and emotion. He felt he had entered another world, a larger-than-life world of heroes and heroines, fairy-tales and mythology. Anything was possible. Her body beguiled him. It was so slight, so fragile, yet its core was steel and the power of her limbs making love to him and the intensity of her emotion returning his passion seemed too strong for that slim frame.

They devoured each other. Like Guinevere and Lancelot, Deirdre and Naoise, Cleopatra and Antony they feasted, bemused by and intent on each other. They were amazed and delighted at the heights they could reach, astounded at their love.

Martha felt whole again. She felt healthy. Her illness was magically in remission and she imagined herself cured. Life flowed hotly through her veins, coursed through her every limb in the powerful consummation of her loving. Only Nonie and Eilish were fully aware of the scandalous affair; Tom and Martha were too besotted with each other to try to dissimulate in front of them. But they, the servants, fiercely loyal, were glad and rejoiced at their mistress's return to health, in spite of the immorality of the liaison. If that was what made her better then they would hold their peace and hope against hope that Tom Gallagher would cure their beloved mistress for good.

No one else noticed. They went together everywhere and everyone said, 'Poor Mrs Tracey and Tom Gallagher are stuck wi' each other over the business with Varina and Roland, God help them.' And everyone agreed they were doing a great job of keeping the peace and making the best of things.

It was going to be a stylish event and Dublin buzzed. Varina sulked and was over-excited by turns. Roland escaped as often as possible and that was most of the time. To his surprise Varina did not chide him for his lack of attention, a fact he found slightly disturbing.

Austin was a more relaxed man these days. Whatever happened now he was all right. He hoped his mother lived a long time.

He sat with Pius Brady over pints in out-of-the-way pubs and discussed plans. Pius deplored how well Martha looked. 'She positively glows,' he said bitterly. 'What the hell's happened, Austin? Tell me that.' He had extended his credit limit, become lavish in his betting on the basis of Martha's early demise and the windfall coming his way and was perplexed by the turn of events. He often forgot he spoke of Austin's mother.

'I'm glad she's better.' Austin sipped his pint. As long as Martha lived nothing drastic could happen. He would be looked after. It was if and when she died that the phoney will simply had to be implemented because then both he and Roland would otherwise be rendered practically penniless.

'But she *said*, she *told* me she had only a short time,' Pius protested.

'Shut up, Pius. You think I want my mother to die?'

'You didn't seem to mind when I first suggested it,' Pius said morosely.

'I don't want Mamma to die. I just don't want

to lose out when she *does.*' Austin looked at the solicitor over the rim of his pewter stein. 'You are a ghoul, Pius, you know that?'

All respect had vanished between them since they had become collaborators. Austin did not fear his boss, the senior partner, any more, and he did not call him sir. Nor did he use 'Mr Brady' when speaking to Pius as he had done formerly. If anything Austin was now the dominant associate, as he was the relation to the testator. In some senses Pius was dependent on Austin and he would have to trust his junior, for although Austin could not cheat Pius out of his share, the possibility that he might try to was an unpleasant constant.

'And what about my da's money? He must have left something?' Austin asked. Pius looked shifty. 'It went back into the business, didn't it?' Austin said accusingly.

'How do you think we've stayed afloat, eh? I went over every detail with your mam, Austin, and she was quite satisfied.'

'You screwed Mamma out of whatever was there, didn't you, Pius?' Austin looked at his god-father angrily. 'You did, you bastard, didn't you?'

'Prove it,' Pius said tranquilly. 'And how dare you imply . . . ?'

'I'm not implying, I'm stating a fact. And how would you fancy an examination of the relevant books? Eh? I have enough on you, Pius Brady, to put you into Mountjoy Prison for ten, fifteen years.'

'You did an' you'd not see a penny. Your mother's original will comes outta hiding and the new one . . .' Pius made a tearing gesture with his hands.

Austin shrugged. 'So?'

'You lose everything, Austin. Just think. Mallow Hall, D'Abru's. The lot. Without me you're scuppered.'

And Austin had to concede. Pius was right. Until Martha died Pius was in control. He looked out of the mullioned windows, through which he could see nothing at all, and he sighed. Life was a bitch, he thought. No one was ever really in control. There was always some unexpected element. Something unpredictable. He took another gulp of the bitter drink, burped and sighed, 'Ah!'

Pius looked at him in disgust.

Chapter Twenty-Three

It was at the wedding that Austin met Shona Donnelly. What came over him he afterwards could not figure out, but there, in the marquee in the grounds of the Royal Hotel in Bray, Austin bumped into Shona and they began to chat.

Austin was best man. Tom Gallagher had walked up the aisle with a very lovely bride on his arm. If Varina looked a trifle frantic, that was expected. 'She's nervous, poor wee lamb,' the married female guests told each other, nodding knowingly under wide-brimmed hats. 'Ah sure, she'll get over that soon enough, God bless her.'

Roland had the father and mother of a hangover. His stag night had lasted three days and nights and one of the boyos said they'd drunk Dublin dry. Tom Gallagher could not hand his daughter over to the plump young man but with an expression of distaste. Roland's eyelids kept drooping in slow motion over eyes that were barely focused. He was not an ideal bridegroom.

Not that anyone noticed. Bridegrooms often looked the worse for wear. Nor did they notice that when Tom Gallagher sat down beside Mrs Tracey he took her hand in his and pressed it, giving her a look so fervent it would have scorched a saint. Even if they had noticed, they would not have thought much of it. Gallagher and Mrs Tracey were partners at this event, bound together by a mutual interest in their children, the marriage of their offspring.

The weather forecast predicted heavy drizzle so the Royal Hotel had erected a marquee on the lawns. Trestle tables squarely surrounded a dance floor. It reminded Roland and Pius of the races, but most of the guests felt chilly and just a little uncomfortable. It would have been much more glamorous if the weather had been good and they could have sat in the sun. The folding chairs were functional, like school chairs, not at all conducive to lolling or relaxing, and the wind from the sea blew the canvas in and out like sails on a ship.

Shona Donnelly was sitting next to Austin, her name on a little card beside her flat, wide champagne glass. They all had name cards with little silver fairy dolls holding them and a heart-shaped chocolate covered in silver paper, a D'Abru chocolate.

Shona was one of the bridesmaids, and next to her sat Orlick Fitzmaurice and on his other side Lydia. These last two were whispering intently to each other — no doubt, Austin surmised, discussing plans for their own wedding. That was all they thought about, these Dublin girls, Austin thought in disgust. Weddings. They *all* had one agenda: to catch a husband.

It was left to Austin to talk to Shona, seeing as how his sister and Orlick would not come up for air. He examined her covertly for several minutes and eventually addressed her with the unoriginal announcement, 'It's really a very nice do, isn't it?' Not meaning it at all.

She nodded, looking at him with large brown eyes, but she said nothing. She had a round face, curly hair and dark lashes and those big brown eyes. Perhaps it was her eyes looking up fearfully at him, or seeming to, that started it. There was, he thought, respect in those large eyes. He was a solicitor, after all, a professional man. It made him feel good, the way she looked at him.

'You Varina's friend?' he asked tentatively.

'Well I'm not Roland's!' she said, surprising him. It was a smart, tart, Dublin sort of thing to say. Showed she was not stupid. She grinned at him then and said, 'You're the brother!'

'Umm.'

'Yeah. You met me before. At Clarie Foley's beach party last year, but you forgot!'

He shook his head. 'Oh no. I remember,' he lied.

'You're best man. You'll be making the speech' she said, knowing he lied.

The wind blew the flap behind them and she jumped. He patted her shoulder, feeling masterful. 'It's okay,' he said. Like, don't worry, I'll protect you. She smiled up at him, batting her lashes, playing the game.

'Gave me a start,' she said, glancing at the flap. Then, 'When's Lydia getting married?'

He shrugged. He was not in the least bit interested in his sister's nuptials. Such thoughts took up no room in his head at all. His sister had very little reality for him, she was a concept and an enemy. 'Dunno,' he said.

'Oh, you're awful,' she cried. 'You've gotta know.'

'I don't think *they* know,' he said casually, giving her a frank once-over.

She blushed under his gaze. 'You're a fine one, Austin Tracey,' she giggled. 'Like what you see?'

He licked his lips and nodded but before he could say anything more he had to make his speech.

While he was making it he could not help but notice how she gazed up at him, the admiration in her eyes. It was a clumsy speech, the jokes heavy and larded with innuendo, but neither Martha nor Tom really heard it. Every time their eyes met it was like diving head-first into turbulence. Every time their fingers touched electric shocks vibrated through them. Each moment was heightened and unreal and what the others said or did could not reach them.

The speeches were made, the toasts over, and the orchestra struck up 'Oh How We Danced On The Night We Were Wed'. Tom at last looked up and saw Roland was a trifle unsteady. He rose and, going over to his new son-in-law, shook his shoulder. He dug his fingers into the muscle but Roland did not feel it.

'Lay off the booze, Roland, God's sakes,' he whispered. 'Drink some coffee, some black coffee. Pull yourself together, man.'

He stared at Roland for a moment in disgust, then he put out his hand to Varina. 'Have yourself in a state to dance with my daughter when we get back,' he hissed, then he smiled at Varina and together they went on to the dance floor.

'Well, pet, how are you?'

Her eyes were nearly as glazed as Roland's and she said petulantly, 'Oh, I don't know, Dadda. I feel so sick.'

'Well, never mind, we'll get you out of it if you really don't want it.'

Her eyes brightened. 'You mean it? Oh Dadda, I think I *hate* him.'

'Just you wait till the baby is born, pet, then we'll sort it,' he assured her, angry for her. Then his eyes sought his love and he gazed across the crowd at her with adoration. Her eyes returned his ardour and his knees felt weak.

At his words Varina had perked up and as soon as he could he returned her to her place at the centre of the table and hurried to Martha. He took her in his arms and felt her melt as they moved on to the floor and he whispered, 'I adore you.' When she pressed her body close to his he murmured, 'Wicked woman!' delightedly in her ear. 'Don't do that here or I'll go mad.'

She laughed, looking up at him with innocent eyes.

'The rest of your life with me?' he demanded.

'You always ask — don't you trust me?' she whispered.

'I do. I'm just pondering the dilemma. We

can't stay here. In Ireland. And I *have* to have you all to myself, alone and apart. Safe in my heart . . .' he half sang, half murmured in time to the music.

The orchestra were playing 'You Stepped Out Of A Dream' and he held her, whispering the words in her ear, meaning every sentimental syllable. 'I'm so happy,' he said.

She nodded. 'Me too. It's beautiful, this moment, now.'

'Not for poor Varina, I'm afraid,' he said. 'And what are we going to do? We can't go on like this.'

'People would talk!' she laughed. 'You know me, Tom. I'm not shockable and I'm afraid I'm impervious to gossip.'

'But Varina and Roland! They'd be so embarrassed.'

'Yes.' She was suddenly sober. 'They are going to find it difficult enough as it is.' He thought maybe not, maybe not. But then he thought, there would be the child.

'You see, I want to marry you,' he told her.

'We can't. I'm sure there's some rule against it. Consanguinity. Affinity?' Sudden tears came into her eyes. I won't be here, she thought. I'll be in my grave. And she clung to his smooth dinner-jacket, suddenly terrified.

'Darling, what is it? What's the matter?'

'We're happy as we are, aren't we, Tom?' She blinked the tears away, looking at him wistfully.

'Deliriously, darling, but it's not enough. I want to wake with you in my arms every blessed morning. I want to sleep close to you every single night.' He put his lips near her ear. 'I want you with me *all* the time. Not some of it, *all* of it.'

She knew she'd have to tell him, sometime, about the illness. But not yet, not yet. Who knew, it might put him off her. He might find the idea of sickness disgusting. God knew she felt that herself. How could she blame him if he felt the same? Suppose he lost interest, how could she bear that?

'Let me take you to Italy,' he whispered. 'Let's go to that lovely land and be together, completely together while we talk over what's to be done.' He wanted to tell her that there was no reason why they should not be married. They were both widowed, available. Only their children rendered it difficult. But Tom Gallagher, witnessing the travesty of the wedding today, could not believe it would last. Varina would have the baby. He'd petition Rome for a separation, an annulment even. These things could be accomplished with money and contacts. Of course he'd have to buy off Roland, but he had no worries on that score. Roland Tracey was, he had no doubt, eminently buyable.

Martha was thinking, why not? Why not? She would like to see Lydia married, but after that, who would care where she went, what she did? She pressed closer to Tom and murmured in his ear, 'Yes, my darling, oh yes. Let's go to Italy. But after Lydia's wedding.'

Austin asked Shona to dance. The waltzes

were over, the romantic music had had its spell, and now it was time for the razzmatazz.

'There's just one place for me. Near you!

It's like heaven to be. Near you!

Times where we're apart, I just break my heart . . .'

Austin was an efficient dancer, capable of executing complicated steps. What he lacked in rhythm, Shona made up for, and the two flew around the floor with stunning aplomb.

'Sittin' at an upright, my sweetie an' me,

Pushin' on the pedals, makin' sweet harmony . . .'

Austin felt at that moment very powerful. He had managed to put Pius in his place, sort out his future, assure himself of a comfortable life and all was well. Lydia was going to marry Orlick Fitzmaurice, and there was old money there, so his sister would not be hard done by. Orlick would look after her, no doubt about that, so all in all he was simply righting a legal irregularity. Things could not be better. And this girl he was twirling was the perfect dance partner.

He smiled at Shona, who grinned back, executing a twirl one way, then the reverse, her hair flying, mouth half open, green silk swirling out around tanned legs.

'You like to have dinner with me some night?' he asked, just like that, out of the blue.

She swirled back to him, her body hitting his with a thunk. 'Yeah. Sure,' she replied breathlessly, though whether from the thought of going

195

out with him or the exertions of the dance he did not know. She certainly sounded casual, and it was that more than anything that made him determined to follow up on his invitation.

The evening ended badly. Roland was too drunk to go anywhere though the couple were supposed to leave for Killarney. There was a crash at the top table and the bridegroom disappeared under it. Austin hurried away to the scuffle, telling Shona to wait for him. His blasted brother was not going to spoil this night for him. With the help of Tom Gallagher he booked a room in the hotel and carried the lolling, senseless body up to it. Dumping Roland on the bed they left him there. Tom then got Varina a separate room and she kissed him at the door. To his relief told him, 'It's better this way, Dadda. I don't think I could have borne him to . . . you know.'

He nodded, pinched her cheek and told her to sleep soundly.

'I will, Dadda. I will.'

Varina had not wanted Roland's embraces that night. She had in fact dreaded them. Pregnancy had put her completely off sex and she had been anticipating the moment they would be alone together with distaste and apprehension. The thought nauseated her and she wanted nothing more than to be left by herself. Her wish granted, she was grateful to slide alone between the cool, fresh sheets and fall soundly asleep.

Chapter Twenty-Four

Lydia was not at all in a hurry to marry. At the breakfast table next morning Martha put it to her that it might be a good idea to arrange an October wedding.

'It will soon be winter, darling and I'm sure you don't want to get married in the cold.' She looked through the window to where the leaves were turning gold and the first few fell trembling to the earth. Time was slipping by so fast, too fast.

'Mamma, that's next month! People will think I'm like Varina and *have* to get married. Besides, I don't want to get married yet. I'll wait till spring.' She paused. 'Or summer would be better,' she amended hopefully.

Martha did not want to remind her daughter that she might not be around next summer so she simply said, 'I'd like it if you married sooner, pet.'

Lydia swallowed and looked resentful. 'Well, if you insist.'

'How does Orlick feel?' Martha asked gently.

'Oh, the sooner the better for him,' Lydia replied reluctantly.

'Then it's settled,' Martha said decisively. 'Don't worry, dearest. You've avoided marriage for so long that you are alarmed about the whole idea of it, and I completely understand. But postponing it will only make your fear worse.'

How to explain? Lydia sighed. No one understood her desire to take things slowly, for things to stay the same. She was happy as she was — why couldn't people understand that? Oh, she herself hated her reluctance to move on. She was being perfectly honest when she said she envied her friends and the career girls they'd become, the young wives and mothers. She only wished she was like them. But she was not, and she supposed she must be wrong to feel as the did. The others, her mother and friends, couldn't all be mistaken, so it must be her.

She'd do what her mamma wanted. She'd marry Orlick next month. It was, when she thought about it, silly to put it off.

Tom Gallagher was becoming more and more impatient. He fretted every moment he was separated from Martha and now that the wedding was over they had fewer excuses to see each other. Both agreed discretion was important, for Roland and Varina's sake.

It appeared that the pair were barely tolerating each other. Roland, living with his father-in-law and wife in her childhood home in Ailesbury Road, was deeply uncomfortable and spent as little time there as possible. Tom had informed his son-in-law in no uncertain terms that he needed to work hard and earn enough money to buy himself and his bride a home, but luckily for

Roland, Tom had become half-hearted about his career. Actually Tom could no longer have cared less. His mind was elsewhere. Nevertheless he went through the motions, threatening Roland with the Drimnagh kiosk, taking a malicious pleasure in watching the boy squirm, and though he could easily have implemented his threats he actually allowed Roland to escape, disappear day after day into the arms of his buddies, continuing the rackety life-style he led before he was married. It suited Tom and it suited Varina, for the moment.

What Roland was going to do when his credit ran out was something Tom Gallagher speculated on with interest. He had no doubt the boy would 'touch' him for a loan and it amused him to wonder how exactly he would behave when Roland plucked up the courage to do so. Buy him off? Ensure he stuck around until the baby was born then tell him to scarper? But would Varina need her husband then? How would his daughter feel? At the moment she could hardly bear him near her and was only too happy to see him dash off every morning as if he thought the Hound of the Baskervilles was yapping at his heels.

And what of his plans for Martha and himself? It was a tangle, but a tangle never stopped Tom Gallagher getting what he wanted and he was not about to be stopped now. He was confident he could work this one out. In the meantime he enjoyed his little power-game with Roland

Tracey. If he lived to be a hundred Tom felt he would never be able to figure out how his beloved could have bred such a lazy, unattractive and bumptious young loser as Roland Tracey.

The weather turned chilly. The evenings and mornings were cold and the dawns and twilights were long, misty and mysterious. Shimmering veils of vapour hung on the trees and the leaves turned gently gold and amber, carmine-red and yellow. Martha felt the cold but she did not feel sick. Each second was precious to her and she too wanted to spend every available moment with her lover. 'I didn't know it was possible to feel like this — so strong,' she told him.

'It's true. I feel it too. Oh my dear, let's not leave it too long to go away. Be by ourselves.'

Granny Kathleen went on a pilgrimage for a weekend to Knock. The effort nearly killed her, but she felt it worthwhile when on her return she was met by a glowing Martha, rosy-cheeked and radiant. 'Who wouldn't believe in miracles? Eh?' she cried when she saw her daughter.

Tom was at Mallow Hall when she called. She laboured up the drive in her long black wool coat with the velour collar, her felt hat pushed down on her head, her fur tippet tightly knotted around her throat. Nonie showed her into the drawing-room where Martha sat with Tom on the sofa in front of an empty fireplace. Tom rose when he saw her and Martha cried, 'Mother!'

'I did the pilgrimage, pet.' She ignored Martha's warning glance, jumping to the conclusion that it was simply a plea for her not to remark on Tom Gallagher's presence. She examined her daughter's appearance, totally ignorant that there could be any mystery about her condition. 'An' don't ye look good.' She stopped, looked shrewdly at Tom then back to her daughter. Smiling, she asked Tom, 'Don't ye think so, mister? Doesn't she?'

'Sure does. I'm Tom Gallagher, Mrs, er, Daly, isn't it?'

' 'Tis so. An' I've heard of you. Are you the one responsible for the glow in her cheeks and the brighteness in her eyes? I wonder.' She twinkled at him knowingly. 'Eh? If so, ye deserve a medal. If ye saw her a while ago, sure wasn't she dyin'. Now she's like a new woman.'

Martha was desperately afraid that her mother would give the game away but there was no stopping her. She could only hope Tom would not take Kathleen's phraseology literally. He was looking from one to the other, puzzled.

' 'Tis you an' Our Lady did the trick, I'll be bound,' Kathleen said, settling herself in a comfortable chair opposite them.

'Put a match to the fire, Nonie, and bring us some tea,' Martha said, a flush on her cheeks, trying to change the subject. 'Mother, you'd like a fire, wouldn't you?'

'Me ould bones are riddled with the damp,' Kathleen nodded in agreement. 'An' the blaze takes the chill outta 'em. An' a cuppa tae would go down a treat, *alanna*.'

Nonie hurried away to get the tea. Kathleen looked over at Tom. 'So what de ye think on the change in her? She's much better, isn't she?' she asked. 'It's not just me imagination, now is it?' Tom opened his mouth to speak, to ask what this was all about, but at that moment and to Martha's relief Lydia and Orlick burst into the room.

'Mamma, Orlick's here. Oh hello, Mr Gallagher.' Lydia sounded breathless.

'Please call me Tom.'

'No. Oh no, I couldn't. Granny, meet my intended.'

'Oh, you must be mad, young fella-me-lad,' Granny Kathleen cried. 'Yer onto a mismatch there. Are ye sure the two of ye know what ye're doin'?'

Lydia shook her head impatiently. 'Yes, Granny,' she answered firmly. 'We do.'

'I didn't go to Roley's weddin'. Not on yer life,' Granny Kathleen said. 'Knew it was a non-starter, if ye'll forgive the racing parlance.'

'Granny, this is Varina's father,' Lydia said reprovingly.

'I know that, an' I know a mismatch when I see one,' the old lady persisted stubbornly.

'Shut up, Mother darling, do,' Martha said mildly. 'We'll have some tea . . .' But it was in vain; Kathleen was not to be silenced.

'I was tellin' yer mother, Lydia, that I'm that glad to see how well she looks now, how she's improved, praise the Lord.' She looked over at

Orlick. 'I did a pilgrimage for my darlin', so I did.' Her voice suddenly broke but she pulled herself together and continued, 'When I last saw her she looked like a ghost, now God bless us she's got a new lease of life. Oh thank you, Lord Jesus, thank you.' To Martha's horror, tears filled her mother's eyes and spilled freely down her cheeks.

Lydia rushed over to the old lady and sank down beside her chair. 'Oh Granny, Granny, don't upset yourself. I'm doing a novena too. I've prayed every morning and evening to Saint Jude, patron of hopeless cases, to let Mamma live. Cure her illness.' Martha closed her eyes and realised the game was over. 'And I've been to morning mass every morning. Father Delaney thinks I should be a nun, I'm so often in the church. He doesn't think I should be married at all.'

'He's not the only one,' Granny Kathleen muttered. 'Please God our prayers worked.'

Lydia continued, 'Just look at Mamma, she never looked better.'

Everyone stared at Martha, even Nonie, leaving the tea things she had brought in on the table beside her mistress and lighting the fire, looked over her shoulder at Martha. Orlick, who was in Lydia's confidence, also inspected Martha. Lydia and Kathleen stared happily and hopefully at the lovely woman with her hand on her heart, her small face suddenly charged with apprehension. Tom Gallagher stared at her too, his face pale with shock.

'Now, now, we're embarrassing her,' Kathleen said. She glanced from Tom to her daughter and back and realised she'd put her foot in it. It was obvious from Tom Gallagher's face firstly that he was in love with Martha and secondly that he had not known she was ill. Well, well, Kathleen thought to herself, beady eyes darting from one to the other and back, so Martha's in love. So my little girl has fallen for this good-looking man who is trying to control the muscles of his face without much success. She had known her daughter was involved with Tom, sensed that they were having an affair, but what she was looking at now was deep love. Well, an' maybe it was the Lord's way of answering their prayers. She hoped so.

But she could not think of anything to say, something clever or subtle to pour balm on the situation. For the life of her she could think of nothing.

Tom sat speechless, stunned by what he had heard, trying to assimilate the news, while Martha tried to be social, asking Orlick and Lydia about the wedding, and they all sipped tea.

Then Lydia and Orlick left. They seemed very content together, so when Granny Kathleen muttered something about them not being suited Martha was able to disagree with author-ity, despite the tremble in her voice. 'Nonsense, Mother. They make a perfect pair. Don't you think so, Tom?' she asked.

There was a white line around Tom Gallagher's mouth. 'Well now, who am I to say?' he asked coldly. 'Sure what would I know about this family, not being party to any confidences?'

Kathleen rose hurriedly. 'I'm weary Martha, me love,' she said. 'I'd be grateful if Mr Gallagher here would escort me home.'

Tom had no choice but to acquiesce and they left together.

Martha, left behind, was utterly devastated. She could see how Tom had reacted and his face had revealed her worst fears. It had mirrored shock and horror when the truth sank in.

'Oh God help me,' she cried and walked restlessly about the room, touching things absent-mindedly, fiddling with the ornaments, gathering the fallen petals from beneath the flower arrangements.

She chided herself mercilessly. She should have anticipated this happening, realised that Granny Kathleen or Lydia might unwittingly betray her, but she'd been too busy living in the present, enjoying herself. She felt sick and suddenly very tired.

She rang the bell for Nonie. When the servant arrived she was shocked by her mistress's appearance. It was as if something in her, some fire, had been extinguished. With a heavy heart she helped her mistress up the stairs, into her room and into her bed.

'Why didn't she tell me?' Tom asked Kathleen.

They were sitting in her tiny living-room in the cottage, the old lady still in her warm coat and hat, the tippet wrapped firmly around her neck.

'Don't be daft, man! Why de ye think?'

He spread his hands. Nice, competent hands, she thought, capable and firm. 'I don't know, Kathleen. I've told her everything about me.'

'*Everything?* I doubt it. None of us tells all. It's not fair to do so. You would be burdening your loved one with stuff they don't need to cope with. There are some things we never say to each other out of consideration.'

She was right. He thought of Roland and how he'd never expressed his true opinion on that score because he did not want to hurt Martha by criticising her son . . .

'I see I'm right.' Kathleen had been watching him closely. 'There are some things we don't share, and why not? Well, I'd say it is because we don't want to take the risk of hurting each other.'

'Oh, I wouldn't be . . .'

'I'm not sayin' you would,' Kathleen interrupted him. 'I'm sayin' we don't because *we think* the other *might* be hurt. We don't know and we don't want to take the risk.' She stared at him, her eyes curiously like the eyes of the geese that had crossed their path outside. 'I'll bet ye didn't tell my daughter that your Varina got a really bad deal? Eh? No, of course not. Though I bet if ye had my Martha would have agreed with ye. No. We can't tell each other everything, *alanna* — if

206

we did we'd be at war all the time. It's called civilisation.'

'But something as important as that?'

'Sit and sup with me awhile,' Kathleen said and shuffled over to the old iron stove and scalded the teapot from the kettle bubbling there. 'Get used to the idea,' she added. 'We're all goin' to die sometime.' He winced. She watched him intently. 'She's goin' te need yer strength,' she said. 'We're all pretending she's going to recover. That she has recovered. *I* believe it sometimes, especially since you've come along, and I know Lydia believes it. It's how Lydia copes with things, believing they won't happen. But deep down I know that Martha is not going to recover. She's not got that long.'

'How long?' he asked, not wanting to know yet having to. 'How long?'

'A year, I think. Nine months. Maybe less.'

She was scooping the tea into the pot as she spoke.

He drew a sharp breath, groaning, his heart sinking, his head drooping on his clasped hands. All the sunlight seemed to have vanished and a chill wind blew on his heart. To find so much love, so much passion, then to lose it so quickly, was unbearable.

'Oh Kathleen, what will I do?' he asked helplessly.

'What were ye goin' to do, this mornin' before I came in an' disrupted yer life?' she asked, pouring the boiling water on the tea.

'I was going to try to persuade her to come to Italy with me. I was going to . . .'

'Well, why don't ye do just that?' the old lady asked. 'Why don't ye just go ahead wi' yer plans? Why not?'

How could he explain what he felt, the hollow inside him? They had been so joyous and now all the joy was gone. There was nothing now but sadness.

He did not think he could endure it, knowing she was dying. He thought the agony of knowing what was going to happen would unman him. Pain coursed through his body at the thought of her, where before the mystery of her had thrilled. Now there was aching, screaming, nerves so acute he almost cried out.

'I know what ye feel,' she said, handing him a cup of tea, black as tar. Then, putting a jug of milk and a bowl of sugar beside him, she stood in front of him. 'My Liam died on me an' I'll never forget the agony till me dyin' day.' She looked out through the small cottage window. 'Sometimes the pain is so fierce it winds me,' she paused, pressing her hands to her heart. 'Even now, after all these years, takes the breath from me body.' She came nearer him, staring at him. 'But ye know what, Tom Gallagher? I'd do it all again, I had the choice. I'd not choose to avoid the pain, never to have known my Liam. Oh no! It's poor Lydia's trouble. No stamina. Great love takes stamina. Takes a stout and a brave heart. Takes courage.' She nodded at him, then went and sat in her rocking chair on the other side of the fire. 'No, Lydia'll lead a happy, peaceful life. Uneventful. That's what she has chosen, and God bless her, mebbe she'd got the right idea. She'll never be tempest-tossed. But it's not for the likes of you an' me, Tom Gallagher. Or Martha. We're passionate people. We *have* the stamina for great sorrow as well as great love.'

They sat there for a long time in silence, Tom sipping the strong black tea, lost in thought.

It had begun to rain outside. It pattered on the windows against the small leaded panes. It was dark now and Kathleen lit the oil lamp. She moved slowly, a trifle painfully about the room. The orange glow of the lamp illuminated the centre of the room, leaving the periphery in shadow. Kathleen piled more logs on the smouldering brickettes and, catching fire, the wood blazed merrily.

Tom sat sunk in debate with himself, not hearing the rain on the window, the crackling of the fire, the ticking of the clock. Kathleen gently rocked in her chair, lost in dreams of long ago when Liam and she had wandered the beaches hand in hand, searched the shore for shells and kelp and made love in the seaweed-smelling caves or on the hot golden sands.

At last Tom said, 'I've been a fool, haven't I?'

Kathleen didn't answer for a moment, then she said, 'Yes, but we all are, time to time. Yer a human bein'. We're all fools led nose and heart by our own selfishness. What *we* want. What we think we deserve. When we should be thinkin' of the other person, the one we say we love. Eh?' She looked at him. 'Well, what have ye decided?'

'I'll go up to her now. Never leave her side again.' Then he chewed his lip and muttered, 'Until . . .'

She stood up. 'Good lad. Now that's the way. It'll be hard, mind. Not easy.'

'But it'll be easier than never seeing her again. Kathleen, you're right. That would be unbearable.'

'It's the choice,' she said, gripping his hands. 'Yeah.'

He walked back in the driving rain to Mallow Hall, striding along impervious to the torrent beating on his face and shoulders.

When he reached the door he pulled the bell, then raced past Nonie when she answered it. He ran up the stairs to Martha's room.

She was lying on her pillows, weeping. When he entered she turned her face hopefully and her eyes lit up when she saw him. He hurried to her, dripping over her pale carpet, and scooped her into his arms. 'My darling, my darling, my own sweet one, forgive me. Forgive me.' Murmuring into her ear, kissing her cheeks wet from her own tears and the rain on his face.

'There's nothing to forgive *you*, my darling. It's me. I should have told you. Oh, I should have told you. Do you still love me? Or do you hate me now?'

He folded her ever tighter in his arms, a hard

painful lump in his throat. 'Hate you? Hate you? How could I ever hate you, my soul, my life, my love? You are the very heart of me, my darling. My own.'

She clung to him, wrapping her arms around him as if they had been parted for days.

'I'll never let you go,' he cried, kissing her eyes and her lips. 'Never, never, never.'

He had made his choice.

Chapter Twenty-Five

It could not be long, Nonie said, shaking her head, before Lydia found out about her mother's gallivanting. Eilish agreed. The other servants were gossiping, no matter how much Eilish and Nonie warned them not to, and soon, they knew, it would be all over the place. Mr Gallagher was at Mallow Hall morning, noon and night these days and he and the missus seemed to have thrown discretion to the winds.

Although the cook and the housekeeper were happy to see their mistress restored, as they thought, to health by his presence, the constant fact of Mr Gallagher *there* confused and muddled them. The status quo was unbalanced.

'Sure 'tisn't right,' Eilish muttered over her stove. 'Don't know who I'm catering for these days.'

'Not decent, 'tisn't,' the gardener agreed, shuffling through with his shears. 'Doin' God knows what above there, breakin' the commandments right, left and centre.'

'Well now, aren't you the one to talk an' you drunk as a sailor on shore-leave every Saturday night and beatin' up yer missus when ye do finally come home.'

'An' sure that's different! That's not agin God's law, now is it?'

So the relief at the improvement in their mistress's health gave way to resentment at the gossip about the family and the position their mistress put them in, bringing shame on the house.

Lydia remained in blissful ignorance. She spent most of her time at the shop or the factory, checking up on things; the rest of the time she was with her fiancé.

Orlick had heard all about the affair his future mother-in-law was purported to be having. He had only to look at Martha's face and into the eyes of Tom Gallagher to realise the gossip was true. But he was not stupid enough to tell Lydia. He knew his hold on her affections was shaky and that the slightest denting of her faith might sever those tenuous ties, so he kept his mouth firmly shut. He believed the bearer of such information to Lydia would not be easily forgiven. Orlick knew what his fiancée was doing. He understood Lydia much better than anyone gave him credit for and he realised that she was testing the water of emotional commitment. If they could strengthen their ties to each other everything would be all right. So even when Lydia rhapsodised about her mother's recovery he did not enlighten her as to the probable cause; he simply decided to be there to catch and comfort her when she did find out.

Orlick's parents were far too polite even to discuss such a state of affairs with their son. Only in the privacy of their bedroom did Dr Fitzmaurice wax eloquent about 'that woman' and her 'wanton ways'. 'Wouldn't you think she'd had enough with two before?' he asked rhetorically. 'Man-eater if ever. And shouldn't she be a little more discreet? Eh? Don't you think? This'll be the third she's got through, cavorting recklessly with every Tom, Dick and Harry. The third! Wouldn't you think she'd have more self-control?'

'Yes dear.' Mrs Fitzmaurice breathed deeply and thought enviously of Martha Tracey and her cavorting and her lack of control. Bebe Fitzmaurice had long secretly fancied Tom Gallagher. Such a big handsome man! He must indeed be a lusty lover. She'd never experienced lusty love and was quite sure that Martha Tracey had. She thought longingly of the fun Martha Tracey must have had, be having. Dr Fitzmaurice, never too hot in bed — too dedicated to his patients, he said — had given up 'that sort of thing' some years ago. ('I'm sure you're relieved, my dear. Only at our age, it's a bit, well, you know.') She didn't know. She felt young and sexy and even though her waistline had long vanished she felt 'the urge', as Dr Fitzmaurice had always called it, strongly and often. But sadly she realised that it was her lot to practice precisely the dictates of the Church and have sex only to reproduce, leaving all the excitement of sinning to the likes of Martha Tracey. Hell or purgatory might just be worth it, and in the event one could always repent and go to confession.

It was finding out about her mother that drove Lydia into the autumn wedding Martha so wanted for her.

Lydia did not much like her sister-in-law. She kept putting off the visit her mother told her courtesy demanded. She had driven to Dublin in her little Ford, called into D'Abru's. She looked over the books for her mamma and then Brosnan Burke gave her a progress report. He liked Lydia and found her a shrewd businesswoman, very *au fait* with what worked and what did not. He was explaining to her that the raspberry fondants were not selling and there were pounds of them left. 'People are going off the very sweet centres,' he told her. 'It's the fashion, I think. It's all steak and salad these days. Texan diet, all the fashion.'

'Chocolates are not Texan,' Lydia remarked.

'No, but the steak and salad is, followed by fruit, followed by a chocolate. But it has to be a truffle, a coffee centre, a milk centre or a mint. Not a sweet centre. We sell loads of butterscotch and toffee centres but not strawberry or raspberry. They're out. What do you think?'

'I think we ought to cut down on production of the fondant centres.'

'Except the vanilla . . .'

'Except the vanilla,' she agreed. 'I'll tell my mother and we'll let the factory know. Step up the truffles and cut down the fondants . . .'

'People say they're always left . . .'

'And we'll see how it goes. I'll tell Mamma.'
She was staring out of the shop window, frowning, thinking. People hurried by, umbrellas up. It was drizzling, soft, penetrating rain. Passersby looked intent, as if mentally they had already arrived where they were going. Then she noticed Roland flanked by two of his mates, Cad Connolly and Fishy Moran — so called because they said he drank like a fish.

Lydia waved. 'There's Roley!' she cried and ran to the shop door.

Brosnan sighed. 'Drunk again,' he muttered under his breath, gift-wrapping a brown and gold-lettered box for a plump woman in green.

Lydia hailed her brother. Roland, hearing his name, swerved around, people parting behind him, Cad and Fishy on either side smirking tipsily at her. Her brother peered at her. 'So, Lydia,' he said. 'How's Ma?'

'She's fine,' Lydia answered, embarrassed by her brother's obvious intoxication. She glanced over her shoulder at Brosnan, but he avoided her eyes, as did the people passing by.

Roland stood swaying in the middle of the pavement. 'You're a smug little bitch, aren't you?' he shouted, suddenly belligerent. 'Never even been to see my wife, visit your sister-in-law. Call yourself Christian? Eh? Miss High-and-Mighty Heiress? Bloody foreign manners. D'Abru! Foreign muck!'

'Nah, nah, nah, leave her be. She's a female, Roley. 'Taint gentlemanly to insult a female.'

Cad, who was not as drunk as either Roland or Fishy, could see Lydia's distress.

She was completely taken aback, not ever having been in contact with her brother when he was this intoxicated. She shook her head in bewilderment as he stood swaying in front of her, alternately sneering, rearranging his face, and peering at her as if she was suddenly far away. His friends were urging him towards South Ann Street where Davy Byrne's was about to close for the holy hour.

'C'mon, Roley, c'mon, 's no use standin' here. People lookin' . . .' Fishy insisted, trying to pull his friend on.

'An' ye don't know about Mam? Eh?' Roland cried. 'Don't know about the cuckoo in the nest? Don't know what the population of Dublin's sayin 'bout sweet Mam? Eh? Miss Innocent.'

'What are you talking about, Roley? You mustn't talk like that in front of . . .'

'Don't mean what he's sayin', Liddy. Not quite himself, see.'

Cad jerked Roland's arm and he suddenly lost interest in his sister and swerved around on one foot, saying to his pals, 'Need a little weaveljuice. A tincture is called for. Forward, me hearties, forward.' And he lunged across the street, his pals in close formation behind him, people scudding out of their way. At the last moment before he turned into South Ann Street he looked back over his shoulder and cried out to her, 'I'm off to Fairyhouse an' I won't see any of you till next

217

week. So how'd you like that then?' Then the three of them vanished around the corner, hot-footing it to the pub.

Lydia went back inside the shop. She began to talk about the order for the factory and the raspberry fondants. She would not discuss her brother or his condition with Brosnan Burke. It would not be seemly. She contented herself with making a list of chocolate sales in order of their popularity.

Lydia decided to drive that afternoon to the Gallagher house to see her sister-in-law. She supposed Roland was right; she had been remiss as far as Varina was concerned, so when she'd finished with Brosnan she set out for Ailes- bury Road. She felt guilty at her neglect of Varina but could not help herself when she speculated whether Varina would notice she had not visited.

When she reached Ailesbury Road she was seized by an embarrassment she could not account for; nevertheless she parked her car in the driveway, noticing absentmindedly that Mr Gallagher's cream Chevrolet was not there but Varina's little red sports MG was. Typical car for Varina Tracey, Lydia reflected sourly, then shook herself. This girl was family now.

Much to Roland's fury, Varina had refused to allow him to drive the MG. She reminded him that her mother had been killed by a drunk driving a car and she did not want her husband to be guilty of the same crime — which he was almost sure to be if he was allowed behind the wheel.

The hatchet-faced Styles answered Lydia's ring at the front door and showed her into the very masculine library-cum-sitting-room. The chairs and sofa were leather, the magazines *Sporting Life* and *Tatler & Sketch*. Lydia sat fingering the gold studs around the arm of her chair, leafing through *Tatler & Sketch* while she waited.

Varina was showing her pregnancy even though she was only in her third month. She looked very pretty, Lydia thought, her voluptuous blonde good looks enhanced rather than spoiled by her increase in girth. The sisters-in-law greeted each other warily. Neither of them was at ease with the other.

'You look great, Varina,' Lydia assured her, very aware that Varina might not realise everyone in Dublin knew she was pregnant.

But Varina said, 'You mean it suits me. Being pregnant. So my father says, but I think I look awful.'

'No, honestly, Varina. You look lovely.' Lydia paused then rushed on, 'I saw Roland today, in Grafton Street . . .'

'Drunk, I suppose.' It was not a question.

'Um. Yes. Has he been awful?' Lydia, always sympathetic, melted a little towards her sister-in-law. Varina saw the concern in Lydia's eyes and she too felt a breaking-down of the barrier between them.

She nodded. 'Yes. He's been drunk since the day we married.' And she began to confide in her sister-in-law, sometimes details Lydia would much rather not have heard.

Varina was astonished that Lydia had not sprung to Roland's defence. It was what she would have done, but Lydia was realistic about her brother and that surprised Varina. Varina was also enjoying her role of newly-wed, a superior position to that of mere fiancée. She had problems that belonged in the grown-up world, the world that Lydia had not yet entered and therefore could not understand.

'Oh, you cannot think what it is like, Lydia,' she moaned. 'They're such bores!'

'Who?' Lydia asked innocently.

'Men, of course. It's not just your brother, Lydia, it's *all* of them. You wait and see.' She nodded her head wisely.

'Oh, I'm sure not *all* of them, Varina. Your father for instance . . .'

'Don't *mention* Dadda! Please don't. The way he's behaving! Second childhood, I call it. It's disgusting, don't you think? How can you think otherwise?' She stared into Lydia's bewildered face. 'You don't know, do you? Jeez!'

At that moment Styles opened the door and brought in a tray laden with teapot and china, barmbrack, scones, jam and cream, butter and a Victoria cake. Varina dismissed her then poured the tea, enjoying herself, leaving Lydia dangling.

It was not that she wanted to hurt Lydia, simply that the power she now had proved irresistible.

'Have a scone?' she suggested, holding out a

plate to her guest. 'No? The great thing about being pregnant is I can eat what I like. My doctor says I must eat for two.' She laughed, dimples playing in her cheeks.

'What don't I know?' Lydia asked.

'Oh come on, Lydia, don't pretend!' Varina knew her guest was in the dark but was enjoying herself too much to stop.

'I don't know what you're getting at, Varina.' Varina's mouth was full of scone and jam.

Lydia afterwards wished she had not pressed to hear, that she had run out of the place. She was not a gossip — gossip changed things and she hated that. Gossip forced one to deal with emotions she was fearful of.

'Oh come on, *everyone* knows. Your ma and my dadda!' Varina opened her blue eyes wide. 'Doing it.' She looked at Lydia's stricken face and, though she felt the first stirrings of shame, continued, 'You know. They're going the whole hog with each other. Bet they're at it right now up at Mallow Hall.' She shuddered delicately. 'It's horrible to think about it, isn't it? Old people like them, at it like animals.' She hoped her father would pay for what he was doing. She hoped Lydia would scold her mother and Martha would throw her father back home to her. Varina was very jealous. This was the father she had owned all her life to the exclusion of everyone else. Up till now there had been no other woman in his life and she hadn't had to share him with anyone.

And she had always been jealous of Lydia, not only because Lydia was what she thought of as a lady, but because she had Martha for a mother. Varina, missing her mother, wished that Martha could belong to her. Part of Roland's attraction for her in the beginning was that he was Martha's son. But now that same woman had taken her father from her. She looked with malicious satisfaction but with shame in her heart at Lydia's now deathly pallor.

Lydia stood, knocking over her cup, tea spraying her clothes and Varina's tasteful mother-to-be dress. Varina was suddenly alarmed and repentant. Lydia's face was frozen in horror and she did not seem to know what she was doing. Varina had the nastiest feeling that she'd gone too far. The sad part was that deep down she would have liked to be friends with her sister-in-law.

Lydia fled from the room, bumping into a table on the way out. 'Lydia!' Varina yelled after her but Lydia had yanked open the front door, having crashed into Styles in the hall and run to her car. She pulled the door open, jumped in, then frantically rolled up the windows so that Varina, who followed her and kept knocking on the window beside the driving wheel, could not reach her. Varina and Styles watched helplessly as Lydia banged her forehead on the wheel of the car and pounded it with her fists, then stuck the key in the ignition and, starting the engine, backed the little car out of the drive, spraying gravel right, left and centre.

'Well!' Styles said, hurrying back inside. 'Well indeed. Some people!' The sharp-faced woman looked sideways at Varina. 'Well, miss, I hope you're satisfied. You shouldn't have told her like that,' she said. 'Yer mam'd turn in her grave!'

Varina realised that when she had exclaimed 'Some people' she was speaking of her.

Styles wagged her finger under Varina's nose, something Varina hated her doing. 'You should learn, miss, that there's no satisfaction in putting down those you envy. It doesn't work!'

'You were listening!' Varina screamed accusingly. 'You had your ear to that door.'

But Styles was not embarrassed. 'Just think if it was *your* mam,' she cried. 'How'd you feel then?'

'My mam wouldn't have,' Varina protested.

'How'd ye know?' the housekeeper demanded. 'Human beings is funny, so they are. Ye never know about things like that. Never think ye know what goes on in people's lives, miss.' She folded her arms. 'And wouldn't Lydia D'Abru have made a fine friend, an ally? An' you with none, Miss Varina, so busy were ye flirtin' wi' the fellows. Eh?'

It was so exactly what Varina was thinking that she snorted angrily.

Styles continued undeterred, 'But she'll likely never forgive you for this. Every time she looks at you she'll be reminded you were the one who told her. She'll forgive her mam — she's the type

— but she'll always associate you with betrayal.'

'Lydia's not like that. She . . .'

'She'll turn the other cheek? I doubt it. Lydia D'Abru is like the rest of us — fallible.'

'You're a bitter old cow, Styles,' Varina struck out angrily, but hot tears stung her eyes.

'I tell ye you'll live te regret this day.'

'Oh shut up, you old witch,' Varina shouted and went into her father's sitting-room. Then she noticed the tea on the carpet and she sat down on a leather pouffe and began to sob.

It was not meant to be like this; her living at home, Mrs Tracey, expecting a baby and still in her father's house. It had never been her room, this study of her father's. His influence was everywhere in the house. Even her bedroom. When she had moved into the larger front room upstairs from the nursery, he had decorated the room. Or rather, had a decorator from Arnott's do it.

She had looked forward so much to getting married, having her own place, chosen by her, with her own taste. Not that she ever told her father about her dreams and aspirations; she was too afraid of upsetting him. He had been so solitary since her mother died. Lonely and alone. She tried to imagine what that must have been like, all those years devoted to her, to his daughter, with no wife at his side to comfort and sustain him. She shivered. Surrounded by the heavy, oppressive furniture, Varina cried for lost opportunities. Styles was right. Lydia D'Abru would have been a wonderful friend to have. She should have respected Lydia, not been so ready to hurt. And she had been so stroppy with her father, not trying to understand his need. After all, he could do as he wished; she was a married woman and it was not his fault that she was unhappy and her husband did not provide for her. Her father had stood no nonsense from her, though. He had told her in no uncertain terms to mind her own business. 'I looked after you, Varina, since your mother died and I enjoyed every moment. I would not have missed tending you, would not have changed things if I could. It was a privilege and a delight. But I am happy now, with Martha, and if you had eyes in your head you could see that and be glad for me. But no, just because you are unhappy you want everyone else to be.' He had looked at her sorrowfully and it was the disappointment in his eyes that smote her heart. 'You had every opportunity, Varina, to do as you wished,' he continued white-lipped. 'I made it quite clear to you that whatever you wanted to do was all right with me.' Tom spread his hands in a gesture of helplessness. 'You married Roland. It's not my fault you are unhappy.'

'But Dadda, I had no choice — I was pregnant,' she had whined.

Her father had held up his hand. 'No, Varina, no. You *did* have a choice. Many choices, but you chose wrong. You did not have to get pregnant. From what you've told me it was not rape.

Having married Roland you could have tried to make it work, but you've made it plain to everyone that you have nothing but contempt and loathing for your husband. Worst of all, you've made it obvious to *him*.'

'But Dadda . . .'

'No buts, Varina. And I've told you time and time again that if you want out of this marriage, I'm happy to do my best to extricate you, though with a baby it will be difficult. Not impossible, though. We can make out a case for one of you having no intention of having any more children. That's grounds for annulment. Or that one of you . . .' Tom frowned '. . . well, it would have to be Roland, was agnostic at the time of the wedding. Or a technicality; the marriage, as far as I know' — he cocked an eye at her — 'has not been consummated *since* the ceremony?' She shook her head 'What happened before is irrelevant.'

'But Dadda, I'm not sure . . .' she had petered out, unable to meet his clear blue gaze. She was not sure she wanted to revert to the single status, find herself unmarried with a child. Being married was classy. Having a rotten husband was something a lot of women accepted, the thing was to *be* married. And if she was on her own again no other man would be interested, not when they found out she had a baby. That would be the worst. Her life would be over while she was still at the beginning.

'Well, Varina, I give up. The solutions are up to you. You're a married woman now, and you must run your own life.' He had taken her hands between his, holding them tight and looking into her face. 'As I must. I'll not have you carping to me about Martha Tracey. I'll not have you in my house and uttering against her, you understand?'

She'd never seen her father so serious. She nodded, reluctantly. Where would she go if she could not remain here at home? She put on her sullen expression, letting him know she'd obey, but reluctantly, and nodded her head.

'Okay, Dadda.'

'I've given you my life since your mother died, Varina, I always put you first. I'll always love you, you know that. But now it is time for me to do what I want, what I need. I'm human too, Varina, and love has come into my life unexpectedly. I'm not going to waste my opportunity to be happy just because I've raised a selfish little daughter.'

'Well, I still think it's disgusting,' she'd not been able to resist throwing at him and flounced off, leaving her father shaking his head.

She'd not wanted to be so nasty, she'd just been incapable of unbending and reaching out to him. She wanted to punish him for her own unhappiness and she was sorry now. She'd missed a golden opportunity.

So many things to regret. Being nasty to Lydia. Antagonising the girls at school so that she had no friends now. She had been so jealous of their mothers, but she'd never said. Particularly Lydia's. But she knew now they would have understood and made allowances if only she had admitted her feelings, but she'd been too proud, too resentful.

Too late now. The horrible thing was, she was left with the results of her behaviour. She could not go back and erase them. There was nothing she could do. Once said, words could not be unsaid the way knitting could be unravelled. She buried her face in her hands and sobbed. It was too late. Too late.

Chapter Twenty-Six

'How is she taking it?' Martha asked Tom. She lay on her chaise, her head on Tom's shoulder. The curtains were drawn against the orange autumn sun and the room was filled with golden shadows.

'Not well,' he replied, 'but it's her problem. She's a big girl now, Martha, she must let me free.'

'They're never big girls, Tom, they're always your children. It's a fact of life.'

'Then what do you expect me to do? Sacrifice myself?'

She shook her head. 'No. No, of course not, my dearest. But have patience with her. She'll come around.'

Their relationship had changed subtly. Gone was the first rapturous and heady lightheartedness. The consuming passion had given way, after Tom had found out about her condition, to an equally intense desperation and solicitude.

'Oh my dearest, the pain in your eyes! It was not there before. I put it there,' she told him. He said nothing. What could he say for it was true.

She too now thought seriously about her condition in a way she had not before due to Tom's ignorance. His lack of knowledge had helped her forget and now he kept the subject at the forefront of both their minds.

He was more in charge now. He deemed it his vocation to look after her in every possible way. Their partnership was dissolved and he became her carer. Their love deepened, but travelled in a different direction.

Their love-making too now had a new dimension. Each time might be the last, but in this, as in all things, he was solicitous of her well-being.

'Oh my darling, I won't break,' she would cry, to make him lose a control he thought he had but which she urged him to abandon.

Talk of how they felt for each other, the poetry quoted, the verbal excesses, had given way to a cautious discussion of plans.

Tom was impatient to take her to Italy. 'It worked for Browning and Elizabeth Barrett — why not for us?' he enquired.

They valued more and more their time together. 'It's a gift,' Martha said. 'A precious gift not to be wasted.' And they were so in love that the time seemed alarmingly short.

Sitting on the chaise, Tom in his shirt-sleeves, Martha in the *robe de chambre* that he loved so much, they held each others hand. 'First time I saw you, *really* saw you, you were wearing that. You floated in like a cloud, disarming me,' he told her and they talked of their plans, their hopes. They held on to each other, reluctant to separate fingers, contact.

There was a fire in the grate, for the weather had turned frosty and Nonie was determined her mistress would not get a chill. They gazed into the glowing depths, murmuring to each other, softly kissing cheek and hand and forehead to punctuate sentences and to reassure each other that they loved. They were unprepared for Lydia's abrupt entrance.

'So then, it's true!' she announced dramatically. Tom made as if to get up from his seated position but Martha's hand on his chest restrained him. 'No. Don't move, Tom. We are doing nothing wrong. Sit down, Lydia.' She indicated the chair opposite but her daughter shook her head impatiently and declined the invitation.

'I won't sit down with that man in the room,' she announced, aware that she sounded childish, yet, wounded to the core as she was, she could not help herself.

'Then leave,' her mother told her, making her gasp in shock.

'Mother! You don't mean . . . ?'

'Yes dear, I do. Tom and I are in love. What's wrong with that? We are both free and unattached. Would you forbid me a little happiness?' Her mother's words made Lydia feel bad, turned her into a spoiled child. But she was resentful, she could not help it. She felt she had a right to be angry at the turn of events but she didn't know why. She could not think of a sound reason, yet she was angry.

Tom stood. He picked up his jacket by the name-tab and slung it over his shoulder. 'I'll leave you,' he said, and before Martha could protest he dropped a kiss on her forehead and exited the room, saying, 'I'll wait downstairs, my dear.'

'What a thoughtful man he is,' Martha remarked when he'd gone.

'Mother, I'd like to get married at once,' Lydia announced firmly.

'Good,' her mother nodded. 'November?'

'I don't *care*,' Lydia exploded. Oh, why couldn't her mother understand? Why didn't anyone?

'Darling, you must not marry poor Orlick because I have Tom in my life. It would be so foolish of you. But you will have to do what you eventually feel is right for you — only don't put the responsibility on my shoulders. I refuse to accept it. You make your own bed, dear child, remember that.'

Lydia tried to swallow this awesome truth. 'Yes, Mother.'

'Look at Roley and Varina. God forbid you'd end up like those two.'

'I *told* you, Mamma, I love Orlick. I really do. And I'll marry him in November. Is that all right with you?'

Martha looked at the scarlet-cheeked, mutinous face of her daughter, saw the confusion there. 'Come here,' she said. 'Come here, pet.'

'I'm not pet any more. *He's* pet.'

'Don't be silly, Lydia. Come here.'

She was hoping her mother would insist, hoping against hope she'd be commanded to accept Tom Gallagher and this ludicrous situation with him and her mother.

232

'Oh love, come here at once.'

She crossed to her mother and sat down and was embraced. She did not yield, not yet.

'I love you, pet, you know that. I'm sorry I didn't tell you about it . . .'

'Well, why didn't you?' Relaxing in the warm embrace.

'Because I was afraid that you'd make it a contest.' Martha looked at her daughter. 'I was right, wasn't I? But it is not a competition between my children and Tom. I love you all. My love for Tom is simply different . . .'

'I don't want to know, Mamma,' Lydia said, but she now yielded completely to her mother's embrace, resting her head on her mother's shoulder. She lay in exactly the same position as Tom had shortly before. 'Oh all right, Mamma, if you must love Tom Gallagher, then I suppose you must.' She snuggled close. 'Let's talk wedding plans,' she said. It was one way to stop her mother telling her things she did not really want to hear.

Chapter Twenty-Seven

Austin executed his triple-step hop, slung Shona out, pulled her back, twirl, out-in-out, with extreme efficiency. He always handled his partner as if she was a robot, like a yo-yo. He fully expected whoever he was dancing with to follow exactly his lead and Shona was first-class at doing his will on the dance floor, twirl, in-out-back. However, sometimes Shona smiled intimately at him on her way towards him and it unsettled him. He wished she wouldn't. Not on the dance floor.

He'd taken Shona dancing quite a few times since the wedding. He'd also taken her to dinner — nothing fancy, he didn't want her to get ideas about his money. Everyone knew his mother had been a D'Abru and no one, in Austin's opinion, would believe he could touch none of the family money. What he didn't know was that Shona, who worked in a bank, was privy to the finances of the D'Abrus, and knew of the lack of Tracey money both individually and business-wise. She knew Roland was a drinker — she'd followed his cheque trail from pub to pub often enough when she'd filed the badly scrawled bits of paper in the Royal Bank of Ireland on College Green. She knew the D'Abru money was Lydia's, and she knew Austin was a gambler. But she had a pretty good idea that Austin and Roland would fight for a share of the fortune and that Martha Tracey would always see her sons had a generous allowance. Better than most.

Irish law and Catholic Church thinking stipulated that the male of the species should be in charge and so in the future, if she managed to capture Austin Tracey, she would not be short of a bob or two.

Anyway, he was better off than most of the fellas available. Oh, there were lots of wealthy boys about, but their families, ever vigilant for fortune-hunters were snotty and stuck-up and guarded their rich young offspring fiercely, freezing out opportunists.

Not that Shona was a fortune-hunter. Heaven forfend! It was simply that she had made up her mind very early that she was not going to follow her mother's lead — and the example of the majority of women in Dublin — and marry some struggling weed with prospects. She was not going to struggle until those prospects materialized, slaving away on a meagre salary, or worse, wage, until prosperity arrived with his pension. How many times had she heard that? 'It's a grand job with prospects and a safe pension at the end of the day.' Well *she* didn't want to wait until she was sixty for her life to begin.

Her father, a bank official like herself, had done just that, promising her mother a trip around the world when he retired, but her mother had died at fifty, a gentle, sweet woman, waiting for the great day when her husband would reap the benefits of a life of dedication. She'd missed the boat entirely. There was no way that was going to happen to Shona.

Shona's father had had no heart for the luxury trip around the world without his wife, and he puttered about the house and garden all day now, a defeated, depressed grey, little man, lonely and alone. No, Shona did not want a fate like that.

Shona's father had been a teller, but that post was not available to women employees. Shona spent the day filing in a six-by-six office in the bowels of the bank, away from the sunlight and air. She did not mind. It did not occur to her to be resentful; that was the *status quo* and besides, she was positive she was not going to end up there. She would not be working for the bank long enough to draw a pension.

She was aware of the alternatives. She could start going out with one of the many boys who tried to date her, but they were all in the category of 'hopeful prospects', working their way up to that pension. Or she could find a husband who had money in his background. She pursued the eligible and the wealthy, but the only one who'd shown any real interest was Austin Tracey.

She did not feel he was the man of her dreams, nor rich and powerful enough really, but there were no other takers, and *surely* Martha D'Abru would look after her sons, see they were living in a manner to which they were accustomed? Shona banked on that.

She liked Austin Tracey. She did not love him, but then she was not a great one for love. Something inside her derided it. The other girls melted over Rock Hudson and Jimmy Dean but she remained indifferent to their celluloid charms. She was too intent on finding an avenue to the real fulfilment of her dreams.

It was not wishful thinking, a fantasy. No. It was, rather, a desperate determination to escape from what she saw as a life of numbing mediocracy and boredom. To rise each morning, as her mother had, nothing but the day's chores ahead of her — wash the dishes, make the beds, hoover the house, cook the lunch (Mr Donnelly had come home for lunch every day), wash up afterwards. In the afternoon do the shopping at the little grocer at the end of the road, come home, do the mending, the ironing, make jam, pies, pickled cucumbers, knit socks and scarves against winter cold, put up her feet then, listen to the radio, drink a cup of Lipton's tea, read *Woman's Own* — the highlights of the day — then prepare dinner, eat it with hubby, tired from his day's work, go to bed, worry about the mortgage, the electricity and gas bills, rates and taxes. Oh no! God forbid!

She went after Austin Tracey like her life depended on it. She found out his likes and dislikes. She discovered he liked to dance and she quickly became proficient, practising in her bedroom. She discovered he liked to complain about his sister Lydia and she agreed passionately with what he told her, nodding and shaking her head in agreement and disbelief when appropriate. She discovered he was eaten up with jealousy over the D'Abru business and she fed his hatred.

She instinctively knew he'd go off her if she went to bed with him, which she was quite prepared to do but, as she found out, was not necessary. She indulged in some heavy petting, finding ways of exciting him and bringing him ecstatic release without, as he would put it 'cheapening herself'.

So she became indispensable to him. She fixed his problems. She was the shoulder he could complain on, she was his only source of pleasure and, like his sister Lydia, Austin saw no reason for things ever to change. Marriage was not on Austin Tracey's mind. He reckoned, however, without Shona's resourcefulness.

He had become used to her ministering to his sexual needs. He had become dependent on this release. After all, he was not interfering with her, she remained *virgo intacta,* and he could hold up his head and claim to be a gentleman. He was not 'taking advantage' of Shona. Eventually, however, his complacency was nipped in the bud and his dependency made obvious to him.

Most people were unaware of what Shona thought about, and Austin was no exception. Austin, though, was not the type to worry about what others thought except in relation to his mother's money. One of his great failings as a solicitor was his inability to really *listen* to his clients, to hear the message underneath what they said. All he knew was that, for the first time in his life, he was reasonably happy, content with his lot and his general situation.

Lydia was getting married. That meant he need not feel responsible for her — Orlick Fitzmaurice would look after her and he need feel no guilt when she lost Mallow Hall and D'Abru's. And he had a girlfriend who suited him exactly. Yes, things for Austin Tracey were perfect. For the moment.

Lydia got married on November the fifteenth. She wore a white satin mediaeval-style dress trimmed with white swansdown. To the horror and disapproval of all present she walked down the aisle on the arm of Tom Gallagher.

The trouble with Martha, Dr Fitzmaurice told his wife on their way home that night, was that she did not seem to care what others thought. Totally indifferent to public opinion, she went her own sweet way and did precisely what she wanted. It was, the guests whispered under their breath to each other, disgraceful. Father Smilling diplomatically feigned total ignorance of the situation.

The reception was held at Mallow Hall and everyone agreed that aside from Martha's shocking lack of tact, flaunting her lover under everyone's noses, the wedding was a big success.

The sun, despite the season, shone gloriously. It was cold and crisp, autumnal colours a gor-

geous conglomeration of ambers, golds, vermil-
ion, ochre, evergreen, and crimson, and the
mountains pale purple in the distance.

The food was superb and a band from Dublin
played romantic music: 'Blue Moon', 'I Love
You For Sentimental Reasons', 'Smoke Gets In
Your Eyes'.

Unlike Roland and Varina's reception no marquee was needed, and couples roamed the
grounds, danced on the terrace under the fairy-
lights.

Varina and Roland were there, ill-at-ease,
looking like strangers. Varina was really big now
and there was a softness about her, Martha
noted, a vulnerability lacking before. As usual,
Roland behaved badly. He was barely civil to his
wife or to Lydia, got drunk quickly, and soon
reached a semi-comatose condition and relapsed
fairly quietly into a morose silence in an armchair in the study.

'What am I going to do about him?' Martha
asked Tom, sighing.

'There's nothing you can do,' Tom replied,
watching her for signs of tiredness. She noticed
that he often did that and it irritated her. 'Don't
watch me all the time, Tom,' she whispered, then
glancing at the dancers smiled, 'Austin, though,
seems much improved.'

Tom, who had known neither boy before and
on acquaintance disliked both heartily, nodded
unenthusiastically. 'He's doing a line with Shona
Donnelly. She seems a nice girl. I believe her

father was in the bank.' A good recommendation. Meant he was trustworthy and therefore his offspring would be. Tom smiled to himself. He had heard on the grapevine that Shona Donnelly was a gold-digger. But he was not worried about that. Austin and Roland, he'd decided, could go to hell their own ways. It seemed to Tom that that was where they were headed anyway.

In the drawing-room, where the carpet had been turned back and the dancers were swirling about under the large chandelier and out through the French windows on to the terrace, the fairy-lights twinkled red and yellow and blue. Austin was wagging his index fingers in the air and hopping professionally, sending Shona flying to and fro with gusto.

Martha sighed. 'Oh, to be young!' she murmured.

Tom laughed. 'There's always something faintly ridiculous about the latest dance. Don't you think?' he asked. She laughed too and smiled at him. 'Don't wish for anything at all, dearest woman.' he said. 'It's perfect as it is.'

'We should do this,' Shona was shouting in Austin's ear every time she neared him.

'Do what?' he asked eventually.

'Get married,' she shouted, smiling.

He stood stock-still on the dance floor, people bumping into him, apologising. Shona went on twirling, waving her hands in the air. She could feel the knot in her stomach. Her gamble might not pay off.

'Move, can't you?' someone hissed at Austin and he automatically commenced dancing once more. When he pulled Shona to him she remained at his chest, pressing her hips against his, gluing her body to his, refusing to move away even when he tried to twirl her. 'Then we can woo-woo all the time,' she whispered sibilantly in his ear. 'Woo-woo' was what Austin called sexual activity.

He *could* have detached himself from her body if he'd mustered up a great deal more will-power than he possessed. It was unbearably sexy, her gyrating against him, and he groaned with the pleasure of it.

'Let's go woo-woo now,' he begged in a strangled voice.

Abruptly she moved away from him and he nearly fell.

'Not till you say you'll marry me,' she said in a matter-of-fact voice. 'No marriage, no woo-woo. Ever again.'

Fatal words! 'All right, all right.' He was in pain, would be until she used her tricks to ease his tension, bring him that sweet, sweet climax. He'd say anything to get that. Agree to murder.

How had it happened? She had learned to pleasure him with an efficiency that both startled and thrilled him. She knew exactly what to do, how long to do it. Like a sorceress she weaved her magic and he wanted more, more, more.

He told her he'd marry her and took her the back way to his room. He could always pretend he had not understood her. Got it wrong. He could wriggle out of his promise afterwards. After the magic. After the woo-woo.

Chapter Twenty-Eight

Lydia was changing into her lilac tweed Sybil Connolly outfit for going away. When the knock came at the door she thought it was her mother. 'Come in,' she called. It was Varina. 'Hello, Varina,' Lydia said.

She could hear the band below playing a Johnny Ray number, one about walking in the rain. She was feeling blissful. She was leaving Mallow Hall and all her problems there. Orlick had put down, with his father's help, a deposit on a lovely little semi-detached in Sandymount. She would live there calmly and quietly with her husband, content to let him care for her, protect her, look after her. She could come and visit her mamma, not have to be involved with all that stuff with Tom Gallagher. She liked Tom, had become reconciled to her mother's involvement with him. She was a reasonable person and she had come around to the obvious fairness that her mother deserved her happiness, was entitled to be in love. But she did not want to *participate* in it. She did not want it happening under her nose.

She would go to the factory and the shop. She would do that because she enjoyed it. She hoped to visit her mother often, but she'd have her own snug little houseen and Orlick to hold and love her. She'd avoid all the scandal, the gossip about her mother and Tom Gallagher. She'd avoid Roland's drunkenness.

And Sean Sullivan.

Mrs Sullivan and Granny Kathleen had been together at the wedding. Granny Kathleen had stared at Lydia as if she'd sold state secrets but Mrs Sullivan understood. She said, 'Sean sends best wishes,' and pressed Lydia's hand. 'So do I, my lamb. I hope you'll be very happy.' Kathleen hooted loudly and went and got a sherry.

Lydia didn't know whether to be glad or sorry that her visitor was her sister-in-law and not her mother. She stared at Varina across a sea of discarded satin wedding things — veil, bouquet, gloves and underwear.

'I want — well, Lydia, I want to apologise. I was mean to you and I have no excuse.'

Lydia smiled readily. 'Oh Varina, of course. You've nothing to apologise for —'

'But I have, Lydia. Don't try to sweep it under the carpet. Pretend I didn't hurt you. I'm sorry I told you like that —'

Lydia turned her attention to buttoning her jacket. She didn't want to talk about her mother, but Varina continued, 'It was mean and spiteful. I was, oh I don't know, jealous, I suppose . . .' Her blue eyes were swimming in tears and Lydia's soft heart was touched.

'Oh Varina, you *can't* be jealous of me. Why, you're the most beautiful girl in town. Oh Varina!' Impetuously she embraced her sister-in-law and they both laughed in relief.

'Remember I caught your bouquet,' Lydia said.

Varina nodded. 'I remember.'

'I never thought I'd be wedded so soon after you, though.'

'Lydia.' Varina hesitated. 'Lydia, when you come back — you know, from your honeymoon — can we be friends?'

'Of course. I'd like that.'

'You're so good, Lydia. I wish I could be as nice as you are.' Varina sounded wistful.

'I'm not nice, Varina,' Lydia said, frowning. 'I'm not at all nice, come to think of it. It's just, well, I *avoid* being nasty. Doesn't mean I'm not.'

'There, you see? You are so nice you don't even think you are.'

'Is Roland still being awful?' Lydia asked because she wanted to change the subject. She didn't really care about her brother.

'Oh, I can manage Roley,' Varina said. She too was not interested in Roland Tracey. 'It's myself I worry about.'

'Mother and your father are coming with us to Collinstown,' Lydia said. 'We're taking the evening flight to Paris.'

'Paris! Oh, lucky you.' Varina smiled ruefully. 'We never made the honeymoon Dadda planned in Killarney. We spent our wedding night in separate rooms in the Royal in Bray.'

'I know. Mamma told me.'

It was then that Martha entered. She looked beautiful in a wine-coloured tweed suit, a silk shirt and a grey chiffon scarf that hovered about her neck. 'Darling, you'll be late. Hello, Varina.' She was surprised to see the girl there but charmingly kissed her cheek then folded her daughter in her arms. 'Oh my darling, I'm so happy for you. This is the day I've dreamed about from the start. I'm so proud of you, pet.' She dabbed her eyes with her handkerchief. 'We'll be late,' she cried. 'You'll miss the plane.'

She did not tell her daughter, and nobody except Nonie and Eilish knew, that she too was taking a plane that evening from Collinstown. At last, with Lydia safely married, her will in Pius Brady's safe keeping, she and Tom could go to Italy. Two hours after her daughter and new son-in-law took off for Paris, Martha and Tom would board a plane to Rome.

PART TWO

Chapter Twenty-Nine

Martha bloomed in Italy. She showed some fatigue in Rome so they hastened to the villa Tom had rented on the coast near Amalfi, just past Positano. It was situated on a slope surrounded and shaded by eucalyptus and cypress. Some Roman general or emperor or more probably senator had walked the old flagstones, having built the villa for summer use, to escape the heat in Rome. The grounds were littered with fallen statuary and the floors of the villa were of green Carrara marble, and there were beautiful mosaics everywhere.

It was warm there, a lovely solid heat that was both fresh and soothing, and the air was full of the scents of flowers and herbs and greenery. The Mediterranean sea was peacock-blue and the bougainvillaea and hydrangea, the wistaria and jasmine and hibiscus were still in riotous bloom.

They settled in and almost at once Martha was transformed. They slipped into a routine. Caterina, the wife of a local fisherman, served them. She was a large, jolly person and they took to her at once. She brought them huge cups of caffé latte each morning and warm, new-baked bread from Positano where she lived, with fruit and wonderful preserves, chunky apricot, thick plum and whole-fruit strawberry.

They ate in the huge old-fashioned bed or on the balcony overlooking the sea. They swam and they walked. They talked endlessly of love and tried hard to live in the present. They usually went to Positano, Amalfi or up the coast to one of the delightful little pink villages for a light lunch, then, when they could, collected an English paper and read in the afternoon. Tom had given Martha the collected works of Elizabeth Barrett Browning and she browsed through the volume, reading about an old love.

Caterina came up in the evening and cooked for them. Her cooking was superb and she used fresh herbs and vegetables. She had four lusty sons whom she'd named after the four apostles, Matteo, Marco, Luciano, and Giovanni. She was immensely good-humoured, called them Mr and Mrs Gallagher and they decided it would be tactful to leave her in ignorance of their true status. She was a devout Catholic and her tolerance might not extend to serving a couple living in mortal sin.

They dined on the balcony under the stars, staring at the moon and each other and the sea, the fabulous gently shifting sea. They drank the local wine, the evening scent of jasmine overwhelming, and every now and then the church bell tolled.

They went to bed early and made love, holding on to every precious moment, living it to the full, utterly in the here and now. Martha abandoned herself to Tom completely and he, plunging into the depths of her both physically and spiritually, became one with her, part of her, and she part of him. They were like the first man and woman in Eden in this Italian paradise, discovering each other in delight, awe and — underneath it all — despair. 'The moments are ticking by,' he said. 'So quickly, so quickly.' He looked out over the sea, a blue heat-haze shimmering in the distance like an azure veil.

'I'm here, my love,' she cried. 'And I'm strong.'

There was no doubt about that. Her eyes were brighter than the stars, her skin like an apricot, tender and warm and downy. She had acquired a touch of tan and it suited her. Her energy increased rather than flagged, her humour was buoyant.

Caterina asked them if they would like to come to an end-of-season festival and they happily agreed. The festival, she told them, was to venerate Santa Pedro, the fisherman, and the end of the fishing season. 'Ana the fac' that the fishin' isa over for the winter,' she laughed, her whole body shaking. 'As if the season ever ends! No! We fish, my Sebastiano, every day!'

The festival had begun with a solemn procession and ended with a dance. Everyone sat outside and gossiped, the older ladies stout in black, the young girls in brightly-coloured dirndls flirting with the local Romeos.

'I wish I was one of them,' Martha whispered.

Tom was holding her hand and he pressed it.

'No,' he said. '*We* are the ones to envy. They may never know a love like ours. I feel sorry for them.'

They danced, copying the others, the fat Caterina showing them the dance with surprising grace and great gusto. At first Tom was awkward and stiff but soon they were carried away by the rhythm, shoulders shaking, feet flying. The party didn't end until late that night when, full of good wine and good cheer, Tom and Martha climbed the hill to their villa, tired and blissfully happy.

'What did I ever do to deserve you?' he asked.

She touched his cheek with tender fingers. 'You just are your wonderful self,' she replied.

'I'm yours now and forever, every bit of me,' he said. 'My heart, soul and body.'

'Hush, my own. Such extravagance is frightening. Kiss me now under the moon.' He touched her lips softly with his. She could sense his tenderness in the meeting of mouth on mouth. So much love, his passion held in check. He pulled a bougainvillaea blossom off a branch and held it against her face.

'Ah yes. I thought so. You are more beautiful,' he said. 'Lovelier than any flower.'

He kissed her again and this time did not hold his passion in check and the bougainvillaea blossom lay crushed between them.

Chapter Thirty

Paris in November was just as delightful as the Amalfi coast. The autumn leaves, red and gold, on the chestnut trees along the Champs Elysée shivered in the brisk little breeze that blew in from the Seine. The sun shone brightly in the crisp afternoon and Orlick and Lydia drank *café au lait* in smoky cafés and watched the world go by outside.

Lydia decided she liked being married. Orlick was a gentle lover and their love-making was a slow discovery, with many mistakes and a lot of delicate satisfaction. Orlick led her slowly into the delights of sexual excitement and her awakening was delicious and protracted rather than tempestuous and passionate.

Neither of them was in a hurry. Both realised they had the rest of their lives to discover all about each other and learn about sex. For the moment they were happy to make love tenderly and exploratively, to eat, sleep and explore the enchanting city, and each act was of equal importance to them.

They did all the tourist things, unselfconsciously. They sat for hours in the cafés, wandered the Louvre hand in hand, shopped in the rue du Faubourg-St-Honoré, climbed to the Sacré Coeur, whispered to each other in Notre

Dame and giggled like teenagers at the naughtiness of the show they saw in Montmartre.

Finally they were both delighted to return home, not because they had not enjoyed themselves but because they were both eager to sample the delights of settling down in their own little house.

And there it was in Sandymount, all ready for them. Lydia felt for the first time really, truly married. Orlick gave her the key and told her to open the door. This is my house, my home, she thought, and inserted the key and turned it. The door sprang open and Orlick lifted her into his arms and carried her across the threshold.

In the hallway he let her down gently and she kept her arms around his neck and leaned against him.

'I really feel married now,' she said. 'I'm Mrs Fitzmaurice, aren't I, Orlick?'

'Sure are,' he told her tenderly.

'Mamma'd think us very banal,' she said. 'Pedestrian. Going to all the obvious places in Paris. Not devouring each other in bed. Being so content with this little home, so dinky, so *ordinary*. Do you think I'm boring, Orlick?'

He laughed. 'You know I don't,' he said. 'I love you. I wouldn't want you to be like your mother at all. I love you just as you are and if that is ordinary, then so be it.'

'I'll be a good wife, Orlick. I promise.'

'And I'll be a good husband,' he said firmly. 'Now, what's for dinner?'

'Yes, at once, my lord and master!' she laughed.

'Mother will surely have left something in the fridge.'

'Oh, it's wonderful having a fridge. We haven't a fridge at Mallow Hall. We have a larder.'

'Well you got one now,' he said triumphantly.

They went into the kitchen. It was painted blue and white and it had every modern convenience imaginable. There was a table covered in a blue and white check table-cloth with two places laid and a bowl of yellow chrysanthemums in a dark blue vase. 'Mother's done this for us. She's great,' Orlick said, rubbing his hands together.

Lydia opened the refrigerator door with proprietorial pride. A blast of freezing air greeted her. There was a bottle of milk, some back rashers, Hafner's sausages, and eggs in little hollows made specially for them. There was a white bread bin with fresh bread in it. 'I'll miss the croissants,' Orlick said.

'Oh, but this is wonderful,' Lydia cried. 'I don't care if I'm the most ordinary person in the world, it's just what I want, this kind of life, this kind of house. And you.'

She took the apron from a hook behind the door and tried it on. 'It suits you,' he said.

'Mother would never be seen in one of these,' she laughed.

'Lydia, you are not your mother,' he told her.

'No, I'm more like Doris Day,' she cried. She

searched for a pan, found one. 'You know, Orlick, none of them understand what I want. They all look at me and decide I must be the greedy heiress to Mallow Hall. But that's not what I want at all. It's too big, too grand for me. I'm so happy with this.' She grinned at him. 'I can manage this.'

She lit the gas, put some butter in the pan. 'Now you go read in the living-room. Do whatever husbands are supposed to do,' she commanded.

He kissed the back of her neck, delighted with her. 'This is what husbands do.' He snuggled up to her, laughing, and she laughed too and shrugged him away. 'No. I can't concentrate when you do that,' she said firmly. 'Shoo! Shoo!'

She fried the bacon and eggs. She was not very good at it but she enjoyed trying. She'd learn. Orlick would always make allowances for her mistakes. He was that sort of husband.

They too fell into a routine. Orlick worked hard in the hospital and Lydia, with her mother away, paid a lot more attention to the business. She went to the factory and the shop on weekdays, and on Saturday and Sunday, Orlick's hours permitting, they went sailing off Bullock Harbour. Orlick had a neat little sailboat called *Cat's Meow* and Lydia and he went out in her with sandwiches and a flask and messed about.

Their tastes were simple. The 'old money' Austin believed the Fitzmaurices had and that he reassured himself would make up to Lydia any loss she suffered at his hands was in fact mostly gone and what was left was barely enough to put Orlick through his last year's medical training after the deposit Dr Fitzmaurice had put down on the house in Sandymount. Though the Fitzmaurices were not rich any more, they were not poor either, and could claim to provide a comfortable existence for Lydia and her husband. She would never want.

Lydia was happy in this situation. She had no ambitions where wealth was concerned and was not an extravagant person. She was wonderfully happy. She felt safe and protected and at peace. Nothing really disturbed her except thoughts of her mother's death, but she did not allow herself to dwell on that.

Varina came to see her, one winter evening in the dusk when the leaves had all fallen and the street-lamps went on at six o'clock. Lydia and Orlick sat before a roaring fire. Varina, to Lydia's surprise had brought Roland with her.

Lydia served tea. She made it herself, thinking how her mother would disapprove. What would her mother do without Nonie? Lydia had discovered she liked feeding people, cooking their dinner, ministering to their needs. She even thought that if anything awful happened she wouldn't mind being in service. The thought shocked her but she indulged herself as she shopped, planning the menus she thought her friends would enjoy, remembering their tastes, their likes and dislikes, cooking the food. Serving it. She liked nothing better than to do the whole job herself.

She was learning fast. She discovered she had a natural talent for cooking. She enjoyed house-wifely pursuits.

Varina commented on the cosiness of the room.

'Yes. We like it.' Lydia glanced at her sister-in-law and her brother. 'It's nice of you to come and visit us.' She felt awkward, not because of Varina but because Roland had his pink beady eyes fixed on her with belligerent intensity.

'And this ginger cake is gorgeous,' Varina cried. 'Did you bake it yourself?'

Orlick glanced proudly at his wife. 'Oh yes. She's a wonderful cook, is Lydia.'

'I'm not surprised, Lydia. You are wonderful with food. Think of the chocolates.' Varina did not know what she was saying. She bumbled on, trying to dissipate the atmosphere her husband was creating in the cosy little room.

She tucked her hand through her husband's arm, smiling at him, and Roland promptly re-moved it without as much as giving her a glance. 'Lydia doesn't *cook* the chocolates,' he said in withering tones.

Lydia hated the cruelty of the gesture he'd just made, removing his wife's hand as if it was a piece of dirt on his jacket. She knew she'd hate it if Orlick administered such a slight in public.

It then emerged that the real purpose of

Roley's visit was not so much to see his sister as to enquire what the hell their mother was up to. Fairly typically, news had filtered through to Roland long after everyone else knew about it.

'What does she think she's doing, pissing off to Italy like that?' he complained and Orlick raised his eyebrows slightly. Roland saw the grimace. 'Beggin' your pardon, little sister, for the language. Oh dear, dear me. Tut tut,' he said sarcastically. 'But what the hell is she doing, off like that without as much as a by-your-leave?'

'Your mother is a free agent, Roland,' Orlick said. 'She can do as she pleases.'

'Oh! Is that so!' Roland opened his mouth to continue but Varina said, 'She did send a letter, Roley.'

'With your da,' Roland glared at her. 'Jesus, I don't know where to put myself when people ask me.'

'No one asks you about Mamma, Roley, I'm sure,' Lydia said coldly.

'Well you're wrong. They do,' Roland insisted roughly. 'Everyone's talking.'

'Oh, I wouldn't say that,' Orlick remarked placidly. 'Time has passed and they are not here. Other things are happening.'

'Oh, and what would you know? Living here in your pesky little house, messing about in that hospital,' Roland remarked petulantly. He'd not taken a drink since his early morning wake-me-up and was feeling terrible — edgy and irritable. 'All I want to know is, what is Mamma doing?

261

Why isn't she home?'

'Mamma is recuperating in the warmth, Roley,' Lydia said firmly. 'We all know she has cancer. Tom Gallagher is helping her immensely and I'm praying that between him and the climate there she'll get better . . .' Tears began to fall and she put the plate of scones down with a bang and ran out of the room.

'Now see what you have done!' Orlick stood angrily. He looked at Roland. 'You are the most insufferable boor, Roland, you know that? 'Bout time you realised it.' He followed his wife out of the room.

Roland snorted, 'Huh!' He looked at his wife but her eyes were firmly fixed on her fingernails and she remained silent.

Roland was uncertain what to do next. He was feeling really appalling now. His teeth had begun to chatter and his hands to shake and he found it impossible to hold the delicate cup and saucer. On top of that, he was sweating profusely and beads were dripping into his eyes, stinging him.

'Better go,' he muttered, getting unsteadily to his feet.

As he turned to go Lydia came back into the room, Orlick close behind her. 'Sorry for that,' she said, and as Roland sat down she refilled their cups then passed around the plate of ginger cake.

'No need to apologise, Lydia,' Varina spoke, looking up at her sister-in-law. 'You didn't do anything.' And she glared at Roland.

'I'm worried about Mamma, just as you are, Roland,' Lydia said with dignity. 'But she is happy just now . . .'

'Happy!' Roland snorted. He shifted about, unable to stop still for a moment.

'Yes, Roland.' Lydia looked at him angrily. '*Happy*. And she has every right to be. Mamma has looked after us for years. She's been on her own and she's been lonely, but that did not stop her from looking after us. Just now she's with someone she loves, who makes her happy. I have to accept that.' She glanced at her sister-in-law. 'But, and I'm sorry to say this, Varina, I have to say I don't like it much. It is not what I would have chosen. I wish Mamma was here with us and I could go see her every day. I wish she wasn't in Italy, so far away. But that's selfish, I know. Your father, Varina, is what she needs at the moment and I have to be happy for her.'

'Well I think it's disgraceful!' Roland said. 'What if she gets ill when she's there? Those Eyeties are useless when it comes to civilised professions like medicine.'

'Oh for heaven's sake, Roland, and you supposed to be a Trinity student!' Orlick's tone was contemptuous. 'The Romans were civilised long before we were. Why, they practically *invented* medicine. Where do you think the caesarean operation came from?' Roland stared at him blankly. 'Good God, man, common sense should tell you.'

Varina smiled. 'Don't enlighten him, Orlick. Let him work it out for himself.'

Roland was beginning to feel seriously ill. He felt his stomach heave and contract — like some damn woman giving birth, he thought. He felt as if there were razor blades in his gut. His hands were shaking so badly now that he sat on them. He would have agreed to have them amputated for a drink. 'All I can say is, you women get away with murder while we men have to pick up the tab. Mother goes to Italy with her lover and nobody gives a hoot, while I have a bit of nookie with a willing partner and . . .'

'I think you better stop right there,' Orlick interrupted firmly.

'What?' Roland looked at Orlick as if he didn't understand. Which he didn't. He was about to make a move to leave, get himself to a pub as quickly as he could when Varina rose and looked at him witheringly.

'You really are very stupid,' she said coldly. 'Excuse me.' She turned and left the room.

Roland was left trying to conquer his twisting gut and keep his hands still.

Varina liked Lydia's house. She liked the neat little rooms, so fresh, so feminine, the starched curtains, the light colours. She was tired of the heavy solemnity of Ailesbury Road.

She peeped into the bedroom. Let Roland wait. Orlick and Lydia had a patchwork quilt on the bed. It looked so comfortable and cosy. The bedroom was small but it had a bathroom off it.

There was sweet-smelling soap in a dish beside the bath and Lydia's shampoo and deodorant beside Orlick's shaving cream. There was something so together about it all that Varina winced.

She sat on the lavatory. It was pale green, like the bath. Softly coloured, pretty tiles with sunflowers on surrounded the bath. Hopeful and happy, she thought and sighed, suddenly feeling like crying.

The baby stirred within her and she rested her hand on her abdomen. How lovely it must be to be in love with the father of your child. She thought about those hot moments in the back of the Morris Minor with Roland and wondered at how insatiable she had been then, how careless, how foolish. She could not understand it now.

Yet she wanted the baby, looked forward to its arrival so much. She just didn't want or love Roland and she would have liked to be able to blink her eyes and find him gone.

But she was lonely too, sighing for a mythical father-figure who would complete her life, a real man, a whole person, an adult. I'm impossible, she thought, and looked up to see Lydia in the doorway.

'How do you stand him?' Lydia asked. They both knew she meant her brother.

'I hardly ever see him,' Varina said. 'I think I'll get a separation, Lydia. When Dadda gets back.'

'I wonder what will happen to Roland then? I'm afraid he'll lose what little grip he has on reality.'

Varina's large blue eyes met Lydia's squarely. 'I neither know nor care,' she said. 'Sorry, Lydia. Can't pretend.'

There was a cough in the doorway and the two women swivelled around. Roland stood there staring at them. For a while nobody moved, then Roland turned and ran down the stairs and they heard the front door bang. Lydia looked back at Varina, who shrugged. 'Neither know nor care,' she repeated. 'It's too late, Lydia. The whole thing's dead.'

After that Roland disappeared. No one knew where he was and, like Varina, no one cared. Even Cad Connolly and Fishy Moran, who were to be seen rollicking up and down Grafton Street at closing time or just before or after the holy hour, when asked by Lydia where Roland was, simply shrugged unconcernedly and said they hadn't the faintest. Lydia would run out of the shop when she saw them pass and their answer was always the same: 'Dropped over the edge,' Fishy sighed, peering at her through half-closed lids, and Cad would shake his head regretfully. 'Pissed off somewhere, don't know where!'

'Don't you *care?*' Lydia would ask but the pair would simply wave and move on.

'Loyalty of drunks,' Brosnan would say, shaking his head.

Roland did not even bother to turn up at Trinity for his tutorials or send an excuse. Nor was he sleeping in Mallow Hall or Ailesbury Road. It was as if after that tea with his sister he'd vanished off the face of the earth.

Chapter Thirty-One

Varina's baby was born the day Martha Tracey died. Varina was alone, her father in Italy, her husband God knew where when the first stirrings and slashes of pain warned her that her baby was ready to be born. She was frightened, all alone like that, for Styles was out shopping so she sent for Lydia. She phoned the factory and they contacted Lydia at the shop and she hurried to the house, ordered an ambulance and went with her sister-in-law to the nursing home.

The girls had become close over the months after the tea party at Lydia's. They often met in Bewley's or Fuller's, visited each other and sometimes went to a movie together. Lydia felt sorry for the girl whose glamour she had once envied. Varina was so very much alone.

Lydia held Varina's hand all through her painful ordeal. It was a quick delivery though and, much to Lydia's relief, Varina bore it well.

There was a rapturous look on Varina's face when the newborn infant was laid on her breast and the young mother looked first in awed amazement at the tiny mortal then with delight at Lydia. 'Did you ever?' she asked incredulously, exhausted but never happier. 'Did you ever in your whole life see anything so gorgeous?'

The little girl was born on 6 March at three

a.m. and on that day and at that time Martha Tracey died in Italy.

'What's your mother's second name?' Varina asked Lydia, who sat beside her sister-in-law, staring with fascination at the tiny mite.

'Rose,' Lydia replied. 'Mother says that Granny Kathleen always said, "First one from the Bible, second one from the heart'. Granny Kathleen loves roses so she called Mamma Martha Rose.'

'Then she'll be Rose,' Varina said. 'I always thought your mam was the most beautiful lady in the world. She was never angry like the other mothers, never shouted 'Stop that at once, Lydia' or anything like that. She was always so gracious. I'll call the baby Rose after her. Rose Tracey.'

Lydia put her cheek against Varina's. 'She's lovely, Varina, so lovely,' she whispered.

'An' you'll be godmother, Liddy, won't you?' Varina continued.

'Oh Varina, I'd be honoured. Look at her little hand, those little fingers, like starfish. Oh Varina, how wonderful it is and how foolish Roland is to miss this.'

Martha collapsed suddenly. The Italian doctor was very surprised that she had survived so long without help or hospitalisation. 'She's riddled with it, *Signor* Gallagher,' he told Tom. 'I don' understand.'

'How do I love thee? Let me count the ways,' she whispered to Tom from the pillows of the big

bed. 'Oh Tom, you've been so good to me, so good for me. I love you so.'

'Don't talk like that, my darling, I'll not let you die,' he said desperately. But she seemed to have reached some plane of acceptance and he could not follow her. 'Don't leave me,' he begged. 'Heart of my heart, don't go.'

'It's inevitable, dearest man,' she said. 'Oh my love, I'm so grateful to you, for everything.'

In anguish he clasped her to him. 'Don't go,' he pleaded. 'I'll be lost without you.'

'You've got to help Varina with the baby,' she said so softly he could barely hear her. 'She'll have no one. Roley is useless. Promise, Tom.'

'I promise.'

She lay pale on the pillows and he felt a surge of anger. What malicious fate had drawn them together to love so much and was now tearing them apart?

'Say the Browning poem to me,' she asked. He tried to keep his voice steady, picking up the book from the side-table. Italy and love had worked for the Brownings, so why not for them? Why not, oh Lord, why not?

He began to read:

'If thou must love me, let it be for naught
Except for love's sake only. Do not say,
'I love her for her smile — her look — her way
Of speaking gently, — for a trick of thought
That falls in well with mine, and certes
  brought

A sense of pleasant ease on such a day' —
For these things in themselves, Beloved, may
Be changed, or change for thee — and love, so
   wrought,
May be unwrought so. Neither love me for
Thine own dear pity's wiping my cheeks dry:
A creature might forget to weep, who bore
Thy comfort long, and lose thy love thereby!
But love me for love's sake, that evermore

Thou mayst love on, through love's eternity.'

His voice choked a little and he repeated 'Love's eternity', then looked at her and saw at once that she was dead. He looked at the clock. He must have been reading to her when she passed away. His voice must have been the last thing she heard. She had been lulled to her final peace, the sound of Elizabeth Barrett Browning's lovely words in her ears.

He sat a long time holding her hand. He felt wearier than he had ever felt before in his life. Somewhere in the distance a church bell tolled. After it the silence seemed endless.

At last he placed her hand on her bosom, went to the window, plucked a spray of bougainvillaea and laid it on her breast. 'Goodbye, my love,' he whispered. 'Goodbye.' And he kissed the pale, cold cheek and sat by her, his head sinking between his hands.

Chapter Thirty-Two

Austin was in a quandary. He had admitted to Shona that he'd made the promise to marry her under duress and laughingly asked her how could she possibly have taken him seriously.

Shona had flounced away and refused to see him. Absolutely no woo-woo.

'I didn't really think you'd take me seriously, Shona,' he told her.

'Well, Austin, I did,' she replied unemotionally. 'So it's like this — let me spell it out for you. I'm *not* your girlfriend and there is no more woo-woo at all until you change your mind and decide to marry me. *And* I'm thinking about a Breach of Promise suit. But we'll leave that on the back burner. Depends on what you do next. First move is up to you.' And she blithely left him, as he phrased it, gawking where he stood.

Mentally Austin thumbed his nose at her but physically he could not help thinking of the woo-woo. He missed the excitement and, though he hated to admit it, he also missed her company. He'd got used to talking to her, bragging a little, swanking about Mallow Hall. It made him feel superior, a chosen man, apart from all the others because of his dynamic qualities. She told him he had dynamic qualities and he saw no reason to doubt her. She made him feel good.

Austin was neither charming nor handsome. If he had been like Sean Sullivan he'd not have worried a bit about Shona's defection, there would have been many eager to take her place. But he was not Sean and the girls did not come flocking — in fact at the next hop he went to both girls he asked to dance turned him down and no one claimed him at the Ladies' Choice. He was truly scuppered.

It was not that the girls were utterly indifferent to him or that he was utterly without attractions, but there were several factors involved.

Firstly there were more men than women available in Dublin at that time so the girls could afford to be selective. Secondly Shona had had a word with her friends and they had put the word around in their set to leave Austin Tracey alone. The girls did not feel that Austin Tracey was worth a breach of friendship. They would have paid no attention to Shona's request if the man in question had been Sean Sullivan or Orlick Fitzmaurice or another of that calibre, but Austin Tracey just wasn't worth it. So poor Austin found himself out on a limb.

He pretended not to care, but when two weeks after the break he bumped into Shona, who just happened to be strolling down the Green when he was turning into the Shelbourne for his evening drink, he found himself *begging, imploring* her for a date, a resumption of their relationship.

'Oh!' Shona looked at him provocatively, putting one hand on her hip and batting her eyelashes. 'Missing your woo-woo?'

'Hush up, Shona, have you no shame?' He glanced right and left, fearful someone passing by would hear. Unabashed she grinned at him. She had this nasty habit of saying intimate things loudly so that people stared at him, thinking God knows what. If he could explain quietly it would be all right, but she stood her ground.

'Come in and have a drink with me,' he implored.

'Are you going to propose to me in there?' she demanded in a voice that could be heard at Nelson's Pillar. A few people looked over their shoulders at him and grinned.

'No, wait, I don't just miss, er, well, *that,* you know . . .'

'Sex?' she enquired, and a group of office girls passing by glanced at him, sniggering.

'Shush! *No.* I miss your *company,* Shona. I miss *you.*'

'I don't care what you miss, I simply want to know if I go in there with you, are you going to propose marriage? If not, I'm off.'

'Well, I'm, I thought we could talk. We could discuss things . . .'

'Goodbye, Austin.' And she sashayed away, wide skirts swirling about her, high heels clacking on the pavement, brown curls bouncing on her shoulders.

Aw what the hell, he thought, and called after her, 'Okay, Shona. You win.'

She turned her head and looked at him. 'You

mean it?' she cried.

'Yeah.' The word was dragged from him against his will.

So he got engaged to her. They sat in the Horseshoe Bar in the back of the Shelbourne and talked, he agreeing to her every demand, smelling her body, craving his woo-woo, mentally crossing his fingers (she had his hands in a fierce grip), telling himself he could wriggle out of it when the time came. He did not for one moment take her threat of a Breach of Promise suit seriously. It was such a humiliating procedure for a girl to have to go through and anyway, Shona was not involved with the legal profession. His friends could blind her with legal jargon enough to terrify anyone, let alone a woman, about the appalling experience the whole thing would be.

But Shona Donnelly began to worry him when the very next morning she turned up at the office, *his* office, bright and early, informing Pius Brady and Eileen Skully that they were engaged to be married and that Austin had promised to take her out that morning to buy her the ring.

'You don't mind, Mr Brady, do you?' she twinkled at Pius.

'Oh, aren't you the lucky girl, Shona Donnelly,' Eileen exclaimed and Pius rubbed his hands together and countered with, 'Nonsense, Eileen! Isn't *he* the lucky fellow. We'll have some champagne on ice for the pair of you when you return. To celebrate. Eileen'll organise that, eh, Eileen?'

275

Eileen nodded and Shona hauled Austin down Grafton Street and manipulated him into buying a huge, expensive diamond solitaire.

Shona was ecstatic as they drove out of town to Mallow Hall, where they announced the news to an indifferent Nonie and Eilish.

'I hope ye don't want lunch, Master Austin,' Eilish said. 'Nonie an' I are just off. The missus gave instructions we'd just be here in the mornings.'

'But she's paying you the same, I'll bet. Wicked women!' Austin's tone was falsely jocular. 'Do a half-day's work, get paid full time. Oh, you're no fools, you!'

Tears sprang to Nonie's eyes and red patches appeared on her neck. 'Now, Master Austin, when have I ever counted hours? You tell me that. Why, when you had the rheumatic fever that time, didn't I sit with you all night, an' you scared outta your mind about ghosties and banshees that —'

'I was joking, Nonie, you know that!' Austin interrupted hastily.

'No I don't,' Nonie replied belligerently. 'You was always an ungrateful little beggar, so you was. Come on, Eilish, let's get outta here.' She clamped a shapeless hat on her head and the two of them left, huffing and tutting to each other.

'Silly old biddies,' Austin muttered, then yelled out as Shona suddenly, there in the hallway at Mallow Hall, turned to him and her hands were all over him. He almost doubled over in the

276

hall. 'Oh Jesus! That is . . . oh my God!'

'I told you you'd be glad,' Shona whispered, massaging, kneading, driving him wild. She had begun to demonstrate what he had been missing.

Chapter Thirty-Three

The news of their mother's death reached Ireland on the day after little Rose Tracey's birth, but Martha's body was not brought home to Mallow Hall until a week later.

Lydia grieved cloaked in Orlick's love, his arms comforting around her, his support strong and constant. She found his strength an enormous consolation and rejoiced that she had him at her side.

Kathleen lamented in solitary agony in her little cottage until Peggy Sullivan heard her wailing and went to her neighbour to try to give succour. They sat in the little front room and swayed together, rocking in each other's arms, chanting, praying, trying to accept the will of God even though it made no sense to them. 'It shoulda been me,' Kathleen cried and Peggy agreed. 'Yeah! It shoulda been you.'

Pius told Austin in the office. He got the phone call from Italy and he sat still as a statue a moment, assimilating the news.

The day had finally come. Sometimes he had felt the whole thing had been a fantasy. Martha Tracey was not dying, had not made a will. But it *had* happened. Martha had passed on and now Tom Gallagher was bringing her body home to Mallow Hall.

For a while Pius felt scared. What he was about to do was criminal. He almost decided to jettison the plan, read the will Martha made, play it straight. However, that honest impulse was short-lived and sprang only from a fear that he would be found out and have to pay the penalty. Within minutes he reverted to type, got to his feet and removed the original will from the safe. He had kept it, as he had told Austin, in case Martha suddenly demanded to see it. That was not going to happen now. It had to be destroyed.

He flipped the intercom. Eileen's voice floated in.

'Yes, Mr Brady?'

'Please see I'm not disturbed, Eileen, will you?'

'Yes, Mr Brady.'

He emptied the ash-tray. It was a large, cut-glass receptacle full of cigar butts and ash. He placed the bottom edge of the will inside it, took out his cigarette lighter and set fire to the document. It did not burn easily. He had quite a struggle with it. It seemed reluctant to be consumed and fought the flames valiantly. Pius re-lit and re-lit and re-kindled until eventually the ash-tray contained only the powdery remains of what once had been Martha Tracey's will. Only a small red ribbon was left.

Pius flipped the intercom again. 'Eileen?'

'Yes, sir?'

'Please get me Mrs Tracey's will from the files.'

'Yes, Mr Brady.'

'And Eileen, is Mr Tracey in the office?'

'Yes, sir.'

'Send him in to me please.'

'At once, sir.'

Austin took the announcement of his mother's death quite well. He felt no great sadness at the news, but rather shock, as if he had not really expected it to happen. He was preoccupied with his feelings about Shona, as it happened, and was agitating about the situation he found himself in with her. But he was not so preoccupied that he did not feel a thrill of excitement tinged with fear as Pius Brady said, winking at him, 'I have here, Austin, your mother's last will and testament. I suggest I read it to the family after the funeral.' Austin saw that Pius had the intercom on so that his secretary could hear them. He joined in the game. 'Yes, Pi— Mr Brady. That would be best.'

'Tom Gallagher is dealing with officialdom — all the complications at the Italian end,' Pius said, and for the first time the actuality of his mother's death hit Austin. He felt a surge of anger rise within him that this man dared to involve himself with his, Austin's, mother, with something as intimate as her death. What had it to do with him? He squeezed his eyes and hands and bit his lip until that feeling passed. Pius's help could not be avoided unless he wanted to end up a pauper. He would just have to grin and bear it.

They could not find Roland. Austin and Lydia

met briefly to discuss what was to be done. They embraced without much affection and decided after a short conversation in Pius Brady's office and with great reluctance to broadcast over Radio Eireann an appeal for Roland to get in touch — the usual message. Unfortunately their efforts bore no fruit and Roland remained missing.

When, a week later, travel-stained and red-eyed from lack of sleep, an exhausted Tom Gallagher arrived at Mallow Hall with Martha's body, Austin refused him entry. He stood militantly on the front steps and told Tom in no uncertain terms to leave the premises. 'You are not welcome here, Tom Gallagher, so go now or I'll have you thrown out.' Tom was too distraught, too heart-broken to argue, and he left without a word and went home to Varina.

He felt he would drown in his grief. There was no will in him to go on, no spark or spring of energy left. But the sight that met his eyes when he opened his sitting-room door lifted him out of the despondency he had sunk into. At least a little.

In his big leather chair, in the glow of the standard lamp, sat his daughter, the baby at her breast. He took in the scene with eyes greedy for the love expressed there, the hope. Varina looked down at the tiny infant at her breast with such tenderness and adoration that it was as if a hand gripped Tom's heart and tugged at it. He could hear Martha's voice clearly in his ear: 'It's all right, Tom, my darling, think of the baby. That's what is important.'

'Dadda, meet Rose. We called her Rose after Lydia's mother. Her name was Martha Rose and that's what I've called this little mite. Rose, meet Grandadda.'

Tom fell on his knees and drew the two precious beings, mother and daughter, into his embrace and wept the first tears he could shed after Martha's death. They were tears of anguish and joy.

Two days later the funeral took place. The church was crowded. There were a lot of people who loved Martha Tracey, mostly people who worked for her, and whom she had dealt with in business. They remembered how fair she was, how kind, how understanding when they were in trouble. J.G. was there and Brosnan and Nellie Byrne. The social circles had always disapproved of her, but they packed the church nonetheless, loath to miss this her final appearance.

Austin had wanted to forbid Tom Gallagher to participate either at the church or Mallow Hall, but Pius reprimanded him and the priest, Father Smilling, had looked at him with contempt and did not deign even to reply.

Pius told him, 'It will look suspicious. Odd. As if you had something to hide. No, Austin, much as you hate it, now is the time to be magnanimous, if you can manage that. So Austin did what Pius suggested though he found it extremely difficult, especially when he had to shake

Tom Gallagher's hand.

The funeral service was lengthy. There was a Papal Requiem from Rome, via Tom Gallagher and the Italian officials.

'Disgraceful, I call it,' more than one person commented. 'An' her livin' in sin, bold as brass. Flagrantly. Does the poor Pope, God bless him, realise what he's puttin' his approval to, I wonder?'

The Requiem Mass, in Latin of course, was said by Father Smilling. Kathleen sat in the front pew with Orlick, Lydia and Austin. Nonie and Eilish sat behind with the other servants. Tom Gallagher, much to Austin's relief, had the tact to take a place behind the servants. He arrived with Varina, baby Rose in her arms, and although Lydia beckoned them to join the family in front they remained where they were. Pius Brady, with Eileen Skully, who had insisted on being there, much to her boss's surprise, stood further back again. J.G., Brosnan Burke, Nellie Byrne and the workers from D'Abru's were scattered about the church, nervous and self-effacing in the fashionable crowd.

It was halfway through the service that Roland arrived. At first the people near the back thought he was an intruder, a tramp looking for warmth and shelter, and the ushers tried to put him out. 'Sure he's only a travellin' man,' someone said. 'Lave him be.'

Then he staggered up the aisle and someone recognised him. It ran like wild fire through the church: 'It's Roland Tracey.' 'It's Roland Tracey.' 'It's Roland. He's drunk.'

He pushed in beside Austin. Varina gasped when she saw him, shocked by his appearance. Unshaven, his dark suit crumpled, eyes bloodshot, whole body shaking, tears pouring down his face, he stood there, reeking of stale alcohol, sobbing audibly.

'Pull yourself together, man,' Austin hissed. Lydia tried to reach across Austin to hold his hand but Austin pushed her back. 'Leave him be,' he muttered to his sister. 'He's bad enough without you encouraging him.' Lydia bit her lip.

The service over Austin, Orlick, Pius and Tom Gallagher shouldered the coffin and Roland tried to join them. Austin was furious that Tom had the temerity to assert himself at this stage, but he himself put a firm restraining hand on his brother's shoulder and forced him back into his seat, whispering, 'Stay there! You're a mess. You are not fit to shoulder your mother's coffin.' There was, however, nothing he could do when Tom Gallagher took Roland's hand and gave his place to the pathetic son. 'Your mother would have wanted it,' he whispered.

At the graveside, to Austin's rage, Tom Gallagher threw a dead spray of some foreign blossom on the coffin, but there was no way of retrieving it and he had to let it lie there. In any event, Pius had a hold on his arm and when he glanced at the solicitor there was an expression of warning on his face.

The March day was full of promise. Daffodils were about to bloom and trees to bud. Tom felt nature spoke for Martha. She wants us to look to the future, he thought, and held tightly to Lydia's hand. 'Your mother's message was clear,' he told her. 'She was so . . .' He hesitated. 'Life-affirming. She lived her life to the full, wasting none of it, and now, with spring about to burst forth in all its glory, her hope would be that we follow her example.'

'But it is difficult,' Lydia said.

'But not impossible.' Tom shuddered suddenly. 'Oh my darling one, goodbye,' he murmured and looked at Varina beside him, her young face shocked by the reality of death, full of disgust as she stared at her husband across from her. The baby in her arms sighed and waved its tiny hand at nothing. 'Goodbye, Martha. Hello, Rose,' he whispered and blinked the tears from his eyes.

Chapter Thirty-Four

They sat in the drawing-room in silence. Around them the debris of the wake cluttered the usually immaculate room and Eilish and Nonie bustled about, weeping silently, glad to have something to do. They gathered empty glasses, ash-trays full of cigarette and cigar butts, plates with the remains of the smoked salmon, brown bread and lemon slices they had served.

They looked a glum gathering, as was appropriate, sober-faced and slightly tearful, but there was an underlying excitement, a tension that revealed itself in sharp, irritable replies, constant smoking and an anxiety to get things moving. Pius hovered in the background, nervously clearing his throat. Austin could hardly contain his impatience with the servants, urging them to hurry up, and it was Pius who whispered to him to control himself. He asked Nonie and Eilish to sit down and join them. Roland sat inert in an armchair, as if in a coma, his hands clasped between his knees. Lydia sat beside Orlick on the chaise, she and her husband the only tranquil people in the room. Varina was becoming impatient, for it was nearing Rose's feeding time and she felt too shy to proceed in front of this gathering. However, her father refused to allow her to leave. 'They are your family too, Varina,' he'd told her. 'And Rose's. You can't slide out of it,' he said. So she'd remained sitting in front of the bookcase, her father standing back against the wall in the shadows behind her.

Kathleen sat stony-faced on a small footstool, sunk into her black coat and her thoughts.

'Everybody ready?' Austin asked at last. There were murmurs of assent. 'Then I'll hand you over to Pius Brady here, who was Da's partner and is our solicitor. He has told us that mother made a will just before she left for Italy. When she discovered she was dying. Pius.'

He calls him Pius now, Lydia thought, surprised, and she held on tightly to Orlick's hand. 'I don't like this, Orlick,' she whispered. 'Can't we go?' Alarm bells were ringing in her head but she didn't know why. Orlick half-rose but Pius was standing in front of the fireplace and had begun to read, so he sat down again.

'This is the last will and testament of Martha Rose Tracey, duly signed by her and witnessed by Nonie McMurtagh and Eilish Ross.' Lydia realised that she had never known the two servants' surnames. She wondered at that, finding it worrying. 'Initialled by them in my presence . . .'

Couched in legal jargon with many florid sentences and complicated phraseology, the will was slowly read by Pius Brady. That everything was to be divided equally was the message that came through loud and clear. Martha said, according to Pius, that her husband's former partner, her two sons and her daughter would have equal shares in Mallow Hall. 'Mother would never use a phrase like that,' Lydia whispered to Orlick. ' "My two sons and my daughter." She'd call us by our names. She'd say Lydia, Austin and Roland, I know.' And the business was to be split four ways and the money divided, everything equal, except for a couple of legacies and generous bequests to Eilish and Nonie.

Pius put the document on the table when he had finished. There was silence in the room. 'I think that it is a very fair arrangement,' he said. 'It will have to be entered in probate, of course, but you will agree it is appropriate.'

'What *you* think is of no consequence here or there,' Kathleen cried, rising from her stool, the picture of indignation. 'That is not my daughter's last will,' she said firmly.

Pius did not bat an eyelid, although Austin looked petrified. 'I'm sorry to inform you, madam, that it is!' Pius turned to Austin, who was nervously puffing on his cigarette. 'This often happens,' he said apologetically. 'There are nearly always members of the family who are unhappy about the deceased's instructions. Obviously not everyone is always satisfied. But you see, madam, we don't always understand our nearest and dearest's last wishes.'

'I understood my daughter's wishes very well indeed,' Kathleen bristled. 'She came to see me about her will,' she announced, looking around her, fixing each one of them with a beady glare. 'Told me what she wanted doing. Exactly.'

'In the event she must have changed her mind,' Pius said firmly.

Varina rose suddenly. 'Excuse me . . . I've got to . . .' And she left the room. Eilish looked longingly at the baby and Nonie said, 'Thank you, sir. You don't need us . . . ? The babby . . .'

Pius cried, 'Just a moment!' and the two women looked at him. 'Are those your signatures?' he enquired, pointing to the last page of the document which he had picked up again. Eilish peered at the place Pius pointed to. She nodded. 'Sure?' he asked. 'Oh yes,' she said. Nonie fished her spectacles out of her battered old handbag, put them on and examined the document. 'Yes, sir,' she affirmed. 'Can we go now, sir?' Pius nodded his head. 'Of course,' he said and they followed Varina out of the room, cooing and clucking over little Rose. 'I think that is all I can do here,' Pius said, picking up his briefcase with an air of finality.

But Kathleen was not to be fobbed off. 'Oh no you don't, my lad,' she cried indignantly. 'You're not gettin' away that easy.'

'I'm sorry, Mrs Daly, this is nothing to do with me. I simply write down what I'm told.'

'What you were *told* to do was leave Mallow Hall and D'Abru's to the rightful heiress. To Lydia D'Abru,' Kathleen finished defiantly. 'What you *did* was . . . well I dunno, but it was *not* what my daughter wanted. I know that.'

Pius glared at her. 'Be careful, madam,' he said in his sternest tones. 'Be careful what you accuse me of.' He stared at her, his eyes for once quite steady. 'I cannot think why I should have not done precisely what your daughter dictated. What possible motive could I have? And you can of course contest the will,' he continued smoothly. 'It is your right. Drag your family through the courts. Have brother fight sister and vice versa in public. It is your prerogative and you are free to commence proceedings at any time.' They all stared at him. He saw Lydia frown, her face pained. 'If I am accused of any inappropriate behaviour I shall of course take action at once to clear my name. I shall sue you for every penny you've got.' He relaxed a little and spread his hands. 'Of course, that would break my heart. Austin and Roland's father was my partner and my friend and Martha was as dear to me as a sister —' His voice broke. What an old ham he is, Tom Gallagher thought, and Orlick, Lydia and Roland watched him in fascinated silence.

There was a sudden shift in focus as Roland rose unsteadily to his feet, glaring first at Austin then at Pius.

'Granny Kathleen is right,' he told the assembled company in a slurred voice. 'It's all a sham. A plot. A rip-off.' There was a stunned gasp. 'A scam!' he cried. 'You louses are trying . . .'

'Sit down, Roland. You are not well,' Pius said severely.

'He's drunk!' Austin shouted. His nerves were in shreds but as the scene unfolded he was gain-ing courage. Pius was giving a superb performance. Roland opened his mouth to speak, then his face changed colour and he seemed to lose the thread of what he was saying. He bumbled a bit, frowned, scratched his head then shook it. 'Gotta get a drink,' he muttered and ran out of the room.

Lydia had watched Roland, her eyes full of pity.

'There you are, you see. Said he was drunk,' Austin announced, relief in his voice.

Now Lydia focussed her attention on Austin. He met her eyes and saw dawning understanding in them. At first she looked incredulous. She gulped a few times, staring at him. He could see the realisation in her stunned expression, the understanding. 'Oh my God!' she whispered. Only Tom and Orlick heard her.

While this was happening Kathleen was in full flow, berating Pius, accusing him of being all sorts of things, and Pius himself was fastening his briefcase, his lips tight.

Then Lydia stood up and Kathleen's diatribe faltered to a halt. Everyone looked at the girl. 'Don't let's quarrel, Granny,' she said quietly. 'Mamma would have hated that.' She looked at Tom for confirmation. 'Don't you think so, Tom?' Her voice sounded wistful. 'Let us try to remember this is the day of Mamma's funeral.' She looked narrowly at Pius. 'If Pius says that that was Mamma's last will and testament then I'm sure that is the truth.' Pius's gaze shifted beneath her candid look and slurred away into the corner of the room. 'What do you think, Austin?' Lydia asked.

She looked searchingly at her brother, who stared back at her. His eyes were cold and hard and he had no trouble at all in replying firmly, 'Of course it is the truth. I'm quite sure of that.'

'Then that's good enough for me.' Lydia seemed to gather up her strength. She took a deep breath. 'Mamma used to say that truth had its own life.' She glanced again at Tom. 'If there are lies they come to bite back. I would not want that to happen. She always said that trust was important, even when there was deceit about. What I do is much more important than what others do. I can be at peace with myself.'

'Jasus, Lydia, you sound like Mamma. Who are you to lecture us? Eh? Uppity little . . .' Austin's face was crimson.

'Austin, that's enough. I don't understand a word she's saying,' Pius protested, 'but her Mother's death has affected her badly. It has affected us all.'

'What she is saying, in Martha's very voice' — Tom Gallagher spoke for the first time — 'is that if there are lies in this room today they'll come back to haunt the liar. That's simple enough to understand.'

Pius looked relieved. 'Well, that is that then,' he said.

'Come then, let's go, Orlick,' Lydia said. She gathered up her purse and gloves. 'What will happen to D'Abru's?' she asked casually.

Austin cleared his throat. 'It will be sold. Sorry, Lydia, but we outnumber you three to one.' 'Oh! You've already talked to Pius and Roley then?' she enquired innocently.

'Er, no. No. But Roland's talked so often about selling that I have no doubt . . .'

'But then, Austin, we don't always understand our nearest and dearest's wishes, do we?' Lydia's voice was smooth as she quoted Pius Brady. 'Come along, Orlick,' she said. She looked at the assembled company. 'This has been a very sad day indeed,' she said. She kissed Granny Kathleen, who was weeping feebly again. 'I'll come and see you tomorrow,' she said. 'Don't worry, Granny, it will be all right.' She looked at the attentive face of her husband. Granny Kathleen saw the look and realised that she might have been wrong. Passion may not be everything, she decided — the love on Lydia's face was bottomless. 'Time to go home,' Lydia said to her husband.

She thought with gratitude of her home, the place where she lived with Orlick. She was glad she didn't live at Mallow Hall. She could feel the dissension in the atmosphere almost like a living being. There would be no happiness here now that Martha's calming spirit was no longer within.

The little house in Sandymount was her real home, her haven that she shared with her husband, and she couldn't wait to get back there now.

Chapter Thirty-Five

'You really think he's cheating you?' Orlick asked.

'Oh, I *know* he is,' Lydia answered calmly. She looked around her neat little sitting-room with a sigh of satisfaction.

'But if he is, then your mother's wishes are not being carried out,' Orlick said logically, looking at her with a puzzled frown on his face. 'Aren't you going to fight for what is rightfully yours?'

'Not if it means fighting my brothers,' Lydia replied. 'In the courts, in Dublin. I can't think of anything worse. Speculation in the papers. Everyone picking over our differences. Oh no! That would be horrible.' She paused, thinking, and he smiled tenderly, contemplating her lovely still face. Then she added, 'And if it means so much to Austin and Roland, then so be it. It won't do them any good. Mother always said what goes around comes around. For years I've thought that I was some kind of a monster to be so suspicious of my own brother.' She frowned. 'I thought I was weird because quite frankly I have never trusted Austin — and Roley just blows with the wind. Now I know it wasn't me. Austin is a terrible person and poor Roley is a drunk.'

'It's still wrong to let them get away with it,' Orlick said. 'Come here, honey, where I can hold you.'

She cuddled up to him on the chintz-covered sofa, sighing softly and smiling contentedly. Orlick said, 'Roland was on the verge of blurting something out, I don't know what it was, but . . .'

'I do,' she replied. 'And it will all come right. Eventually.'

He stared at her, perplexed. 'How do you know?' he asked.

'Darling, I love you. Don't let's talk about it any more.'

'Yes, but I can't help thinking . . .'

She sat up sharply, looking at him anxiously. 'Does my losing my fortune make any difference to you?' she asked him.

He laughed. 'Good God no!' he replied spontaneously. 'Hell no! If you were as poor as a church mouse I'd love you to death. But I'm not a fool about money either, and I believe it shouldn't be treated cavalierly. Also, I hate cheats. They shouldn't be allowed to get away with it.'

'He won't,' Lydia told him, meaning Austin.

'Are you going to fight him then? I thought you decided to turn the other cheek.'

How to explain? She did her best and used the same words to her grandmother the next day, the same words exactly, sitting in the little cottage talking earnestly.

The old lady had taken her to task for her lack of action, her acceptance of what they both knew was Austin's duplicity. 'It's like *not* going into battle, Granny. Mother always said that entering a fight rarely paid off. It generates hatred, feuds, resentment, vendettas. Sometimes letting go is the best thing to do, though it seems feeble. It might look the least courageous, but it is the best. It was what Jesus did. Mamma was so wonderful, Granny, so wise, but people thought her impulsive and thoughtless. And she wasn't. There was logic as well as love when she married my father. She wanted to get out of here —' She glanced suddenly at her grandmother. 'Oh, I didn't mean . . .'

'I know you didn't, child. Go on. What you say makes sense. You know something; you sound exactly like her. She could always make me see things clearly.' Kathleen wiped a tear from the corner of her eye.

'Thank you, Granny,' Lydia smiled, thinking of Martha. 'I want to be like her. Mother rose *above* things, Granny. She never stooped to the same level as her opponents or her critics. She never said you've done this to me so I'll do that to you. So you see, engaging in a law suit, a contest against my brothers in this case, is not, I think, what Mamma would have done. Not what she'd want at all.'

'It wouldn't come to that. Austin and that corkscrew character Pius Brady are guilty as hell. You know that. I know that. They'd back down before it became . . .'

But Lydia was shaking her head. 'I can't take that chance, Granny. I think liars come to believe their lies. Really truly believe that their lies are the truth. I think by now Pius Brady and Austin have persuaded themselves that they are doing the right thing, that in law Austin *should* be custodian of the house, the business, the money. I'm a mere woman, after all. Only poor Roley —' She paused, then continued, 'No. I sat in that room yesterday, the room I always see Mamma in, and it was as if she was there with me. I *knew* what she wanted me to do, how she wanted me to behave. It was as if she'd lent, or given, her wisdom to me.' She smiled at her grandmother. 'How could that be?' she asked.

'She was with us there, *alanna*. She was there,' Granny Kathleen said sagely. 'I've felt her presence vividly since she died. When she was in Italy I couldn't sense her at all. Now she's all around us.' Lydia nodded. 'And you think she'd not want you to fight?' the old lady asked.

'Austin and Pius know that I know. They know I'm aware of what's going on. They know I won't do anything. They read me like a book. But, Granny, they are uneasy, so uneasy.' She looked over at her grandmother. 'No good will come to them from this,' she finished. 'No good ever comes from a dark deed.'

It was a gloomy day. It drizzled rain and a chilly breeze blew. Granny Kathleen had a fire in her grate. 'I'll set a fire here from now on,' she told her granddaughter.

Lydia laughed. 'You mostly have one,' she said.

'Well, I'll have one all the time from now,'

Kathleen replied. 'Old bones are cold.'

Lydia realised that the old lady was telling her something. The will to live was slowly flickering out, and days to Kathleen Daly now seemed long and joyless.

It was dark in the little room. The blue and white delftware on the dresser seemed the only colour in the dim interior except for the glowing coals. 'I'm cold, *alanna*,' Granny Kathleen said and shivered. 'A ghost walked over my grave just now.'

Lydia found a shawl and tucked it around the old lady's feet. 'There, Granny. That better?'

'I don't know, Lydia pet. Will I ever be warm again? Martha took the glow with her. She took the rock 'n' roll.' She smiled sadly at Lydia.

'I'll get Varina to bring you Rose,' Lydia said. 'She'll brighten your eyes again.'

'My great-grandchild!' Kathleen drew in a deep breath. 'Oh God, how wonderful. I saw only a bundle yesterday, I was too angry to look. Ah child, you're right. Anger blinds us to beauty. All the beauty that's there. It clouds our vision so that all we can see is evil.'

So they reached an understanding and the will went uncontested. Lydia was never sure what drove her — all she had was a belief that this was the way her mother would have wanted her to act and a firm knowledge that, as she said, dark deeds never paid off. Now there would follow a time of waiting for the will to go through probate.

Chapter Thirty-Six

Pius had influence and was able to push things through, and exactly one year later D'Abru's was sold to an unnamed businessman who kept his identity secret. The workers in both the shop and factory were worried sick about their future but for a long time no one could shed any light on who the new owner was or what he intended to do about the business.

The intervening year was rich in incident. Varina, encouraged by Lydia, took Rose to see her great-grandmother and there developed between the ex-glamour girl and the old lady a firm and loving bond. Varina liked the old lady's brisk honesty and straightforwardness.

Lydia, that summer of sunshine and love, became pregnant. The three of them were often to be found sitting under the apple tree beside Granny Kathleen's cottage, playing with a naked Rose who sat and fell, then toddled and fell, on a rug spread at their feet. The three women watched in contented bemusement as the infant tried to catch the butterflies and stared in fascination as the leaves overhead shifted and cast dappled patterns over everything. They drank tea and talked about fashion and the latest movies, Sybil Connolly's clothes and the new music by the Beatles.

After her third month Lydia stopped going to the shop and factory. She found it depressing. The staff and workers were terrified about their jobs and there was an air of desperation bordering on panic. There was nothing she could say to reassure them for she knew as little as they did. Brosnan Burke was typical: 'I got three kids now, Miss Lydia. Little Janie needs medical care an' this job is the only thing between me an' penury.'

'Maybe the new buyers will keep you on, Brosnan.' Lydia squeezed his arm sympathetically. 'I'll ask them to do that, but I can't promise they will.'

'It's awful,' she told Varina and Granny. 'Those people have worked all their lives for our prosperity and now they'll probably find themselves jobless. Out in the cold.'

'You love that company, don't you, Lydia?' Varina asked and Granny Kathleen darted a quick glance at Lydia. Lydia nodded.

'Yes I do. I remember when I was a little girl, about five years old, and Mamma taking me on my first visit to the factory. Imagine, I was a child whose mother ran a chocolate factory! Wow! Then she took me to the shop and we were given a truffle each and we went up the street to Bewley's and I had a hot milk with mine and Mother had a coffee. I wore my pink nap coat with the brown velvet collar and my matching hat attached to the name-tab at the back with tape.' She laughed. 'So were my gloves,' she said. 'Attached to me with tape.' She tickled little

Rose under her chin. 'Will Mamma do that to you, little pet, I wonder?' she cooed.

'Old acid-face did that to me too,' Varina giggled. 'My mam was dead and old acid-face, as I called Styles, sewed my mittens to the sleeves of my coat and I never wore them. Put them on, I mean, the gloves. Just left them dangling there.'

They all laughed, thinking nostalgically about childhood, pausing, each one, in her own thoughts. Then Varina lifted Rose and held the baby to her breast. 'Why don't you set up your own factory and shop?' she asked Lydia.

'How do you mean?'

'Like my old dad did,' Varina said. 'Why not?'

'But I'd be setting up in opposition to myself.'

'Not now it's sold you wouldn't,' Varina said.

'It would be too much.' Lydia shook her head.

'No it wouldn't. Da would help. It would give him something to do that would remind him of your mother. He's so depressed these days. Lost interest in everything. Except little Rose. But, oh Lydia, he's not himself at all.'

Tom Gallagher was a changed man. The light had gone out of him; his vitality, once so palpable, had vanished. He moped all day; his only interest, his business, had become a bore to him.

Then one midsummer day he'd gone to the kiosk in Booterstown and in a fit of loneliness asked his employee there, an eager young chap called Paddy Mac, for a drink.

'Don't usually at this time, sir,' the young man replied virtuously, wondering nervously if this was a test. He'd been told about Tom Gallagher's pouncing methods and did not want to be caught out. Besides, it was true. He did not imbibe much at all and certainly not this early in the morning.

However, Tom insisted and took the young man around the corner to the local pub. It was dim and smoky, a place where old men gathered and muttered and sucked on clay pipes or chewed on evil-smelling tobacco. He bought Paddy a pint and, returning from the bar, trying to avoid knocking his head against the beams, he glimpsed Austin Tracey and Pius Brady, sitting in a booth at the back, hunched over short ones. There was something furtive in the way the two, half-concealed, were whispering together, something conspiratorial. Tom avoided them, he did not understand why, but he got the impression that this was a secret meeting and intruders would not be welcome. All of which was very odd indeed as the men were co-workers in the solicitors' offices they shared — what the hell were they doing in this out-of-the-way pub whispering together? Then Tom shrugged. It was unimportant and none of his business. But he tried not to let them see him.

'Have you ever thought of going into business for yourself, Paddy?' he asked, putting the pint before the astonished boy.

'Well, sir, I'm, er, happy with you, sir,' Paddy wondered again about tests of loyalty but Tom interrupted him.

'Oh come off it, Paddy, I really want to know.'

The boy stared at him doubtfully.

'Look, Paddy, why don't you buy the kiosk from me? I'd let you have it for a very fair price.'

Paddy Mac, who had just got married, gulped. 'Janey Mac, Mr Gallagher I'd jump at the chance. If the bank will give me a loan —'

'I'll help you with that, Paddy. Recommend you —'

'But, sir, if I can ask, why?'

Tom glanced around. He just caught sight of Pius slinking out of the back door. He looked over and saw Austin, head low over his drink, and something in the slant of his shoulder or the tilt of his head reminded Tom of Martha and his heart twisted with the pain. He drew a deep breath.

'See, it's like this, Paddy. I've done all the work, built up the business. There's no stimulus for me any more. So I thought I'd unload some of my assets. I'm losing interest, Paddy, and that can only be bad for the business. I need, the business needs enthusiasm to succeed and it needs drive and a desire for success. You, Paddy, have those qualities.'

'Yes, sir. Oh yes, sir.' Paddy had two hectic spots of red on his cheeks. An offer like this happened once in a lifetime and Paddy Mac was not going to miss his opportunity. 'I'll have to talk it over with the missus, but she'll agree, I'm confident.'

Tom liked the word, liked the way the boy used it. 'Well, let me know, won't you?'

'You'll have my answer very soon, sir.'

And he did. Tom helped arrange a loan with monthly payments guaranteed that he knew Paddy could manage. He sat back and waited for the others, the more adventurous and ambitious ones, to come forward, put in requests to buy the kiosks they ran so well and profitably for Tom. And they came, thick and fast, from all over the country as the news spread. Tom Gallagher was selling out.

Tom was kept very busy arranging all this, advising the ones he felt would be taking on more than they could handle, who would, he felt, fail, persuading them not to invest, and encouraging the ones he thought would succeed, but every so often he remembered Martha and the darkness settled over him like a storm cloud.

Lydia, who often visited Varina and Rose in Ailesbury Road, found him, one day, alone in his study, head between his hands. She went to him and put a hand on his shoulder. He looked up and there were tears in his eyes. 'I miss her so much, Lydia,' he said.

'I know. So do I,' she replied.

'You've got Orlick,' he said.

'I know. But I still miss her.'

He looked up contritely. 'I'm sorry, Lydia, that was selfish of me. It's just that —' He paused. 'It's just that she seems to be slipping away.'

'Let her go, Mr Gallagher. Let her go.'

'You see, Lydia, I don't want to let her go,' he said.

'I know.'

'I can't bear to lose her.'

'Maybe she wants to be set free. Wherever she is.' He looked at her, puzzled. 'What I mean is, we go on. When we die. We go on. Maybe she feels you are holding her back. Maybe you should let her go.'

'You mean forget her?' His voice was angry. She shook her head. 'No. Oh no! We'll none of us ever forget her. But we have to accept she's gone. Let her free.'

'I seemed to see her the other night,' he said meditatively. 'It was very dark and I could have imagined it. The curtains were billowing out and she was there. I thought it was a figment of my imagination. I still think so — I dare not think otherwise or I'll be dabbling in the occult and mediums and all that nonsense. She said, 'It's all right Tom. It's all right.' Then she was gone.'

'I don't think it was your imagination. The exact same thing happened to me. Those same words. "It's all right, Liddy. It's all right." '

'Are you serious?'

'Perfectly. Only I know it wasn't my imagination. She'd come to reassure me. She always used words like that.'

He hung his head again. 'Perhaps you are right,' he said.

'I know I am.'

'There's such a long time to go, so many days and nights to put in before . . .'

'Before you see her again,' she whispered.

'Yes. It's so boring, filling in the time.'

'There's Rose,' she told him.

He nodded. 'Yes, there's Rose.'

'It's what Mamma would have wanted, you to be happy with Rose. The next generation. I'm sure she had something to do with me getting pregnant. She hustled God up there, wherever she is. Prompted him.' She laughed.

Tom took her hand. 'You're a comfort to me, Lydia. You are so like your mother.'

She smiled tremulously. 'Thank you. There is nothing that could make me happier than to be like her.'

They remained like that as the light faded and the evening came.

Chapter Thirty-Seven

It was a rainy day in late April when Eileen decided to enlighten Pius Brady as to what was in store for him, what her plans were.

She wore for the occasion a red and white checked cotton dress, with starched collar and cuffs, white high-heeled shoes and a little white Pringle cardigan. Pius was startled when she came into his office. His secretary usually wore sensible shoes, a plain linen or wool suit, navy or black, and a neat little blouse, white or cream. The red and white check took his breath away and his look of amazement she mistook for admiration.

'Oh sir, Mr Brady.' Now that the moment was actually here it was harder than she had imagined.

'Yes, Eileen, what is it?' He looked at her quizzically. 'I must say that dress is very . . . fetching. But do you think it is, er, suitable for your position here?'

'Well, sir, I may not *stay* in my position here much longer.'

His heart plummeted. She was, as Martha Tracey had said, a treasure. Young girls, secretaries, nowadays did as little as possible, their minds on boys and rock 'n' roll. Eileen would be hard to replace.

'Oh Eileen, I hope you are not thinking of leaving,' he began but she shook her head vehemently.

'Oh no, no, no, Mr Brady.' She flashed him a wide, toothy smile and he realised he rarely saw Eileen Skully smile. He decided it was perhaps better that way. Eileen's smile was curiously shark-like. Voracious. And she smelled heavily of Coty *L'Aimant,* when usually she did not smell at all.

'Well then?' he asked, mildly perplexed.

'I think we're . . . you and I . . .' It was much, much more difficult than when she played this scene in her dreams. By now he should have leapt to his feet and cried, 'Yes, Eileen, oh my darling, yes. I've thought of you secretly all these years but I never dreamed you felt the same way.' But he just sat there, a puzzled expression on his face. 'You see, sir . . . I think you and I have a lot, a great deal, in common.'

He shook his head. 'I'm afraid you've lost me, Eileen. You're not sick, are you?' It was her woman's time, he decided, and it had hit her rather harder this month than ever before.

She sat down in the chair in front of his desk, the chair that Martha Tracey had sat in well over a year ago now. Pius Brady was suddenly alarmed. This was unprecedented. Was Eileen having a nervous breakdown? He sincerely hoped she'd leave his office before it actually happened. He shrank back into his chair, away from her, and an expression of distaste crossed

308

his face. Eileen saw it and it hardened her resolve. So he was going to be difficult, was he? Well, she'd soon sort him out. He'd be glad enough later on, when he got used to the idea. Okay, so it was a shock. She did not expect him, not really, to embrace her right off — that only happened in dreams — but later he'd adjust, learn to appreciate her wonderful qualities, just as he'd done when she had gone for the job.

He'd not been that keen to employ her, twenty years ago. Like all men, he went for looks, the façade instead of the intrinsic *worth* of the applicant.

The Agency, Dublin's only one, had sent her and five others along for Pius Brady to choose from. She had taken one look at him and made up her mind. He was it. The one.

She had, by devious means — spilling her coffee the next day into the receptionist's lap, running through the Agency's files marked 'current' while the receptionist cleaned her dress — copied the telephone numbers of the other applicants for the job. Those names and numbers were etched on her mind. Each card had a passport-type photo fixed to the right-hand corner so there was no room for error.

Eileen had phoned all these applicants and, imitating the receptionist, had told them that the post was filled. She had turned up in Pius Brady's office next day with the news that all the others had found jobs elsewhere and she was the only one prepared to work for him. Her implication was that he was lucky she had not gone elsewhere and thus had begun their long association.

At first she had waited breathlessly for him to notice her *that way*. After all, it happened in all the films. But he never did. She made herself indispensable to him and prayed for the moment when she could save the day, or his life, and thereby command his attention, his gratitude and eventually his love. But it never happened. The years slid one into the other. She wept into her pillow and many a night she cried herself to sleep. She was frustrated yet eager; hope never deserted her.

And she waited. The years flew by. He came to trust her and rely on her more and more. But instead of coming to his attention as she had hoped, she became more a part of the background. The wallpaper. She had his company all day, every day, and despite the negative situation, she had still believed it was only a matter of time.

Her only competition, Dolly West, was not a candidate for marriage and merely disgusted Eileen. Dolly West was not a contender worth consideration.

Now the day had finally come, the moment was here. Oh, it was not what she had planned but, just as she'd become invaluable to him in his work after his initial reluctance to employ her, so he would become content in his marriage to her after a temporary disinclination.

'We're going to get married, sir — er, Pius. You and me.'

There was a moment's stunned silence. 'Have you gone mad?' Pius asked incredulously. His voice squeaked on a high note he'd never before heard himself use.

She shook her head. Now that it was out she felt much better and rushed ahead. 'It's obvious, sir, Pius. We're meant for each other. Like peas in a pod, you an' me.' She flashed him her toothy smile. 'I love you, Pius, I always have. You've never noticed. You've been too busy, but I knew this day would come. Oh, if only you knew how I've ached for you, Pius.' The Christian name now tripped easily off her tongue. She had used it so often in her dreams.

'Shut up, *Miss Skully*. I think you have taken leave of your senses.'

'Oh no, Pius. We're to be married, no doubt. As from this moment, we're engaged.'

'As from this moment, Miss Skully, your employment is terminated.' He stared at her, bewildered. 'I'll pay you to date . . .' But she was shaking her head decisively. It bothered him that she kept on smiling despite his rejection. She seemed so calmly sure of herself.

Her next statement winded him. 'No, Pius. We'll marry all right. Unless you want the world to know all about your handling of Martha Tracey's will.'

He sat very still while the clock in the corner ticked uncommonly loudly and this alien Miss

Skully, painted and glammed up, stared un-blinkingly at him across the desk.

'I don't know what you are talking about.' His voice sounded feeble even to himself.

'Of course you do!' she replied briskly in that voice she always used to reassure him, a tone he was always grateful to hear. Until now. Oh Lord, until now! 'You "doctored" Martha Tracey's will and now you are hurrying it through probate so you can claim your quarter of the proceeds,' she told him calmly. 'After the sale of D'Abru's, of course, and I believe that will go through smoothly.' She smiled at him again. Oh, that smile. It gave him the shivers. She, his right-hand woman, his confidante, the one person he trusted apart from his mother, now gave him the shivers.

'You are being ridiculous,' he said without conviction.

She shook her newly permed hair. He noticed it now for the first time, the frizzy hair fluffed up around her head. It gave her an odd look, like a lewd and ageing cherub. Good God, she'd had a perm for the occasion!

'No, Pius, I'm not ridiculous. You are. I'm simply telling you what's what. I expect to see our engagement announced in the *Times* and the *Independent* as well as the *Evening Herald* and the *Mail*.' Her voice was suddenly strident. 'If I don't, I intend to go to Lydia D'Abru with a copy of the original will which I've got, safe and sound.' She gave him that awful smile again.

'*Stole,* if you prefer, as we are speaking frankly. You see, you burned a *copy* in that ash-tray.' She pointed to the pristine-clean, cut-glass receptacle and they both stared at it. 'You see, Pius, I'm the one who has been careful all these years. I'm the meticulous one. You didn't even *check.*' Then she stood. 'You know the deal, Pius.' And as he opened his mouth she put up a halting hand. 'No. It is non-negotiable — you taught me that phrase, Pius. Non-negotiable.' She repeated it with relish. 'If the announcements are not in tomorrow's papers or the day after at the latest, then Martha Tracey's genuine last will and testament will be made *public.* Even if Lydia D'Abru, beg pardon, Lydia Fitzmaurice, doesn't want to know her mother's last wishes, which I very much doubt, the papers will. The courts will. The Law Society will. Your professional peers, whom you always accuse of jealousy, will. That will *will* surface. The ball, Pius, is in your court!' And she flashed that terrible smile at him and flounced out of his office, leaving the scent of Coty *L'Aimant* and triumph hanging heavily in the air.

Chapter Thirty-Eight

Pius told Austin about Eileen Skully's astonishing proposal over a couple of short ones in the sawdust pub in Booterstown and to his disgust Austin seemed amused.

'You'll have to marry her, Pius.' Austin could not disguise the glee in his voice. 'Nothing else for it, old chap.'

'Aren't you at all afraid?' Pius asked.

'Not about that.' Austin shook his head. 'A wife can't testify against her husband and all that. You'll marry her all right and then we'll have nothing to fear from her. No, the person I'm worried about is my brother.'

'Roland?' Pius asked incredulously. 'That helpless sot?'

'Yes. Bloody Roland. He's a loose cannon, Pius. You heard him at the reading. He was just about to blurt it all out, only he felt sick.'

'That was ages ago and he didn't, and no one would have listened anyway.'

'I think they might, Pius. I just hope you are right.'

'Look, Austin, if he'd been going to he'd have done it by now. He's somewhere, no one knows where, drinking himself to death. No, we've got nothing to fear from him.'

'Suppose he surfaces all fresh-cheeked and recovered and sells us out? What then?'

Pius hooted derisively. 'And pigs might fly!' he cried. 'Alcoholics do not just get better, Austin.' He shook his head. 'No, forget him. But, Austin, I *can't* marry Eileen Skully. She's weird!'

'Blast! There's Tom Gallagher at the bar. Lean this way. I don't want him to see us.'

'Why not?' Pius asked, but obeyed Austin nevertheless. 'We're entitled to meet. I was your father's best friend, after all. I'm your godfather. Your employer.'

'It looks funny, us meeting here. It wouldn't look funny in town.'

Pius stared at him a moment. 'You're getting neurotic, Austin, you know that?' Pius was serious. 'Paranoid. Jesus! Come on, let's go.'

'And you'll marry the bitch?'

'What choice have I got?'

'None,' Austin said decisively, smirking to himself as Pius slid out the back door.

Pius put the announcement in the papers and Eileen Skully withdrew one thousand pounds from the firm's account, using her power of signature. She informed Pius of what she was going to do. She went to the same Grafton Street jeweller as Shona and purchased a diamond solitaire identical to the one Lydia wore with her gold wedding band on the third finger of her left hand. Pius groaned and wondered what hell he had traded himself into, what terrible future lay in store for him in this appalling union.

Eileen told him he had to give up Dolly West,

315

announced it calmly. He sprayed his coffee all over the papers on his desk in astonishment as she gave him the ultimatum.

'But . . . but . . .' *No one* knew about Dolly. He'd been so sure. No one, yet here Eileen was, the secret name tripping easily off her tongue, casually, as if she said it every day.

'You think I don't know?' she asked complacently. 'I know *everything* about you, Pius Brady.' She wagged a finger at him.

It was creepy and he felt exposed and humiliated. She stripped him of dignity, self-confidence and power with her every utterance.

She gave him no time to think, to plan, to take a breather. With her usual swift efficiency she arranged the wedding — a quiet ceremony in the church in Grafton Street. She knew no one would come so she contented herself with telling him the arrangements. She was feverishly excited and he listened in horror as she ordered him to have Austin Tracey as his best man. She had an old friend from school to be her bridesmaid. Truth to tell, the old friend from school had forgotten her and was taken aback by this sudden request, agreeing to it only because she couldn't think fast enough to refuse.

So Eileen Skully became Mrs Pius Brady and settled into the house in Clontarf with Pius's mother. She proceeded to rule the roost without mercy or any consideration for the needs of either Pius or his mam. She moved through their lives like a tornado.

The house was redecorated, money spent, mealtimes and menus changed and reorganised without consultation and with the merciless efficiency Pius had once admired her for.

Pius Brady lost his bounce. He found his beloved race courses and the bookies banned to him. If he disobeyed he was threatened with exposure and a particularly nasty fate. He could not prise the document from his wife, she would not tell him where it was. She smiled that wolfish smile and told him it was in a safe place.

He was a man in prison, a man whose freedom was only an illusion. He was a man in hell.

Chapter Thirty-Nine

Austin, for his part, brooded. His thoughts, night and day, centred on Roland.

Where was he? What company was he keeping? Austin went as far as asking the police to look for his brother. When they failed to turn up anything he employed a private detective to scour Ireland for him. The detective, a big, tough ex-garda called Mark McEvoy, assured Austin that his brother would be found. 'Unless he's skipped the country,' he told Austin. 'In whatever rat-hole he skulks I'll find him.'

'You just tell me where he is,' Austin said. 'I don't want you letting him know you're on to him. This *is* confidential, isn't it?' Austin's tone was anxious. The Gardi had been suspicious. They had asked awkward questions like why would Roland want to disappear, and was there anything troubling him? Austin did not want the police nosing into their affairs. No, siree.

The big detective nodded. 'Yes, confidential,' he said.

'It's just that I don't want to let the family know I'm chasing him,' Austin explained. 'I want to assure myself that he's okay. They've thrown him out, see.'

The detective didn't want to see. He hated when the clients tried to justify themselves. He'd heard it all before. The people who owed money and got roughed up after he'd found them. *They* often told him the poor chap had come into money. Jesus, some people! The phoney excuses and the genuine article, he could tell the difference from the very first utterance. Even before the client spoke he could spot the real thing, could tell the agonised family trying to find a lost and loved member from the evil-intentioned, and Mr Austin Tracey smacked loudly of the latter. However, Mark McEvoy was in the business to make a living and, his not to reason why, he promised he'd set to to find Roland Tracey.

'What if you don't find him?' Austin asked anxiously.

'You have to pay me anyway,' Mark McEvoy replied calmly, staring straight at him. 'Tough,' he added, seeing the expression of disgust on his client's face.

'It's a swizz,' Austin remarked and the big man shrugged.

'You want the job done, or you don't. It's up to you, makes no difference to me.'

Austin paid him.

He knew Roland inside out and he knew that the drunk had not the stomach to keep up the deception. His brother was weak and so full of self-disgust that it would take very little for him to blab. Shit, he'd almost done so at their mother's funeral. It made Austin break out in a cold sweat just thinking about what might have happened if Roland had completed his sentence, if Roland had remained *compos mentis* for another five minutes. No, more and more he came to see his brother as a threat. A very serious threat.

After that meeting at Mallow Hall Austin had seen his brother only once. Roland had come by the office a few days later, looking for money. He had rolled in reeking of alcohol, uttering threats and demanding cash. Austin and Pius had hustled him into the back room — Eileen was out shopping at the time — and encouraged, no, *pressed* him into signing the consent for the sale of D'Abru's. They had refused to part with a cent until the document was signed and then got rid of him by giving him five hundred pounds. Pius said he would open an account for him at the Bank of Ireland where money would always be available to him. Roland had suddenly burst into tears and told them they were too good, too kind. He slobbered all over Austin, thanking him, and the solicitors finally managed to hustle him out through the back entrance and into the lane behind the offices. It was the last they had seen of him. The last Austin *wanted* to see of him, except — except! There was that worry. It was a constant anxiety, a worm curled beneath everything he did. It lived with him, inhabited his head, his heart, his mind.

Shona was planning the wedding. She was dashing around Dublin looking for a wedding dress. When he cancelled yet another date with her to talk over plans she got angry.

'I never see you these days, Austin,' she told him tersely.

'I'm working to make sure we have a good start. A good life.'

'No! Don't give me that crap any more,' Shona shouted down the phone. 'You're going to behave yourself, Austin Tracey, act like other fellas do. Or else!'

'Or else what?' Austin demanded defiantly. What could she do? he asked himself. He was not in Pius Brady's position. She was nothing, had no power over him at all.

Anyway, he had no time to think about sex or Shona just now. He had other things to think about, more important things. His libido was dead as a dodo and the mere idea of woo-woo disgusted him.

The days and weeks passed and still no sign of Roland. Austin spent most of his waking hours preoccupied about his brother, in a cold fury. He got in the habit of thinking about Roland's movements, speculating, wondering. It made him uneasy. He acted automatically, did the right things, ate meals, went to the office, took on clients, conducted his business and even occasionally took Shona out, but his mind was absent. He had no recollection of any of his activities, walking through his life as if in a dream — yet driven by a fierce energy. While he ate and slept and talked his mind was obsessed, his head full of Roland, Roland, Roland. What Roland would, could, might do, say, let slip. Where, when, how he'd let them all down. It was Roland, Roland consuming his every thought, in bed with him, in the office with him, at meals with him, all, all the time.

He was best man at Pius wedding but could remember nothing of it the next day. Apparently he conducted himself impeccably, but though his body was there his spirit was not. In feverish haste Austin mentally ran ahead of himself all the time. He was never fully present in the day, but constantly in yesterday or tomorrow, thinking about Roland, his mind racing, racing, racing.

All roads led to Roland, so when late that September the news came through that the will had been probated and filed all Austin could think about was whether Roland would find out, how he'd find out and what he would do. They would put D'Abru's up for sale, they had his signature of consent for that, but endless possibilities flitted through Austin's over-active brain about his brother's reaction if indeed he discovered what had happened.

Then Mark McEvoy phoned to tell Austin that he had located the party he was interested in. Roland's whereabouts were discovered. But what now?

'You want me to keep an eye on him?' McEvoy asked when Austin came to his office.

'No.' Austin was decisive. 'No. I'll, em, no, let him be.' He looked into the clear eyes of the big man and tried to keep his own gaze steady. 'He's on the road to self-destruction,' he told him. 'I just want to know where he is in case he needs me and I can help.'

In a pig's eye! McEvoy thought, watching Austin's conflicting emotions cross his face.

'You see, he's drinking himself to death and the family —'

'Yeah, yeah, I know,' the ex-policeman interrupted. 'The family. Is that it then?'

'Yes.'

'Okay. Thank you, Mr Tracey. Glad to do business with you.'

Austin left the detective's office, shivering, trying not to think. He knew what was simmering in his head but he did not want the thoughts to surface. They lurked down there subliminally, deep, deep at the bottom of his mind, squirming like snakes in the mud. In the last weeks the black thoughts had woven themselves into his dreams, become part of his fantasies about his brother. The black thoughts were thoughts of death.

Chapter Forty

Death and Roland. Roland and death. So convenient, so appropriate.

And his brother was courting it, no question of that. He was drinking himself into an early grave. Anyone with a weaker constitution would have been dead long ago. And Roland *wanted* to die, there was no question in Austin's mind about that. He was hell-bent on it. Now, if he had been a healthy, vigorous man, if it was, say, Tom Gallagher, or Pius even, then Austin told himself he would not dream about such an eventuality as death. Certainly not imagine it as a possibility. But Roland! Roland was half dead already.

He was living in North Great Georges Street. A hovel. It was a disused cottage around the corner from Dorset Street, tucked in between a huckster shop — which incidentally sold rot-gut on the side — and a garage used as a storage place for the pub on the other side.

End of September and the leaves falling again and a cold wind off the Liffey. Austin walked past the windowless little hovel. You'd never think anyone was in there, but that was where McEvoy said his brother was. Roland would die in there before the winter was out, no doubt about that, but Austin was in a hurry. D'Abru's had been up for sale, then sold. It had been on the radio, constantly in the news. Had Roland got a radio? Did he in his drunken stupors read the newspapers? When he was sober? *Was* he ever sober?

Austin had to find out. His nightmare was that Roland would talk to someone in a bar, tell them about screwing his sister out of her inheritance, and where would they all be then? Behind bars was the answer to that.

Austin went to Georges Street every day. He lurked, staring at the nasty little pile of bricks, thinking, scheming, a prisoner of his thoughts, his speculations. He would drive the car to Findlater's Church, park it just down from Belvedere. He walked the rest of the way to the hovel. Watched it, smoking constantly, hard-heeling the used butts under his shoe, grinding his teeth. Every fibre of his body was clenched.

At first he'd decided Mark McEvoy had conned him and his brother was not there at all. He had been there, watching the place on and off, for days and days. And nights. Watching and waiting, going over and over in his mind how he would sue the detective for misleading him, how Mark McEvoy would live to regret his association with Austin Tracey. 'Bastard, bastard,' he'd mutter, pulling on his cigarette. 'Bastard.' He'd insist on getting his money back, drag him through the courts, ruin his reputation.

Then one day he saw Roland shambling out of the tumbledown place and into the huckster shop next door. The breath left his body and he relaxed for the first time in months. There was Roland, large as life, before his very eyes. Nothing bad had happened. Nothing yet.

But he was horrified at his brother's appearance. No more roly-poly boulevardier, no more the jaunty stride, the dandy's dress. His clothes hung on him and he looked like a skeleton. Even at this distance he looked crumpled and filthy.

Roland emerged from the dingy little shop moments later, holding what was obviously a bottle wrapped in brown paper.

'Couldn't even wait till he gets off the street,' Austin muttered as Roland pulled the paper from the top of the bottle and, leaning against the side of the shop, put the mouth to his lips and took a swig. The way he did it disgusted Austin. He took the bottle between shaking hands as if it was his mother's breast, as if he was receiving Holy Communion, and gulped it greedily. It slopped over his mouth and chin, which he wiped with the sleeve of his jacket. Oh God, to be so dependent! How appalling. For a second, stirrings of pity tugged at Austin's heart, but he stifled them firmly and disgust returned. This was his brother, a Trinity student, supposed to be a gentleman — a pathetic drunk!

Yes, Austin thought, squashing his cigarette stub out under his foot, rotating it hard on the pavement, yes, there was no place for his brother here. The world would be better off without him.

Chapter Forty-One

Roland had few moments of full consciousness and when he did they were terrifying. He knew then where he had sunk to and what he had become and that was unbearable. Better the delirium tremens, better the nightmare illusion he lived through, hallucinating and passing out. The half-waking delirium he spent most of his time in was not nearly as bad as being aware of his situation. But not quite. The surface thoughts, dreams, fantasies, nightmares, call them what you would, were bad enough, but deep down on another level altogether he knew he was imagining it all. The dark, macabre place where insects crawled all over him was of course the DTs. He knew that; but there was nothing he could do about it so he accepted it as part of his plight. Then, when the craving always with him now became unbearable, he could take another gulp of the poison and win himself a few hours', moments' respite before the horror commenced once more. Depending on how strong the tincture was. Depending on how weakened his body was.

They'd joked about this, Cad and Fishy and himself, assuming the odd victim of alcoholic poisoning they met *had* any control, had any choice in the matter, not realising in their arrogance that there was no choice whatsoever once a certain invisible boundary had been crossed. But the worst of all were those fleeting moments of clarity when he saw his position, rose above himself, as it were, and saw the pitiful, ageing young man, unshaven, unkempt, writhing on his urine-stained mattress in the bare unfurnished room with the naked light-bulb that did not work because there was no electricity. It swung creakily to and fro in the breeze from the paneless window. He could stare at the moon through the broken frame until it multiplied, blurred and turned into blood. Then developed a face, a nameless, horrible face grinning at him, looming down upon him, trying to get him.

Covered in an ice-cold sweat while his body burned at a temperature of one hundred and three degrees, he looked with horror on what he had become. How disappointed his mother would have been in him, her dear youngest. Lovely Martha. How she would have mourned Roland. He was glad she was dead and had not lived to see what he had done with his life.

Yet it seemed to him he'd had no choice. One day he could take it or leave the alcohol and the next he could not exist without it. He'd always enjoyed it, wanted to get pissed, only now he didn't even like it any more yet he had to have it, needed it to stay alive. The booze held him in thrall and squirm as he might there was no way out.

Chapter Forty-Two

He lay on the mattress on the floor, in and out of his hallucinations, weeping, gagging, vomiting green bile and blood and half the time totally out of his mind.

He knew he was dying. It was not possible to live like this. He'd get pneumonia or TB or something else lethal and croak and that would be a relief. What he was trying to grasp was the something he knew he had to do *before* he croaked. It came to him, then slipped away, hovered tantalisingly on the edge of his brain then got pushed aside by the ants.

The ants were large and wanted to invade him. They swarmed all over his body, trying to crawl up his nostrils and into his eyes. It took him all his time to keep them off. Sometimes he lit matches and burned them off. His body was covered in scar tissue and suppurating sores.

What was it? What the hell was it? Then he would see the sweet face of his sister Lydia. Then the intent faces of Austin and Pius, talking about the will. Oh Jesus, the will. It wasn't right. They must not screw Lydia. He'd have to find Austin, tell him.

Then one day at the end of September he opened his eyes and saw his brother standing above him. 'Aus,' he whispered. He tried to smile at his brother. Was Aus disgusted with him? Roland was not sure how long Austin had been there, what he had seen.

'Aus, gotta tell you . . .'

'What, old fella?' Austin sounded kind and he was smiling.

Roland groped for sense. 'Don't sit there, Aus,' he hissed. 'Ants!' he added, nodding his head, concerned for his brother.

'No. I won't.'

'Will you help me, Aus?' There was a chap he'd met went to Alcoholics Anonymous and beat the booze. He'd scoffed at the time but filed away the information just in case. It was just before he'd really crashed out, knowing he was falling, looking at Cad and Fishy, telling them, 'I can't dance your dance any more. The music's gone phut!'

Austin could help him clean up, get help. Phone the friend. What was his name? Ray. That was it. Austin would know — he was a solicitor too. Doing well since he'd stopped drinking.

But there was something else first. 'Aus,' he croaked, 'Aus, listen. We can't do this thing with the will.' He sounded quite lucid. He grabbed his brother's hand. 'Please, Aus. I can't live with it. It's evil, screwing Lydia, not doing what Mamma wanted. Aus, you hear?'

He could feel himself slipping back into the nightmare. He drew on whatever feeble strength he could muster and looked up at his brother. 'Aus,' he pleaded. 'Help. Help me.'

There was a blackness after that, red demons,

such fear in his gut, such terror. All he could think was, oh Aus, help. Help me. Please.

His brother was carrying him. Oh how good, how blessed. Aus would get help for him, he might even get better. He was in a blanket. How tenderly his brother carried him, how he had misjudged him. Blood was thicker even than money.

He was in a car. The leather was sticky against his cheek. He was slipping again into the nightmare but this time underneath it all was hope. A tiny ray of hope. Austin would help him sober up. His brother would help.

He felt the water on his body like a balm. It was so cool, so fresh. It was soothing. Austin must be bathing him. He could see water-lily pads and the cool shade of a weeping willow, green and restful. Like the lake at Mallow Hall. Austin was helping him down, down into the cool green depths, the shimmering waters under the lily pads.

There was a bursting sensation in his lungs, a terrible pain. Maybe the pain was necessary so he could get better. He felt his face surface. He opened his eyes and looked into the eyes of his brother. 'Oh, Aus. Thank you,' he choked, then 'Mamma!' Then that fierce pain again. His heart swelling, a feeling of happiness. He'd done the right thing about Lydia.

Then nothing. Blackness.

Chapter Forty-Three

No one knew who had bought D'Abru's. The staff worried themselves silly. Nellie Byrne, whose mother had worked alongside Bernard D'Abru himself and who was one of the best workers there, moaned to Lydia, 'It's the uncertainty. I can't take the uncertainty, missus. It's killin' me.'

Nellie Byrne, like a lot of the others, took pride in her work, and like the others needed to know what was going to happen. 'We depend on my wages, missus,' she told Lydia. 'An' I got to know if they're gain' to stop an' me be outa pocket.' Lydia did her best to placate them and for the time being everything went on as before. Word came through the bank that they were to proceed as usual, the new owner had no immediate intention of deciding what he wanted to do with his acquisition — a statement Lydia could not bring herself to believe. When she told the bank manager as much he raised his eyebrows and shrugged.

Speculation was rife and Lydia was confused. What was she supposed to do? In the event she did nothing, partly because she did not want to close the outfit prematurely. She waited.

She basked in Orlick's concern for her condition, his support and his love. She told Granny Kathleen, 'I'm so happy, Gran. I feel guilty that I am because Mamma is not here, but I tell myself that she would be glad for me.'

Kathleen pursed her lips. 'An' I'm glad yer happy, *alanna,* an' it's obvious ye are, an' bloomin' like a rose. Still,' she added stubbornly, 'I say ye need a bit of excitement in yer life. A bit o' danger.'

'You can keep your excitement and your danger,' Lydia said tartly. 'I like peace and quiet and I've got it with Orlick.'

Granny Kathleen hooted derisively. 'Much peace an' quiet you'll get with a babby around. Hah!'

'Oh Granny, I don't mean . . . I mean . . .'

'I know what ye mean, love, I'm just teasing,' she said in placating tones. 'I was never like you, though. I wanted the electricity. The tension.' She cocked her head sideways, 'Put the kettle back on the hob; here comes Varina and little Rose.'

It always puzzled Lydia how her grandmother knew of someone's arrival at her home before they entered the cottage door.

The girls greeted each other and Varina deposited Rose in Kathleen's lap. The old lady brightened and began to coo over the baby. Lydia made the tea and the three sat sipping.

'You know where your husband is?' Kathleen asked Varina, who shook her head.

'No, Granny Kathleen. Haven't an idea. Last time I saw him was at the funeral.'

Kathleen's shrewd old eyes narrowed. 'I

wonder what he was about to say that day, the day of the funeral?' she asked innocently.

Lydia rebuked her harshly. She knew what her gran was up to. 'I told you, Granny, I don't want you stirring up trouble.'

Kathleen shook her head. 'God 'n' ye run from it, don't you, Lydia? Like a hare before the hounds.'

'What's that, Granny Kathleen?' Varina asked, watching Rose with adoring eyes.

'Trouble — Lydia'll travel a soul's journey to avoid a scene, God help her.'

'I think she's got sense,' Varina said. Lydia flashed her a grateful look. Granny Kathleen could be a single-minded old bore when she chose to.

'I mean, all the worlds wars and misery would cease if everyone was like her,' Varina continued.

'Anyhow, I've had trouble enough not knowing what to do about D'Abru's,' Lydia protested. 'Those poor people, Brosnan and J.G. and Nelly Byrne, they're riddled with uncertainty. Don't know from day to day what to expect. How's that for tension, Granny, eh?'

'I told you before what I'd do,' Varina said and for the first time Lydia looked at her seriously and did not brush her off.

'You really mean that, don't you?' she asked.

'Mean what? What does she mean?' Kathleen asked.

'Sure I mean it. Dadda is in the process of selling off all his kiosks. He's lost the heart for the whole thing. He'd help, and to tell the truth I'd like to see him involved in something else. He'd get a new lease of life out of a new enterprise. The challenge'd do him good. Specially something to do with your mother.'

'So what are you suggesting exactly?' Lydia asked.

The little room was dappled with bright shafts of light that poured through the cracks in the door and the small windows. The baby gurgled and tried to catch the shimmering beams. The old woman rocked and hummed through her gappy teeth and the two smartly dressed young girls sat on stools, their skirts and petticoats billowing out around their high-heeled strappy shoes.

'What I'm suggesting is, you get a small shop wi' space in the back and you go into business for yourself. Make your own chocolates. Call it Fitzmaurice's Fine Chocolates. Or, better, Lydia's Fine Chocolates. You could start small at first, but I bet it would grow and grow.'

Granny Kathleen was not listening. She said, 'I wonder about Roley. I wonder where he is.'

Varina shrugged. 'I don't *care*,' she reiterated. 'I just hope he doesn't come back to bother *me*.'

Lydia glanced at her grandmother. 'What is it?' she asked.

Granny Kathleen shook her head. 'I dunno, pet. Just a feeling. A feeling about him. Sadness. That poor little boy.' She shivered. 'But then wi' this wee mite in the house how could there be sorrow?' she asked and all three looked at the baby waving her arms and legs and they smiled.

A day or two later Lydia was shocked when she received a letter on a sheet of notepaper headed 'IEL' with 'Irish Enterprises Ltd' printed underneath and an address in Manchester. The letter informed her in complicated business jargon that D'Abru's was now part of the MacMillan & Co Ltd Chocolate and Toffee Manufacturer. They had bought D'Abru's, and the management should prepare itself for changes. Changes, they informed her, that would update, modernise, mechanically upgrade and streamline the old business.

Changes began the following day and after that they came thick and fast. Lydia's services were terminated, as were those of J.G. and Brosnan Burke — summarily dispensed with. They reeled with shock at the suddenness, one day fully employed, the next out on their ears. J.G. nearly wept and Brosnan was so angry he hurt his hand banging it on the counter.

A new manager, a brisk Mancunian with slicked-down hair and a brown three-piece suit, arrived and more redundancies followed swiftly. Desperate employees queued outside Lydia's office in Grafton Street, waiting to know what they should do, where they should go, and she received despairing letters by every post.

Another portly, red-faced man in a navy pinstripe three-piece came to her office and told her that they were putting the shop up for sale at the end of the week. 'I'm sorry, dear lady,' he told her, his eyes and voice full of a sympathy he obviously did not feel. Why should he? He rubbed his hands together and licked his lips nervously in the face of her composure. 'D'Abru's, the shop, is defunct now, I'm afraid,' he told her, 'It's unnecessary, see. MacMillan's will keep the logo, the name on the boxes. We intend to manufacture six times as many sweets as you have been doing.'

Lydia muttered, 'They are not *sweets!*' but he continued, 'We intend a huge expansion, the installation of machinery to do the jobs *people*' — he muttered the word contemptuously — 'did before.'

'The chocolates, Mr Bestwick-Scoff, are *handmade*. They are quality. That is why they are so popular and so expensive.'

'Oh, we'll bring down the prices, make a fortune.' He smiled at her. 'And in the factory it will be a hand that pulls the switch, a hand that guides the boxes on their merry little passage, a hand that pushes the carts.'

'And the rest of the workers?' she asked.

'The floor workers have nothing to fear. Provided they can keep up. Machinery is, you must know, much faster than the human being. Hence our desire to revolutionise the industry. No, if they want to keep their jobs they'll have to pull up their socks. There'll be no place for slackers. We expect everyone to work much faster. Time and motion, you know. Time and motion.'

'Chocolates are made with love,' Lydia re-marked.

Mr Bestwick-Scoff smiled and shook his head pityingly. 'Not any more, Mrs Fitzmaurice, not any more. It is mass production these days if you want to increase the profits.'

'D'Abru's has always been famous for quality,' Lydia put in mildly.

'People don't want quality like that any more. The day of the high-priced product, luxury goods as they are called, is over. The man in the street is being catered for these days and the man in the street doesn't know quality from pig-shit, if you'll pardon the expression. The man in the street has not got sophisticated tastes.'

Lydia thought of the newspaper man who shouted 'Herl er Mail' on the corner of Grafton Street and who came in for his D'Abru truffle once a week to have with a coffee in Bewley's. She thought of the workers who appreciated so much their free box at Christmas. She thought of the bank clerks saving up to give their girlfriends a box of D'Abru chocolates for birthdays. She thought of the medium-paid husband doing ditto for his wife.

'You don't have a high opinion of the *hoi polloi*, do you, Mr Bestwick-Scoff?' she remarked.

'Oh, don't get me wrong, Mrs Fitzmaurice. They are our bread and butter, the men and women in the street. But they are not *refined*. Their taste buds won't know the difference between a quality chocolate and a mass-produced one, believe me. No.' He waxed eloquent. 'The day of D'Abru's is over. Everybody wants everything these days and they want it at affordable prices. Tellies, cars, nice clothes, make-up and perfume, all at affordable prices. Chanel No. 5 will go the way of D'Abru's, believe me. So will Christian Dior. Their days are numbered. The public are demanding equality and by God we'll see the demand is met. Everyone will be able to afford D'Abru's chocolates, we'll see to that.'

'But it won't *be* the real thing,' Lydia protested mildly. 'It's a con trick, Mr Bestwick-Scoff. And surely there should be room for both, the expensive and the cheap?'

He shook his head. His face was smooth as silk and he smelled of some sickly aftershave, certainly *not* an expensive one, Lydia realised. 'You don't realise what is happening, Mrs Fitzmaurice, if you'll forgive me for saying so, tucked away in this little backwater here. In England your average Joe and Jane are getting what they want. Their heart's desire. I'm wearing Gilbert Macabelly's Catalogue for Gents. Every bit as stylish as Gieves & Hawkes, but cheap. Affordable.' He looked at her for confirmation but saw none in her face. Undaunted he continued, 'Mary Quant, Laura Ashley, Marks and Spencer, Terence Conran, Barbara Houlinickey — they all provide affordable goods, satisfy a demand, get very rich.'

'Any of those make chocolates?' Lydia asked.

Mr Bestwick-Scoff shook his head. He was becoming a little impatient. Time was money, money was time.

'No. But MacMillan does. We intend to expand distribution. Our outlets should reach Great Britain as well as Ireland, and eventually America.' His eyes lit up at the mention of the USA. 'And that's where the *real* money lies.'

'So that's the priority,' Lydia remarked. 'Money.'

'Of course. What else? Money is power, power money.'

'And quality is secondary?'

'Who cares about quality these days, Mrs Fitzmaurice? I'm afraid you are living in yesteryear. We'll make a fortune.'

'Well, good for you,' Lydia said sarcastically. 'You can run a slogan, "You too can afford D'Abru's chocolates".'

He took her seriously. 'What a splendid idea. I'll remember that. Sure we can use it.'

Lydia was angry. She telephoned Varina as soon as the pompous Bestwick-Scoff had gone and her sister-in-law said to come right over. 'I've talked to Dadda and he's a little half-hearted about it all at the moment, Lydia, I'm afraid. So do come. He needs prodding.'

'Well I don't know, Varina — if your Dadda is lukewarm maybe we should forget the whole thing.'

'No, Lydia, this is the best idea I ever had and

it is going to be perfect for him, do him the world of good. I'm determined to go into it with you. I'm that excited. So come on over at once.'

Chapter Forty-Four

Varina had been thinking. Lydia's life in the factory and the sweetshop seemed to her the height of style. She looked back on her life as a pretty doll dependent for her happiness on men — her dadda or a husband. The thought depressed her. She had been brought up to be an ornament, nothing more. Dressing up so the boys would wolf-whistle now seemed to the young mother demeaning. I'm worth more than that, she decided, and the idea of going into some class of business and becoming financially independent seemed very appealing. D'Abru's entered her mind and took hold of her imagination.

She had suggested it to Lydia that day in Granny Kathleen's without giving it deep consideration and afterwards it began to appear to her as an answer to all her problems.

She knew her Dadda would never see her want for anything but that was no longer enough. She had seen Lydia buying this and that without thought, without reference to anyone else. She had envied Lydia her little house in Sandymount, decorated in the way Lydia herself had chosen. She disliked having to ask her father for every blessed thing she wanted for little Rose. She'd seen Lydia open the till in D'Abru's and say to Brosnan, 'I didn't take my full salary on

Saturday, Brosnan. I'll just grab fifteen now and you can enter it and let me sign the book,' and Varina realised that Lydia got money every month that she could do anything she liked with.

Lydia commanded a salary! It seemed amazing to Varina. She got *paid* to do something she liked, *loved,* and it made her independent. Varina had watched and learned from her sister-in-law. She liked what she learned and made up her mind to grab herself a slice of the cake. She expected to work hard for it. She wanted something to work hard at and make her feel useful.

Tom Gallagher in his dark living-room drew in a sharp breath when Lydia entered, Varina in tow. Varina could no longer call Styles 'old acid-face' for the housekeeper had melted for Rose. The baby had wound itself around the severe woman's heart and thawed her completely. She dripped over the baby, doted, cooed and in general lost all her sharp edges. She took every opportunity to look after Rose and had her now on her lap in the kitchen.

Tom thought for a moment that Lydia was his beloved Martha returned to him. In the dim lighting of the room Lydia was a carbon copy of her mother, so it was a while before he could marshal his thoughts and catch the drift of what his excited daughter wanted him to do.

'Oh no Varina,' he cried firmly when he twigged what she was about, 'I've just sold off the last of my kiosks, I'm not about to go down that road again.' 'Then what *are* you going to do?' his daughter demanded. 'Sit here day after day moping? Waiting to die? You'll get senile, Dadda, and I'll have to look after you. You'll die of boredom and become a grouchy old man before your time.'

Tom looked at his daughter in surprise. He'd never known her to be so incisive, so determined. 'This, er, enterprise you girls want me to invest in, I'll, er, think about it,' he said, looking at them from under beetle brows.

'Oh no, no, no!' Varina stamped her foot. 'It will be too late then, Dadda. I want you to make IEL an offer *now* for the shop in Grafton Street. See, they've put it on the market and . . .'

'You see, Mr Gallagher, it was where D'Abru's started,' Lydia said, 'We can get a small staff and operate from there. If my ancestor did it, so can I. Some of my workers will want to help me I know that. They are artists, like mother was.' Tom glanced at her sharply. Did she know how it affected him when she spoke of her mother? He supposed not. He thought of Martha, what *she'd* want. Was she here in this room prompting him?

'You see, Mr Gallagher, I can't agree that people don't care about quality any more. And I think the public can taste the difference. I do not underestimate the "man in the street" as Mr Bestwick-Scoff tried to tell me.'

'Mr Who?' Tom looked at her in disbelief.

'It was his name. Bestwick-Scoff.'

'Jesus!'

'He's going to mass produce D'Abru's chocolates in an extended factory using machinery instead of people.'

'But they are *hand-made* Lydia. How can you have hand-made chocolates produced by machine? I ask you!'

'Well they'll taste like any old chocolates you can buy in one of your kiosks Mr Gallagher,' Lydia said, 'They'll become ordinary. Not something special any more.'

'All right, all right,' Tom cried, capitulating and Varina and Lydia whooped in delight. 'You win. But I tell you girls, it's not going to be easy. It will be an uphill struggle.'

'I know. I know, Dadda, but we'll put our backs into it . . .'

'I hope not literally, Lydia, in your condition,' Tom permitted himself the warning with a smile.

'Mr Gallagher, I can run the whole thing from my Mamma's chaise,' she cried, 'and that, I hope, will not be necessary. I know the business inside out. I'm healthy. I'll have Varina to help.'

Varina, sitting on the leather sofa beside Lydia nodded. 'Yes, Dadda. We have it all worked out.'

'I'm going to get together a small dedicated staff, my best workers, the ones who don't want to stay with MacMillan's. We'll produce the finest hand made chocolates. I'll . . .' She glanced at Varina. 'We'll,' she amended, 'give them shares in the company so they'll be happy to work hard, make it a success. It will give them an incentive. The harder they work, the more chocolates we sell the more money they'll make. I'll

put it to Brosnan to stay. He's a brilliant manager and trustworthy. Varina and myself can
pitch in, half a day each, look after the customers.'

'You can't keep the name though can you?'
Tom asked regretfully. Lydia shook her head.
'Pity,' he said.

'No. I think the premises are more important,'
Lydia told him, 'People are used to buying chocolates there, in Grafton Street. They'll not notice
the name change.'

He thought how pretty they looked, the two of
them, his daughter and Martha's beautiful child
sitting there like stars shining in the gloom of the
room. They were full of hope and vitality. He admired their enthusiasm and although he could
not summon up a like enthusiasm he pledged
himself to help them all he could. In a moment of
utter bewilderment he felt a rush of air (from the
open window? the door?) and a sigh and a long
yessss.

Chapter Forty-Five

The bid was made in the name of Tom Gallagher's business. Under the name Gallagher Kiosks a competative offer was made for the premises in Grafton Street. No one guessed where the bid came from. No one dreamed that the shop would remain unchanged, the premises used for the production of hand made chocolates. It was assumed that Tom Gallagher would sell cigarettes there and people tutted and said it would lower the tone of Grafton Street. And when the word got out in the business world people nodded their heads sagely and murmured how sharp Tom Gallagher was. 'Bet he got it for a song, from Lydia and those awful brothers,' they said, 'He sold up all the tacky little kiosks he had all over the place, little gold mines they were so he could rise in the world,' they whispered, 'Grafton Street no less!' and they waited for the façade to change.

It did. The brown and gold turned to deep wine-red and gold and to the amazement of the curious Lydia D'A's Fine Chocolates appeared over the frontage and the D'Abru girl, Mrs Fitzmaurice as she had become proudly pregnant, and her sister-in-law, the bold Varina Tracey whose husband had taken to the bottle were to be seen conducting business as if nothing had happened, as if D'Abru's hadn't been sold out from under them at all. It was a very strange kettle of fish indeed.

Brosnan was only too happy to stay on and was thrilled to find himself possessed of shares in the newly formed company. Some of the factory workers, lured by the higher wages and the MacMillan promise of all sorts of perks remained in the factory under the new management. Rumour had it that they were pressurised into working so fast that they spent all their time dazed in a zombie-like condition. Nelly said, 'Sure it's not the Irish way at all God help us, now is it Mrs Fitzmaurice, I ask you.' A handful of oldtimers and younger women who did not trust the new slick management were eager to come to work with Lydia and they too were given shares which energised them in a way Mac-Millan's could not. They were determined to make a go of the enterprise.

It was a nice place to work, everyone pulling together. The atmosphere in the little shop was light-hearted yet busy. Customers came, as they always had as if nothing had changed. Business never ceased, the takings remained high and a lot of people were unaware that anything at all had happened or that there had been a change at all. Sometimes Lydia herself forgot this fact.

If the front of the premises was cheerful and busy so was the cramped space at the back. Lydia and Nelly Byrne taught Varina how to roll chocolates and the two girls and the workers collapsed in laughter at her initial efforts. They worked to music and they worked hard, much harder than they could be persuaded to in Mac-Millan's. They were playing for high stakes and all were determined that they would succeed.

Tom Gallagher often visited. It cheered his bruised heart to see the laughing girls working so hard, so eagerly, the customers leaving with smiles on their faces, the radio playing music or Joe Linane chatting and the warm succulent smell of chocolates permeating everything.

He examined the books and found them healthy. He left the management to Brosnan as he had always done with the managers in his kiosks. He found himself completely in tune with Lydia; 'Always give them responsibility' he'd say and she agreed. 'It was what Mother always said.' He admired her straightforward way of doing business, her acumen.

She was a peacemaker, he realised, a healer, a loving spirit and she drew people together, poured balm on wounds and forgave easily. He had a shrewd idea what had happened about D'Abru's and Mallow Hall and while at first he'd been outraged at her submission and refusal to fight for her rights as time passed he began to see how intelligent her tactics were.

She was happy. From what he could tell she had all she needed and wanted. Life, for her was sunny whereas fighting would have put her under a terrible strain, a depressing arena and the dishonesty, the fraudulent machinations of Roland and Austin had certainly brought them no happiness, no rewards, no peace.

Lydia, Tom decided, whether consciously or unconsciously was wise beyond her years, and the girl had her priorities right.

It was not long before Varina and Lydia had their own accounts in the Royal Bank of Ireland on College Green along with a loan to the firm of Lydia D'A's Fine Chocolates. That was being paid off promptly and much quicker than expected.

Tom was surprised at how much he enjoyed the shop, how happy he was driving to the city meeting cronies for a drink then popping down Grafton Street to Lydia's. He would entice Lydia or Varina, whichever one of them was there, to take a break and have a coffee or lunch with him in Bewley's or Jammet's then return to the house in Ailesbury Road to Styles and Rose and the joy of that child. He had never see Varina so happy, so busy, so fulfilled.

MacMillan's were furious when they realised who had bought the shop in Grafton Street and for what purpose it was going to be used. According to Nelly Byrne heads rolled. The pompous Mr Bestwick-Scoff was 'axed' she quoted.

Nelly was having an affair with J.G. and leaving the factory had not halted it and he told her what went on there. 'He's workin' himself inte the ground,' she told Lydia, 'Poor fella. He's no good te me any more, if ye know what I mean. Man says that sometimes he thinks the bloody machinery is running ahead o' them. *It's* in control of them, not the other way around.'

But there was nothing MacMillan's could do about Lydia's enterprise. They were flooding the market with D'Abru's brown and gold boxes, a slightly inferior quality box it was true, but after an initial flurry of excitement and a jump in sales things had slumped and it seemed a lot of people preferred to trudge to Lydia D'A's Fine Chocolates to purchase the quality product. 'They're not eejits y'know,' Nelly Byrne protested, 'The public. They're not fools. The chocolates MacMillan makes taste gastly! I know they're cheap, but people who can't afford ours prefer to pay the extra and buy Cadbury's or Bourneville or some other medium-priced chocolates. I think they've bitten off more than they could chew. For all their talk of time and motion and cheap available goods they've forgotten that people are not idiots.'

Lydia tried the offending product and although they were tasty they could not compare with the original hand made product and had a tendency to leave a bitter taste in the mouth.

Varina came to the shop every morning for one week and every afternoon during the next. When she wasn't there Lydia was. They boxed and cored the chocolates and sold them as fast as they could produce them in the back under the supervision of Brosnan. It delighted them that they were beginning to make money and Varina was thrilled to have an interest outside the home. Lydia had always had this outlet but Varina particularly appreciated the escape from domesticity. She loved little Rose to distraction but it was wonderful nevertheless to get out and really do something creative, communicating with other people, the chat, the craic, the ups and downs of other's lives mingling with her own.

The little group were duly rewarded with success. They were wise enough to know that provided they did not become greedy as their rivals had done they would do very well indeed. As time passed the enterprise became more and more successful, more and more solvent.

Lydia's baby was born. Orlick waited with Tom and Varina, Dr and Mrs Fitzmaurice in a state of near panic, but a smiling nurse came to announce that Mrs Fitzmaurice had had a fine healthy eight-pound baby boy.

With Orlick's blessing she called the baby Bernard after her father. Orlick was so happy, so proud of her, so ecstatic at being a father that, he said, he'd not care *what* she called him. Dr and Mrs Fitzmaurice were a bit miffed but they could not disrupt such evident content and harmony. Bernard Fitzmaurice opened his eyes and became part of one of the happiest most loving households in all Ireland. 'He's a lucky little beggar,' Tom said. 'Only he knew.'

Chapter Forty-Six

Austin sat in the sawdust pub with Pius Brady. They had fallen into the habit of meeting there for a drink. The conspirators. But no Roland.

Pius had been sitting in their usual booth muttering to himself about the unfairness of life when Austin put a hand on his shoulder, startling him out of his monologue.

'Jasus Mary and Joseph,' Pius cried, 'You put the heart across me!'

'Never mind that,' Austin's tone was tense, but Pius interrupted him, 'Listen to me, I'm having the grimmest time imaginable. You can't imagine how that woman, that bitch . . .' Austin dutifully listened as Pius droned on and on hardly pausing for breath listing a catalogue of mind-numbing grievances mostly about Eileen. He did not seem to realise he was boring Austin to death and in any event his partner was only half listening to him.

'She's a monster Austin! Medusa isn't in it. No, Medusa was a saint compared to Eileen. Lucretzia Borgia is nearer the mark. No Irma Greck. Jesus, Mary and Joseph, my poor mam! She's beside herself. Gone into a decline so she has and who's to blame her? It's war Austin. Total war. The two of them'll kill each other one fine day. Not that that would be a bad thing. I'm sick to death of the both of them. Reaching the end of my tether. Time was, Austin, a man could come home from his days toil and find peace. A meal, hot and appetising would be served; a good tasty stew, a casserole full of goodies, or my Mam's *pièce de résistance,* dumplings in a beef hot pot. Oh my God,' he cast his eyes up to heaven in ecstacy at the memory, then looked at Austin, 'We eat *salads* all the time now,' he said despairingly, '*Salads,* I ask you! I *hate* salads. Steak and onions, God what wouldn't I give for a juicy T-bone and fried onions of an evening, but she's forbidden them. She never lets me outa her sight, counts every penny I spend, asks for receipts! Can you believe it! Buys herself Sybil Connelly dresses and French perfume. *French* perfume, mind you, at a fiver an ounce. Jasus!'

Austin watched him as he talked. He had aged, Austin reflected, his face lost its golf-course weathered look, the skin faded, grown greyish and wrinkled, the eyes poached-egg and the chin sagging. He knew himself to have grown pale and haggard too. It did not seem fair that the dividends, the money in the bank were not reaping a happier reward.

If only he could forget that face, those words. 'Help me!' 'Thank you, Austin.' They rang in his ears, reverberating down the dark days and nights of his life. 'Help me!' 'Thank you, Austin.'

And that face, that face beneath the water, bloated, the eyes popping, that grisly vision haunted his dreams and would not go away.

He was so tired all the time. Utterly exhausted morning noon and night. Whenever he passed Lydia D'A's Fine Chocolates in Grafton Street he thought about how he would feel if he was his sister. He could not imagine how she must feel. Yet he tried to console himself that she looked happy. He'd glimpse her glowing face, alive and vibrant, animated, full of excitement and laughter, lit up from within. He'd forgotten what it must feel like inside to look like that. If he'd ever known. What did she have? What spark made her glow so brightly? What fund of joy dwelt within her to have it flow abundantly over and out into other peoples lives? Austin could not imagine. He'd say to himself, well we didn't do her any harm, did we? And wonder at his despondency, his despair. There was no light in his life. And he would walk on past as if he was a fugitive. He never went in to the shop. He remained outside, outside the circle of light, alone and isolated.

He lived alone at Mallow Hall. Shona had gone long ago, left him with bitter words. He missed her dreadfully. He had a nasty suspicion that he was in love with her. He could have found her again, phoned her, pleaded for a reconcilliation endeavoured to change his behaviour, but he was afraid.

Afraid all the time. Afraid of any close relationship, afraid he would talk in his sleep, let slip something he shouldn't know, afraid of the demons that beleaguered him and would not be shaken loose.

He went on a pilgrimage to Croagh Patrick. He climbed the mountain barefoot, the stones cutting his feet to ribbons. He bled and it was agony and that helped. In the misty dawn he wept and the poor priest thought he might be a saint. He smiled at the priest who blessed him telling him he was God's beloved child and he felt the balm of mercy for a short while, but it did not last. The priest said no peace would come unless your conscience was clear and Austin's very essence was riddled with 'Help me' and 'Thank you Austin'. He felt healed but it did not last and the haunting continued.

He had money now, all he needed, all he could possibly want but he could not think what to spend it on. His taste for the good life had evaporated. Food did not interest him, neither did drink. He might get drunk and blab and he could not afford to do that. He could not afford to relax even for a moment.

Roland would have talked. He was going to, Austin was certain, he'd said as much before he died.

Before he died. That was the nub of everything. That was what Austin could not get out of his mind, that death. Oh Jesus that terrible death. 'Help me' 'Thank you Austin'. The piteous face of his brother, the trusting face.

No, he did not need the money now, there was nothing he wanted to spend it on.

And Mallow Hall was lonely. Unoccupied, it had fallen into disrepair. It needed attention badly. Austin could have spent some money on that but he couldn't be bothered. It needed enthusiasm and he was bereft of that. The house had become damp and musty, dusty and neglected and the gardens once Martha's pride and joy were overrun with weeds. He wondered sometimes why he had ever wanted the place and could not remember.

He packed Eilish and Nonie off. They might hear him say something incriminating. It was unlikely but he did not dare to take a chance. They were glad enough to leave. The house was no longer the happy place it had been when Martha was alive and Lydia brought her boyfriends home and they had their bequests to console them. They had no desire to remain in the dark gloom of the big house any more.

Then he heard that Nonie had gone to work for Lydia and Tom Gallagher had coaxed Eilish out of retirement to help Styles with little Rose and the housekeeping by doing the cooking. Styles had elevated herself to the position of nanny and as she had never been anything other than a tolerable cook Tom was pleased as punch when the cook from Mallow Hall, creator of those delicious and inspired meals came to work for them.

So Austin lived alone at Mallow Hall and the roof began to leak and the bedrooms smelled damp and the gardens collapsed into chaos and all its beauty was disguised. A creeping decay began to eat away at what had once been beautiful, warm and welcoming, and in the lake behind the trees a body decayed and in the house a man's soul began to rot.

Chapter Forty-Seven

Then one morning in the post Austin found that Shona Donnelly was bringing a lawsuit against him. She was suing him for Breach of Promise, a humiliating class of a situation for a solicitor to find himself in. That was the purpose of this meeting with Pius, to discuss with his fellow conspirator how he should deal with the lawsuit. But Pius was droning on and interminably on about his terrible wife.

'. . . And if she comes into my bedroom in the middle of the night telling me she has 'the urge' I'll . . .'

'Shut up, Pius, and listen. What should I do? About Shona?' Austin demanded.

'You should have married her. Or never proposed to her,' Pius, irritated at being interrupted, replied succinctly.

'I could deny it all. Say she was lying.'

'You could. But she'll call me and Eileen to testify that we heard her say you were engaged. And I'm not going to perjure myself,' he said piously. Austin hooted giving him a contemptuous glance and Pius amended, 'Well even if *I* did to save your skin, Eileen wouldn't. God she's a hard one that . . .' 'Shona,' Austin interrupted wanting to keep him on the track. 'Well unfortunately she's got Owen Moore, the snotty little git, so smart he'll cut himself to represent her. He'll prove you didn't *deny* it that day in the office,' Pius said. 'That's all he's got to do. And you got her a ring, didn't you? That was a mistake old fellow, a bad mistake.' He shook his head and added, 'Put you right in the shit old chap, no mistake,' and he laughed.

Austin turned and grabbed the lapels of his jacket roughly. His red-rimmed eyes were blazing. 'Don't you laugh at me you bastard,' he hissed. Pius gasped at the murderous expression in Austin's eyes. 'Jesus!' he shrank back from the burning eyes, 'Take your hands offa me Austin Tracey or I'll have you arrested.' Austin let go so abruptly that Pius nearly fell off his seat. He looked at Austin with horror. 'What the hell's the matter with you? Jesus man have you lost your marbles?' 'Arrested! You'll have me arrested! Don't make me laugh! You don't want the Gardi poking about in your life now do you?' Austin leaned close to Pius and the older man could see his companion was possessed by terrible inner turmoil. It emanated from him like an aura. There was something not normal in Austin's eyes, a wild look Pius did not trust. He began to feel nervous.

Ever since his mother's death Austin seemed to Pius to become more and more obsessive. Paranoid almost. Insanity lurked behind those eyes. Pius stared back. 'You all right Austin?' he asked in placating tones. No reply. There was silence as Austin stared at his pint morosely. Pius cast about for something to say. 'How's Roland? You catch up with him?'

If he'd hoped to placate his friend he failed. To his terror Austin drew back his lips over clenched teeth and snarled at him, 'What makes you ask that?' he whispered hoarsely. 'You been spying on me?'

'No, Austin. Course not. I just haven't seen Roland and I wondered had you? Has he been up to Mallow Hall? Claim his inheritance?'

Austin was staring at him fiercely. 'You bastard. Yes. He's at Mallow Hall.' He lowered his voice and leaned closer to Pius. 'In the lake. Roland will bother us no more.' Austin's flushed face, filmed with sweat, his eyes glowing like hot coals, swam before Pius's astonished and horrified gaze. It took a minute or two to assimilate what he had just said. Once he'd digested it he sprang to his feet, knocking over his pint. 'I don't want to hear this,' he said, calmly as he could, but decisively, 'I'll not listen to your ravings, Austin. Pull yourself together, man, for God's sake.' Austin grabbed at his jacket again. 'But listen, Pius,' he cried wildly, 'You've got to hear. You are the only one I can tell.' Pius pulled his coat free of Austin's grasp. 'No, Austin,' he said firmly, loudly, 'I do not *want* to hear this. Understand?' And as Austin opened his mouth he cried, 'Go to Clarendon Street to confession, but not to me. I want to hear nothing of your jabbering. Absolutely nothing, Austin. And I think it better we don't meet again. Okay? Goodbye.'

Austin tried to catch him again but Pius was suddenly calm and firm and strong. 'Get hold of yourself Austin, I beg you. And remember I'll deny anything to do with you or your family so keep your mouth firmly shut.'

And he marched out of the pub, ducking his head as he went to avoid the beam. Austin was left alone, his head sunk low on his chest, demons gnawing at his brain.

Chapter Forty-Eight

Tom Gallagher decided it was time he tidied things up. Varina could not live forever in limbo, married but alone, not knowing where her husband was, whether he was alive or dead. He decided to investigate the whereabouts of Roland Tracey so that he could sort things out and perhaps have his daughter's marriage annulled. In order to expedite things as quickly as possible he went to see the main man in Dublin for this sort of thing; Mark McEvoy.

The big ex-cop nodded when Tom explained his mission, but hesitated, then told Tom, 'Look I don't want to cause a family squabble but I've already been asked to find this person, Roland Tracey. I did the job and as far as I know, that was that.'

'Oh?'

'Yeah. Can't tell you who was looking. Unethical. But what I can tell you is *where* he was found. Where I found him.' He gave Tom the address and Tom had to be content with that.

He found the hovel, could not believe anyone could possibly exist in such a place but when he made enquiries in the vicinity he found out that Roland Tracey had, indeed inhabited this terrible place and for some time. But, the neighbours said they had not seen him around for a long time now. 'It's not surprisin' though,' the little man who owned the huckster shop next door told Tom. He had his hand in a strategically receptive position, moving it under Tom's nose, palm cupped upwards.

Tom pressed a ten shilling note into it and the little man's eyes widened. He wrinkled his forehead and said, 'Now dat I tink of it, 'twas the last time I seen him, a fella took him away in a green coupe.'

Austin. That was Austin. Had to be. Austin had a green Buick coupe. Not many of those cars around, besides it was the odds. Who else would want Roland Tracey?

'Haven't seen hide or hair of him since dat night,' the man said, 'Stoned outa his mind he was. Like always. Rat-arsed. Leanin' on dis fella he was. Fella dragged him inte de car, de fella dat owned de coupe.'

The ten bob note had disappeared and the cupped palm was once more waving gently beneath Tom's nose.

'What he look like,' Tom pressed another ten bob note into the eager hand. 'The fella owned the coupe?'

'Him? Oh he was a big fella. Heavy set. Sandy red-faced fella. Coulda been a working man only he was dressed proper. Professional like.'

Austin. Had to be.

So where had Austin taken his brother? It was damned suspicious.

'Can you tell me exactly when this was?' Tom

asked the little man. The hand was empty again and it rose now, palm upward once more, posed gently beneath Tom's chin. 'Wha?' Tom put another note into it. 'God bless ye mister. Yes. 'Twas last year. The last day of the month. I remember cause 'twas de day I got me new brogues. I get a pair once a year. Me feet hurt somethin' shockin' standin' all day and 'twas dat evening I saw de big fella drag poor ould Roland to his car an' him paralitic. Three sheets!'

At home that night Tom told Varina his news.

'I don't care Dadda,' she said, 'It doesn't matter to me where he is.'

'Well I think it will,' Tom replied, 'Eventually. You'll not remain alone all your life, please God, so darling I think we should get things sorted now so that when and if you find someone else you'll not have a lot of obstacles in your way.'

'I don't want to meet anyone Dadda. Men are awful!'

He grinned at her. 'Oh I don't mean you,' she told him, 'But most of them are and I don't want to go through all that pain ever again.'

'Some men are trouble, I agree. But think of Orlick. Lydia and Orlick have a wonderful relationship.'

She shrugged, 'I suppose,' she hesitated, 'I suppose you are right Dadda. But I've no intention of letting any fella take me for a ride again.'

'So I'll go ahead? At the worst it will free you from Roland, pet. Give him no legal rights over little Rose.'

'Oh Dadda, yes. That would be good.'

'So the bold Roland was last seen being driven away by his brother from that grim little slum in Dorset Street,' Tom mused.

'What'll you do, Dadda?' Varina asked indifferently.

'I don't know, darling, I don't know.'

There was nothing more Tom could do and Mark McEvoy advised him to let it rest. 'I've followed every lead but they go nowhere. It's a full stop Mr Gallagher.' He smiled at Tom. He liked him, the straightness of him, the honesty. 'I'll keep my eyes and ears open for you and if anything turns up I'll let you know.'

'Thank you,' Tom said.

'See, it's a puzzle. All the dates are correct. I told Mr Tracey, the brother the week before where Roland Tracey was. Gave him the address just as I gave it to you. So he musta gone and got him.'

'What I want to know is where he took him. I want to find him because . . .' Here we go again, thought the detective and sighed, '. . . married to my daughter. She's not seen him since the wedding. Well, *hardly* seen him and only in the company of others and I think she should get shot of him once and for all.'

Mark McEvoy looked into the clear blue eyes of his client. He had long decided that Tom was one of the good guys but there was nothing he could do for him at this moment in time. 'I don't know how to help you sir,' he said, 'But I'll try.'

Then as Tom opened his wallet he shook his head, 'No. No sir, I won't take anything from you now. Let's see if I turn up anything first.' And Tom Gallagher had to be satisfied with that.

Things rested there for a while. Tom heard about the breach of promise suit and shook his head. How had his beloved Martha produced two such idiots he wondered. Austin and Roland, so grandly named, such messers. Both had failed miserably in their relationships with the opposite sex. He could only think it was the lack of a father that had pushed them into the mire.

Time passed and life caught up with Tom. Surrounded by Rose and his daughter and the business he was busy, and so he found little time to mope. It was what Varina and Lydia hoped would happen.

Varina insisted on redecorating the house in Ailesbury Road. 'It's old and dark and dismal Dadda,' she told him, 'We haven't decorated since Mamma died and I want a nice cheerful place for Rose to grow up in.' As usual Rose swung the argument. Tom liked his dark home. For him it was a tranquil place, but the use of Rose as a weapon invariably worked so he shrugged and gave in and soon the house was swarming with painters and decorators and he felt like a stranger in his own home. To his surprise he found he quite liked the change. It gave him a sense that something new was happening, the change would bring a more cheerful future.

But the constant presence of workmen and people milling around was eventually more than Tom could stand so he proposed that they take a house for the summer and leave Ailesbury Road to the workers and enjoy what promised to be a glorious holiday away from it all. 'We'll not return until it is all done and the place comfortable and habitable again.' They say if you want to give God a good laugh tell Him your plans.

Chapter Forty-Nine

The house they rented was in Portmarnock. Lydia, Orlick and little Bernard joined Tom, Varina and Rose. They insisted Granny Kathleen came with them which she was only too pleased to do, being unable, she said to do without the children. 'They've brought new life to me,' she told Tom, 'An' it would be grand now to spend time in the house with them. An' Portmarnock was where I went once with Liam. 'Tis a lovely place.'

Nonie and Eilish had to come with them for how would they manage without? Styles who never left the house in Ailesbury Road and who disapproved of the changes there was prevailed upon to come as well. 'You'll go mad and kill one of those poor workmen,' Tom told her. 'You can't stay there by yourself. You'll do something you'd swing for. Besides, what will you do without Rose? And more to the point, what will Rose do without you?'

'Mebbe darlin' little Rose'd say somethin' an' I'd miss it,' she agreed. Tom told her they couldn't manage without her so they all set out in high old form.

They were lucky that they could leave Lydia D'A's Fine Chocolates under Brosnan's capable management and Tom drove up to Dublin once a week to check on things, see everything was all right.

The long summer days by the sea slipped by and Varina and Lydia swam and mothered their children and lazed in the sunshine. It was glorious weather, the sun sparkled on the gentian-blue water and the sand lay like a silver silken blanket beneath them. Lydia got a tan but Varina, careful of her milk-white skin remained under an umbrella her hair protected in a scarf topped by a straw hat, her eyes behind sunglasses.

Lydia and Orlick went sailing a lot. Orlick had sailed the neat little *Cat's Meow* down from Bullock Harbour and they spent many happy hours aboard her. He joined the family whenever he was off duty at the hospital and their love deepened and grew and they were like sturdy plants in the sun growing together healthily and happily.

Week folded upon week. The children thrived in the relaxed atmosphere and Varina lost whatever prickliness left over from her relationship with Roland. But their stay ended abruptly.

Tom came down to the beach one Friday on his return from a visit to Dublin. He removed his shoes and socks and let his feet sink into the soft hot sand. Shading his eyes with his hand he could see the two families on the beach and his heart warmed. Varina lay under her parasol in the cool shade, dreaming what dreams he did not know, could not guess. Under a striped canvas awning they had erected for their babies Rose and little Bernard played, watched over by Styles and Granny Kathleen. Nonie and Eilish were preparing supper in the house and Lydia and Orlick were swimming strongly like young porpoises out in the distance completely at home in the water. Tom thought how lucky he was to have these people to return to, how blessed. But, as he watched he saw Granny Kathleen slowly, so slowly keel over and lie inert on the sand.

He knew instantly she was not well. He shouted back to Nonie to call an ambulance and rushed to her side and found that she was dead.

Lydia, looking towards the shore, sensed that something was not right and called to Orlick to return. When Orlick checked he confirmed that she was dead. 'It looks like a heart attack,' he said, 'Of course I'll have to verify that.' Then seeing his wife's stricken face he added, 'Her heart probably just stopped. She would have known no pain.'

'Oh how can you say that?' Lydia cried. 'How can you possibly know?'

'Look at her face,' Orlick said. 'It's so peaceful. Happy almost.'

'It was the best way for her to go,' Tom consoled Lydia. 'Both your mother and Granny Kathleen have had lovely peaceful deaths. They were very lucky, my dear.'

Lydia wept and allowed herself to be consoled by her husband. He was so comfortable, so reliable. They telephoned Mallow Hall but Austin

371

did not answer the phone. He heard it and knew it to be important, else why did the caller persist? But he let it ring and ring and ring. If he had answered it he might have saved himself, who knows? But he didn't and therefore he precipitated the tragic but inevitable ending to the chain of events that he and Pius had set in motion so long ago.

Orlick was advised by Lydia to telephone Peggy Sullivan and ask her to go up to the Hall and rouse Austin and tell him the sad news. 'He'll have to be told,' Lydia said. 'You'll have to break the news to him that his grandmother has passed on. He can't be left in ignorance. Peggy? Can you go up there and tell him? Thank you. We're grateful.'

Chapter Fifty

It was such a gorgeous day and hot so Peggy Sullivan took her time. It was a shock, Kathleen Daly passing on. They had been neighbours since Peggy was a girl and she was fond of the old dear. But Peggy was a realist. She had lived in the country all her life and her natural disposition was cheerful, so she accepted things. Birth and death, sickness and health, love and hate, they were all part of living, of life and should be accepted on a daily basis and not elevated into positions of overwhelming importance. Everything was of equal importance and should be dealt with on a day-to-day basis. So although it had been a shock to be told that Kathleen Daly was dead, Peggy decided it was probably her time to go and as she was with the good Lord now there was no need of exaggerated grief.

She gathered bunches of wild flowers planning to leave them at the door of Kathleen Daly's little cottage. '*Requiescat in pace,*' she whispered as she went along. 'Welcome into Your kingdom the soul of Kathleen Daly, wipe away all her tears. Let her see You in all Your glory, and may she rest in peace in Your presence, Amen.' She gathered Queen Anne's Lace, and cornflowers, daisies and tied the bunch with thick blades of grass.

A bird sang a piercingly sweet song as she strolled along up the boreen to Mallow Hall by the back way. Sure wasn't it the easiest, quickest way, past the lake to the big house. It was not the way anyone else came but it was the best way from the cottages.

She dawdled along, truth to tell because she dreaded having to beard Austin Tracey in his lair. The idea of coming face to face with him made her very nervous. He had got a reputation these days for unpredictability and irascibility. He was possessed, the people hereabouts, in the vicinity of Mallow Hall had decided. Unhinged. Lumbering about the land, mouthing curses if you greeted him at all. And she was fearful of the anger in him, obvious to all, anger that could turn murderous and she alone in the cottage and Kathleen Daly gone to her rest. Peggy loitered and sent up pleas to the Almighty that Sweet Jesus would protect her through the storms and vicissitudes of life. Sure wasn't this a vicissitude and no mistake? Granny Kathleen dying unexpected like that in Portmarnock and himself not answering the phone and they all knew he was there and she having to break the news and God alone knew how he'd react. She'd rather die than make this journey and see that terrible demented man.

She dallied, and told herself it was hot. She was hot. It was a heavy, sultry day and that made her dawdle, sure enough.

As she meandered along she noticed as she approached the lake that, even though the day was heavy and sultry, there were still more flies than there should be in a Catholic country. Flies like that gathered in hot heathen lands, but not in Ireland. Bumble bees, wasps, bluebottles and flies were zooming around like dive bombers thick in the foliage massed overhead and in groups beside the lake. It was funny. She'd never seen so many flies. The air was thick with them.

She waved her hands about over her head and face and took a deep breath and that was when she got the smell. It hit her so she nearly gagged. It was foul, a putrid stench, the pong of rotting flesh, like dead fish or decaying eggs or worse.

She was passing the lake. The hot sun had dried it out around the edges, and the water was lower than she'd ever seen it. The periphery for about two feet was cracked, dried mud, splitting in the sun. Then she noticed the concentration of flies in one place, through the bullrushes. She frowned, worried, disgusted by the foul stink, and she looked through the bullrushes and saw it and screamed. A decomposing body, lying there, covered in crawling things, smelling to high heaven. Oh Jesus, oh God.

She could hear a phone ringing through an open window up at Mallow Hall but she ran back to her own cottage. She decided she did not want to see Austin Tracey just now nor give him any news at all. Let someone else do it. She'd had shocks enough for one day and she rang the police grateful that she could lay the whole thing

375

in their hands. How glad she was that Sean had insisted she had a phone in her home so that he could call her. She rang Seargent Belton and reported that there was a corpse putrefying in the lake at Mallow Hall. Then she rang her son Sean.

Their lives were disrupted and the calm sweet days were over. The Gardi were everywhere and Austin Tracey was arrested and taken away in a black Mariah.

Lydia did not find out about her brother's death until the day after the discovery of the corpse. She was busy helping Tom attend to her granny's last journey to Dublin, notifying the church where she'd lie overnight and the undertakers who would receive her and look after her and transfer her to the church after they had collected her from the mortum. Orlick had arranged a post mortum and Lydia was totally preoccupied with a hundred and one details that needed her attention. She missed her mother more than ever and felt maturity thrust upon her reluctant shoulders. Only Tom seemed able to relieve some of the stress and reassure her that she was not the only one responsible for the arrangements.

The news of Roland's death did not shock her as much as Orlick expected. In fact she seemed to accept the fact of it quite calmly.

They had left Varina and Styles and the servants behind them in Portmarnock to shut up the house and follow them in a day or two. Varina said, 'I'll be back for Granny Kathleen's funeral. I wouldn't miss it Lydia. I loved that old lady,' and Tom had assured his daughter that the funeral would not take place before Monday. 'They don't bury people on Saturday,' Tom told her, 'Messes up the clergy's itinerary.'

Tom told Lydia about Peggy Sullivan's grisly discovery. 'We don't know the details yet Lydia, but they think Austin did it.'

'Oh God!' Lydia's face paled and she suddenly looked ill, 'Oh God Tom, what's happening? What's going on? Everything is falling apart.'

'Lydia, you've been so sure for so long that certain things will not touch you. But sweetheart I'm afraid that no one can guarantee that. And you know what they say — a house built on sand will not last. I'm afraid Austin has built a life upon deception and fraud and that will inevitably be discovered.'

'What is happening Tom?' Lydia asked again.

'It's called scandal my dear,' he said, 'I'll protect you all I can, and Orlick will too, but this one you'll have to tackle yourself.' He took her face between his hands, 'But don't worry Lydia, we'll be behind you one hundred percent.' He sighed, 'However don't jump to any conclusions. Let's bide our time.'

Lydia shivered. For the first time in her life she could not run away, could not tidy the problem under the carpet. It was, as Tom Gallagher told her, grown-up time. She had no control over events and had no recourse but to bow to fate.

She took a deep breath and decided to do her best.

To her surprise she managed quite well under the strain. She found facing up to it not nearly as alarming as she had thought it would be. Strangely too, when she looked squarely at events it was as if she had been aware that something like this could happen. Underneath everything she understood. 'You've always been fearful,' Tom Gallagher told her, 'And now you've discovered as the man said, there's nothing to fear but fear itself.'

Events moved swiftly. Varina, Nonie and Eilish closed up the Portmarnock holiday house and returned to Dublin with Rose. Detective Inspector Gaffney came to talk to Lydia, and though she could not help him, the picture became clearer.

It appeared that Roland had been living in some slum off Dorset Street drinking himself maggoty. According to witnesses, the Detective Inspector told Lydia and Orlick, Austin came looking for him. He was seen watching the house for days. Mark McEvoy testified to that. Then one night he collected his brother and Roland was never seen again. 'But that doesn't prove anything Detective Inspector,' Lydia protested. She felt safe here, Orlick's arm around her his hand over hers. They could tackle anything together. She glanced at her husband and thought triumphantly, 'I can deal with anything with this man beside me, I really can.'

They all sat in her front room. It was bright and fresh, the voile curtains blowing in the breeze. The floral coverings on sofa and chairs were cheerful and there were bowls of Michaelmas daisies and yellow jonquils everywhere.

Lydia sighed and wondered why she was not more upset. 'I know that Mrs Fitzmaurice,' Detective Inspector Gaffney replied calmly, 'But how do you explain, er, how will *he* explain, your brother Austin, the fact that several people saw his car, the green coupe drive through the village that evening and the pathologist puts the time of death as near as makes no difference as being that night. And we cannot trace your brother after that date. And to top it all, when Sergeant Belton went up to Mallow Hall after Mrs Sullivan phoned him, Mr Austin Tracey's first words were, "So you've found the body then?" ' The detective spread his hands.

'He could have decided Roley was dead and when he saw the policeman jumped to the *right* conclusion. That Roley had killed himself drinking.'

'Umm. But it is unlikely Mrs Fitzmaurice, especially as it appears the cause of death is . . .'

'Drowning?' Tom Gallagher hazarded. 'The drink could have led him to fall in the lake and drown himself.' But the detective shook his head. 'No. He was partly strangled. There were marks, unmistakable, around his neck.' The detective stood. 'Anyhow, we're still investigating.

379

Putting it all together. Mr Tracey is simply helping us.'

'Can I see him?' Lydia asked.

Detective Superintendent nodded, 'I don't see
why not,' he said.

For a moment Lydia felt swamped by the actuality of what had happened. One of her half-
brothers had most likely murdered the other.
She remembered Roley, the fat little baby, her
mother's adored youngest, playing on the lawn at
Mallow Hall. She thought of Austin getting his
diploma and how proud her mother was. But as
she thought she had to acknowledge that she had
never really liked either of them. They had never
been kind to her, they had always been at war.

She wished for her own sake, selfishly that she
cared more, cared about Austin, cared about
Roley, but in her heart there was only anger.
Anger at the wasted lives, anger at the scandal,
anger that they were so careless with love and responsibility. What the bloody hell had they
thought they were doing? She wondered whether
she was partly responsible.

She decided calmly and rationally that she was
not going to accept blame. She was going to
remain above events, forbid them to touch her,
refuse to allow her feelings to dominate her. It
would not be fair to Orlick or Bernard.

No, she would do as her mother would advise
— behave with dignity and keep her priorities
strictly in order.

Chapter Fifty-One

Granny Kathleen's funeral took place after Austin's arrest. They delayed it so that Roland could be buried at the same time. There was a post mortum on Roland and that held things up.

They were buried beside Martha in the little churchyard at Mallow Hall.

Lydia wept and wondered. Half her family, no all her family gone in one fell swoop, for Austin was as good as lost to them. Detective Inspector Gaffney laughed when she asked him if Austin could be allowed to attend the funeral. 'Not in a million years Mrs Fitzmaurice,' he told her, 'Why who can tell what tricks he might get up to. Old family retainers waiting to try to help him escape.'

'We don't have old family retainers,' she told him wearily. It made no difference, Austin was to remain incarcerated until his trial. He was refused bail much to the annoyance of his lawyer, a sworn enemy of Pius Brady called Ignatius McBroderick.

'They won't allow him out, better make up your minds to that,' he told Tom and Lydia, 'Not for a million quid.'

So, of the family, there was only Lydia at the funeral. Tom was there of course and Orlick, Dr and Mrs Fitzmaurice, Eilish and Nonie, Peggy

Sullivan, Varina and a few others, some from the firm, some from the estate.

It was a sad day, a misty Irish day, and no one felt cheerful at the wake. Lydia was shocked at the condition she found Mallow Hall in. 'The state of it,' she whispered to Tom. 'Gosh, Mamma'd turn in her grave if she could see it now.'

'Sure the missus gave life to it,' Nonie said, tears in her eyes. ' 'Tis a dead place without her.'

Wet branches of unpruned trees beat against the windows of the house and Lydia could not wait to return to her home in Sandymount.

Chapter Fifty-Two

Mountjoy jail was not a pleasant place to visit and it frightened Lydia to go there. When the door clanged behind her she jumped and Orlick who had insisted on going with her held her hand tightly in his own. Truth to tell he too was scared but he did not let on for Lydia's sake, murmuring soothing noises in her ear. 'It's all right dearest, it's all right.'

They were led to the visitors' room where they sat behind, or in front of, depending on how you looked at it, a wire mesh partition in a bare stone-walled room. There were cigarette butts on the floor and a single hundred watt bulb swinging on a wire overhead.

Lydia and Orlick exchanged a glance but did not speak to each other. Lydia had never seen such a place.

Austin was brought in. He was flanked by two Gardi and he was handcuffed. Lydia gasped when she saw him.

He had changed. He was rail-thin, gaunt-faced, unshaven, and he had aged. 'Oh Aus!' Lydia ran forward. Whatever differences she had had with him evaporated now. 'Lydia?' His lips trembled and he sat down abruptly. The guards came and stood beside him. He shook his head and she bit her lip. He looked so shaggy and un-

383

kempt. Lydia's eyes filled with tears.

'We'll get you out of here,' she said. 'I know you are innocent.'

He shook his head again. 'No, Lydia. I'm not. I'm not innocent and you know it.' She was crying, tears pouring down her cheeks.

'If only you knew!' he said.

Orlick joined his wife. 'Austin, don't say anything,' he advised hurriedly. 'Anything at all. It's foolish.' 'Pius Brady said that to me. Last time I saw him,' Austin seemed preoccupied as if his attention was elsewhere. 'He's right,' one of the Gardi beside Austin nodded, 'Better not say anything Mr Tracey. Keep calm. You've not been tried yet.' But Austin would not listen. 'They'll find it all out sooner or later Lydia,' he said, 'They always do,' and he pulled at his chest, hitting it with clenched fist, 'I was wound up so tight for so long. Since I was born. I can't bear it any more. It's too heavy for me.'

'No hush Austin. We'll get you a good lawyer. Pius Brady will help.'

Austin threw back his head and let out a loud hysterical guffaw. The two Gardi jumped. 'Oh Jesus!' he cried, 'If only you knew! Oh God!'

'Don't let him say any more,' Lydia pleaded and looked at her brother pressing her hands on the wire mesh that divided them. 'Oh Austin I love you. I won't let them harm you.'

He stared at her solemnly and a huge sob tore at his chest making him shudder from head to foot. 'Oh Liddy! If only I'd trusted that.'

'What, Austin?'

'Your love. Mamma's love.'

'It will always be there, Austin, you know that.'

'No.' He shook his head regretfully. 'No. I've forfeited it. There was a time, a time . . .' He faltered. 'But I blew it and you are only telling me this now to console me. You pity me.' She realised that what he said was probably true. She would feel this sympathy for anyone in Austin's plight, but she rallied defiantly. 'It's not up for debate,' she told him.

'I stole your inheritance,' he said.

She nodded, 'I know,' she replied. He stared at her, astonished.

'What?' he said, then 'Oh, the pity of it!' He looked at her, puzzled, 'Yet you came to see me? You don't hate me?'

'Of course not. It was only things. Money.'

'Liddy . . .'

She smiled tremulously at him. 'I know,' she said. 'You wish . . . I know.'

'If only,' he said.

There was the sound of keys rattling and another guard came into the stone room on Lydia's side.

'Time's up.'

'Okay. Don't lose heart, Aus. Promise.'

Austin nodded but he did not promise anything. He watched his sister leave and there were tears in his eyes.

But it was too late. He shook his head. It was so easy, he thought, letting go, loving. He'd never

385

realised how easy it was. He wished idly that someone had told him, then thought that they probably had and he had not listened. All his life he had been busy with the greed in him, comparing himself to his sister, weighing assets. He had missed so much. A huge despair descended upon him and his shoulders and every bone in his body drooped downwards.

To love was like putting on a warm soft garment that kept out the cold and heated the heart and soul and spirit. It was easy to love and he knew now that you didn't need success or assets to feel good if you had love. Why had no one said?

He returned to his cell and wondered at his own stupidity and the waste of it all.

He remembered that day when he'd found Lydia and Sean Sullivan the other side of the hedge and how he'd not understood their innocence, their joy, their comradeship. He misconstrued their relationship because his mind was so full of his own venal desires. He'd been a fool.

If only then he'd understood. That was what it was all about. Not money, not possessions, not houses or businesses or any of those *things,* but a reaching out in weakness and dependency to another human being for the warmth of their love and concern.

He thought of Shona. She had loved him and he had thrown it away. Or maybe she had not really loved him but had had designs on him. He suddenly thought, so what? He could have earned her love, they could have been happy. But every person in his life that mattered, or should have mattered he had driven away.

'Help me.' 'Thank you Austin.' He buried his head in his hands and wept. The Gardi looked at each other. One of them shrugged. 'They're always sorry when they're caught,' he said.

Chapter Fifty-Three

The whole sorry business made headlines. It was publicity of the most hurtful sort for Lydia and her family, this turning the spotlight on their private lives. The prying and poking and speculation in the papers, some of it wild about them all, particularly Martha was imaginative to say the least. And it inferred weird and wonderful scandalous goings on though never actually stating anything libelous.

Martha was described in one tabloid as 'the much-married beauty who rose from the mire of a slum cottage, from the degradation of poverty to the grandeur of a stately home'. 'This lady' the paper announced, 'had the ability to seduce all men and she did not deprive herself. Her lifestyle was opulent, she always had men around her and she died in Italy in the arms of her latest paramour.' Martha was unrecognizable to those who knew and loved her and what exactly she had to do with Austin's guilt or innocence was a mystery.

Tom Gallagher bit his lip, well aware there was nothing he could do. He held his peace but he suffered deeply and only the time he spent with his daughter and Lydia and the children eased his anger.

Lydia spent as much time as she could with

her son in the nursery. She would not allow them to hurt her. She decided she'd not permit their grubby innuendos to spoil their lovely life. With determined dignity and lofty purpose she rose above it all, held her head high and cancelled the papers. But the headlines kept the rest of Dublin riveted for weeks and months.

Eileen Brady, efficient and astute as ever had seen the end coming. She had secretly been transferring large sums of money to banks in Switzerland and Jersey. She had always felt insecure about the Tracey brothers. Naturally suspicious she did not believe their fraudulent behaviour would remain secret. Like Austin she felt that Roland was a loose cannon, unpredictable and untrustworthy, and when in his cups was very likely to blab. She had gradually been laying plans to leave Ireland, put distance between herself and the Tracey family and when Austin was arrested she panicked Pius into immediate flight. He came home one day to find his bags in the hall, his mother in tears and his wife in her mink with tickets in her hand and a taxi outside. He was bundled into the taxi and they drove to the airport before he could rightly assimilate what was happening. He found himself in London, then on a ferry to Jersey.

The swift change was too much for Pius. After that he went downhill rapidly. He did not like Jersey. He felt utterly separated from all he cared about, all that was familiar, his home town, his profession, his chums, the familiar habitat. He yearned for the bars he had drunk in, the people he knew, the routine he was used to. He was lost.

He hated exile, felt alien in a strange land. He did not understand foreigners, as he called them, and sadly lacking in charm, he failed miserably to make new friends.

His hatred for his wife grew yet he was chained to her by insoluble ties of deception and fraud. He disliked being separated from his mother. The old lady wrote piteous letters from home pleading with him to return. The press, she said were harassing her and she did not know what to tell them. 'They are hinting terrible things about you son, so leave that one behind and come home to your loving mother'. He was beside himself, fully aware that Dublin was the last place he could now go. He felt trapped and frightened inside his skull but could think of no way out. He cursed the Tracey brothers, forgot it was he that had proposed the plan in the first place. Most of all he cursed Eileen. He was not at all grateful to her for saving him from what she told him daily would have been a fate worse than death. He could not imagine a fate worsc than the one he was living through at this moment.

Pius blamed everyone but himself. He was the kind of man who believes that the circumstances were different in his case and that excused his dishonesty. He bemoaned his plight and wallowed in self-pity.

There were beautiful golf courses in Jersey but he could not bring himself to play. There were no races and he complained of the lack though he would not have attended a meeting anyway. He felt imprisoned and persecuted.

It never once occurred to him that it was all his own fault. He sat in the magnificent house Eileen was renting and sulked. The sun scorched that glorious summer but Pius Brady brooded and saw no beauty.

Eileen however thrived. Unlike her husband she made new friends; well, new acquaintances. She played bridge, joined the local socialities. She let people know she had money to spend, discreetly of course. She was very quickly recruited to various charities, committees, got elected to the boards of organizations devoted to the raising of funds for good causes. She attended charitable do's, fund-raising events, became a person to be reckoned with and thoroughly enjoyed herself. She decided on a long term plan to jettison Pius.

Then all at once the good times came to a sudden halt. It all stopped. Suddenly all her appointments were cancelled. Just like that. One day she was queen bee, the next no one wanted to know her.

The phone never stopped ringing, the calls came fast, one after the other from secretaries regretfully cancelling the appointment, the invitation. They could not make it. They were ill. The event was cancelled. They had discovered Lady This-or-That had prior claim to open the fête, preside at the dinner, arrange the event, introduce the celebrity. Eileen stared aghast at her little black book, at the lines she had had to draw through date after date after date. Nothing remained but a tea with dotty old Antonia Markham-Bell who was quite deaf and not really a person of consequence in Eileen's estimation.

What had happened? Eileen felt sick. She felt as she used to on the days when she knew Pius was seeing Dolly West.

Since she'd married Pius everything had gone her way. She'd got the bit between her teeth and had galloped ahead blissfully in her new-found position. At last she could do as she liked. No more 'yes sir' 'no sir' 'at once madam'. She could do as she pleased, sleep late, buy what she wanted, spend Pius' money.

She'd organized the house, the old woman (Pius' Mother) the salting away of the funds. She'd purchased a wardrobe of new designer clothes, had her hair styled by the best hairdresser in Dublin and led the life of Riley.

Austin Tracey's arrest had given her the excuse she needed. Dublin society would never accept Eileen Brady née Skully, she knew that. And the Tracey family were ever present haunting her, a threat to herself and her husband. Then there were Pius' cronies, his clients, people she'd called sir or madam. Dublin was too small to be able to reinvent oneself. So when Austin was arrested she was able to hustle Pius out of the country, leaving behind horrid old Mrs Brady whom she loathed, the Tracey brothers whom she hated, all the past, the memories and begin this new and glamorous life where no one knew her and she could swan about, the rich Mrs Brady, wife of the solicitor and cut a dash with the local elite.

And now this! She wondered what on earth could have happened and speculated wildly about rumours and gossip and libel and character assassination.

She sat on the terrace in the shade wearing a multi-coloured wrap over a matching bathing suit in the latest polyester fabric. The three piece was brightly coloured and the colours matched the vivid acquamarine of the swimming pool. The sun cast a myriad sparkling spangles of light on its surface.

The house she'd rented was large and open-plan, terribly modern, a film-star sort of place, pale furniture, marble floors, glass sliding doors all around. It was the sort of place she'd seen a hundred times in the magazines, Film Fun, and Movietime. Eileen adored it.

So she sat in her designer leisure outfit on her padded reclining Laz-E-Boy leisure chair, feet up on a sheaf of magazines on the table beside her wondering what she had done wrong.

The servant brought the papers on a silver tray, not the Jersey ones, they came early, but the overseas ones, *The Times*, the *Manchester Guardian* from England, and from Ireland the *Irish Times*, the *Independent*. She did not want them. She was not interested in reading anything from

Ireland, but Pius insisted.

The houseboy had a funny expression on his face as he laid them carefully beside her. He gave an imperceptible sniff and disappeared around the back of the house.

And there was Pius, his face, large as life all over the front pages of all the Irish papers. And under the photographs of Pius, none of which were flattering (he was smirking in an unpleasant smarmy sort of way) was printed in huge black capitals: WANTED FOR ALLEGED FRAUD.

Eileen choked on her gin. The only reassuring thing she could find was the word alleged. She could tell herself and the world that nothing had been proved. Nothing.

Furious she smashed the cocktail glass on the marble floor, ground her teeth and thought.

Such headlines did not get printed unless there was solid evidence. She guessed instantly that Austin Tracey was, in Jimmy Cagney's immortal phrase, singing.

She did not waste much time in thought. As soon as she had assessed the situation she hurried inside and began to pack her bags. Again.

The accounts were in her name, she had made sure of that. She dressed quickly, phoned the bank, instructed them to transfer all her funds to Switzerland, told them she would call in that afternoon and sign the authorization.

She packed a case. She draped her mink over her shoulders even though the day was hot (if Joan Crawford could do it so could she), put her jewellery into her make-up case and walked out of the house blowing a kiss over her shoulder as she left.

It was not Eileen Brady née Skully that they were looking for. She still had her passport with her maiden name on it. They'd left Ireland in too much of a hurry for her to change it. She would leave Pius behind to face the music. He was the guilty one after all. She had done nothing wrong.

She'd go to Switzerland, leave all memories behind. She would have nothing there to remind her of the past, no Traceys, no Pius and wasted love, no subservient secretary image to overcome, no disgrace.

Pius had proved such a disappointment to her. Once she had got him she found out she did not really want him. He was not worthy of all that passion, all that yearning. He'd proved himself to be a lousy lover, a hopeless husband, spineless and weak, a real moaning minnie. Eileen knew she'd be far better off without him. She was so much cleverer than he was in spite of his degrees and college education. What she'd ever seen in him became obscure and she regretted all those wasted years of devotion and slavery.

But Eileen was not one to waste much time on regrets. She consoled herself with the thought that without her tenacity and the man himself she would not have the money now, would not be able to run away like this; desert the sinking ship and win out. Survive. In style. He had enabled her to climb this far and now the world was her oyster. Pius Brady had served his purpose. She was up and out and away. Today a modern summer house in Jersey with a professional man, tomorrow a Sir, a Marquis, a Prince even and a villa, a schloss, a palace, who could guess? After all she was very rich.

Chapter Fifty-Four

Austin did not heed the advice he was given and confessed all. In fact he seemed desperate to do so. A dam burst and he could not stop talking.

The result of his statement was that the Gardi got in touch with Scotland Yard and they contacted the Bureau in Jersey and Pius was run to ground. They discovered him rigid with fear, cowering in a corner of the film-starry house and he was arrested and returned to Dublin under escort. Discovering Eileen's defection he'd been too terrified and indecisive to try to escape, too petrified to mobilise himself to formulate a plan of action. Even to run away was beyond his capabilities and he sat frozen in a corner of the living room until they came and took him away.

The trials caused a stir. Dublin was agog. Daily news of scandalous doings entertained the populace, but because of Austin Tracey's confession the whole thing passed pretty swiftly. There was no real defence put up. Austin sat in the box and blabbed.

Lydia, Tom and Varina went to give support to Austin, but they soon realised that he was hardly aware of their presence. He seemed cocooned in a world of self-disgust and shied away from their clear speculation.

They all protected Lydia. Tom and Varina particularly. Anything that threatened her security they kept at bay, firmly out of her way.

Tom forbade her to go to the shop. Varina went though and though some people knew who she was, most didn't and left her alone. She told her father that as she intended to keep working after the trial, stopping would only make matters worse when she started again. 'Better keep going,' she said, 'People get tired when the excitement wears off.' They left the running of the place to Brosnan who turned up trumps. Tom asked Brosnan to promote Nelly to take Lydia's place.

'I think we can expand,' Tom told Lydia. Brosnan agreed.

'We can't make enough chocolates to sell. We've got orders piling up. It's only great,' Brosnan told him.

'What should we do then?' he asked.

'Sure Mr Gallagher, half the old staff is dyin' to cross over to us,' Brosnan told Tom, 'They're that disillusioned wi' MacMillan's, you can't imagine! It'll be only too asy to take on extra. But we need bigger premises.'

'There's a disused factory in Dorset Street. I saw it when I went to look at where Roland spent his last few weeks. I'll put in a bid for that.'

Life had to go on. Tom felt awkward when he thought how his mind had worked when he saw this appropriate place in the middle of tragedy.

So Tom set about procuring the premises and Nelly was promoted and Varina and Tom supported Lydia through her difficult patch.

Lydia took no newspapers while the trial was on. She did not listen to the radio. She grew closer and closer to Orlick and Bernard and Tom and Varina and Rose. They were drawn together by their relationship with the Tracey family. Nonie and Eilish were there, helping, proud that they were relied upon, and in their own way relishing every moment of the tragedy that had overtaken the family they had served. They were treated with new deference by shopkeepers and traders, listened to when they expressed an opinion, especially one concerning the Tracey family.

And Mallow Hall fell to the mercy of wind, weather, damp weeds, looters and plunderers.

Lydia spent long afternoons in her garden playing with little Bernard. Although Eilish often prepared the evening meal when they were all together she liked to cook for her family. She read and listened to music. She was at peace and the only blot on her horizon was her brother's plight.

She gave evidence. She told an astounded courtroom that she'd known Austin and Roland were cheating her but she had done nothing to stop them. 'I chose not to,' she said calmly. 'They are family after all and it's not right, family member fighting family member. All my brothers' lives they knew that they had nothing and I had everything,' she said. 'I would have looked after them, but they did not know that. I should have told them. It was very hard for them.'

'That hardly excuses murder,' the prosecuting barrister said, somewhat sharply.

'No. It doesn't,' she agreed.

About the murder she knew nothing. 'It could have been an accident,' she told them, 'Roland was always drunk and Austin is, or was, obsessed. Demented, I'd say.'

'It wasn't an accident. I killed him,' Austin shouted and was rebuked.

What was terrifying Lydia was the possibility that Austin might get the death penalty. Sometimes he seemed to want that extreme punishment. He told the court precisely what he had done and pleaded to be put down like a dog. 'It's what I deserve,' he said.

The court did not agree. In the end, he got life and in the fraud trial that followed Pius got ten years in prison.

Each of them reacted to the verdicts in his own way. Austin gave a long shuddering sigh but seemed resigned. Pius wet his pants.

Chapter Fifty-Five

It was during the trial that there was a ring on Lydia's doorbell. The jury was out and the girls were waiting for the result. They were anxious but too frightened to remain in the court to hear it read.

'I couldn't do it, Tom,' Lydia told him. 'It's too much to ask. I think I might faint, pass out, and that would make it even worse for Austin.'

'It will be bad for him anyway,' Varina said. 'They're not going to find him not guilty! They can't! He's pleaded guilty, God's sakes!'

'No but . . .' Lydia faltered. 'If they sentence him to . . .'

'Death you mean. They won't. He'll end up in Grangegorman.'

Varina and Lydia waited in the garden. Tom was in court. He said he'd let them know what happened as soon as possible.

They were sitting at the table drinking tea, the children playing around them. The garden was walled, protected by trees, sycamore and chestnut. It was full of spring flowers; daffodils, crocus and snow-drops around the base of the old oak tree. There was a fountain playing in the middle of the lawn, a cheeky little cherub holding a fish from whose open mouth water streamed and the sparrows were cavorting happily in the glittering jets. They darted in and out shaking their feathers pleasurably and chirping. 'It's so silly,' Lydia said, 'All of it. So futile. None of it need have happened but it is too late now. We can't go back.'

'I know. Don't you think I haven't told myself a million times Lydia. I should never have married Roland.'

'That wouldn't have changed anything. Poor Roland is, *was* an alcoholic. He was basically a nice if silly bloke. At least little Rose is legitimate. You've saved her that discrimination.'

Varina nodded and sighed. They could hear Dusty Springfield singing on the radio, 'You don't have to say you love me . . .'

It was quiet in the garden and the music floated out to the two young mothers. It was not very warm yet and they wore soft angora twinsets over gathered fine wool calf-length skirts. Neither of them had had the courage to get into the new miniskirts. They both had single strands of pearls at their throats.

Varina had taken to copying Lydia. The latter did not mind, in fact was flattered when Varina told her, 'I've always thought you and your mam were the bee's knees. So stylish! So elegant! I tend to be a bit . . .' she wrinkled her nose rejecting the words *tarty* and *sexy* and said 'Obvious!' 'No Varina, you were always *glamorous!* I always envied *you*. How stunning you looked. All the guys turned their heads when you came into a room.'

'Go on!' Varina gasped, digesting this information with avidity. 'Wow! I *love* it! Oh Lydia, you never!' But she copied her sister-in-law just the same.

When the bell rang Lydia's cheeks paled and she looked swiftly at Varina. 'The verdict!' she cried.

'I'll get it for you,' Varina offered rising.

'No, no. You stay there.' Lydia stood, straightening her shoulders. 'I'm being silly. I'll deal with it.'

It was not Orlick, she knew that. Orlick was working in the hospital and in any event he had his key. It could be Tom.

She went to the front door. She could see, through the stained glass the silhouette of a large man and for a moment she paused, then took a deep breath, steeling herself for whatever happened next.

She opened the door and was instantly swept into the arms of an older and if possible even better looking Sean Sullivan.

He lifted her off her feet, swung her around, kissing her cheeks, chanting, 'Lydia me darlin', Lydia me love, Lydia, Lydia, Lydia,' and laughing as he called her name.

At last he put her down. 'Let me look at ye,' he cried and held her at arms length, 'God yer still as beautiful as ever. More so.'

'I was thinking the same thing about you Sean,' she laughed back at him, 'Gosh I'm happy to see you. So happy.'

'I came as soon as I heard, Lydia. I didn't hear until the other day. I been in America. Jasus, Lydia, what have those two brothers of yours been up to? Can I help? Please let me help.'

'No, Sean. There's nothing you can do. It's all in the hands of the good Lord now. We're just petrified Austin might get the death penalty.'

'Send for Mr Pierpoint?' Sean frowned, 'They'll never do that. We're not barbarians here, are we?'

She burst into hard sobs in the hall. She had been holding onto herself and this warm, loving presence had undone her. He put his arms around her and held her to him. She sobbed into his jacket for a while, grateful for the comfort of his arms, then raised her tearstained face up to him. 'I'm sorry Sean,' she said.

'You never have to say sorry to me Lydia, you know that.' She nodded, 'It's so good to see you Sean. Come in, come in.'

He took her hand and she led him out into the garden. The sun shimmered over the placid scene. Varina had chased little Rose down to the oak tree and the little girl was crowing with delight as her mother tickled her. Varina's blond hair fell over her face and she pushed it back and looked towards the house her blue eyes full of laughter, her wide mouth in a grin.

'Are you okay Lydia?' she cried.

'And who is that?' Sean asked staring at the young mother.

'That's my sister-in-law,' Lydia said looking

from one to the other, smiling, 'Roland's widow. Come and meet her.'

But he turned to Lydia and said, 'You're a mother now too, I hear.'

She smiled at him, 'A wife and mother,' she told him. 'Yes. My Mam told me. Happy? My Mam swears you are. I kept writing to her asking her, telling her, if Lydia is unhappy count on it, I'll come and rescue her,' they both laughed, 'And I think Mam hoped sometimes you'd be unhappy so she could get me home.' They sat down at the table on the terrace.

'You gave your Mam a phone, didn't you?'

'Yes. And you were the reason. But I was in America and failed to be there for you when it most mattered,' he grinned at her ruefully, 'I didn't telephone my Mam from America. Had trouble getting through.'

Varina was still playing with Rose at the bottom of the garden and they both watched her. Lydia glanced at him and saw such a tender, sweet expression on his face as he watched Varina and Rose tumble together under the spreading branches of the tree. She felt a momentary pang of jealousy. Sean had been exclusively hers all her life. Then she silently chided herself. They had loved each other but had never been in love. Sean Sullivan was to her the brother Austin and Roland had never been. He'd been the brother she'd have chosen. Nothing could ever change the way they felt about each other and she would not want Sean as a husband.

Too volatile, itchy feet. He would always escape her. She could only be happy with a stable, reliable man like Orlick. She smiled to herself, thinking about him.

'You *are* happy then Lydia?' Sean asked her.

'Oh yes,' she said, 'I'm very happy Sean. You needn't worry on that score.' She inspected him, 'You look prosperous,' she said and indeed he did. He was wearing a beautifully cut Harris tweed jacket, a yellow cashmere pullover over a fine cotton shirt and hand made brogues on his feet.

'Ah, I struck lucky,' he said, 'Got my own haulage business now. Own fleets of trucks in England. And now, America. We go everywhere. Oh I did all right, no mistake.'

He glanced at her. 'Heard about you though. Done out of your inheritance.'

'Well Sean, it didn't work out too bad for me, even so. In fact I'm doing just fine. Orlick is a dedicated doctor and eventually he'll make a very nice living and he has a trust fund with a little something in it from his parents. And Lydia D'A's Fine Chocolates is making a tidy profit now. Orlick will be finishing in the hospital soon and setting up his own practice. With his father. I've got everything I want.'

'You were never greedy Lydia,' Sean told her, 'You amaze me. Other people, this thing would eat them up, but not you. You are very special, know that?'

'I'm happy,' she said and they smiled at each other.

'Who would have thought, that day I left Ireland, that we'd end up like this?' he mused.

'I would. I *knew*, Sean. I believe we can make our own lives much more than we think we can. I for one do not believe we need be blown about like the autumn leaves.'

'But you always knew what you wanted Lydia. And you got it.' She nodded, 'Yes,' she said.

Varina brushed down her skirt and took Rose's hand and moderating her steps to the child's toddling she was coming towards them up the garden path.

'Varina and I are in it together,' Lydia told him, both of them watching her progress up the garden path.

'Really? In the business I take it you mean?'

'Yes Sean.' The last vestige of possessiveness vanished and she said, 'She's lovely Sean, lovely.'

He thought how soft these women were compared to the women he'd met overseas. There was something vulnerable and unguarded about them. They were trusting and spontaneous and he welcomed them in his heart, the lovely girls of Ireland.

'She's been wonderful to me,' Lydia continued, 'We started it together. It was her father's backing that made it possible. He was my mother's . . .'

'I know,' he said swiftly, 'Mam told me.'

'God those phone conversations must have been riveting!' Lydia smiled.

They were silent awhile, watching Rose who

had fallen and was crying into her mother's neck. Varina was soothing her with soft words and comfort.

'Remember that day I left?' he asked. Lydia nodded, 'You didn't want anything to change? Seems to me you've had a lot of changes in your life since that day.'

'I was afraid Sean. I didn't want to grow up. Then I married Orlick and I found out there's nothing to be afraid of. Varina's father always says there's nothing to fear but fear itself.'

'Roosevelt.'

'Who?'

'Roosevelt said that.'

'Well Tom Gallagher told me and I found out it is true. Having Bernard helped.'

He looked for the first time into the pram beside them where the infant slept, oblivious to the world.

'This little mite? Can I pick him up?'

'Sure. It is just about time for him to wake and demand sustenance.'

But before he could do so Varina arrived at the table.

'I'd like to meet her,' Sean whispered to Lydia.

'Introduce us,' Varina said, smiling at the handsome stranger. Lydia complied and left them together to go into the kitchen to make some fresh tea and get Bernard's feed prepared.

She watched through the window. Sean had picked Bernard up and was lifting him up and down carefully, gently rocking him from side to side. Bernard was rubbing his eyes and yawning in a leisurely fashion. Sean glanced covertly every now and then at Varina who was smiling gently to herself. They'll make a stunning couple she thought and the last vestige of the old Lydia slid away and died as she let go of her girlhood.

Orlick found her there, staring out at the scene, the kettle boiling unheeded, the teapot losing its heat.

'Who is . . . ?'

'Shush!' She turned in the circle of his arms, putting her finger on his lips and whispered, 'That's Sean Sullivan. You remember.'

Orlick smiled, 'The fella I was jealous of?'

She laughed softly, 'Hush! Hush. I think those two are getting things together,' she whispered. 'Just look at them. Like a family aren't they?'

'Darling you are incorrigible. You want everyone to be happy like you.'

'Varina is not everyone,' she breathed as he kissed her cheek. 'And it would be so lovely.'

'Well, hold your horses, pet.' He tilted her chin and stared at her for a moment, then said seriously, 'It is okay darling, the verdict is in.' He saw the colour leave her face and he added quickly, 'Life. He got life.'

'Thank God. No Mr Pierpont.'

'No,' he said, 'I spoke to one of the jury . . .'

'Orlick, you were there? I thought you were at the hospital?'

'I took time off. They were quite happy for me to do so. Sweetheart, I was worried about you. I needed to hear for your sake, you know . . .'

'Oh darling, you . . . thank you.'

'Well I spoke to this jury member. He said he believed Austin was not, as he called it, all there. The others agreed. That was why they gave him life. He said no one sane would do that, *could* do that.'

'Orlick?'

'Yes sweetheart?'

'I love you very much. You know that?'

He nodded, 'I know my darling, I know.' He kissed her warm lips. 'And I'm just mad about you.'

They looked at the couple in the garden. The babies were in their arms and they were laughing together. Rose was jumping on Varina's knee and Lydia could see little Bernard's face peering over Sean's shoulder.

'I think they might make it,' Orlick said, smiling at her. Her face became serious for a moment. 'Do you think it might have all turned out differently if I hadn't done as Mamma said? You know, turned the other cheek?'

Orlick frowned. 'We'll never know, Lydia. It seemed to me all set right from the beginning, like it had to happen. It's a waste of time, looking back, wondering if, if, if. You know what they say, look back but don't stare. No, darling, what happened, happened,' he said. 'Each one of the protagonists behaved logically at the time and you did your best. What more can anyone do?'

The back gate opened and Tom Gallagher

came striding up the path. He waved to Lydia and Orlick and stuck his thumb up in the air in a gesture of success. He mouthed, 'Life!' and Varina ran to greet him, Rose at her heels. Sean looked over his shoulder at her in the kitchen and winked. Bernard had begun to howl.

Orlick took her hand and together they went out into the sunlit garden to their friends and children.

We hope you have enjoyed this Large Print book. Other G.K. Hall & Co. or Chivers Press Large Print books are available at your library or directly from the publishers.

For more information about current and up-coming titles, please call or write, without obligation, to:

G.K. Hall & Co.
P.O. Box 159
Thorndike, Maine 04986 USA
Tel. (800) 257-5157

OR

Chivers Press Limited
Windsor Bridge Road
Bath BA2 3AX
England
Tel. (0225) 335336

All our Large Print titles are designed for easy reading, and all our books are made to last.